A PROMISING INVITATION

She did not protest when Storm approached, his hands closing over her shoulders. Against her hairline, he whispered, "My Cleopatra . . . my Tallie . . . why do you wear this ugly scarf? I want you to stop . . ." As he drew it down, Tallie attempted to retrieve it at once. But she could not keep her long golden tresses from escaping the coarse fabric. She spun, her eyes dancing as he gathered the tresses in his hand and held them gently.

Tallie put distance between them, then twisted her hair and dropped it into the back of her dress. "I am not *your* Cleopatra or *your* Tallie, Storm Phillips. Leave me alone, will you?"

He crossed his arms, then leaned against the door. "I see you found my rose, Tallie. It reminded me of you." He crept behind her once again, he whispered, "Come and meet me tonight, Tallie."

Tallie spun toward him and hit him in the chest. He laughed, then withdrew, and she saw him flip his hat onto his head as he crossed the clearing.

Was his invitation to enjoy the cool night or did he want more? Would he will her mouth to his to be captured in a hot, passionate kiss? She wanted to feel the sweetness of his breath upon her cheek, taste the honey of his mouth, surrender to his passions. Yes, that was what she wanted . . .

The door opened, startling him from his thoughts. A lantern, held by a dark-clothed man, forced him to bring up his arm to shield his eyes from the painful light. Then the door closed again, the light remained, and a familiar form dropped cross-legged before him. Silence spanned a few moments of time before the visitor made his identity known through his peculiar manner of speech, a comfortable blend of eastern brogue and the regional accent of the Blue Ridge mountain range.

"I'll probably need your help getting up from this position, Storm."

The voice of Judge Isaac Grisham, the man who had sent him to this hellhole, brought a strange relief to him. "Come to see me suffer, eh, Judge?" he asked. Then, "You know I didn't rob that train, damn you."

"In my heart, I don't believe you did. But I had two witnesses on the stand who said you did. I did not find you guilty . . . I merely sentenced you according to the law. What in hell did you expect me to do?"

"Believe *me* instead of *them.*"

"I did believe you, Storm. The jury didn't."

"Because they were white and I am a half-breed bastard."

"You are *not* a bastard!" Judge Isaac Grisham took notice of the gauntness of Storm's visage, the swollen eye, the blood still crusted at the corner of his mouth. "I've got a proposition, Storm."

"I'm in a perfect situation to listen to one," Storm immediately replied. "I'm pretty much up against a brick wall."

Isaac Grisham ignored the moment of sarcasm. "You've served seven months of a ten-year prison sentence. Looks to me like you and prison life aren't getting along too well." He awaited a response, but none seemed forthcoming. "How'd you like to be back in the mountains."

"I won't marry that ugly niece of yours, Judge Grisham."

Grisham laughed. "I wouldn't ask the lowest swine to marry poor, mean-spirited Hester."

"Then what, Judge?"

* * *

"I hate this goddamned place!" Storm Phillips pressed his knuckles to the tight line of his mouth and fought back the scream of rage curling in his throat. The guard had just locked the door, and Storm didn't know when—or if—that door would be opened again. The last time he'd been tossed in solitary confinement, the guard had not returned for three days . . . at which time he had thrown a tin plate of rancid mush inside the door and promptly closed it for yet another three days.

Storm frequently got hell from the other prisoners because of his Cherokee blood, and had spent most of the last seven months in solitary confinement as punishment for instigating fights with some of those men. Sometimes it was a blessing to be separated from convicts who hated prison as much as he did, and at others, it was a curse. Though he liked to be alone—and always had—he liked spending it in the vast freedom of the Blue Ridge mountain range.

So, he looked around the familiar cell with its bed of straw covered with a flea-infested blanket in one corner and a pot to relieve himself in the other, then sank down against the wall and dragged his wrists onto his drawn-up knees. He watched the door well into the night through the one good eye that had not been blackened in his latest bout of fighting, heard the stirrings of guards and the clinking of their keys far away through the thick mortar walls. He had not slept a wink when the sun cast a thin line of light along the wall from a high, narrow window. Another day passed, and another night dragged its heavy shadows over the silently seated prisoner.

He dreamed of the gentle mountains that were his home, of ravines and ridges painted red and gold in the autumn season, of sunsets and peace luring the solitary traveler into the contours of the hills and valleys. He imagined sparkling pools and cascading water falls, high, broad, fertile lands cleared many years ago by the settlers. He thought of mysterious, contorted forms of trees when the mountains had been covered in ice.

her face in the shadows of a head scarf, but if the flawlessness of her hands mirrored the rest of her, she was much younger than the others.

"Judge Grisham?"

He looked to Sister Joseph, an apologetic grin widening his mouth. "Yes, Sister, you were asking about a good, reliable man. Most of our able-bodied young men work as loggers in the mountains. I would like to help you but . . ." An idea came to him as quickly as an unexpected slap in the face. He sat back, his fingers skimming through the thick hairs of a snow-white goatee as he realized he could help the women and pacify his conscience at the same time. Leaning forward, he spoke directly to Sister Joseph. "I do have a young man in mind, someone who might do just the job you need. I must confess, though, I am not sure of his religious inclinations. I need to talk to him first. Where will you be staying in the meantime?"

"The Collins family has kindly agreed to put us up until we travel to the site of our new church, a place, I understand, that is of tremendous beauty."

Judge Grisham knew the spot well. His good friend, Dr. Hiram Frick, had donated the property to the women after meeting Sister Meade in London. Sister Joseph had been most persuasive, stating that the Lord had directed the sisters to go to these mountains to establish a church in a place where He was greatly in need. Being a religious man himself, Dr. Frick felt that the area needed the healthy influence of a new church. Isaac Grisham felt there was a sufficient number of established churches in the region, but then, he and Hiram seldom agreed on anything.

When Sister Joseph came to her feet, followed swiftly by the other four women, Isaac Grisham rose and leaned across the desk. "As soon as I talk to the young man in question, I will ride out to the Collins place."

"And if this young man is not agreeable?"

Isaac Grisham nodded thoughtfully. "He will be, Sister. Yes, indeed, he will be."

Chapter One

Under the best of circumstances, the request would have been a difficult one to grant.

"We need a man of good, reliable character, who places great stock in our Lord. . . . A man who doesn't have to go home to a family every night, one who will take orders from women and will work for two dollars a week. We need him to build a church."

Judge Isaac Grisham now looked over the seated women who had introduced themselves as Sisters of the Way. He thought it strange that they would call themselves "sisters," since they were not nuns, nor of the Catholic faith. The one in charge, Sister Joseph, was a most unprepossessing figure, tall and gaunt, with a giant patch covering her right eye. Sister Meade had a harsh, pockmarked face, and was trying to hold a nervously yapping terrier on her wide lap. Sister Michael was a stout woman, who giggled incessantly. Sister Pete looked quite masculine, and was deep-throated. Judge Grisham had watched the women closely these past few minutes and thought she might be the most zealous of the group. But the last one . . . he hadn't seen her face, because she kept her head low enough to conceal

ZEBRA BOOKS are published by

Kensington Publishing Corp.
850 Third Avenue
New York, NY 10022

First Printing: September, 1995

Printed in the United States of America

CAROLINE BOURNE

WHITE LACE

ZEBRA BOOKS
KENSINGTON PUBLISHING CORP.

A clattering of wheels in the corridor just outside drew Storm's attention. Presently, the door opened and a cart was shoved into the cell. The aroma of potatoes and beef wafted immediately toward Storm, and he looked into the gray shades of the guard's face. The fierce narrowing of his eyes warned Storm that if, indeed, this luxury was for him, then there would be hell to pay for it later on.

Storm looked to Judge Grisham. The older gentleman said, "Take the food, Storm. You need the strength."

Storm wasted no time. Returning to his crouched position against the wall, he ate hungrily of beef, potatoes and gravy, early peas and hot biscuits, and drank the fresh milk straight from the pitcher, even though a cup had been provided. He knew the meal had come from the warden's table, and he knew that Judge Isaac Grisham had ordered it.

The food was good; under more favorable circumstances it would have been enough to feed three healthy men, with left-overs for a dog. Storm was so grateful that, in between bites, he told Isaac to lay out his terms for release.

Isaac Grisham felt his heart sink in as he watched this starving man eat the first good meal he'd had in seven months. Wiping the sheen of tears from his eyes before Storm could see, he continued, "I've got a bevy of church women who've arrived in the mountains to build a church compound. They have limited funds—love offerings, they call it—they've received through donations from English sources, and must stretch what they have as far as it will go—"

"English women?"

"American . . . broadly traveled to collect the offerings. You build that church, Storm, and provide protection for the sisters and I'll suspend your prison sentence."

"That doesn't sound so bad. But there has to be a catch," Storm said with a noticeable degree of suspicion. "And what makes you think I wouldn't take off?" When Isaac didn't respond, Storm asked, "What's the catch?"

"I talked to Hiram Frick last evening. The women are apprenensive. They're worried about the length of time it will take to build a proper church and solicit additional donations to complete the job."

"So . . ." Storm set the empty plate aside, his dark eyes piercing the span of space to settle on the judge's paler ones. "You want me to do the worrying for them as well?"

"Wouldn't hurt to take up the burden, I suppose," he answered matter-of-factly. "The catch, Storm, is not only the length of time you will work for the sisters, but—"

"I've got a ten-year sentence here," Storm replied without hesitation. "Any length of time up to that would hardly be a catch."

"You'll work for the sisters for five years. I trust that is agreeable to you."

"It is."

"And convert your beliefs to the way of their church."

He frowned. "I can *convince* them I've converted." Storm sat forward, his slender fingers raking through his unkempt, shoulder-length hair. "You can tell me how long to serve them. You can't tell me how to believe."

"That's right . . . I can't tell you how to believe. But I can tell you that you'd better convince them you're a believer. They insisted on a believing man."

"And a train robber?"

"They don't have to know you're—that you've been here, or for what crime."

Storm half reclined now, his back grazing the rough stone walls. "So, what you're proposing, Judge, is that if I serve church women for five years, convince them I'm a believing man, build a church and provide protection for them, then you'll suspend my prison term."

"That's what I'm telling you."

Storm grinned, the first time in months he'd had the strength to do so. "Just tell me where I sign and I'll let the door of this hellhole hit me in the butt on my way out."

* * *

Tallie awoke screaming, her hands thrashing through the darkness of the room in her insensible haste to protect herself. Suddenly, she felt arms surrounding her, heard a door being rushed open and a light coursing a brutal path into her eyes. Regaining her senses, she fell sobbing into Sister Pete's arms.

"There, there—what has frightened you so, Sister T?"

She said nothing as she tried to forget the nightmare, but it was simply not possible. She'd been rushing along Whitechapel Road in London's East End, a dark mist had clung to her ankles, traveling over her skirts with such force that it had ripped the basket of flowers from her hands, then a face, grim, macabre and without features, had suddenly loomed before her. The knife had slashed down and she'd seen her severed arm fall to the mist, which had suddenly developed long, sharp teeth, to snatch the arm into its black jaws. Then she had awakened, and now she sat sobbing in the hard, masculine arms of the sister who had been sleeping beside her on the wide bed.

Sister Joseph approached now, the lantern swinging almost recklessly from one of her hands. "Is she all right? Is it the usual nightmare?"

Sister Pete nodded, and Tallie said, "I'm so sorry. I shouldn't have eaten the pork for supper. It always causes nightmares."

"Poppycock on the pork!" Sister Joseph immediately argued. Her nerves jumped when Fanny Collins approached, golden hair loose and disheveled and catching in the lapels of the robe she was attempting to close around herself. "It's all right, Mrs. Collins. Sister T is prone to nightmares. I do apologize for the disturbance."

When Sister Joseph had withdrawn and the door closed, Sister Pete rose to light the lamp on the table with a match from the box. Now she returned to the edge of the bed and took Tallie's hand within her own. "You must *tell* someone what happened, Tallie. No one is going to believe for long that you are one of us. You . . ." She shrugged lightly. "You are different and pretty in a nonecclesiastic way. Such prettiness cannot be hidden long in the shadows of our plain black garments. You must tell someone why you left London in such haste. There are good people here who will protect you."

Tallie dragged back her waist-length tresses and began twisting them nervously between her fingers until they were a single tight knot curling around her hand. "I cannot, Sister Pete. Oh, I do apologize for placing you and the others in danger, and I'm so grateful for your protection, but—" Tears sheened her hazel eyes once again. "The Crown has a far-reaching influence. I can *never* tell what I saw. *Never.* I swear, if he finds me here, I shall leave your group so that you will not be in danger. I swear I shall."

"Our Lord wouldn't want you to swear," fussed Sister Pete without true feeling. "You let us worry about future dangers."

Sister Pete recalled the morning—aboard ship halfway across the Atlantic Ocean—that she'd first laid eyes on the frightened Tallie Edwards. She'd just seen a man in the dining salon and was making a hasty retreat when she ran into their group in a narrow corridor. Being in the midst of people dedicated to God, people she immediately decided would be her willing friends, she had broken down and told them over a two-hour period what terrors she was facing. The sisters had taken her into their fold and made her one of them, and for the remainder of the trip she had evaded the attentions of the man who had followed her aboard ship in Southampton. His name was Farrand Beattie, and he was guarding the interests of Albert Victor, the duke of Clarence, Queen Victoria's grandson and, as the firstborn son of the Prince of Wales, first in line for the throne of England.

Tallie had witnessed a horror so unspeakable that it had given her nightmares, such as the one she had suffered tonight. Sister Pete, overcome by emotion once again, drew Tallie into a loving hug and whispered gently, "Don't worry, dear girl. One day you will be able to return to your beloved Cora and Ellie in London. That despicable man would not dare follow you here.

Perhaps . . ." She drew back now, forcing a smile to her mouth, "perhaps he has given up and returned to London."

Tallie didn't think so. "Yes, perhaps, Sister Pete. Let us hope that he did. I would rather die than place you—all of you in danger. You do know that?"

"There'll be no need for dying." Gruffness entered her voice as she drew up, then turned and went to her own side of the bed. Smoothing back the covers, she said, "Now, let us get some sleep, for tomorrow we shall meet our new American handyman." Then, clasping her hands firmly, she said, "Let us pray he is a God-fearing, non-drinking man."

There were times that McCallister Phillips wanted to give up his hatred for Storm. It was a time-consuming burden and he had let it get out of hand. But since Storm's mother, Rachel, had died giving birth to him, he had made it a habit of directing his hatred toward Storm.

He also had mixed emotions about Judge Grisham releasing Storm from prison. He had gone to a lot of trouble—had a couple of his ranch hands rob a train and blame it on Storm, he did—just to get him out of the mountains. There was no need to reassign Storm to the church women. He could have sent men from his ranch to do the work needing to be done. He didn't want Storm roaming the mountains again and, as he'd threatened, filing court documents to claim part of the Phillips Ranch lands. He'd paid two men handsomely to lie in the witness box that Storm was the man who had robbed the mail train. The strongbox taken in that robbery was safely tucked away beneath the floorboards of his barn, its contents—more than fifty thousand dollars—still untouched.

So, he sent Bart Johnson over to the Collins place to talk to the church women. John Collins made no bones about the fact that he didn't want any of McCallister Phillips's men on his place, but he reluctantly agreed to let Sister Joseph talk to Bart. The two met in a cozy, though overly warm, parlor, sparsely furnished with pieces John Collins had made in his furniture shop.

''What do you wish to see me about, Mr.—did you say, Johnson?''

''Yes, ma'am.'' Removing the pillow from a tidy side chair, he sat across from Sister Joseph. ''I work for McCallister Phillips, and he wanted me to tell you about the man Judge Grisham has hired to work for you.''

''How very thoughtful. We don't even know the gentleman's name. In fact, we know nothing about him at all.''

Bart Johnson was a big, barrel-chested man, with a ruddy complexion pitted with scars. He liked the way the old woman looked at him, as though she did not seem to find him repulsive, as most women did. ''His name's Storm Phillips, and he—''

''Phillips? Any kinship to your employer?''

''My employer don't claim none, ma'am.''

Obviously the man was a relation to McCallister Phillips, or this odd statement would not have been necessary. Rather than open a subject of controversy with Johnson, Sister Joseph fussed, ''Ma'am won't do. You may call me Sister Joseph.''

''Yes, ma'—uh, Sister Joseph. The man, Storm Phillips, he's a convict at the state prison, an' he's a half-breed Cherokee an' he don't believe in Jesus and all that, like you and the other sisters do. He's a heathen, ma'—uh, Sister Joseph.''

She nodded thoughtfully, her loose jowls giving way to gravity as her head bent and rose. ''I see. And why would Judge Grisham send such a man to help us?''

''He thinks he didn't rob that train last year, an' it's his way of lettin' Storm out of prison but still requirin' him to pay his dues what was give to him by the jury.''

''A train robber, Indian, and heathen.'' Sister Joseph should have been horrified. But she was simply suspicious of an unseen gentleman's motives for sending this information to her. ''Tell your employer, Mr. Johnson, that I thank him for the information.''

''Then you won't be requirin' Storm's services?''

"I'll talk it over with the sisters." She arose now, her way of letting Mr. Johnson know that she was ready for him to leave.

"Good day, ma'—uh, Sister Joseph." Bart Johnson nodded his head imperceptibly, then moved through the house in a swift departure.

The sister returned to the divan, plumped the pillow beneath her elbow and mulled over what Bart Johnson had told her. Perhaps the man *was* a heathen and a train robber . . . but she could not believe that Judge Isaac Grisham, a man she had initially thought kind and accommodating, would endanger the lives of five helpless women in a strange and distant environment. McCallister Phillips must have had ulterior motives for sending that Bart Johnson to her with facts Isaac Grisham deliberately withheld, and it was up to her to weigh the importance of the issue . . . a duty she was prepared to do without delay.

She was a God-fearing woman, dedicated to bringing His word, and the teachings of her church, to this new region. Her first instinct was to forgive, and to trust mankind, even if her second was to worry. What better time to begin the act of forgiveness than now?

She rose just as Sister Michael entered the parlor, her wide mouth breaking into a smile. "Company, Sister Joseph? Do we have company?"

"He's gone, Sister."

Disappointment edged into Sister Michael's bulbous features. "I thought, perhaps, it was our new man."

"It wasn't." Sister Joseph's voice grew terse. "Just a well-wisher, Sister Michael." Looking at her, she said quietly, "Don't pout. We'll meet the new man tomorrow. Never fear." Moving toward the foyer, she continued with haste. "Now we must do what we can to help Mrs. Collins with supper. She has, after all, five extra mouths to feed."

"And is doing it so tastefully," giggled Sister Michael,

bouncing up beside her. "I do believe I've put on a few pounds since I've been here."

"God forbid," mumbled Sister Joseph, engaging herself in peeling the new potatoes sitting on a side board.

Tallie sank beside the clear, cool pond, her gaze catching the shimmering moonlight upon the water's surface. Tears stung her eyes and she caught her lip between her teeth to keep it from trembling.

She should be inside, helping the sisters prepare the evening meal, but she knew her melancholy moods annoyed them. She missed her aunt and dear little Ellie, and she wasn't sure how she could survive the days and weeks and months separated from them.

Then the moonlight caught upon a sad sight and she rose slowly, moving across the slight rise of the hill toward a small plot of earth. The two little headstones surrounded by a wooden fence stood scarcely a foot high. One read *Beloved Sarah,* the other *Precious Jason,* and the single date on both stones, *July 1, 1879,* indicated that the twins had been born and died on the same date. She wondered if the babies had belonged to John and Fanny Collins.

How she hated death! Why did it have to be part of the "natural order"? These two little ones could today be getting under foot, exasperating their parents and enjoying their love.

Death made her think of Collar and Cuffs, which Eddy was called behind his back. Eddy thought himself more a country gentleman than a prince, and prided himself on his flair for personal fashion. He was more conscientious of his looks than the most vain woman ever imagined.

And she hated him! Hated everything he stood for. Hated his superior ways! Hated what he did to her poor friend, Mary Kelly!

That was a sight she would never forget, and thinking about

it now made her shudder with revulsion to the point that she felt sick at her stomach.

Storm stood back and watched her from the darkness of the pines. He had ridden back to Granger with Judge Isaac Grisham this afternoon, and though he knew he was meeting the women tomorrow, he couldn't help riding out here to get a look at them beforehand. The one standing beside the small graves was tall and slight, and there was a grace about her that seemed contradictory to the coarse black unadorned garb she wore. A white shawl, the only light thing on her, stood out in the darkness, and a glimmer caught by a sudden moonbeam indicated that her hair was pale. He tried to see her face . . . the face of a woman who would dedicate herself to an unseen god, but she kept her back to him.

His horse suddenly sniggered from the darkness behind him and he pressed himself to the pine just as the woman turned sharply on her heels. He tried to see her features then, but the shadows of the forest fell completely across them. When she called, "Who is there?," he thought her voice so crisp and beautiful that for the moment it stunned him. He immediately attached alluring youth to her.

Tallie noticed the slightest movement in the overhanging darkness of the pines. She thought perhaps that someone's horse had escaped from its pen; it never occurred to her that she might be in danger, for the greatest danger to her had been left back in London, hiding in the royal palace behind his grandmother's skirts, a world away from the quiet mountain meadow where she now stood. But could Farrand Beattie possibly have followed her to these remote mountains?

Her gaze scanned the dark timberline, her mouth slightly trembling as she let the fear grab her inside. She imagined that small, glaring eyes were watching her, and she could almost catch the whiff of a man's distinct aroma.

Suddenly, she wanted to flee back toward the Collins house, but her feet seemed firmly rooted to the soil at the foot of the tiny graves. Her slim hands moved discreetly to lift the heavy black skirts she wore a fraction, and she caught her breath, hoping to avoid detection.

Then she expelled the breath, with a scolding, "For heaven's sake! There is nothing there . . . nothing at all. Stop being a foolish girl!" But the fear stayed with her, and she could feel the roots growing through the bottom of her shoes, gluing her feet to the earth. She could just imagine Sister Joseph having to come out here with a shovel.

Then an aggravating series of yaps suddenly took away the peace. As she turned to the house, she could see the blur of Sister Meade's terrier charging toward her with the ferocity of a wild bear.

Storm wasn't sure why he didn't make his presence known. He needed only step forward and introduce himself. Surely, the young woman had been made aware of the connection he would soon have to the sisters and they would, after all, be spending a lot of time together. It seemed a good enough moment to begin the relationship and, perhaps, take the edge off the appointed meeting between them tomorrow. He wasn't sure how the women felt about it, but he was nervous as hell.

Inwardly, Storm laughed. He loved women, loved being around them, loved having them in his arms, loved how they made him feel.

His horse sniggered again, interrupting his thoughts. As he pressed himself further into the rough bark of the pine, the young woman turned and fled toward the dim lights at the windows of the Collins house.

Storm wasn't sure why, but he stood there for a long, long

while, watching the house for some sign of activity, and worrying about his immediate future.

He really wasn't sure if he could take orders from women.

He really wasn't sure if he could keep his vow to Judge Isaac Grisham not to take off and lose himself in the vast foliage of the mountains.

He was sure, though, he thought, remounting his horse as the yapping of the little dog grew louder in its approach of him, that he would give it one hell of a try.

Chapter Two

Storm returned to Judge Grisham's house on the hill just outside of town to face the blackest rage he could have imagined in a man usually so calm and benign of disposition. The judge was standing on the porch, his pale-blue eyes livid, his arms crossed, and the toe of his left boot tapping rhythmically against the planked boards. Storm was sure that the longer hairs of the judge's goatee were standing rigid against the cool breeze blowing up from the valley.

"Where the hell have you been, Storm?"

"Out," he replied shortly, lowering his gaze as he attempted to skirt past the older man on the porch.

Judge Grisham immediately blocked his path, his short, gnarled fingers now closing firmly over Storm's shoulders. "*Out* simply won't do. I left you here with Martha and went into Granger for half an hour. When I returned you were gone . . . and you took my best saddle horse at that!"

"I brought him back," replied Storm, managing a cockeyed grin. "And all in one piece, I might add."

Judge Grisham forced a moment of calm as he reminded Storm, "You're a convict, Storm. For the next ten years you will be a convict . . . or *five,* if you do your job for the church women as I've arranged. And until then *I* am your warden, not Martha, and not the sisters. You will obey orders, or I'll put you right back behind the solid walls of the penitentiary. Do I make myself clear?"

The fingers pressing into the bones of his shoulders were beginning to hurt. Storm tried not to let it show, nor would he shrug off the judge's hands, as he had a mind to do. "You make yourself clear, Judge," replied Storm in a soft, polite voice.

"Then where did you go?"

"I wanted to see the church women. I rode over to the Collins place."

"And you saw them?"

"Just one," he said, relieved as the judge's hands slid off his shoulders and into the pockets of his trousers. He moved toward one of two chairs on the wide porch and sat down. "I was curious," he continued quietly. "I've never seen women who dedicated themselves completely to their religious beliefs."

"Your curiosity could have gotten you locked up again. If I'd gone into Granger looking for you, I'd have used that dag-nabbed phone at the mercantile to call the warden."

Storm kept his gaze down. "You want me to go call him, Judge?"

"Don't get smart with me, Storm!" He sat in the chair beside the younger man, his fingers now caressing the smooth, worn wood of Martha's favorite rocker. "I don't want you to mess up, Storm. Hell . . ." He hesitated only slightly, "I hated to see your father so dang pleased with himself because you were locked up. I know he's the one responsible for this . . . I know those two witnesses worked for him."

"You know what I wish, Judge?"

"What is that?"

"I wish some man would walk up to me one day and say, 'You know you ain't his son. You're my son. Me and your ma, we really loved each other, and when she was unhappy in her marriage to her husband, well, she and I—we got together and we decided to seal our love by having a child together. You're *my* son, not *his.*' "

"Don't wait for that to happen, Storm. Your ma was faithful to your father, even when he turned his back on her when she was carrying you. Don't you ever doubt you're Mack's son. Just look at him, Storm. Look at what you'll look like in thirty years or so." Isaac Grisham looked to Storm, a man only twenty-nine years old, whose dark eyes held a thousand years of bitterness and hatred, his tall, slim body, under normal conditions, a good twenty pounds heavier, his dark hair long on his shoulders—the judge remembered when he wore it short and neat, swept across his ears in the white man's fashion. His left eye was swollen from the beating he'd gotten a couple of days ago, and the cut on his mouth dragged down to his chin. He remembered the night Storm had been brought into the world. He remembered his good friend, Dr. Hiram Frick, entreating him and Martha to take the child and raise him as one of their own. Martha had been with child herself at the time, terribly ill the whole term, and she had not felt that she was strong enough to take another baby. As it was, their own son, born three weeks later, had been stillborn, but by then Hiram Frick had sent the child to live with his sister.

Storm was well educated; Hiram and his sisters had seen to that. But rather than doing something with his education, he had returned to the Blue Ridge Mountains. Isaac figured he'd done that just to be near his father in his obsessive hope of someday being accepted by him. He had tried for years, had even visited him at his ranch once, but the elder Phillips had run him off. Thereafter, Storm had brooded over the rejection, then had done the one thing Isaac had prayed he wouldn't do. He had fallen in with bad company and gotten himself in trouble.

Isaac refused to accept that Storm would never make something of himself. Storm tried to convince people that he cared about no one and nothing, with the exception of roaming the mountains freely, but Isaac was well aware of Storm's sensitive and caring nature. He had heard about the time he'd brought a wounded fox cub to Dr. Hiram Frick for medical treatment, the time he'd carried the little Williamson girl back home after she'd broken her ankle crossing the log over Holler Creek, knowing full well that her alcoholic father hated any man with Indian blood running in his veins. Hiram Frick's sister had left Storm well provided for when she'd died, and Isaac remembered the "anonymous" donation Hiram had told him about—for the little girl's surgery in Boston when the broken ankle had healed improperly.

To be fair, though, Isaac had to agree that Storm had his faults, as well. He distrusted most people, but Isaac hoped that would change when he got to know the sisters. And Storm wasn't a religious man. Perhaps the sisters would be a good influence on Storm.

"You're being quiet."

Issac cut his moist gaze to the younger man. "I was just thinking," he apologized.

"About me, I suppose?"

Issac nodded. "About you, indeed." Then, "What are we going to do with you, Storm?"

"Hell if I know, Judge." A small grin turned up his mouth. "Worthless horses and old dogs are taken out in the woods and shot. Maybe that's the best solution for train robbers—"

"You're probably right, Storm. But don't start counting down on your days. You're not entitled to humane destruction."

Storm smiled, though it was fleeting and a little sad. "Thanks, Judge."

The old man stood up, then began stroking his goatee in his usual way. "It's late, Storm, and the mosquitos are early this year. I'll bet Martha's inside, pacing the floor and wishing we'd go on to bed so she could get a little rest herself."

Storm looked up, unable to discern the judge's expression,

though the twinkle in his eyes could not be hidden by the cover of dark. "Mind if I sit here for a little while?"

"As long as you sit, Storm, and don't go gallivanting off into the mountains."

"I'll stay right here," he promised. "You have my word."

The judge started to enter the house, but immediately turned back to Storm. He said nothing for a moment, as though he were composing some small thought, then spoke in a low tone. "Those three small cabins sitting up there on the land Hiram donated to the sisters . . . do you think you could make them suitable for them to live in while the church and new living quarters are under construction?" Before Storm could respond, he continued, "Until the work levels out, I could hire a worker for you . . . perhaps Old Potts. He could really use the work and maybe it'll keep him off the bottle for a while—"

"That'd be like keeping a beaver out of a river," Storm replied. "I'll fix up the cabins first thing. And you don't have to pay Old Potts. I'll give him my two dollars a week. I have a good bit of money left in the bank in Charleston . . ." Lest the judge jump to the wrong conclusions, Storm immediately offered, "And it isn't the train payroll, Judge. It's my money . . . the money Doc Frick's sister left me when she died."

"I told you, Storm, I never believed you robbed the train. Now—" The screen door creaked, the judge's hand falling to the inside latch, "you come on in soon and get some sleep. After you meet the women tomorrow, you'll have a lot of hard work ahead of you. I'll look up Old Potts in the morning. He's been sweeping the boardwalk in front of the mercantile every day for two bits." He paused again as he prepared to enter the house. "Doc Frick has a wagon at his place that he's donated to the women, but it's not in good shape. Everton says you can use one of his wagons anytime you want. You'll be needing one to haul supplies for the women."

"I'll go see Doc after I meet the women in the morning."

"You be polite to them, Storm." He nodded imperceptibly, a gesture the judge did not witness. "You hear me, Storm?"

"Yes, sir . . . I'll be polite."

"Good night then."

"G'night, Judge." At last Storm was alone; he sat back and dragged his palms up to press them against his eyes. But the pain of the beating made that uncomfortable, and he instead cupped one palm gently over the swollen eye.

He sat like that for a few minutes, then arose, stretched back his shoulders, and entered the overly warm parlor of Judge Grisham's house. The bed in the small room behind the kitchen soon gave some comfort to his aching body, and sleep came quickly upon him.

Tallie had one of her usual nightmares. But this time she was able to shake it off without awakening Sister Pete. She sat up in bed, fanning her face with her fingers and hoping that the fire in her cheeks would not explode. The nightmare had been just as vivid this time, and she could almost feel the slicing pain of the knife her attacker had wielded against her.

She was angry and resentful of the circumstances that had driven her from London. She should be safely tucked away in the apartment she shared with Ellie and Aunt Cora over the modest flower shop that provided enough money to pay the rent and put food on the table. Why had she left the security of home and family that evening? She hadn't seen her friend in a half-dozen months and she really wasn't sure why Mary had wanted to see her that night. Her missive, sent by one of the street children of the East End, had sounded so urgent. Could it have had something to do with the man who was killing the prostitutes of Whitechapel? A man whose identity Tallie now knew.

Tallie was certain she would not be able to sleep. So, she let thoughts and reminiscences scatter through her head as she sat slightly forward and hugged her drawn-up knees. The night seemed pale and luminescent within the room, and the gauze curtains stirred, caught by a light wind whipping through the open window. She thought of her husband, perhaps because he'd hated the wind when it whipped through the fine, limp strands of his hair before the customary oils had been applied.

She remembered the morning they had met. He had stopped by Aunt Cora's flower shop to purchase fresh roses for his mother. He had been charming, eloquent, and, after meeting sixteen-year-old Tallie, he had more or less forgotten about his mother and his urgency in returning home. They had started courting. When he asked her to marry him four months later, Tallie had been concerned because he'd never taken her home to meet his parents. He had confessed with great shame that his parents refused to meet "that doxie from Whitechapel." They had refused to attend the wedding and, even months later, had refused to acknowledge that the marriage had ever taken place.

The one night she'd spent with her husband before his batallion had been sent to India had been sweet, gentle, and wonderful. Unlike many of the women who'd grown up in the wild streets of London's East End, Tallie had been a virgin on her wedding night, and David Alan Edwards had taken that into consideration, taking special care to make the night memorable for her. Though David had been a tad stiff in his manner, he had shown many tender moments and had even kissed her once in the streets, though he didn't care for public displays of affection. Aunt Cora had liked him, her opinion perhaps intensified because of the creamy chocolate candies in floral boxes he'd often brought her. She had been ecstatic when David had asked her for Tallie's hand in marriage. He was from one of the "better" families, and Cora had seen his social standing as Tallie's escape from the East End of London.

Then he had died in India. Tallie had come home to the small apartment crammed with furniture above the flower shop, and life had continued. She had decided that she never wanted to be married again, because she was convinced she would never find a man as wonderful as David.

Tearing herself from her memories, she looked now to the

sleeping Sister Pete, feeling guilty for thinking of love and sex in the company of such a chaste and moral woman. So, she forced her thoughts forward through the year. She had accepted her life and had worked with no complaint in Aunt Cora's flower shop. She'd given birth to Ellie nine months to the day after her husband had departed for India, and the child had been her one true blessing. Ellie . . . dear, sweet Ellie. In just a few months she would celebrate her eighth birthday, and Tallie was filled with sorrow and regret that she wouldn't be there with her. Aunt Cora's gentleman friend, Mr. Leggett, had acquired a spotted pony from a farm east of London and had asked Tallie's permission to present it to Ellie on her birthday. Tallie wished she could see the light in her daughter's eyes when she saw the gift Mr. Leggett would keep for her in his livery on Commercial Street.

If she'd stayed home that night, she wouldn't have witnessed the gruesome deed in Mary Kelly's apartment, and her life would not be turned topsy-turvy now. She would be hugging Ellie and telling her how much she loved her, and she'd be enjoying cinnamon tea with her dear aunt.

Thinking of Mary made her think of Farrand Beattie, and she couldn't help wondering where he was right then.

Farrand Beattie had lost track of Tallie Edwards aboard ship. Only after he had studied the passenger's manifold was he able to put two and two together. Four church women had booked passage and were staying together in a starboard cabin, and yet when they had left ship, there were five of them. He had culled his information from his talks with the captain several days after disembarkment, and by that time the women had disappeared into the countryside.

He had gone to all of the public transport stations in Charleston, South Carolina, offered large bribes for information and had eventually learned from a young stage clerk that he'd overheard five dark-clothed women discussing a new church they would established in the Blue Ridge Mountains near Granger.

Farrand Beattie knew he would find Tallie Edwards there, and he had to get close enough to her to—

His old horse stumbled on the narrow mountain trail. Dressed in dark minister's clothes he'd purchased at a second hand store in Charleston, he gathered up his cumbersome black robes and drew the horse up, preparing to dismount. He had wired London for replenishment of his expense account, but so far the duke's accountants had not replied. He had asked that the funds be sent to the town called Granger, the place he'd learned was little more than a village occupied by ignorant mountain folks and savage Indians.

He simply had to protect Eddy's reputation and convince Tallie that Eddy had come upon the scene *after* the murder of Mary Kelly. He had been as horrified as Tallie, and even more so when he had realized she believed him to be the fiend. Farrand had been with the young prince for almost seven years now, and he would do anything to shield him from the outside world, and the gossip-mongers so notorious in the newspapers of America. He didn't know what the girl had already told her traveling companions, but he hoped she was fearful enough for her life that she'd kept her mouth shut. She was a commoner; her word would not carry the same weight as that of a prince. It was imperative that he get to her, that he stop her—

"You there, havin' trouble?"

Farrand Beattie turned quickly, his narrow English features pinching in his moment of apprehension. North on the trail he faced a man as physically vile as any he'd ever seen in London's Whitechapel district. The man wore some kind of odorous fur across his shoulders, and his britches were so soiled that he could see the dirt being dislodged in chunks as the man moved. His hair was long and bushy, and a scraggly beard hid most of his face. When the American creature paused some ten feet away, Farrand Beattie announced, "Everything is fine, chap. I was merely allowing my horse sufficient time to rest."

Old Potts had never seen such a proper gentleman, all dudded up in black with a stiff white collar. He was wearing a brimmed hat that Old Potts thought would look good on his own head. He had no coin in his pocket, but perhaps the man would take something else. The only something else Potts had was the ever-present fifth of whiskey tucked into his back pocket. Removing it, then handing it out to the man with the strange accent, he said, "Trade you a swig, mister, fer that fine black hat."

Darkness suddenly fell heavily over the mountain trail, either that or Farrand Beattie was so scared that he was suffering a bout of his habitual hysterical blindness. He thought as rationally as he could under the circumstances. The man was a barbaric native of these mountains. If he wanted the hat, and Farrand didn't give it to him, he would simply shoot him and take it. He wanted to flee, but he was so frightened that he felt his shoes were glued to the trail. He gave a jump when the whiskey bottle hit lightly against his arm, and his senses returned to him in one swell swoop.

Slowly, so that he would not startle the grizzly mountaineer, he eased the hat from his head. "I do not drink the devil's brew, chap, but you are welcome to the hat. It's a little too snug as it is."

Old Potts wouldn't harm a fly. If he'd known that the man dressed as a preacher was scared out of his wits of him, he would have done one of two things, depending on his mood. He'd have rolled on the ground in laughter or he'd have looked drag-eyed and teary, his feelings hurt. Taking the proffered hat, he dragged it on to his dirty, unkempt hair, then crushed it down so that it would stay put. "Mighty 'bliged. Say . . ." He grinned, betraying jagged black teeth. "You a preacher man?"

Suddenly, a series of shots rang out. As Old Potts ducked with a hastily yelled, "Goddamn!" the man dressed as a preacher let out a pained yelp and slumped across his horse's back. "Goddamn!" yelled Old Potts again, looking to the fallen man, then, hastily untying the leather case from his saddle that might hold untold treasures, he lit out for the woods. So quickly did he run that he lost the fifth of whiskey that was as much a part of him as the foul odor following in his wake.

The horse skittered before Farrand Beattie could right himself and catch the reins and hold fast. Fire moved like an echo through the side of his chest, and as he dragged himself to his feet, another shot rang out. Pain exploded through his skull as he fell, and the darkness enveloping him was quick.

Bart Johnson's horse stumbled over the half-dead form on the trail shortly before midnight. Dragging the man across the back of his horse, he took him to the bunkhouse. Then he sent one of the young hands up to the house to tell McCallister Phillips that he'd found the man Pokey had accidentally shot when he'd been aiming for Old Potts.

McCallister had let Bart hire Old Potts to do odd jobs around the ranch. When he'd been found snooping in the barn, Mack was sure he had seen the train loot beneath the floorboards. He was probably drunk and didn't know what he'd seen, but Mack couldn't take that chance. He wanted him dead. Missing the shot was one too many mistakes for Pokey. McCallister had him hauled up to the post in back of the bunkhouse and whipped, and the housekeeper, Thea, was sent out to take care of the wounded stranger.

He would live, Thea told her employer, but he'd require a few weeks under her care.

Thea thought he wasn't a bad-looking man, rather tall and big-boned, with hair that was thick and short. The head wound was serious, though she did not think the bullet had entered his skull, and his right cheek was badly cut. A second bullet had passed through the flesh of his right side, missing all vital organs. She now took up needle and catgut to stitch the wounds. Thankfully, he was unconscious; if he hadn't screamed from the pain of the needle, he'd have surely screamed when the alcohol had flooded the wounds.

Bart Johnson partitioned off a section at the end of the bunkhouse, and that is where Thea took care of the Englishman, who lay still on the cot Johnson had placed there. She had surmised his nationality sometime in the night, when delirium had engaged his mouth in senseless motion. She assumed by his attire that he was a preacher man, though she had never seen this precise manner of dress. She was appalled that McCallister would order the killing of Potts. She also couldn't help wondering how Pokey could have missed Old Potts and hit the Englishman, when he was the best shot in McCallister's employ. She imagined the young ranch hand was wishing about now that he hadn't been so careless.

She was also wondering why McCallister wanted Old Potts dead. He was a harmless man, given to drink, and never had a coin in his pocket, unless one of the good citizens of Granger took pity on him. She imagined that Old Potts knew something McCallister didn't want him to tell.

She had worked for McCallister Phillips for twenty-three years, and in those years she had seen and heard things that, if he didn't trust her implicitly, would have given her employer reason to have her killed, also. She pretended to see nothing and hear nothing; she took care of the house and the cooking, and did not question what McCallister did. She knew his men had robbed the train, and she knew where he had hidden the money taken in that robbery. But that information would never leave her lips, and she knew that McCallister Phillips counted on her loyalty. He would take a whip or rifle to her just as quickly as he would to a man. Besides, she had her son, Matt, to think about—

"How is he, Thea?"

She started, looking across her shoulder as Bart Johnson entered the partitioned area. His hand dragged on the soiled green blanket he had helped her erect just that evening. "Thea gave him her assessment of the situation. He'll be sore when he wakes up, but I think he's going to make it," she ended. Then, "How's Pokey."

"Achin' like hell. You might want to put some salve on those whip wounds before they turn green."

She liked Bart Johnson. Though she knew he was loyal to McCallister, he would not fault her for her curiosity. So, she did not hesitate to ask him, "Why'd he want Old Potts dead, Bart?"

The foreman's hand fell to the shoulder of the rail-thin woman. "That ain't for you to know, Thea. An' it's better if you don't."

"I reckoned that's what you were going to say, Bart." A tired hand dragged back a wisp of light auburn hair. "You know he's mean as hell, Bart."

"I know that, Thea. He's set in his ways an' he don't want nobody crossin' him. Old Potts, he shouldn't have—well, that don't matter noways. Besides . . ." He grinned now, his voice lowering. "I know you've been hankerin' for him for years. You're a fine-lookin' woman, Thea. You ought to fix your hair real purty-like, and maybe put a little color on your lips. He'd notice you. I know he would."

Thea was thinking that McCallister had certainly noticed her once. "He notices nothing!" she contradicted her thoughts hotly. Bitterness edged into her voice; she suppressed the rage and regret swelling within. "He noticed my sister Betsy when she came to visit a few years back, the way he once noticed me. But he don't have time for a woman growing old and haggard."

"I heard him say somethin' real nice about you the other day, Thea—"

She laughed sardonically, sitting forward to adjust the covers over Farrand Beattie. "He said I was the best damned cook in the mountains. Real nice, Bart."

The big man shrugged. "It was somethin' anyways. Women like you, they usually take compliments where they can get them."

To most women, Bart's choice of words would have been an insult. But she knew what he meant, simply that she was getting older, the wrinkles were easing into her face, and her body was not as firm and youthful as it once had been. She was only forty-three, but sometimes she felt twice that age. "I suppose you're right, Bart. Women 'like me' should take compliments where they can get them."

"Aw, Thea—" His hand again touched upon her shoulder, his thick fingers squeezing lightly. "You know what I meant. I think you're a real swell woman. Hell, if I weren't so ornery an' mean, I'd of taken you across the threshhold years ago—"

With a small smile, Thea covered Bart's hand with her own. "I wouldn't have gone, Bart. No offense, but you're right. I've had a hankerin' for Mack since I first laid eyes on him, all those years ago when I was young and pretty . . . and a virgin."

"That boy of yours, Thea," Bart hesitated to continue, "have you ever told him that McCallister's his pa?"

"It's not something he needs to know, Bart. You're the only person in this world, except for me, who knows."

"How do you think he'd feel if he knew he had a breed half-brother?"

Thea drew a deep, weary sigh. Mack had tried to teach her son, Matt, to hate the Indians, as well as most people in general. But it had been like trying to teach a toddler to be an executioner. "I don't know, Bart." Then, "How do you feel about Storm—deep down in your heart? Do you hate him like Mack does?"

"I let Mack think I do. I really don't know what I think about Storm. He's never done anything to me, so I can't say as I hate him. I really don't s'pose that Mack hates him, either. Sometimes I think if he weren't so damn stubborn, he'd a reached out his hand to Storm years ago . . . an' give up this feud. But when Storm threatened to lay a claim to Mack's land here . . . well, Mack, he got kinda mad—"

McCallister Phillips entered the area, causing both of his employees to drag in a heavy breath as they wondered how much of their conversation he had heard. But if he'd heard any of it, his actions did not indicate it.

"Will the man live?" he asked Thea, moving into the glow of the single lamp.

"I think he will," Thea replied quietly.

"Good," said McCallister. "I don't like strangers at the ranch." His gaze cut to Bart. "Don't forget to go into Granger in the morning and pick up the new halters. I want those wild horses broke and ready to ride by the end of the week. We'll leave on spring roundup bright and early Monday morning."

"Yeah, Mack," answered a dutiful Bart Johnson as he tipped his hat. With a glance in Thea's direction, he moved across the planked floor of the bunkhouse and exited into the cool night.

Outside, McCallister said to his foreman, "Come on up to the house and have a whiskey." And as he moved up beside him, he added matter-of-factly, "If I ever hear you speak that bastard Cherokee's name again, I'll take the whip to you, Bart. Do you understand?"

"Yeah, Mack," replied Bart.

"Good! I'd hate to have you laid up when I need you on the roundup."

Chapter Three

Tallie couldn't believe how excited the sisters were to be meeting the new man—with the exception of Sister Joseph, who viewed the matter as a duty to be gotten over with quickly. Sister Michael had washed her hair that morning and fussed over a blemish that had appeared overnight on her rather prominent chin. Sister Joseph berated her for the moment of vanity and sent her to pray in the small alcove of the parlor.

Sister Pete thought the whole matter of the handyman rather mundane, though she readily admitted she was excited that he was visiting, and Sister Meade knew she would be much too busy calming her dog to even have the chance to meet the man.

So, when Storm Phillips rode the big bay gelding up to the porch of the Collins house shortly after ten that morning, Sister Michael was barred from the meeting until she could learn humility and Sister Meade locked herself in a bedroom with the dog. That left Sister Joseph, Sister Pete and Tallie, or Sister T, as the women called her, to meet the tall, brooding handyman, who acted as if he'd rather be anywhere on earth than in the tidy parlor.

Tallie kept her head low and her features half shaded below

the rim of her ever-present head scarf. She thought Storm Phillips a most unprepossessing American man, quite handsome in a wild, uncivilized sort of way, and strangely soft spoken. She'd expected the uneducated brogue they'd encountered among the mountain folk, but his voice was warm and refined, and hardly matched his rugged, bronze exterior.

Sister Joseph could hardly believe the man had been in prison for robbing a train. He seemed very polite and somewhat humble. She did wonder, however, who had been angry enough with him to beat him so badly. "So, Mr. Phillips, you are to be our handyman."

"I told the judge I would be," he responded politely.

"And the two dollars a week is sufficient pay?"

"It is."

"And you are not a drinking man?"

"No, ma'am."

"Let's begin with proper introductions, Mr. Phillips. I am Sister Joseph, not *ma'am*, this is Sister T and Sister Pete." She motioned to each of them in turn. "And the others who are not present are Sisters Meade and Michael. We will none of us wish to be addressed as ma'am. Simply 'Sister' will do quite nicely until you learn our names."

As you wish, Simply Sister. Storm wasn't sure this was going to work. He didn't like being lectured by a crotchety, gravel-voiced old lady. "Yes, ma'—umm, Sister Joseph." Nodding in the direction of the silent sisters, he said, "And Sister T and Sister Pete." He thought T a strange name for the young one he'd seen in the darkness last evening. He wondered what it stood for.

"You don't smoke or chew tobacco, do you, Mr. Phillips?" Sister Joseph continued.

"No, I don't. Filthy habits. Blackens the teeth and stinks the mouth."

"And you're a believing man, Mr. Phillips?"

His gaze had been dragging along the edges of the carpet

beneath his boots, but now he looked up, his eyes darkening, if that was at all possible for eyes as black as his.

Tallie immediately noticed his hesitation, even as the other sisters did not. They accepted his slight nod as affirmation that he was, indeed, a believing man. Tallie, however, instantly knew better. She imagined that the kindly judge had instructed him to fib if the matter was brought up.

"You don't curse or mutter vile oaths against our Lord?"

"Haven't made a habit of it." His attempt at humor was met only by a narrow stare and Sister Joseph's mouth pinched so tightly Storm thought it would meld together. So, he simply amended to, "No, Sister Joseph, I don't curse or mutter vile oaths."

"You're a competent carpenter?"

"I can do most anything I set my mind to."

"Will you be able to handle the job alone?"

"I won't have to," he was quick to answer. "The judge is going to get Old Potts to give us a hand."

Sister Joseph gasped, her deeply veined hand rising to cover her black-garbed throat. "We cannot afford to pay another man—"

"Don't have to. The judge is taking care of it. Says it will be a donation to your cause." He chose not to tell the sisters he was giving Old Potts his own two dollars a week . . . because Old Potts needed it, whereas he did not.

Sister Joseph's smile was stiff, though still sincere. "The Lord has touched his heart."

When a moment of silence entered the conversation, Sister Pete asked, "What happened to your face, Mr. Phillips?"

Without betraying the circumstances of his imprisonment—the judge had told him to be silent on that—he replied noncommittally, "A couple of fellows got upset with me."

Sister Joseph had not told the other sisters about the visit of Bart Johnson and the fact that Storm had been in prison. She felt it was something no one needed to know but her, and she planned to keep a keen eye on the young man.

Right now, she didn't like the way he was looking at Tallie. She was doing as she'd been told, keeping her face well covered, but the young man seemed intent on seeing into the shade of the head covering. Tallie hardly looked the part of a religious woman. She was lovely, had a habit of holding her mouth in a very seductive pose—something Sister Joseph often lectured her about—and her eyes mirrored everything she was . . . young, lonely, and frightened, hardly the emotions of a woman whose only concern should be setting up a new church. Sister Joseph wished Storm Phillips had been an older man, one less easy on the eyes. She knew there was already trouble brewing here, because Tallie's hazel eyes were moving purposefully over Storm Phillips's tall, muscular frame in the way a humble woman of the church could—or should—scarce accomplish.

She loudly cleared her throat, catching the full attentions of both the women. Nodding to Tallie, she said, "You may be excused now, Sister T. Sister Pete and I will go over the week's agenda with Mr. Phillips." When Tallie had arisen, immediately turning away from Storm, Sister Joseph suggested that she join Sister Michael in the alcove for a few minutes of prayer. "There you might repent of any sins that might have entered your heart," she said with bowed head.

Tallie was at once furious, though she did not let it show. She had graciously accepted the protection of the women and this new and strange role as one of them, but she did not feel Sister Joseph had the right to inflict the punishment of "prayers" upon her for her hidden sins. She had, after all, donated all of the money her aunt had given her to the coffers of their "love offerings," and felt that she had properly paid for their protection.

Thus, for the first time since she'd hidden among the sisters, she took issue with Sister Joseph's unwarranted lecture and defied her. Rather than joining Sister Michael for prayers, she moved to the back of the house and soon exited into the cool outdoors. Breaking into a run toward a narrow trail dipping into the woods, she flung off the head scarf, dragged up her heavy skirts and let her legs show from the knees on down.

Soon, she dropped to the cool, damp bank of a pond stocked with fish, her long tresses free for the first time in weeks and catching the crisp wind moving all around her. Tears touched her eyes so quickly that she could not staunch them before they fell over the flushed curves of her cheeks.

She would not be sorry for looking at Storm Phillips as a man rather than just a worker. And she would not be sorry because he brought all the emotions of a red-blooded woman to her surface. So, she had looked at him with admiration. What was the harm in that? He certainly had not been aware of it; she had been careful enough to be sure of that. Because she had assumed the role of a religious woman in order to hide among them did not mean that she *was* a sister. Certainly, she had none of the feelings of one.

She wanted to go home to London, she wanted to deliver flowers for her aunt's flower shop, she wanted to enjoy a cup of cinnamon tea, she wanted to hug Ellie . . . Oh, how lonely she was! She wanted to hear Mr. Campbell, the butcher, refer to her as The Duchess of Whitechapel, and hear Mrs. Ogden, who sold special blends of Oriental tea in the doorway of her boardinghouse, tell her that she was sure she'd descended from heaven to brighten their dreary lives. She wanted to bat her eyes playfully at young Jones, who worked at the iron-works and always stopped at the flower shop to tease her in the early-morning hours. She wanted to see Mrs. Muncie's entire bulk wobble when she laughed.

She was sure her aunt Cora was worried sick about her. After all, when her gentleman friend, Mr. Leggett, had driven her to Southampton to board ship, her destination was to have been the home of Mrs. Hawley in New York City. But when she'd seen Farrand Beattie aboard ship, and learned that he was circulating her penciled likeness among passengers and crew in his attempts to locate her, she had secreted herself with the sisters and changed her plans. She was sure Mrs. Hawley had written her aunt that she had never arrived, and Sister Joseph had said it would be too dangerous to send a letter to her aunt. Surely, her apartment in London's East End was being watched by the duke's men.

She was confident that she had eluded the dapper Mr. Beattie once she'd blended in with the women. Perhaps he had boarded a return ship for England, thinking that the duke—and his reputation—were safe now.

But was *she* safe? She should have taken her chances in London, in her own environment. There were any number of people there who would have protected her, and she could have gone to Scotland Yard. Or could she have? After all, it was the duke of Clarence, good old Collar and Cuffs, she'd seen standing over the dismembered corpse of her friend, Mary Kelly. To protect the royal family, would Scotland Yard have committed her to an asylum, perhaps even performed a brain operation that would have rendered her insane? Her tearful aunt, in explaining why she had to leave England, had said it was a very real possibility. So, she had ordered Mr. Leggett to drive her to Southampton, and had sent Ellie to friends in Liverpool until the matter died down. Tallie had wanted to keep Ellie with her, but Cora had said that the two of them traveling together would have been too conspicuous.

Tallie drew her scarf beneath her cheek and sobbed against the coarse fabric. Life had turned topsy-turvy and she didn't think it would ever be righted again. She didn't think she would ever see her aunt again, or hug her beloved Ellie. She didn't think she'd greet the friendly residents of Whitechapel again, or be teased by Mr. Campbell and young Jones. She didn't think she'd ever feel a cool English breeze wafting through her hair, or feel the tasty heat of Aunt Cora's spicy cinnamon tea upon her mouth. She would die here, away from everything and everyone she loved so much—

A twig snapped underfoot, very nearby. Her head jerked up, her tears immediately staunched in her moment of fear. She saw nothing but the deep shades of the forest, heard nothing but the raucous calling of a hawk circling overhead, and her heart quietly slowed its painful thumping. She was in a strange country, surrounded by strange people with strange customs, and every sound was a threat.

The moment of fear, however, overshadowed the sadness that had caused the rush of tears. A slim hand made a swipe at the offensive moisture, the pressure adding a little color to her pale cheeks. She took the time now to relax. She'd enjoy being alone, and try not to think her sad thoughts and grow melancholy again. Some good would come of this horrible ordeal—she just knew it—something that might improve the lives of her dear aunt and her precious Ellie.

So, she smiled, for no other reason than to make her feel good again. She saw hope where none existed before, and yet she did not know why. She felt confidence, but there was no logical source for it. And the morning—indeed, the world—looked brighter, even if just for a moment or so.

She sighed deeply, the breath she drew into her lungs cool and refreshing. She arose now, deciding that dropping to her knees in prayer beside Sister Michael might not be such a bad idea.

Then, just as quickly as confidence and hope had filled her, a deep, dark foreboding grabbed her within. She paused on the trail that would take her the short journey to the Collins house and looked all around. She was sure the sky had darkened, and that a hand had fallen heavily to her shoulder.

Feeling the rush of tears once again, she quickly pulled the great scarf over her long tresses and resumed her journey to the alcove, and the prayers she now felt something of a desperation to accomplish.

London's East End

Mr. Leggett had immediately sent for a doctor. But there was very little hope. Cora Dunton was quickly slipping away.

The kind old gentleman stood back, watching Dr. Gwynn in his ministrations of Cora. She had suffered a massive stroke in the night, and her prognosis was not only grim, but futile.

In her last moments, she called Peter Leggett to her bedside and told him why she'd had to send Tallie away. Tears misted his eyes as she spoke, clinging to life in her desperation to make the situation known to him. Then, with the final dregs of her dying breath, she told him the secret she had kept from Tallie for twenty-eight years. She told him of the threat made then that could rob her precious Tallie of her life.

He was holding her hand when she drew her final breath, and when the young Welsh doctor approached to offer some comfort, Peter dropped his forehead against Cora Dunton's shoulder and wept quietly.

He wanted to be angry with her for not telling Tallie the truth, so that she could have sought protection from the ruthless fiend, but he had loved the dear woman too much. Why did she have to die like this, when all she wanted was to live her simple life, loving her flowers, her niece and Ellie, and her lifelong friends in the East End.

As Peter Leggett stood away from Cora's death bed, he silently vowed that he would find a way to help Tallie. For now, he would journey to Liverpool and present Ellie with the pony he had planned to give her for her birthday.

He knew that Cora was waiting to hear from Mrs. Hawley in New York that Tallie had arrived safely. He would tell their postman to deliver all Cora's mail to his own rooms, and when the letter came he would follow Cora's dying wish.

He did not want to tell Tallie, because he did not want to frighten her, make her constantly watch across her shoulder. But could he keep such a secret from the woman who had a right to know everything? Could he withhold this vital information from Tallie, when the truth might save her life?

"Are you all right, Peter?"

Peter's gaze connected to the sympathetic but professionally detached one of Dr. Gwynn. "Yes, thank you . . . and thank you for coming so quickly to Cora."

"If it is any consolation, Peter, she would not have lived even if you had been here when she suffered the stroke."

"I will not have you gaping at the sisters, Mr. Phillips. If you cannot conduct yourself as a gentleman, then you simply will not do for this job."

The one thing that stifled a vicious retort was the idea of being returned to prison. Effecting a degree of calm, he replied, "Sister Joseph, I do not gape, nor am I at all interested in the sisters, except in a professional capacity. It is my desire to do a good job for you, and I believe my attitude as I perform the job will meet your requirements. Now . . ." He looked up, his anger strong but held within, "I understand that you and the sisters will be wanting to live in the three cabins on the property while the church, and your permanent living quarters, are being constructed. May I have until the end of the week to make them suitable for your occupancy?"

Sister Joseph weighed his words carefully for a moment, finding them quite appropriate under the circumstances. Then she said, "The end of the week will be just fine, Mr. Phillips. We have established an account at the mercantile in Granger. You may pick up whatever you need to ready the cabins."

He nodded, immediately lowering his eyes. "Then I should be on my way."

"Not just yet, Mr. Phillips." Redirecting her attentions, she said to Sister Pete, "You might give Mrs. Collins a hand in the kitchen. I wish a word in privacy with Mr. Phillips."

Sister Pete slapped her knees through the bulky fabric of her skirts. "Yes, Sister." And to Storm, "Good morning, Mr. Phillips."

He rose in deference to her gender, and when she had quickly exited, returned to the divan. He said nothing, but waited for Sister Joseph to say whatever it was she had to say in private.

Thinking that she might again launch into a lecture, he allowed his moment of irritation to darken his features.

"I had a visitor yesterday, Mr. Phillips," Sister Joseph began in a quiet voice, stacking her open hands upon her lap. "It doesn't matter who he was, but he told me that you have been in the state prison for robbing a train. He also said that you might be a heathen. One of the emotions expected of our order, Mr. Phillips, is compassion. That I am willing to give you. Whether you did or did not rob the train does not matter. But I'll not have you speaking out against the teachings of our church, nor are you to be vocal in the event you are, indeed, a heathen. Judge Grisham believes in you, and he is a man I am inclined to trust."

For a long, thoughtful moment, Storm dropped his forehead onto his linked fingers. When he again looked up, he asked, "Do the other women know about my imprisonment? If they don't know, please don't tell them. I don't want them to be frightened of me." He wasn't sure where the sudden emotions came from, but he felt the salty heat of tears glazing his eyes. "I want you to trust me, Sister Joseph, and to be assured that I will protect you . . . all of you. I was sentenced to ten years for the robbery, but as your God is my witness, I am innocent. Judge Isaac Grisham told me that if I'd serve you and the other women for a period of five years, build the church and protect you from harm, he'd consider my sentence served. And I'm willing to do that. But . . . please, don't tell the others if they don't already know."

Sister Joseph smiled, her thin, gnarled hand patting Storm's, as a mother might pat a child's. "They don't know, Mr. Phillips. And there's no reason why this can't be kept between the three of us—you, me and Judge Grisham." Drawing away now, she met Storm's dark, hooded gaze. "You said, 'your God,' Mr. Phillips. Am I to assume then that you are, indeed, a heathen?"

"I don't consider myself a heathen," he responded truthfully. "I consider myself a realist, giving credit to human nature and logic rather than the divine intervention of an unseen being. That's not to say, Sister Joseph, that I'm not subject to change."

She nodded slowly and thoughtfully, as if she'd just come to a realization. "You've had a hard, painful life, have you not, Mr. Phillips?"

"Actually, I was pampered and spoiled by Hiram Frick's two sisters. When the one who lived here in the mountains died, I was sent to live with the other. I couldn't have had a better life—"

"I sense that you are an angry man, Mr. Phillips. I would like to know why, if you feel inclined to tell me, and why a man like McCallister Phillips would be hostile to you."

"Mack's—McCallister Phillips's reasons are well known in this region. I don't like to talk about them, but if you want to know . . ."

"I do, Mr. Phillips."

"Mack is my father, but he has never acknowledged that I am his son. He married my mother, believing her to be white, because her skin was as white as yours—but she was full-blooded Cherokee. I've been told that Mack saw his parents murdered by Indians when he was a boy, and if that's true, then his dislike of the Cherokees might be justified in his eyes. But I'm still his son, and there is no justification for hating *me.*"

His anger screamed out with his quietly spoken words. Strangely, the small history he'd just given Sister Joseph endeared her somewhat to him. She smiled. "Would you mind if we called you Storm? We'll be together for a long time, and I'm sure that you would prefer not to be called Mr. for a full five years."

"Does make me feel kinda old," he replied, laughing for the first time in a long, long while. "I'd much prefer to be called by my first name."

"We'll try to contain this justified anger you feel, won't we, Storm?"

The moment of humor faded so quickly it might never have

existed. "I won't be angry around you and your sisters. For now, I've told more about my life to you than I do to most people. I'd rather not be subjected to interrogations on my personal life in the future."

Sister Joseph stood, at which time Storm, also, came to his feet. "One day when you know me better, Mr.—Storm—I hope you will learn to trust me. I will always be here to listen, if you wish to talk. If I do not have an answer, then our blessed Lord will, and I will carry your name to Him in my prayers. As for now, you believe as you wish . . . but please, keep it to yourself. The sisters would be shocked and dismayed to know that you are a heathen."

He bowed politely, then took up his hat from the divan and moved toward the door. When he had stepped out to the porch, he turned to Sister Joseph and asked, "Are there any necessities I can pick up for you in town when I go for the first haul of supplies? For when you move into the cabins at the end of the week?"

"Mr. and Mrs. Collins have collected a very generous love offering of household items from the kind people here. The only thing we really need is a teapot. Will you see if you can find one? Something plain, but delicate. Also . . ." She leaned toward Storm. "Sister T is an avid reader. Perhaps you could find some books for her."

"What kind of books, Sister Joseph?"

"Something with a little romance, I would think. Something with a little adventure, as well."

Though surprised by the request, he still found the moment to smile, easing his hat onto his head as he moved down the steps toward his waiting horse. "I'll see what I can do." *Now, what would a zealot want with books about romance?* he thought as he mounted the bay gelding. Tipping his hat to Sister Joseph, he said, "I'll send word to you when the cabins are ready. I looked them over on my way to see you this morning. They're not in bad shape at all."

Sister Joseph nodded. "Storm?" He halted, looking toward

her. "I thought you should know . . . Sister Meade has an aggravating little snip of a dog. No matter how much it might annoy you . . ." A crooked finger came up to shake at him, "You're not to 'do it in' or so your mountain neighbors say. And, please, tell that to the man who will be helping you at the building site."

Again, Storm nodded, and when he had pulled the bay around to move into the woodline, she was joined by Sister Michael and Tallie. In a critical tone, Sister Joseph asked, "Have you said your prayers?"

To which Sister Michael responded, "I've prayed so long that our Lord is probably sick of me."

"A small prayer, Sister Joseph," Tallie offered. "It was all He had time for after Sister Michael took so much of His time."

Sister Michael giggled. Though the matriarch of the sisters gave them her most accomplished look of disapproval, she could not prevent the smile that slid onto her face. Adjusting her eye patch, she turned to the house, ordering in a light tone, "Let's all help in the kitchen, Sisters. It's only fair."

To which Tallie, holding back, replied, "Mrs. Collins asked me to bring in a ham from the smokehouse."

"Then be on your way, Sister T . . . and don't dawdle," Sister Joseph admonished in a stern tone, even as she smiled at Tallie across her shoulder.

Dr. Hiram Frick was at the judge's house when Storm returned. When Storm politely proffered his hand in greeting, the older man pulled him into a rough embrace.

Storm had received more fatherly love from Hiram Frick than from any other man in his life. He had not abandoned him, had always provided the nurturing a man needed from a father figure, and Storm had known that Hiram would be glad to help him with any problem. Never a week had passed that Hiram Frick hadn't gone to the prison to see him, though only once in the last six months had he been allowed in. The warden had always gotten a perverse pleasure in telling Storm that no one had visited a "vile breed" like him, but from the window of the small, narrow cell to which he'd been confined he had been able to see the front gate. From there, he had watched the arrival of Dr. Hiram Frick, and within moments, his departure. This man was important to his life; he had no doubt that if his wife, Martha, hadn't been so ill during her pregnancy in the months after Storm's birth he would have been raised as a son by this kind man. He had cared enough, though, to see him well cared for by his maiden sisters, and for that Storm would always be grateful.

The judge appeared from the kitchen, carrying a tray of coffee. "Glad you're back," he said, discreetly casting his glance aside as the bear hug between the men was terminated. Hiram Frick, always at home at the judge's house, immediately began preparing his coffee with cream and sugar, the way he liked it, then looked toward Storm, who had found a comfortable perch in the judge's favorite overstuffed chair.

When the judge gave him a stern look, Storm chuckled, "You said to make myself at home, Judge."

"But *not* in my favorite chair, young man," he fussed, immediately settling into another with his coffee.

For a moment, Hiram thought about the beautiful woman who had been Storm's mother. She had been taken in as an infant by a white family after her mother, their Cherokee housekeeper, had died, and she had been raised as their daughter. She had been beautiful, her skin strangely pale, had not looked Indian at all. He had not been pleased to learn that she was going to marry McCallister Phillips, and had tried to talk her out of it. But how did one talk a woman in love out of marrying?

His thoughts snapped back. He realized that Storm and Isaac Grisham were watching him. "Don't fuss at the boy." Hiram picked up their previous conversation. "You can be a temperamental old puss at times."

What thoughts had sent old Doc Frick into a world of his own? Storm wondered. No matter. He chose to amuse himself with the banterings of the two lifelong friends. He liked these men . . . yes, even Isaac Grisham, who had sentenced him to ten years at hard labor.

He couldn't hold that against him, though. He'd been up against a brick wall, and a hard-nosed jury.

After polite amenities and small talk, Storm rose, announcing, "I've got to get into Granger and get a few things for those cabins in need of repair." And to the judge, "Did you see Old Potts?"

"I did," the judge said, approaching, then discreetly pressing a few bills into Storm's hand. "An advance on your wages," he whispered. "You'll need a little money."

To which he replied, "I'll get some funds from my bank account and pay you back."

The judge's features drained. "You don't have any money, Storm. The state seized your account in Nashville and your funds to repay the railroad company. I'm sorry I didn't tell you when you first mentioned your bank account. I didn't know how."

Storm grinned. "That's all right. Because that wasn't the only bank I had money in. Don't worry . . . I'll pay you back. I told you I don't need money and that old Potts can have my two dollars a week that the sisters are paying."

Judge Grisham nodded his approval, then returned to Hiram Frick, who was pouring a third cup of coffee.

"See you, Doc," called Storm as he exited into the morning.

"Don't forget to ride over and collect that wagon I donated to the sisters," Doc Frick called through the door.

Storm had already mounted his horse and was moving northward onto the road toward Granger.

An hour later, he'd loaded the wagon with the supplies he needed to work on the cabins, run into Old Potts and told him to meet him out there in the early afternoon. He now made his way to the mercantile to pick up the books as Sister Joseph had asked.

After he'd purchased a few toiletries for himself, a straight razor and soap and a bottle of spice cologne, he made his way to the rack and table which contained the few books Mr. Chadwick kept in the store.

He wasn't sure what Sister T would like in the way of reading material, so he chose titles that he thought sounded "romantic." He picked up *The Gates Ajar,* by Elizabeth Phelps, and *The Last Days of Pompeii,* by Lytton, because of the romantic female figure perched on the bow of a boat just inside the front cover. On a small table in the back of the mercantile, he found several books by a Mrs. Southworth, and two by Miss Pardoe, all the titles fitting what he perceived to be the category of "romance." This was a job much easier than he'd thought as he eventually dumped the load on the mercantile counter.

"Plan to do a lot of reading, Storm?" mused the merchant, Mr. Chadwick. "I don't remember you ever selecting those frilly things the ladies of the North write."

"They're not for me. They're for—" Suddenly, and he wasn't sure why, he didn't want to embarrass the sisters. He had been about to tell Mr. Chadwick that the books were for one of the church ladies and to put them on their bill. Now, he wasn't so sure that was a good idea, and he wondered if Sister Joseph had realized how potentially harmful the gossip could be if Mr. Chadwick, true to form, told the first customer to come in that the righteous sisters read scandalous romance novels. So, he struggled with an answer for a moment, then said, "All right, you caught me. They're for me. And I'll pay for them." Taking out the few bills Isaac Grisham had pressed into his hand that morning, he peeled off enough to pay for the books.

"Only need half the cover price," Mr. Chadwick said in his usual monotone. "Wife says I have to get the vulgar things out of the store." Then, "Heard from the judge that you were out of prison and working for the sisters."

"Thanks for the sale price," said Storm, not wishing to talk about his misfortunes. He quickly paid for the books, then dropped them into the canvas sack he'd brought into the mercantile with him. "Do you happen to have a teapot?" he asked, remembering the final item on his list.

"Just that plain blue one on the shelf over there. Want me to add it to the list?"

"Yes," replied Storm, fetching the dusty thing from the dustier shelf and setting it on the counter.

Chadwick wrapped it in heavy brown paper and gave it to Storm to add to his purchases in the canvas sack. As Storm prepared to leave, he asked, "You're not going to tell the ladies about town that I read these silly books, are you?"

To which a flustered, crimson-cheeked Mr. Chadwick replied in his haughtiest tone, "I'm not a gossip, Storm Phillips. Now, good morning to you."

Thought Storm as he exited, *Sure, and a fire won't burn you!*

Chapter Four

"Who was he?"

Old Potts had just told Storm quite a story, and Storm wasn't sure whether to believe him. The stories Old Potts had told in the past had turned out to be whoppers he'd invented while drunk out of his skin, and this seemed to be the same kind of tale.

Old Potts steadily handed the nails to Storm, who stood on a small ladder leaning against the middle cabin, replacing rotten boards around the single window. "He was some kind of preacher man, Storm," the grizzled old mountain man told him. "He was all dressed in black and this here—" As Potts swiped the black hat from his head, "He give me this here hat. I'm tellin' ya, Storm, we wuz standin' there on that trail, and—whoosh!—them bullets ripped right through the trees and cut 'em down. I went back later that night, but he wuz gone." He chose not to tell Storm that he'd taken the man's portfolio, thinking it might have contained money. "He must'a got drug off by a big ol' bear or somethin' real fierce-like."

"Did you go tell Mr. Black?"

Crispin Black was the Granger town marshal. "Yeah, I tol' him, but he says I should go sleep it off."

"Hellfire and damnation!" Storm's thumb, struck hard by the hammer, now went into his mouth for instant relief. "Don't you hate it when that happens?" he said, grinning at Potts after a moment.

"Yeah, when somebody don't believe me—"

"Not that," Storm chuckled. "When you beat the hell out of your thumb with a hammer." Storm studied his thumb, which was already turning blue beneath the nail.

Despite the small injury, the job was quickly finished. When Storm climbed down from the ladder, then set it aside so that he could replace the sill, Old Potts moved off a few feet to take a swig from his whiskey bottle. Soon, he returned to Storm, then started handing nails to him from the tin bowl.

After the sill had been replaced, Storm wrapped a long, bare arm across Old Potts's shoulders and urged him to the front of the cabin. "Judge packed sandwiches for our lunch. You hungry?"

"Sure," Potts grinned, "as long as I can wash it down with some whiskey instead of that sars'prilla I seen in that sack."

"You won't be able to drink that stuff when the church women move into the cabins," Storm reminded him for the tenth time that day. "They don't take to drinking, smoking, cussing, and just about every other worthwhile vice a man might be inclined to enjoy."

"That include pokin' around on women?" Potts said, grinning again, adjusting his crotch as he dropped to the narrow porch.

"That includes women," laughed Storm, tossing one of the sandwiches, wrapped in a linen napkin, toward him. "Judge says I got to bring back the napkins, so don't be wiping yourself with it."

Relaxing with his own sandwich and a bottle of sarsaparilla, Storm began to think about what Potts had told him. He wondered if the bullets he claimed had cut down a stranger—a stranger whose body had disappeared by the time he'd returned—had been meant for Potts. The only person hereabouts who would order a killing was McCallister Phillips, for whom Old Potts had worked, cleaning out stables and other small jobs on his ranch for a few weeks. It was only last week, the judge had told him in conversation yesterday, that McCallister had sent him packing, after he'd passed out drunk and let one of his employer's prize thoroughbreds break out of a stall. By the time the horse had been found in the possession of a poor man north in the Blue Ridge Mountains, it had been gelded, thus ending the plans McCallister had for it to cover his expensive mares and sire a ton of money for his coffers.

Storm was suddenly startled from his thoughts by Pott's graveled voice.

"Ya know, Storm, I think that feller what got kil't on the trail was an Englisher. Talked real funny-like an' called me a 'chap.'" Potts's head suddenly cocked to the side. "Storm, what is a . . ." He said the word slowly, pronouncing each syllable, "cat-e-chi-sum."

"Catechism," Storm quickly repeated the word. "In the context in which you heard the word, I'd imagine it's religious instruction. Where *did* you hear it?"

"Mr. Everton at the hardware, when I went for these here nails. He said one of 'em Bible ladies was in there, astin' 'bout young'uns in the mountains for a cat-e-chi-sum class."

"He must have been mistaken," Storm mumbled. "Catechism is a Catholic thing. I doubt the women used that word." Then, "If they want to give religious instruction to children, I'd like to know where the hell they're going to hold it, because these cabins are much too small."

"Ain't fer now, I reckon," Old Potts surmised. "Reckon it's for when this here church they be wantin' is built up."

Storm watched Potts settle against the cabin wall, his arms crossing and his knees drawing up. As he did yesterday, he would probably sleep for the rest of their meal break, which gave Storm time to ponder the subject of his father. He wondered if McCallister would kill a man over the loss of a horse's sexual appetite. He was sure that if McCallister was responsible, then Potts was the intended target, and not some strange Englishman.

He didn't like to think that Mack would have ordered a killing. He was still his father, no matter what he felt for him, and he liked to think that somewhere beneath Mack's rough, mean, unforgiving, and ofttimes ruthless exterior there was some degree of compassion. He had been wondering these past months if Mack might have been responsible for framing him for the robbery and sending him to jail. It was possible, he supposed, since just a few weeks before the crime, he had encountered Mack in Granger and had told him he was going to court to lay claim to part of Mack's ranch. That land had, after all, been purchased with money his mother, Rachel, had brought into the marriage. Mack had been mad; he'd said that if Storm dragged his name through court proceedings he would make him pay.

Perhaps he did.

So loudly were the thoughts ricocheting through his brain that he looked toward Potts, to make sure he wasn't listening to them. But he was fast asleep, as evidenced by the loud snoring now robbing the day of its silence.

They had done a lot of work in the last two days. Two of the cabins were almost ready for occupancy, and the third, in the worst condition since it took the full force of the north wind, would be completed by late tomorrow afternoon. It would need a new roof, and that was a job Storm would have to do by himself, since Potts was not steady enough to climb a ladder.

The judge had donated a few things for the comfort of the women: a new potbellied stove for preparing hot meals, table linens and towels, a case of soft tissues for the outhouse, dishes, bowls, pots and pans. Doc Frick had gone through his house, as well, setting aside items that he and Martha hadn't used in at least a year. Storm had installed the stove in the larger of the three cabins, with proper ventilation to the outside, and the boxes of donated goods were waiting for the sisters to organize.

There were still things to be done to make the place suitable for the sisters. Top priority on that agenda was breaking Potts of the habit of relieving himself against the trees. He imagined that could cause an apoplectic attack in even the youngest of the sisters.

Ah, yes. That would be Sister T, the shy little one. He wondered what horrible, personal calamity in her life had prompted her to seek the divine veil of a church. Perhaps a man had broken her heart at a tender age, perhaps her parents had died, instructing her to be sent into some religious order for guidance and nurturing. He wondered how old she was, if she had family—

A sudden gust of the February wind whistled across the porch, catching his dark hair and attempting to tear it from the bandanna tying it back from his face. He had just risen and stretched back his shoulders when he heard the plodding of a horse's hooves approaching on the roadway a hundred yards or so from the cabin. As he watched, a horse turned toward the cabins, and he recognized the dapple mare Hiram Frick always rode. Storm watched him halt and turn the horse, and presently another horse pulled up beside him from the road. Storm noticed the heavy black clothing that even the wind could not stir, and presently he recognized the masculine, deep-throated Sister Pete.

In deference to the woman, Storm pulled on his shirt. As he fastened the buttons, his boot edged out, hitting Old Potts against his thigh. "Get up, Potts," he ordered. "We've got company."

With a low growl that was more like a bear being disturbed from hibernation, Old Potts climbed to his feet, scratching at his head as his gaze turned in the direction of the road.

Presently, Hiram Frick climbed down from the dapple and Storm moved to help Sister Pete down. As her feet touched the ground, she said, "Bless you," then lowered her gaze.

"What brings you out," asked Storm, turning toward Hiram Frick.

"One of the sisters was ill. Sister Pete came in to fetch me since Mr. Collins was not at home."

"Oh? Is she all right?"

"A bit undone, I'm afraid. Unaccustomed to our changing weather."

To which Sister Pete added, "Sister T does not adjust to new climates as well as the others of us who are more traveled. And she is a worrier, which adversely affects the constitution. But, not to fret, Brother Storm. We are all praying for her."

"I see" came his reply. Since he'd been thinking about Sister T just moments ago, he felt a bit of color easing into his bronze features. "Would you like to see the work we've done?"

Potts now stood forward, removing the hat from his head as he did so. Bowing politely, he introduced himself. "Howard Potts, ma'—uh—" He immediately recalled that Storm had told him not to address the sisters as ma'am, and quickly amended to, "*Sister.* I'll be helpin' Storm with the work around here."

"So I understand," she responded, flicking dust from her dark clothing. Catching the overpowering odor of liquor, she quipped, "But you won't be helping for long if you don't stop drinking." Then, "Let us see what kind of job the two of you have been doing around here despite the vices of your helper, Brother Storm."

Her manly voice grated on Storm's nerves. Sister Pete moved into the nearest cabin, during which Storm discreetly tidied up the mess he and Potts had made of their lunch.

While Potts moved about, organizing the nails, shingles, and tools for the new roof, Storm accompanied Hiram as he followed Sister Pete through their labors. Occasionally, a grunt would be heard from the woman who appeared to be about fifty, or a hand would swipe over a particularly dirty area of one of the cabins. At times she would say, "This is good or," "It'll pass Sister Joseph's muster," and sometimes that latter statement was followed by a quieter, "Perhaps."

Then the inspection became personal, as Sister Pete rudely pointed out the bandanna Storm had tied around his head and asked, "Is that the mark of a savage, Brother Storm?"

It was all he could do to maintain his composure as he swiped the bandanna from his head. "No, Sister Pete, it catches sweat, which is what a man does when he works hard. It also controls my hair in this wind, since it is long and tends to get in my eyes—"

"That'll have to change," she snipped. "It isn't proper to wear your hair long and untidy like that, and Sister Joseph doesn't approve."

Hiram Frick saw that Storm's temper was heating. Laying a hand gently on his arm in an attempt to bring calm, he said, "Don't take offense, Storm. The sister does not mean to criticize."

His dark eyes narrowed. Pressing his mouth for a moment, he dismissed himself with a curt, "Excuse me, but I have much work to do before nightfall."

In his retreat, Sister Pete had noticed what she thought was a birthmark below Storm's left ear, but, in truth, was nothing more than a little grease. "That mark . . . it is the sign of the devil. I will have to pray for the young man."

To which Hiram Frick, losing his patience as well, shot back, "I brought that young man into this world, and he has no marks. What you see is a little dirty sweat." Then, with mustered patience, "We no longer live in the dark ages, Sister Pete, so we know there is no such thing as the devil's mark upon a person." Dragging in a breath that did nothing for his anger, he continued, "Sometimes I am amazed at human ignorance!"

Sister Pete gasped, drawing her hand to her throat in her moment of shock and dismay. "I did not mean to offend anyone."

As Hiram Frick moved form the dark interior of the cabin into the outdoors, he replied, "It is a human vice that we often speak without thinking, Sister Pete. We are all occasionally offensive and I must apologize for my harsh words."

* * *

Tallie would never have agreed that Sister Pete was offensive. The stout woman had become her closest friend, and she wished she were here right now. She really needed a confidant, and she did not feel comfortable talking to Sister Joseph, who was much too critical, or Sister Michael, who giggled nervously, even when the matter being discussed was serious, or Sister Meade, who cared about nothing but her little dog.

She was sorry Dr. Frick had wasted his time coming to see her. She didn't feel she was physically sick, but she was so sick at heart that she wasn't sure she would survive. Tallie had a dreadful feeling something was wrong, and she wanted to return to London and home. It no longer mattered that she might be in danger; she wanted only to assure herself that Aunt Cora and Ellie were all right.

She knew that Sister Pete would talk her out of going; perhaps that was what she needed from her right now. She couldn't imagine dear, beloved Ellie being left alone if something should happen to her—if the duke's men should be waiting for her to return to England—and Aunt Cora was getting up in years. She'd been nineteen years old when her younger sister—Tallie's mother—had been born, so as Tallie stopped to calculate in her head, Aunt Cora was sixty-nine years old. She'd never really thought about her age before, but now it was very important. Suppose something should happen to Aunt Cora while she was here in America? What would become of Ellie?

Then she remembered Aunt Cora's gentleman friend, Mr. Leggett, who had never let them down. Just before she'd moved onto the gangplank of the ship in Southampton that would bring her to America, she'd elicited the kind man's promise to look after Aunt Cora and Ellie. She had no reason to believe he wouldn't do just that.

He had also warned her that she couldn't write to them. The duke's men could possibly be watching the post and would intercept any suspicious mail to her aunt. But there had to be a way; Tallie simply had to think of a way to get word to her aunt that she was safe.

Of course! Mrs. Hawley in New York! She could write to Mrs. Hawley, and their American friend would be able to send a second letter to Cora through her London agent. She trusted Mrs. Hawley to be discreet.

But did Mrs. Hawley even know that she was to arrive at her country home near Tarrytown? Tallie tried to think. Aunt Cora had instructed Mr. Leggett to take her to Southampton and put her aboard ship so quickly that she wasn't sure if Mrs. Hawley had been notified. She tried to remember if Aunt Cora had said anything about it. Think! Think, Tallie! she mentally scolded herself. Instantly it came to her. Aunt Cora had posted a letter to their American friend, Tallie remembered, because her aunt wasn't sure which would arrive at Mrs. Hawley's town house first . . . Tallie or the letter. There was no question now. The letter would definitely arrive first. Perhaps it already had.

So, with renewed spirit, Tallie arose from the bed in which she'd been resting—doctor's orders—and moved into the parlor and the small alcove where the writing desk was located. There, she found the stationery Sister Pete had arranged in an orderly fashion on the desktop and took up pen and paper. She heard the stirrings of the sisters and Fanny Collins in the kitchen. So that she would not be disturbed, and thus commanded back to bed, she gingerly pulled the door to, then returned to the desk.

For half an hour she labored over the letter. Though she did not have to start over, she did pause for long periods of time to compose her thoughts before condemning them to paper. She told Mrs. Hawley everything that had happened, in the event that she had not received Aunt Cora's letter, then entreated her to inform her aunt of her whereabouts in a discreet manner, so that the duke's men would not find out. By the time she had added her signature to the end of the letter, she had seven pages written in her tiny handwriting. For a few minutes, she read over the letter, making sure she'd used proper grammar and had spelled all the words correctly. Assured that she had—her aunt had always been proud of her command of the English language—she wrote a second short letter to her aunt, sealed the pages in an envelope, addressed it and tucked it into the pocket of her skirt. She would not be able to tell the sisters she had written the letter, because they would not allow her to mail it. She didn't like being sneaky and going behind their backs, but she knew she had no choice.

Dr. Frick had promised to look in on her later in the afternoon; she would ask him to post the letter for her in Granger. But, how would she ask him not to tell the sisters without stirring his curiosity?

Well, she had the rest of the day to think about that. Feeling confident that she was taking the first step to reestablishing contact with her family—and her past—she now settled onto a small, narrow deacon's bench against the wall of the alcove. The Collins house was comfortable; she couldn't believe how much room it contained for the comfort of just two people. The apartment she shared with Aunt Cora and Ellie in the East End was small and cramped, and her aunt kept entirely too much furniture in the three small rooms, most of it cast-offs from people she knew who were a little better off. But it was a happy place, those three small rooms, and Tallie would give anything in the world if she were there right now, having tea with her aunt and scolding Ellie for trying to be the center of attention.

Thinking of Ellie made her remember that she'd missed Christmas with her two months ago. She hoped that their friends in Liverpool had provided a happy holiday for her young daughter; she felt confident that Aunt Cora and Mr. Leggett had gone to Liverpool to be with her and had taken the gifts Tallie had bought for her, adding a few of their own as well. She hoped that Ellie wouldn't think she had abandoned her, that she knew she would come home to her as soon as she was able, and that she would make up for the time they had missed together.

She recalled the brief, hurried conversation she'd had with

Aunt Cora as she'd packed to leave with Mr. Leggett. To this day, she was confused by the subject her aunt had brought up: the death of her mother on Christmas day in 1862, the same day Tallie had been born. She'd spoken of it bitterly, even mentioning the midwife whose negligence had caused her mother's death. Tallie had always felt guilty that her life had cost her dear mother her own, though she knew it wasn't her fault. So many things between her life and her mother's had been similar: both their husbands dying in the Royal Service soon after marriage, both giving birth to daughters several months afterward, and other small things that Tallie had selectively recalled over the years but could not now put a finger on. Even their handwriting had been similar. Tallie had loved reading the letters her mother had written to their father while he was away serving the Queen—letters that had been returned to her with his effects after his death. Her own poor husband had died before he could write even one letter for Tallie to keep as a special memory of him.

Looking out the window, she saw that small patches of frost still clung to the shadows at the edge of the woods. Mrs. Collins had said that the signs of spring were upon them, but Tallie couldn't see them. Mrs. Collins had said she'd seen a flock of robins the day before, but Tallie had missed the glorious sight, the "herald of spring": when the robins came, the warm weather was not too far behind. Dark, gloomy clouds hung on the far horizon, moving imperceptibly upon the mountain where the Collins house sat.

She was so absorbed with this painful separation from her family that had her sick at heart. The very idea that she was "brooding" might send the sisters into the alcove to pray for her everlasting soul, and she simply couldn't have that. They spent entirely too much time there as it was, especially Sister Michael, who seemed to have more sins than the rest of them.

What a dismal turn her thoughts had taken! It was one thing to think about home and family and to be lonely for them, quite another to be absorbed with the subject of sin. So, Tallie attempted to redirect her thoughts, though that direction proved just as futile. For as quickly as she put the issue of sins from her mind, the pinched, typically English features of Farrand Beattie popped into her thoughts. Still, she was hopeful that he was now just a very bad part of her past, for she was sure he had given up the quest and was even now returning to dock in Southampton. She smiled, though there was little mirth in it. She could imagine the rage of Collar and Cuffs when Beattie admitted he'd lost her and that she could be anywhere by now.

Yes, indeed, Farrand Beattie was floating somewhere in the mid-Atlantic, spending his days trying to come up with some excuse to give to his beloved prince.

Tallie was obsessed with that night she had gone to Mary Kelly's room. But now that she thought about it, in the fleeting, fearful moment she'd faced him down, she'd not seen a single drop of blood on Eddy's clothing. Could he have killed her and remained so clean and tidy? She thought not. If he was innocent, then how had he happened to be there? If he had not killed Mary, why was Farrand Beattie after her?

Of course! He thought *she* thought he had done it and that was the misunderstanding he wanted to prevent. Tallie wondered if there might be some chance that Farrand Beattie did not intend to kill her.

But, she knew in her heart, that she was grabbing at straws. Eddy *did* kill Mary, and Farrand Beattie *was* after her. She was in mortal danger, and so very, very fearful of dying at the hands of Farrand Beattie.

At the moment, Farrand Beattie just wanted to survive. He was coming to on the humble cot in the bunkhouse at McCallister Phillips's ranch six miles to the north. He hurt like the dickens, and he wasn't sure what was causing the source of his distress. Fire rippled through the right side of his chest, and his head and arm felt numb. And there was a most remarkable-looking woman perched in the hazy darkness over him, rather like an angel as he reached for some degree of lucidity.

"Who are you?" he asked the woman named Thea.

She told him her name, then, "You've been shot, and I am taking care of you."

"Have I, indeed? And since you have the advantage, will you tell me my name as well?"

A grimace claimed his features as he attempted to lift his head from the pillow. Instantly, Thea's slim hand went beneath his hair and the pillow was adjusted. "What do you mean . . . tell you your name? I was hoping *you* would tell *me*." Then, "I wouldn't move around too much. You'll open your wound."

The Englishman's thoughts were hazy; he wondered if it was natural not to know one's identity, because for the life of him, he could not remember his name, or even if he had one. For some strange reason, though, it failed to alarm him. He was rather proccupied with the woman, who was probably around forty years, tall, slim, and delicate, but a bit tired looking. Her pale auburn hair was unstreaked, and that which had come loose from her combs fell in wisps around her features. Her eyes . . . yes, eyes the color of caramel, were suddenly looking at him as if he'd lost all reasoning. "Do forgive me," the Englishman said quietly. "For a moment I was lost in my thoughts." Shrugging, he added, "Just as well, since I have lost my name, as well." Then, "Are you sure you have no idea?"

"I'm sorry. You had no personal papers on you when you were found" came her short explanation. "You have been out for a few days."

"A few days?" he repeated.

To which she replied, "Three, to be exact." Then, "What is an Englishman doing in this part of the world?"

"I'm English?" he asked, a little confused. "Yes, I suppose I am."

"You must remember something." When he failed to respond, and his face moved into an expression of confusion, she continued with haste, "Well, perhaps when you're fully recovered it'll all come back to you."

"It does seem a reasonable assumption." And with less conviction, "Of course, it will all come back."

Thea arched a pale, pencil-thin brow. She could see tremendous worry lining the man's features, and she wanted to offer him some comfort, some reassurance that he would eventually remember who he was, and how he'd come to be on the trail that night. She was thankful he had no memory of that, because she would hate to be faced with the decision as to whether to tell him who shot him, and why. She wouldn't like to tell him that Pokey had been aiming for another man and shot him instead, and that Pokey was the one responsible for his injuries and his loss of memory. She didn't have to tell him any of this, at least not for the time being. Perhaps losing one's memory could be a good thing.

"You were dressed in a preacher-man's attire," said Thea after a moment. "Does that bring back any memories?"

"None at all," he said, shrugging, then immediately feeling the pain of the move. "I do hope I do not have a fine woman somewhere worried about me."

"If you do, we'll find her," said Thea, attempting to show a little conviction. "Shall I place a paid advertisement in the Granger newspaper? Perhaps someone will come forward—"

"But suppose . . ." the Englishman shuddered at the possibility, "that I am a wanted man, running from some heinous crime?"

"You hardly look like a criminal," Thea said, lightly laughing. But she could see that he was deadly serious. "Well, perhaps the advertisement is not a good idea."

The Englishman thought the woman was as smart as she was pretty. Perhaps he didn't remember his identity, but he liked to think that he knew his character. Surely, that would not change. He was sure that if he were trying to deceive her she would be able to see right through him. He was sure he was an honest man, and he wouldn't be very good at lying. He was sure that any attempt to nourish a deceipt would simply be met by mental starvation. He honestly could not remember his identity, and he felt a desperate need for one.

Thea's fine eyebrow arched again as she looked into his eyes. "Have you remembered something?"

"No, I am afraid not, my good woman. It appears I am alone in this world, save for your tender mercy to me in this time of personal crisis." Farrand Beattie gave Thea's hand a light pat, withdrawing almost immediately. "Tell me, my good woman, where am I in?"

"You are at the Phillips Ranch."

"I mean, what borough am I in?"

"Borough? If that is like a state, this is Tennessee, the Blue Ridge mountain range near Granger."

"That is the nearest town? Yes, you did mention it a few minutes ago." With a warm smile, he said, "This unfortunate chap wouldn't mind a little nourishment, if it isn't asking too much." Then, "Sorry for my boldness. Do I have any money to pay for a meal?"

"You had a little on you," said Thea. "But there is no need of money here." Moving toward the curtain partitioning them from the bunkhouse, she continued, "It is the least we can do for a foreigner in our mountains."

Then she was gone, and the Englishman listened to her retreating footsteps, missing her almost at once.

He was strangely at ease over the loss of his identity. It seemed somehow a relief to him.

Chapter Five

Tallie liked the small, comfortable cabin to which she and Sister Pete were assigned at the site of the new church. The larger cabin was flanked by the two smaller ones, and all the cooking that would be done there would make the long, single room warm and cozy when they were sleeping at night.

Sister Joseph had chosen a lovely site for the church, at the top of a wide hill, with a sheer drop-off to the valley three hundred yards beyond. A line of strapling oaks sat like ships' masts against the azure sky, and the young trees were all that would keep them from stepping off into eternity. For that reason, Tallie had suggested that a good, sturdy fence be built before a lot of activity commenced at the site of the church, in the event a child should wander too near the precipice.

Sister Pete cast a critical eye toward Tallie as she unpacked her small canvas bag and placed the items in the lower two drawers of the chest they would share. ''Sister Joseph . . .'' Her voice raised as she said the single world, ''surely,'' then lowered again, as she finished, ''doesn't know what you wear beneath your dress, Sister Tallie.''

She made a rather dismal effort to tuck the lacy undergarments beneath the edges of a heavy woolen neckscarf Sister Michael had given her for chilly evenings. "What do you mean?" she said in a tone that indicated she was trying to be effectively naive. "One must wear underclothes, mustn't they?"

"And the underclothes that a Jezebel wears, Sister Tallie?" Sister Pete retorted, her mouth twisting, but not in a smile. "You should drop to your knees and pray to Jeeuzus for forgiveness!"

Tallie hated the way she said "Jesus," as though she were trying to give it a third syllable. Sister Pete was, unquestionably, the most devout and zealous of the sisters, but she was also the first one to understand that Tallie was *not* one of them, and had interests other than the church they were establishing here in the mountains. Sister Pete also had a wonderful sense of humor, as Tallie had observed on many occasions. "I wonder how hard it would be to legally change my name. I think I would like to be named . . ." Tallie paused for effect, her mouth widening into a smile as she ended, "Jezebel!"

Just at that moment, a knock echoed lightly at the door. Tallie spun, nearly upsetting her balance, then covered her mouth as her gaze cut to Sister Pete. Suppose it was Sister Joseph, and she had heard what she'd said—

Raising her eyebrows dramatically heavenward, Sister Pete moved to the door. There stood Storm Phillips, one muscled forearm propped lazily against the door facing. He smiled, indicating that he had heard Tallie's declaration, though he discreetly said nothing. "Sister Joseph wants everyone to come to the clearing and give their approval of the dimensions for the foundation. Also, to choose a location for the Lodge of Sisterhood."

Had she detected the slightest note of sarcasm as he'd spoken the name of their permanent quarters, yet to be built? Sister Pete replied, "Of course," and Tallie lowered her head, turning gracefully until her back was full to Storm.

Storm stood aside while Sister Pete moved past him, then began to close the distance between the cabin and the other three sisters, already standing reverently at the site, awaiting them. Storm looked toward the "shy little one"; unbeknownst to him, she was waiting for him to leave before emerging from the cabin.

Tallie took a long, slow breath. Though she could not see him, she knew he was still there; she could sense his presence as surely as if he stood in a dark East End alley, waiting to pounce out and attack her in the deadly twilight.

In a small voice, she said, "You may go, sir. I will be along presently."

Storm immediately sensed that she did not want to be near him. It both amused and annoyed him, and he took a special delight in replying, "I don't mind waiting."

So Tallie, taking another breath, drew down her head wrap, lowered her gaze and ducked past him in the doorway, her footfalls at a quick pace as she tried to outdistance him.

But he would not allow it. Storm's long strides easily kept pace beside her, and she discreetly turned her face away from him.

Breathing a sigh of relief as she stood with the other women, she now watched Storm Phillips rejoin Old Potts. She had wanted to talk to him, smile at him, even share a joke or two with him, but Sister Joseph had warned her that she must not draw attention to herself. She had to keep in the background, if they were to effectively protect her from her human demons.

Now that they were all together, Sister Joseph adjusted her garguantan eyepatch and then clasped her hands firmly together. "Well, Sisters, this is to be it, the new church our beloved Lord and Protector has sanctioned. We shall drop our heads in prayer for the kind love offering of Dr. Hiram Frick." The prayer was brief; Tallie was the only one who did not lift her head, not so much because she felt her prayer should be longer, but to avoid the intense gaze of Storm Phillips.

Storm was well aware that he unnerved the young woman who did not want him to see her face. He was sure her coarse wrap stood out a full foot from her forehead in order to hide beneath the shade of it, and yet he still caught the twinkle in her eyes. He could see her eyes, though not their color. The wisp of hair, caught by a rare glint of sunlight, was pale, almost like spun gold. He watched her slim hand slowly rise, to tuck it beneath the heavy material of her head-covering.

He wanted to talk to her, but he also did not want to anger Sister Joseph, who had been tolerant of his past and willing to give him a chance to prove his worth. And proving his worth did not involve the "shy little one."

Shy little one, indeed! She *was* shy, but for a reason he did not yet know. Though she was very slender, she was also tall for a woman, so she could hardly be described as "little," as a petite woman might be. He thought her pretty and graceful, though he had not gotten a good look at her features, which she seemed to guard zealously. And it annoyed the hell out of him that she was one of the sisters. Very seldom did he see a woman who sparked his interest the way she did.

Tallie was not really listening to the chatterings of the sisters. Though her eyes were upon them, she was listening for the smooth, mellow voice of the man named Storm Phillips. She could vaguely see him out of the corners of her eyes, and his gaze seemed to be upon her. He was quiet, his mouth pinched, his eyebrows furrowed as though he were deep in thought. She thought him a terribly intense man, and an intriguing one. It was all she could do to obey the sisters and avoid him.

"Sister T, are you well? Your face is terribly flushed."

Startled, Tallie drew her palms up to cover her features. Fear shot into her gaze as her attentions turned to Sister Meade, whose inquiry had dragged her from her intimate thoughts. "Of course," she said, lightly laughing, then fanning herself with her fingers. "It is only the sun shining upon me. I feel quite well." Instinctively, her eyes cut to Storm, though briefly, and she saw that he was talking to Old Potts in a quiet voice she could not discern.

She deliberately redirected her thoughts, to something mundane but important, the subject of the letter she had asked

Hiram Frick to post for her. She remembered the way he had looked at her, as though he were questioning her integrity, and she had hastily explained that Sister Joseph felt they should settle in well before they let their families know they were all right, but that she simply couldn't wait. "Please don't tell her, for I wouldn't want her to think I am being a baby," she had implored.

He had asked her if he was wrong to assume that she was expected to give up her private life, as Sister Joseph had told him, when she had joined the "Sisterhood." She had merely shrugged, explaining that "things are different now. Our service should be a joy, not a sacrifice."

He had smiled, patting her hand in a way that she remembered Mr. Leggett patting it just before she'd boarded ship in Southampton. She had known that Dr. Frick understood, and that he would be discreet. Mrs. Hawley would receive her letter in a few weeks and she, too, Tallie was sure, would be discreet in getting the second letter to her dear aunt in London.

A hand wrenched her shoulder back. With a small cry, Tallie felt powerful masculine arms scoot around her waist from behind her and jerk her body against him.

A trembling Storm Phillips held her close, even as the other sisters moved swiftly toward them. Storm whispered to Tallie, "Couldn't let our favorite Jezebel fall to her death," then when the women surrounded them, he explained, "She was about to step off the cliff."

Tallie saw at once the small spanse of space between the saplings that would have taken her over the incline. As she peeled herself from Storm's grip, then turned to face the sisters, who looked at her as if she'd gone completely mad, tears welled in her eyes. Completely embarrassed by the carelessness that could have caused her death—as well as the fact that Storm had heard what she'd said to Sister Pete in their cabin—she broke into a run toward the sanctuary of four plain walls.

With a grunt and a nod, Sister Joseph ordered that a fence be erected immediately, "so that this will never happen again."

"Potts and I will get right on it," Storm said.

As he started to move away, Sister Joseph said in a stern, heavy voice, "Brother Storm, you are never to touch one of the sisters again. Is that understood?"

He did not turn, though his hands moved up to rest on his hips. "I should have let her walk off the cliff?" he asked in a controlled tone.

"You could have spoken sharply and gotten her attention. She would have halted."

"Perhaps." Still, he did not turn. "And perhaps, Sister Joseph, instead of asking me to build a fence, you would now be asking me to dig a grave."

Tallie was so embarrassed she thought she would faint. She dropped heavily against the inside of the door, attempting to slow her breathing so that the dizziness would go away. She really didn't mind so much, now that she thought about it, that Storm had heard her refer to herself as "Jezebel," nor did she mind that he had saved her from certain death. What did worry her, though, was that she could not remember approaching the cliff, and certainly could not remember advancing upon the vast openness of the sky that would have resulted in her death. Parted from her loved ones in England, did she have a secret desire to die? Not knowing frightened her. Believing that she wanted to live more than anything in the world made what had happened all the more horrible.

And she was confused. Storm Phillips had held her close to him, and she could still feel the commanding, trembling warmth of that embrace. True, his first intent might have been to keep her from walking off the cliff, but then when he could have let her go, he had continued to hold her close, until the approach of the sisters had forced him to relinquish his possession of her.

He had been even more gentle than her tragic young husband. Life with David, had he lived, might have been perfect, had it not been for his parents. They had never forgiven their only son for marrying a "common street girl" and, thereafter, had chosen not to know their granddaughter. She suspected that it was because of the distance they would have had to travel to see the child; she did not want to think it was because of the differences in their social classes, though she suspected that it was.

Oh, but why was she thinking about her dead husband and his family, when it was the bronze, brooding Storm who filled her wildest imagination? She touched her waistline, sure that she could feel the power of his embrace still upon her. She eased her head back, sure, too, that his warm breath still tickled against her hairline. She listened to the silence of the morning, the faraway mutterings of the sisters, and she was sure she could hear Storm's voice. *Couldn't let our favorite Jezebel fall to her death!*

The girls in the East End had loved boasting of their "romantic" conquests. To hear their stories about how the right man could make her feel, she had thought that the "right" man in her life had died young and tragically, leaving her alone in a world where she would never find another like him. She had imagined all these years that she was correct about that.

But right now, her imagination was running wild through the mountains with Storm Phillips. What would his arms feel like surrounding her? How hot would his flesh be against her own, how strong would his arms be? She wondered what his body looked like without the barrier of clothing—

"What are you thinking, Sister T?"

She spun so rapidly that she lost her balance, her buttocks landing upon the bed firmly enough that she felt the springs through the thin mattress. She faced Sister Michael, standing in the doorway like an enormous bully, her hands drawn to her hips. Tallie expected to hear excited giggles, but Sister Michael might have been preparing her for the sacrifice, so stern and implacable was her narrow scrutiny. "I wasn't thinking about anything." She shrugged now, her sweating palms drawing discreetly along the lines of the blanket. "I was wallowing in self-pity, I am afraid, terribly embarrassed by what happened, and I do not know when I shall be able to face the sisters again. All of you must think I am an idiot."

"Our Lord wouldn't let us think anything of the sort, Sister T," said Sister Michael, her mouth now moving cautiously into a smile. She did not want Tallie to think she was laughing at her. "We are all very concerned, and do hope you aren't thinking about . . ." She hesitated to continue, "killing yourself."

"Heavens forbid!" retorted Tallie, drawing her hand up to the wisp of hair escaped from the wrap. "I do not know why I went so near the precipice. I want only to see my daughter and my aunt again. What would happen to them if I were to die?"

"Good! Then we needn't worry about you in that regard." Sidestepping a small-rug, lest she trip, Sister Michael now said to Tallie, "We are going into town. Will you be all right?"

"The handyman is taking you?"

"The old gentleman called Potts. The young fellow has already begun setting the posts for that fence along the cliff."

Shamed because she was the cause of his additional labors, Tallie dropped her head. She would have to remember to apologize to Storm when—or if—she was ever allowed to speak to him. "I do not have to go with you, do I?"

"No, Sister Joseph says you are to rest. Then it will be up to you to see that the evening meal is prepared for our return."

This cool tone of voice was so unlike Sister Michael that Tallie silently studied her round features. She wasn't sure if the lack of emotion was deliberate, or whether something had been said to make her so reverent. Tallie was worried, but not enough to interrogate Sister Michael on her uncharacteristic severity. "I shall have the meal prepared," she said after a moment. "And I shall make some pastries with the fine apples Mr. Phillips brought us yesterday."

For a moment, Sister Michael's usual exuberance returned. "And fine tarts they'll be, too, since we all suspect that Brother Storm pilfered the apples from someone's orchard."

Tallie smiled. When Sister Michael had withdrawn, she settled back on the cot and drew up her knees. Soon, the rumbling of the wagon could be heard, as well as Sister Joseph's authoritative lectures as it was swallowed by the road and the forest.

Just at that moment, a slight knock echoed upon the hardwood door. Tallie came immediately to her feet, deliberately straightening her garb and hair as she answered the knock. Even as she called, "Yes, who is it," she knew there was no need. The man, Storm Phillips, was the only one remaining at the site with her.

Lowering her gaze, she opened the door. Indeed, there stood Storm Phillips in the shadows of the porch, holding a small canvas sack, which he proffered to her.

"Sister Joseph had asked me to pick up some books for you to read the other day. I forgot to give them to you. Sorry."

Taking the sack, she said, "Thank you," then attempted to close the door.

Storm's hand moved swiftly to keep it open. "Are you all right?"

Tallie did not turn toward him. Focusing on a small framed print Sister Pete had hung over her cot, she said, "I am fine. Thank you for asking."

Though her dismissal was polite, Storm did not like it one bit. He drew himself up, and his forearm moved along the facing of the door. "I don't know how you and I have gotten off on the wrong foot, Sister T, but I've gotten to know all the women except you. Could we at least be tolerant of each other?"

"I am quite tolerant of you, Mr. Phillips—"

"And that's another thing. Everyone calls me by my first name . . . except you. I don't like being called Mr. Phillips. Makes me feel like an old man. I can't be that much older than you—" Why in the name of everything that meant anything to him did he feel a sudden compulsion to kiss her, he would never know. It surprised, and embarrassed, him as quickly as it came upon him. Though he did not act on his impulse, he experienced the moment just as if it had actually happened.

So, he turned away, preparing to leave, once again denied

the sight of her eyes, her nose, her mouth, and her smooth crimson cheeks. He had seen her features only from a distance or deep in the shadows of that ugly, ever-present shawl, and they had seemed flawless and lovely. But if he were to run into her on a street in Granger in pretty, feminine attire, he would not know who she was. She was the ''shy little one,'' the one who would not let him see her face, and the one who treated him as though he were the last person on earth she wanted to know. He wasn't sure what he had done, or perhaps if some horrible episode in her past had made her leery of men, but he was obsessed with knowing what she looked like.

Once again, though, that small privilege was denied him. He walked away and did not see Tallie come to the door of the cabin and look longingly after him.

She drew a deep sigh, then quietly closed the door. Throwing herself upon her cot, she fought back tears with little success. When she finally fell asleep, she dreamed of London, Aunt Cora, and Ellie.

And a dark-eyed rogue named Storm Phillips.

Fanny Collins came to see her that afternoon, disturbing her from her nap. She had seen the sisters in Granger, had spoken at length with Sister Joseph in the small restaurant at the end of Main Street and she had given her permission to visit Tallie.

''I know you are not one of them,'' Fanny Collins said, politely accepting the cup of coffee Tallie had brewed while she waited. ''And Sister Joseph feels that you need some excitement before you lose your mind. So—''

Tallie was concerned, not only because Sister Joseph had told Fanny her problem, but because by doing so it appeared that she did not believe Tallie's danger to be valid. Settling across the table from Fanny, she asked, ''What kind of excitement do you have in mind?''

''Every February, to celebrate the approach of spring, there is a winter ball at the Granger Social Club. John and I have never missed one of them."

"A winter ball," Tallie quietly repeated. "You are asking me to go?"

Fanny had noticed her hesitancy, and she was a little confused by it. Tallie herself was a puzzle to Fanny. She claimed to have been raised in London's East End, and Fanny had once seen a play in which one of the characters—a street woman—played her scene in the East End. But the character and Tallie sounded nothing alike. Recovering her thoughts, Fanny said, "Sister Joseph says you'll be safe."

"It sounds wonderful, but I really don't know. I admit it would be nice to wear a proper dress again, put a little color on my lips . . ." Suddenly, her brows furrowed, "I really must talk to Sister Joseph before I give you an answer."

Fanny seemed a bit disappointed. Covering Tallie's hand with her own, she said, "Then let's just pretend for a moment that you are going. What would you wear to a ball?"

Tallie thought for a moment, then smiled. "I really do not know. I have nothing fancy enough for a ball."

"In the event you decide to go—and you have two weeks to think about it—why don't you leave the matter of a costume to me, Tallie. You can come to the house later this week and we'll fit you for a dress. I have several that I've worn in the past, as well as matching masks and the fanciest head pieces you've ever seen—"

"Masks! It is a costume ball?"

"Did I fail to mention that? Because it is a costume ball Sister Joseph feels you will be safe."

"Oh, it sounds won—" Color rose in Tallie's cheeks as she came to her feet, cutting her sentence short as she tried to contain her enthusiasm, because she really did not feel that attending such a function would be appropriate. She was also fighting the impulse to give Fanny an answer right now.

* * *

Storm was not eavesdropping. He had just brought a bucket of water to place on the small table outside the kitchen door and he'd heard Sister T and Fanny talking about the winter ball. He'd also heard Fanny call her "Tallie." He liked the name; he could imagine whispering it against her cheek.

Storm wanted to look in the window and get the glimpse of Tallie he'd been aching for, but he could not do so without detection.

Even through the barrier of wood, he could hear the tilt of her voice, the excitement and the anticipation of going to the ball, even as she had tried to suppress it.

He had also heard the fear.

He didn't like big crowds of people, but if Tallie went, he knew he would be there, as well. If, that is, he could talk Judge Isaac Grisham into allowing it.

"As I said, Fanny, I'll give you my answer after I talk to Sister Joseph about it."

Fanny set her coffee cup down and arose. "I know just the costume for you, Tallie. You'll be the belle of the ball."

Tallie hugged her tightly. "Thank you, Fanny. Thank you so much for inviting me."

A frown touched the thin, pleasant features of Fanny Collins. "There's just one thing. Sister Joseph says that if you do go to the ball you aren't to tell the others, or anyone else for that matter. I'll invite you to spend that weekend with John and me, on the pretense of teaching you some mundane domestic chore. Is that agreeable?"

"It is," said Tallie. Following polite amenities, Tallie saw Fanny to her surrey. She waved farewell and watched the buggy disappear into the forest.

Storm had read Tallie's reaction accurately. She was excited at the prospect of going to a ball, but fearful at the same moment.

She knew she would not be able to return to her nap. Since she was alone, she dashed a little of her favorite perfume behind her ears, a luxury Sister Joseph had forbidden, then went to the small kitchen and began preparing the evening meal.

But as she peeled potatoes and put a little honey and sauce over the ham, she started thinking about Sister Joseph's leniency in terms of protection. Tallie had suspected for some time now that the eldest sister had thought she'd overreacted to the presence of Farrand Beattie aboard ship and that, perhaps, he had not meant her the harm she so feared. Perhaps this was Sister Joseph's way of weaning her from their protection, of forcing her to return to her own way of life, that of a "civilian," as she often referred to women not of the sisterhood.

She thought about the ball, wondering who might be there. Would she fit in? And the costume? Would Mrs. Collins dress her as an overstuffed chicken? Or perhaps a clown or a court jester? She was thinking that she might go to the ball as a queen or a fairy-tale princess, but suppose Fanny Collins had other plans? A chicken costume would certainly add the humility to her life Sister Joseph said she lacked!

She hoped that, after her talk with Sister Joseph, she would be able to give Fanny an affirmative answer. She wanted to go to a costume ball. No matter the lesson Sister Joseph was attempting to teach her, she was determined that, should she go, she would have a good time. She imagined that Dr. Frick and the judge would attend the annual ball. She smiled as she thought of the dear old men, then resumed her duties over the food she was preparing.

A knock sounded at the rear door opening onto a narrow back porch. She turned swiftly, just as Storm Phillips pushed the door open without awaiting her response. A potato fell to the floor; she did not turn as Storm's few steps brought him to the table, but she saw the shadow of him as he bent, picked up the potato and returned it to the tipped collander from which it had fallen.

Silence claimed a few moments as he stood there. Then he said, "I just wanted you to know I'll be cutting some saplings out of sight of the settlement. I won't be far away should you need me."

She bowed imperceptibly, saying nothing.

Another moment of silence allowed Storm to wonder if her hair was cropped off short like the other women, who did not always wear head coverings, as Sister T did. "Could I bring wildflowers for the dinner table?" he offered.

"That would be nice." Her voice was scarcely above a whisper. "Thank you, Mr.—Storm."

He smiled, though she was not looking toward him. As he began his withdrawal from the kitchen, he caught the delicate whiff of her perfume and turned back, the smile returning. "Is that perfume you're wearing, Sister T?"

She flustered, crimson rising so quickly into her cheeks that she thought they might explode. "No, no indeed! It is your imagination."

But he knew it wasn't his imagination. The "shy little one" . . . Tallie . . . was wearing perfume! He couldn't help himself. Returning to her, he took her elbow and dragged her to him.

Tallie's voice caught in her throat, even as she fought to issue a protest. Storm Phillips was holding her close, giving her little room to lower her head without her face touching the broad expanse of his chest. The musky, manly scent of him assailed her senses, and it stirred something strong, wild, and wonderful within her. What was she to do . . . and what did *he* plan to do?

She was to find out, at once. Storm's right hand moving swiftly up, he pulled the heavy scarf from Tallie's head, watching the mounds of golden hair tumble from the bindings of coarse fabric. When her livid hazel eyes lifted to him, her full, parted mouth gasping in a breath, he grinned, dipped his head and touched his mouth to her own.

"If you're a church woman," he murmured against her tousled hair, "then I'm Abe Lincoln . . . and he's been dead for years."

Then he was gone, and Tallie, dropping into the nearest chair to still her tremble, drew her finger to her mouth, to touch the hot gentleness of Storm's kiss.

Chapter Six

Tallie sat beside Sister Joseph on a small bench at the edge of the clearing, angrily drawing her hand away when the older woman attempted to touch it. "Now, Tallie, I am not saying you were lying about being followed, I am saying only that we have been here for weeks and I've seen no danger. You are a young woman, a civilian, and you must satisfy a civilian's craving for satisfaction beyond the needs of our Lord. Go to the winter ball with John and Fanny Collins. Have a good time, then come back and tell me all about it . . ." Remembering she didn't want the others to know about Tallie's special privilege, she added, "In private." The way Tallie pursed her mouth gave her face a childlike quality. "And don't pout, Tallie. You cannot tell me you don't *want* to go?"

Tallie did not want to give her the satisfaction of being right. So she said, "I shall go, if you insist, but if I am killed, will you notify my aunt and see that I am properly buried? Up here where I will always be near you and the sisters?"

Sister Joseph laughed lightly. "You are not going to die, Tallie." Her hand swooped out, capturing Tallie's before she could avoid it. Patting it roughly, she said, "Suppose we talk about what you think you saw in London that night you went to Mary Kelly's room?"

"I saw Mary, hideously murdered, and then I saw Eddy."

Sister Joseph paused in thought. "And how did Eddy look?"

"Immaculate, as always, a little wild-eyed—"

"Immaculate and wild-eyed. No blood on his clothing? No weapon in his hand? If I were an investigator, Tallie, and I came upon the scene, and this young suspect were still there, I would look at him, I would see that his clothing was free of blood, that no weapon was in his hand, and probably not on the scene, either, and I might tend to believe he'd come upon this heinous crime, after the fact, just like you did."

Tallie pressed her mouth for a moment. "You are not English, Sister Joseph. Why do you defend the Crown? Why can you not believe that the prince might be guilty?"

"I didn't say that he definitely was not guilty, Tallie. I am only telling you how I view the possibilities. You said yourself that Mary had many friends and that the prince frequented the East End. Perhaps he was one of Mary's many friends—"

"Well, I know for a fact that he was. Mary was proud of her friendship with certain people of social class and stature." A thought came to Tallie. "If you believe I am not in danger, then why do you not suggest that I return to England?"

Sister Joseph adjusted the patch over her eye. "To be sure, Tallie. We would never forgive ourselves should you return home and some dreadful fate came upon you."

"You would never know," Tallie pointed out.

"I'd know." Sister Joseph slowly nodded. "Of course, I'd insist that you keep in touch by post, and when I didn't hear from you, I'd know. Now . . ." With a final squeeze, she relinquished Tallie's hand. "Go to the winter ball with John and Fanny and have a good time. Will you do that for me?"

Tallie had never been to a ball. The closest she had come was the dance held by the boarding school Mr. Leggett had sent her to, "so that you will not sound coarse and common, Tallie, like the girls of the East End." At that event, the girls at the school, twelve to fifteen years of age, had sat on one side of the long, narrow room, and the slightly older boys from another school had sat on the other. With a small, worried smile, Tallie said, "Yes, Sister Joseph, I shall go." Rising, she said, "I must return to the kitchen. The biscuits must be rolled out and baked." Gathering her hands against her waist, Tallie moved swiftly toward the kitchen.

Sister Joseph, sitting alone now, drew a small breath. When Storm approached on her blind side, she gave a start. "Sorry," he apologized. "Is she going to go?"

"She is," responded Sister Joseph. "And you must keep a very close eye on her. Don't let anything happen to our Tallie."

"I won't let her out of my sight."

Sister Joseph sniffed, "And don't get familiar with our Tallie, Brother Storm. It will not be tolerated!"

Storm tipped his hat, a smile curling his mouth as he put distance between them.

John Collins came for Tallie at three o'clock Friday afternon. As she swiped off her apron, Tallie, with a downward gaze, explained to Sister Pete, the only one in the kitchen with her, that "Fanny Collins wants me to teach her how to make monkey bread," then rushed from the kitchen and into the waiting surrey before questions could be asked.

Seeing a half-naked Storm Phillips at the woodpile, his dark, narrowed eyes intently watching the surrey, she discreetly turned her face away as they entered the road. The rogue had kissed her . . . she still had not forgiven him for that . . . and for not doing it again.

Sister Joseph had ordered that he always wear his shirt, but even in this chilly February weather, he often went without one, especially when he was hard at work. She imagined that one of the sisters would soon lecture him on his "ungodly indecency," and demand that he clothe himself.

"So, how are you today, Tallie?"

She looked to John Collins now, his wide mouth turned into a smile as he anticipated her answer. He looked different, perhaps because he had tried to draw the thin, scant remains of his hair over the bald patch above his forehead, greasing it unattractively down. "I am doing wonderfully, Mr. Collins. Thank you for asking."

He touched Tallie's hand, then held it in a way that made her feel very uncomfortable. Politely, she withdrew it, on the pretense of straightening her scarf. She wanted to remove the covering, but Sister Joseph had said she must wear it in public. Public! There wasn't a soul on the road winding through the dense woodlands of the Blue Ridge Mountain Range, so how could this possibly be construed as "public?" She kept the scarf over her hair anyway, in deference to Sister Joseph's wishes.

"You'll be very pleased with the costume Fanny has chosen for you," John Collins continued the conversation. "It's been a few years since the wife fit into it, but—" His eyes moved boldly over Tallie, "it will fit you, snug and nice."

Tallie could scarcely believe the overly thin Fanny Collins could once have been smaller without the first heady wind carrying her away. Proffering a small smile, Tallie made no comment. She was relieved when they pulled up to the porch of the Collins house half an hour later. Tallie hopped right down and was met by Fanny at the door. "I've just made a pot of tea. Come in and make yourself comfortable." When she saw the fleeting moment of disappointment cross Tallie's face as she moved past her and into the house, Fanny's arm went over her shoulder. "Then again, perhaps we should look at your costume first . . ."

Tallie fought to maintain her reserve, but in these two days since Sister Joseph had insisted she go to the ball, she could not help but allow her excitement to be dominant. "Could we?"

Fanny moved swiftly toward a small back room where she had laid out two costumes on an unused bed. She immediately picked up the more modest one and hung it over the door of an armoire. "This one is mine. I'm going to the ball as Princess Marigold, the daughter of King Midas, who wished that everything he touched would turn to gold."

"Yes," said Tallie with a small laugh. "He hugged his daughter, who turned to gold, as well."

Tallie's gaze now fell upon the beautiful costume spread out on the bed, a gown, a headpiece, costume jewelry, and shoes. She knew as well as her own heart the historical figure the costume represented, and as she picked it up, she remembered reading everything she could about the ancient queen who had so enthralled her and never seemed quite real to her. When she turned to Fanny, holding the gown up to her dark-clothed body, tears misted her eyes. "This is what I'll wear, Fanny?"

"That is what you'll wear," Fanny chuckled good naturedly, "if it meets your approval."

Pulling off her scarf and tossing it to the bed, Tallie picked up the headpiece and adjusted it over her hair that had been mashed flat by the coarse black fabric. Approaching the cheval mirror, she again adjusted the dress against her figure. "It's beautiful. Are you sure you don't mind if I wear it?"

"Let's try it on, Tallie." She chose not to tell Tallie that the costume had never been worn, that John had brought it, especially for Tallie, from a costume shop in Nashville, and that she had insisted John back up the small lie that the costume belonged to her. She did not wat Tallie to feel guilty that she might have gone to a little expense for her. "There's also a wig that goes with it, and a mask. I was just trying to find it when you arrived." She began to dig through the clutter in the bottom of the chifforobe, soon coming up with a small velvet drawstring bag, where she had placed it so that Tallie would believe the costume really was hers. "Yes, it should be in here, and the wig, too." Even as she spoke, her hand eased into the fabric and emerged, holding the two items. "Climb out of that dowdy garment you're wearing, and let's transform you into a thing of beauty, Tallie."

But Tallie was so dumbfounded that she didn't hear a word Fanny Collins uttered. She was looking at the elaborate costume through tear-sheened eyes and thinking how awed her beloved Ellie would be. And though she was happy to be going to the ball, she would trade that experience for just one hug from Ellie.

The eve of the ball was upon Tallie so quickly she couldn't believe so much time had gone by. Sister Joseph explained to the sisters that Tallie was going out into the mountains to "minister to the poor," which, of course, elicited responses such as, "Why?," and "She's not one of us; she shouldn't be going", and "Some mischief is in the works!" Sister Joseph decided to "come clean," as Sister Pete had boldly suggested.

"Tallie is attending the annual costume ball in Granger," she finally revealed "You must remember that she is a young civilian smothered by our attentions—"

"And our protection," snipped the usually jovial Sister Michael.

"She must have some small part in the outside world if she is to survive," Sister Joseph explained. "She has been very helpful to us these past few weeks and, I might add, without receiving a single penny for her work. So we should unbegrudgingly give her this happiness."

"Of course, you are right, Sister Joseph," Sister Pete replied.

Sister Meade, holding her dog, remained quiet, though the dog did not.

And Sister Michael hung her head in shame that she had envied Tallie her night at a fancy ball. As self-punishment, she volunteered to pray for forgiveness, which, Sister Pete realized only later, was an act perpetrated in her desire to avoid kitchen duties, which would have been Tallie's job that evening.

* * *

Unbeknownst to Tallie, Storm Phillips would be going to the ball as her bodyguard, should she genuinely have a need for one. Sister Joseph had not told Storm the manner of the threat to Tallie as she had insisted he always keep her in his sight. She had not told the other sisters that Storm would be gone that night, nor had she told Tallie she might possibly see him there. Though she was certain Tallie liked surprises as much as any normal woman her age, Sister Joseph didn't think she liked Storm Phillips very much.

Storm had gone to the judge's house to change into his costume. By the time he emerged from the spare bedroom to meet a judge dressed as Henry the Eighth, he had managed to transform himself into something he was sure would suit his image.

Judge Isaac Grisham was not at all amused. "You're going to the ball dressed like that, Storm? I've already come under fire from the governor for letting you out of prison, and he's going to be there tonight."

"He always says he's going to come, Judge, but can you think of a single year he's actually shown up?" Storm reminded him. Storm pulled the hood of his costume over his head now, so that in a matter of moments all that showed of his face were his dark eyes. He wielded the heavy executioner's axe across the leather vestment of his outfit, then stood with his booted feet apart. Then he gave the judge the once-over, grinning beneath his mask. "How can a man wearing a codpiece that would cover an elephant's second brain complain of my costume?"

In one swift move, Judge Grisham removed the piece from the costume, revealing the thick, wrinkled folds of the ivory material hanging against his loins. "Was intending to remove it," he half pouted. "The women would surely have fainted if I'd arrived with my privates charging into battle."

Storm grinned, again hefting the axe into his other hand. "All I need now is the poor, tragic Anne Boleyn, Judge. Perhaps there'll be one at the ball who won't mind losing her head to me. Again!" Then, "I should have dressed as a stuffy Scotland Yard detective, since it is the beautiful Tallie I am to protect."

"Keep your eyes off Tallie, Storm. The young woman has trouble enough without you."

"I was ordered to keep my eyes *on* her. Besides, Judge, I'm not interested in Tallie—"

"Bull! You've always been a bit of a loner, Storm. I've never known you to attend one of these balls, which you have referred to as silly fluff! Yet, you willingly attend this year?"

"All right, dammit. I'm not attending simply because Sister Joseph asked me to. It *is* because Tallie will be there!" retorted Storm, slinging back his shoulders and puffing his chest. "This costume shows off my physique, don't you think, Judge?"

"You're incorrigible," mumbled Isaac Grisham, smiling in spite of himself. "The most decent incorrigible man I've ever known, Storm Phillips. Bring the buggy around, will you?"

Storm left at once, giving Judge Grisham the moment to sit a spell and ponder his thoughts. The younger man was getting a little too cocky for his britches. But, damn, he was such a likable fellow, and Judge Grisham had been devastated when he'd had to send him to prison. Sister Joseph had attested to the fact he was working well for the sisters, and Judge Grisham felt that he deserved the chance to redeem himself. He suspected in his heart that McCallister Phillips was somehow responsible for Storm going to prison, and if it was the last thing he did he'd prove it!

A rumble of buggy wheels echoed nearby. Presently, Storm reentered the house, announcing, "Buggy's around, Judge. Let's get to that shindig before the spiked punch is all gone."

Judge Grisham rose with little effort, the chair keeping the imprint of his body in the plush leather. When he entered the coolness of the night, he looked toward dark clouds hugging the trees and said to Storm, "Think it'll rain, boy?"

Storm's immediate annoyance at the way the judge addressed him prompted him to reply, "Boy doesn't think so."

And Judge Grisham, smiling, moved his hand onto the taller man's shoulder and gave it a paternal pat. "You'll always be our boy, Storm . . . mine and Hiram's." Soon, the buggy moved onto Main Street for the short journey to the town hall where the ball was being held.

Tallie loved the way the late-evening clouds caressed the far horizon. She loved the way the cool wind whispered across her features, catching in the thick, coarse strands of the black wig she wore. John was in the front seat of the surrey, urging the mare on when she'd just as soon stop to nibble at early grass. Tallie and Fanny sat on the backseat, their costumes, for the most part, covered by two of the older woman's woolen capes.

Tallie felt beautiful and alluring. She wanted only to mix with other attendants at the ball and be herself again. She wanted to laugh and not feel that she'd committed a mortal sin by doing so, to bat her eyelashes at a particularly handsome masculine face, if that was what she chose, even to flirt and share a joke and a bit of the spiked punch Fanny had told her always managed to show up at such functions. She wanted to dance, hear music, see gaily dressed ladies and gentlemen . . . she wanted to have a good time and forget about the troubles that had brought her to this wild country. Because she had never attended a fancy ball, she had allowed her imagination to run wild these past few minutes.

So, when they eventually entered the social hall, Tallie lost herself in the thrill of it. She danced with several young men, all of whom managed to get a little too familiar for her taste, and eventually ended up at the banquet table, tasting something from every platter. Then Hiram Frick and Judge Grisham came to save her from the advances of a cocky young logger dressed as a trout—and quite a convincing one at that—and Tallie found her hands filled with a cup of the spiked punch from the other end of the banquet.

"It'll loosen you up," promised Hiram Frick, motioning to his wife through the sea of heads.

Hiram and Martha were dressed as George and Martha Washington. "Your costume is lovely," Martha Frick said.

And a smiling Tallie, before she could complete a quiet "Thank you" was dragged onto the dance floor by that charming old bachelor, Judge Grisham.

"You dance well." She laughed as she delivered the compliment.

"For an old man, you mean," he laughed in turn. "Thank you, young lady. I feel like a spring chicken tonight."

The last thing in the world Tallie expected this night was danger. Her mood was light and carefree and she was having a wonderful time. With a smile, Tallie leaned forward and said, "I know a little about historic costume, Judge. Sorry to have to tell you this but—" She leaned forward then and whispered against his ear, "Your codpiece is missing."

Storm couldn't believe his eyes. Dancing in Judge Grisham's arms was the most beautiful vision ever to come to him, and he knew at first glance that it had to be Tallie. A golden light seemed to surround her suddenly, so that the other guests, even Judge Grisham, in whose arms she danced, vanished into the blinding glow. So authentic was her costume that she could truly have been the great Egyptian queen, Cleopatra. Her gown was blue charmeuse and glistening gold fabric, a shimmering snakeskin patterned bodice was elaborately decorated with gold medallions, her royal skirts were embellished with swirling golden cobras, and she carried a sistern, an ancient musical instrument, in her right hand. Jewelry adorned her slender wrists, a twining serpent and bangles painted to match her costume, and a splendid necklace with stones of aqua, scarlet, and diamond surrounded the slim column of her neck. Upon her straight black wig sat a golden tiara of cobras inlaid with rich enamels, which Storm recognized from books as a symbol of Egyptian royalty. He knew, without a doubt, that she was a queen as surely as if Cleopatra had suddenly been reincarnated into the body of this exquisite beauty.

Tallie knew that the tall, slim man dressed as a black-clothed executioner was studying her intently. She felt a little awkward, though extremely flattered, and suddenly prayed that Judge Grisham would waltz with her to another part of the dance floor and away from his close scrutiny. But through the hieroglyphic-covered mask hiding most of her face, she was as fascinated by him as he evidently was by her. When he began to move toward her through the crowded room, her courage could only have come from the supportive arms of the gentle old judge.

Storm felt as giddy as a schoolboy with his first crush on a girl. At the same moment he approached, the dance ended, and Judge Grisham, giving her hand a paternal pat, rejoined his friends, giving Storm a surreptitious wink.

Now Storm stood beside Tallie, trying to see her eyes beneath the fancy golden mask. They were lovely and hazel-colored, outlined in kohl, her eyelids shadowed in pearlescent aqua. Her lips were a hot and sultry red, and if he could have seen her face, he imagined that a most charming shade of pink would have graced her cheeks.

And now, the music was beginning to play again and dancers were flooding onto the floor. "Would you like to dance?" he asked softly.

Tallie nearly fainted; the voice belonged to Storm Phillips. Still, she was able to sufficiently recover her surprise and offer her hand. "I would," she said, trying to disguise her English accent, but feeling the effort a dismal failure.

Storm immediately came up with a plan. He would not reveal

to Tallie that he knew her identity. As he took her in his arms, he said, ''You're from South Carolina, are you?''

Lowering her head, she smiled. ''Yes,'' she lied. ''From Charleston, to be precise. How perceptive of you.'' She and the sisters had spent a few days in Charleston before traveling to Granger, and Tallie had taken special notice of the way the ladies there spoke. She couldn't believe she had so effectively picked up the dialect that Storm did not recognize her English accent. Feeling a little more sure of herself, she moved into his arms for the beginning of the new waltz. After a moment, she said, ''You're a fine dancer, Mr.? . . .''

''Phillips,'' he replied. ''But you can call me Storm. And who are you?''

She thought he didn't know who she was; that alone made her feel giddy as she carried the deception into the first moments of the dance. Momentarily, she said, ''And I am Corrine Edwards.'' Actually, it wasn't a lie. Storm Phillips knew her only as Sister T, or he might have heard one of the sisters refer to her as Tallie. Corrine was her middle name.

''Strange,'' replied Storm. ''You don't look like a Corrine.''

Tallie laughed. ''And so I am not, sir. Tonight I am Cleopatra, the alluring queen of Egypt. I plan to enchant every man in attendance tonight.''

''You've already enchanted me,'' said Storm without pause. ''I would be willing to lie down at your feet and have you crush me beneath those golden sandals. I have a proposition—''

''Oh? And what is that?'' The southern accent continued effectively.

''You forget about all those other men, dance every dance with me, and you can enchant me all night. That is, if there is not a Mr. Corrine Edwards hovering nearby.''

''None,'' she responded, his instant smile reminding her of their kiss. He had a wonderful mouth, full and wide, expressive . . . and she oh, so dearly wanted to—

Embarrassment flooded her. Suppose he had heard her thoughts?

Storm was thinking, at the moment, that there was no place on earth he would rather be than in Tallie's arms. She was alluring and beautiful, as enchanting as a goddess come to life. Without planning the compliment, he said, "I think you are enchanting me, my Cleopatra."

Tallie laughed. "It seems I have *already* enchanted you, Mr. Storm Phillips. Your axe just slipped from the back of your belt and you danced right over it."

He remembered now hearing it clang to the planked floor, but it didn't occur to him to retrieve it. Then he saw Doc Frick paddle through the flood of dancers, pick up the weapon and take it away to a place of safety. "Someone just stole my axe," he kidded Tallie. "I suppose now that I'll not take the trophy of a queen's head this night."

"Oh? Was it in your plans?" she asked with a careless laugh. Had her true accent surfaced? She looked into Storm's dark, penetrating eyes through the holes of his black hood. If it had, he had not seemed to notice. She simply must be more careful.

"Well, I was looking for Anne Boleyn, who ordered an axeman from France for her execution. But she hasn't made it to the ball yet." Last year, Mrs. Kingsley had appeared as Anne Boleyn, and, instinctively, he looked around for her. Ah, yes, there she was now, dressed in a Roman toga and wreath of leaves. Storm wasn't sure what she personified, but he imagined that the flowing garment would fit her "condition," since she appeared to be expecting still another child. She already had a dozen. When she looked in his direction, he waved his hand, but he knew the expression upon her face was that of a woman who did not know who was doing the waving. Still, she nodded pleasantly.

Storm turned his attentions to the goddess in his arms. The music had swelled in volume, then had dropped to a near hush. When the Queen of the Gypsies pirouetted very close by them, creating a breeze, he suddenly got a whiff of his Cleopatra's perfume. He discreetly moved his face closer to her hair, so that he might get a stronger whiff.

He pulled back suddenly, his dark eyes beyond the hood attempting to see through her mask. Royal-blue eyelids kept him from seeing her eyes, the hieroglyphics covering the mask made it impossible to see through, even though the material composing it was relatively transparent. The snakeskin bodice of her costume had poufed out, giving him a modest view of the snowy mounds of her bosom, and when she suddenly lifted her gaze, he cut his own, immediately acknowledging another dancer who he recognized. Then he saw the judge and Doc Frick deeply engaged in conversation, even as their gazes followed Storm and his Cleopatra. The judge was nodding thoughtfully, and a ruddy hue had taken possession of Doc's unmasked features. Storm couldn't help but ponder the subject of their conversation. Perhaps one or the other—or both of them—was considering relieving him of his beautiful dance partner? Let them try! he thought, unconsciously strengthening his grip around Tallie's tiny waist.

The move must have startled her, for the tiara of cobras suddenly shifted, then clanged to the floor. When Storm immediately started to retrieve it, at the very same moment that Tallie bent forward, their foreheads met in a head-on clash, reeling Tallie backward and into the arms of a black-clothed gentleman. She turned, preparing to apologize, even as the injury to her head had her senses reeling, and she looked into one exposed, watery blue eye so horrifyingly familiar that she almost fainted. It was Eddy's bodyguard, the persistent Mr. Beattie! The way his long, bony fingers moved firmly over her wrist told her for certain that it was.

She remembered the first time she had seen him, alone on Berners Street, the site of one of the murders. Had he been with his beloved prince then? She had seen him near Miller's Court that night she'd seen Eddy. Then she had seen him aboard ship and now, here he was, in a room crowded with partygoers, holding so fast to her wrist that she didn't think she would ever escape. Without thinking, she opened her mouth and screamed as though hell itself was burning at her feet. He quickly released her, then disappeared into the crowd.

She was suddenly so crushed by people rushing to her aid that Storm Phillips could not get through to her. She looked up, saw the familiar face of Judge Isaac Grisham and allowed him to escort her from the crowded dance floor. Moments later, they disappeared into a council room and the door promptly closed, but not before Hiram Frick managed to enter with the two of them. A bolt was slipped, and Hiram Frick was forcing her to settle into a hard oak chair.

Tallie did not protest as her mask was removed. She did not see the surprised look on both of the men's faces as they witnessed her ashen horror. She could not speak, but merely flashed a frightened look between the two pairs of worried eyes, trying desperately to find her voice.

He was still after her, that despicable man who wanted only to protect his murderous prince.

And she knew that she was doomed.

Storm had retrieved Tallie's tiara and now looked desperately around for her. He was sure she was the one who had let out that godawful scream, and he knew it was not because they had bumped heads. Enough time had passed to assure him that was not the source of it, though if her head felt like his did right now, she was in a bit of pain. He asked several people if they'd seen where she'd gone, but only Mrs. Kingsley seemed to have kept a keen eye.

"Judge Grisham and Dr. Frick took her to one of the council chambers."

Storm had pulled off his hood and now moved in that direction, the delicate tiara tucked carefully beneath his right arm. He knocked on each door before opening them to darkness. Then he saw the judge moving toward the ballroom. "Where is Tallie?" he asked Judge Grisham.

The judge had never seen Storm so interested in a woman

before. And he was certain it was not only because Sister Joseph had asked him to protect her. After a short pause, he said, "Doc Frick is taking her—" He'd been about to say home, but the doctor was actually taking her to Fanny Collins's house. So, he redirected his train of thought and asked, "Is that her tiara?"

Storm brought the headpiece forward. "Yes, it is."

"I'll return it to her," the judge said, attempting to take it from Storm.

But he would not allow it. "I will return it to her myself. Where can I find her?"

Judge Isaac Grisham looked intently into Storm's dark, waiting eyes. "Don't get involved with Tallie Edwards, Storm. You will only get hurt. Concentrate on the job that got you out of prison and ignore the cravings of your loins. One day, you'll be in a position to—"

Storm's hand moved swiftly out, catching the judge's arm. "My concern has nothing to do with my loins, Judge. Something frightened her, and I feel responsible for her. Dammit, where is she? And what made her scream like that?" Isaac didn't know the entire story surrounding Tallie Edwards and the reason the sisters were protecting her. Meeting Storm's expectant gaze, and noticing at once the angry set of his mouth, he said, "I am sure she will be taken back to Fanny's house. Please wait until tomorrow, when she is back on the sisters' mountain, to talk to her."

For now, he had other things on his mind. Just before Tallie's little episode, Hiram had told Isaac that McCallister Phillips and some of his men were roaming the street outside. He had to think of a way to get Storm out of the building and back to the church site before McCallister learned he was here. McCallister had chosen a very bad time to confront the judge about Storm's release from prison and Isaac needed to find the marshal before trouble started. Everton, from the mercantile, approached, then drew the judge aside for a moment. He whispered something to him.

He had assured the judge that McCallister and his men were

gone. The judge now returned to Storm. "Why don't you go on back to the site, Storm?"

"All right. But if I find out that Tallie is hurt in some way . . ." His words halted before they became a threat, and he moved swiftly toward the exit.

"Judge!" A dark-clothed figure moved toward the two men. The mask he snatched revealed to them the features of Marshal Crispin Black. "Is the young lady all right? She stumbled into my arms and I thought she was going to fall. I took her wrist to help her, but she looked up at me and screamed like an enraged banshee—"

"That was you?" Judge Grisham uttered, shocked by this revelation. "But she thought it was . . ." His words immediately ceased, because he wasn't sure who she was afraid of.

"Yes, that was me. Who did she think I was . . . Jack the Ripper?"

"You must have given her a bit of a fright. Perhaps your costume took her unaware . . ."

It *was* a grisly costume, the judge now noticed, the marshal's portrayal of a scalped and murdered Jesuit quite realistic. The costume was in the worst taste he had ever seen. The long, dark wig was pulled across one part of his head, and a realistically painted lump of soft clay attached to his scalp actually looked like exposed bone and blood vessels. It was no wonder Tallie had screamed.

Chapter Seven

Doc Frick took Tallie back to Fanny Collins's house and was surprised to find the still costumed couple standing on the porch awaiting them. While John explained that he'd seen what happened, Fanny dropped a comforting arm over Tallie's shoulders and drew her into the warmth of the parlor. There, a pot of steaming tea was poured into matching china cups, and one of them, sweetened the way she liked it, forced into Tallie's hands.

"You saw him? Are you sure?"

Tallie had told Fanny a little about the man following her, though not the reason for his pursuit. Only the sisters knew about that horror affecting her life. Now Sister Joseph would see that she wasn't imagining things! "It was him. I would recognize those eyes anywhere." Only he would have chosen such a ghastly costume. He looked like a murdered Jesuit."

Fanny instantly paled. "Black-clothed, his wig brought across his scalp and clay made to look like a wound stuck to the side of his head?"

Tallie's eyes widened. "Yes, that was him. You saw him, too?"

Fanny slumped, her head dropping forward, then lifting again. "Tallie, that was Marshal Crispin Black! Every year he tries to make his costume more gruesome. He has made a game of seeing how many women he can frighten or who will faint dead away at the very sight of him."

The silence following her words was almost deafening, then the coldest flood of humiliation washed through her. Tears welled in her eyes, her bottom lip began to tremble, and a pale, shaking hand rose to her head. "I believe I lost my tiara. I am sorry—"

A comforting hand covered Tallie's. "It will show up. Things like that are always turned in at city hall to be returned to their owners. Don't you worry about it at all."

"Perhaps my dance partner has the tiara."

"Do you know who he was?"

She smiled shyly. "It was Storm Phillips. I don't think he knew who I was, though. I'm afraid . . ." Her small smile was apologetic, "I didn't tell him the name everyone knows me by. I gave him my second name—Corrine. I am sure the omission is as good as a lie, but . . ." She shrugged daintily, "Sister Joseph would have been very upset if I'd been too friendly with him."

Fanny, too, smiled. "I'm afraid, Tallie Edwards, that you were friendly nonetheless. And I would imagine Storm Phillips was very aware of your identity."

Tallie hated to think he might have made a fool of her. "Do you think so?"

"I think so, Tallie. And you were very flirtatious. I saw how you were dancing with him, how you smiled at him and . . ." The smile became a light laugh, "John and I danced close enough once that we heard that coy southern accent you were employing."

Tallie allowed herself to smile. "If I did not fool him, then I simply made a fool of myself."

"I don't think so. He was enjoying himself immensely." Just at that moment, John and Hiram entered the parlor, their muttered exchange ceasing when they saw the women. "Would you care for some tea?" Fanny asked.

"Hiram and I are going to have a glass of that peach brandy you bottled a couple of years ago," John said. "Do you mind?"

Though the brandy was generally kept for special occasions, Fanny politely consented. "Just don't drink it all up. You know how your aunt Beatrice likes a bit of it when she visits on the holidays."

When Hiram and John moved into the alcove where the small liquor cabinet was located, Fanny returned her attentions to Tallie. She said nothing to her for a moment, but simply watched her downcast eyes. She could tell that she was thinking of Storm, because there was a light in her eyes she had never noticed before. Granted, Storm was a handsome man, but Tallie could do better. He was likable, for sure, but a loner, and he'd gotten himself in a fair amount of trouble these past few years. Tallie needed to be very careful in her choice of companions . . . or husbands, if that was her ultimate goal.

Tallie might have been surprised at Fanny's perceptiveness. As she absently sipped the tea, that had now warmed to suit her taste, she was thinking of Storm Phillips and the way he had held her as they'd danced. She was thinking of the words he had spoken, *Dance every dance with me, and you can enchant me all night.* She wasn't sure why she was so attracted to the rascal. He was bold; he had already stolen a kiss. She imagined that Storm Phillips would hold her close, awaken her passions and kiss her tenderly, warmly, commandingly . . . all the wonderful emotions that romance novels were made of—

"Tallie Edwards, what are you thinking about?"

Her nerves jumped; pale, passion-glazed eyes turned full to Fanny, instantly recalling her words. "Thinking? Goodness . . ." she lied, "I really do not know. Nothing of any substance, I would imagine."

"Why, I do believe you were thinking about him!"

Her nàiveté was certainly feigned. "Him who?"

"Storm Phillips, that's who. He is wheedling his way into your soul, Tallie Edwards."

She flustered. "Do not be preposterous." But there was no effective argument in her voice, and she could see that Fanny saw straight through her. Therefore, she felt the need to reinforce her stand. "How could I possibly be attracted to a brooding American male? Why, it is simply preposterous! I am accustomed to the proper gentlemen of London, and I could never be attracted to a man like Storm Phillips."

Fanny caught her smile before Tallie could notice it. "You're being much too defensive for an innocent woman." When she saw anger fleet across Tallie's pretty features, she said, "I'll not press the issue. Now . . ." Setting her tea aside, she continued, "I suppose you'd like to get all that makeup off your face. I believe I have a jar of cold cream."

Tallie arose. She'd heard very little of Fanny's response, because she'd been thinking of her own statement, *proper gentlemen of London.* The truth was that she was accustomed to the lowest human vermin of the opposite gender walking the streets of London's East End, men who swilled cheap wine, relieved themselves against the walls of row houses, and passed out drunk in the doorways of lodging rooms procured for bawdy trysts. She was accustomed to vile cursing men grabbing for the breasts of whores as they stumbled down the alleyways, or digging at claps through filthy trousers while accosting decent Londoners for a penny or two to buy liquor. *Proper gentlemen of London,* indeed! Tallie saw very few of them, and they were the ones who patronized her aunt's flower shop, giving her little more than a polite nod with the unspoken message, *Be thankful you even got that, dodsey!*

So deep were her thoughts, Tallie only now realized she was sitting at the small dressing table in Fanny's bedroom, absently knocking over toiletries which she just as absently righted. She'd smeared Fanny's cold cream on her face and was waiting for the makeup to soften. Taking up the washcloth Fanny had handed her, she found that the kohl surrounding her eyes was very stubborn and didn't want to come off. By the time she was able to see her complexion, she had rubbed it red and her eyes were almost bloodshot. The bump on her head was painful, too, and she imagined that Storm Phillips might possibly have a matching one.

There she was! Back to thinking of that rogue again!

Fanny left, then returned with cucumber slices. It was much too early for cucumbers—or too late, whichever way one looked at it—but Tallie remembered John remarking one day that they often forced the growth of vegetables in a small greenhouse behind their house. Leaning her head against the plush fabric of the dressing-table chair, Tallie allowed Fanny to place the slices over her closed eyes. All the while she sat there, feeling the coolness of the cucumber taking away the burning of her eyes, Fanny changed from her costume and moved about the chamber, straightening whatever appeared untidy to her.

The silence gave Tallie a moment or two to think of the tall, bronze Storm Phillips, and the almost possessive heat with which he'd held her to him when they'd danced. She'd never felt so beautiful as she had then, held in his powerful arms, feeling the shallow rise and fall of his chest through the heavy leather of his costume. His eyes had been dark, bold, and alive, and she'd loved the way they had looked at her, assessing her, admiring her . . . claiming her—

But thinking about the dance she'd shared with him made her remember how foolishly she'd misidentified Crispin Black. He'd had the same moist blue eyes, the same build, and she'd truly thought he *was* Farrand Beattie, come to take her life. Sister Joseph's argument a few days ago—that she may not have seen what she thought she saw—had absorbed Tallie's thoughts, and she was beginning to think the old sister might be right. And the very idea that Mr. Beattie might have followed her this far was preposterous. He'd probably gotten lost at the docks in Charleston, perhaps even New York, where the first America-bound passengers had disembarked. She was letting fear make her edgy, seeing threat in every human face. She was usually stronger than this.

"I think those cucumbers can come off your eyes now," said Fanny, her hand coming to rest on Tallie's left shoulder as though to capture her attention in case her voice did not.

Tallie's head moved forward, and she allowed the cucumbers to fall into her waiting hands. Looking into the mirror, she saw that the redness was, miraculously, scarcely more than a shade of pink. By morning, her eyes would be back to normal and she would be none the worse for wear.

Fanny was still straightening the room as Tallie continued her thoughts. Then she began to feel guilty. She was thinking of herself, the good time she'd had at the ball, and had scarcely given a thought to Aunt Cora and Ellie. Thinking of her loved ones made her remember the letters she'd sent to Mrs. Hawley in New York, and she wondered if she'd received them yet. She knew that Mrs. Hawley would find a way to get the letter to Aunt Cora, without the duke's men finding out about it. Tallie felt confident of that.

The widow, Maxine Hawley, had been the first one in the row of townhouses on Tammany Street to have gas run directly indoors for lighting the chandeliers and wall fixtures all through the house. She'd never really liked it much, because the gas smoked up the pale-blue walls of her fancy parlor. There she lay now, in her finest gown, the rose-colored one with the ivory lace cascading down its bodice.

Her son thought the gown perfectly matched the satin lining of the coffin in which she lay. Their friends had gathered around this late Friday evening, to pay their last respects, and to tell Fred Hawley how sorry they were that the gas leak had killed his dear mother. She had died quickly, they'd assured him, and there would have been no pain. Little consolation to the son who had loved her so deeply.

As she had directed in her last wishes, in the event they

should die in common, her little Scottie dog, Peachie, had been placed in the coffin alongside her. Fred had often caught his mother napping on the divan in this very parlor, with her arm wrapped around the sleeping dog, as it was now in the downy interior of the coffin.

Fred touched his mother's cheek, finding it ice cold. He jerked his hand away as it neared the nose of the dog, who had always snapped at him when he got too near "his mistress." Fred hadn't liked the dog and wouldn't have minded at all if the nasty little beast had been the only one to fall victim to the gas.

His mother's maid, Hazel, was still in hospital after being sickened by the gas, but fortunately she was expected to make a full recovery. Hazel had taken care of his mother as completely as if she had been her mother, and had been as influential in raising him as his mother had been. His mother's will stipulated a small monthly pension be paid to Hazel until her death, and Fred had made the first payment to Hazel's husband just this morning. His mother would have wanted it that way.

For a few minutes, Fred accepted condolences from recent arrivals at his mother's wake, then he felt the need for some solitude. Quietly, he moved into the corridor and to the small antechamber where his mother's ornate French desk sat, still meticulous, the outgoing mail neatly stacked in one place, the incoming in another neat stack. He sat at the desk, sure that he could still feel the warmth of his mother's slender form in the plush fabric of the chair, and moved his hand fluidly over the rich carving of the desk. Absently, he sorted through the letters, wondering what he should do with them. The first order of business, he supposed, was to let her friends know that she had passed away, and to assure her creditors that their bills would be paid in due time.

What is this? Fred picked up the envelope and looked at the delicate writing, obviously a woman's, and the postmark in the town of Granger, Tennessee. The envelope had been opened by his mother's darling hand the very day of her death. He knew, because responses to items received the prior day when he'd seen her were already in the outgoing mail. He looked in the envelope, finding still another, unopened, addressed to his mother's friend, Cora Dunton, in London. The two women had met several years before when his mother had traveled to London, and had corresponded ever since. He knew that his mother had been fond of Cora and her niece, Tallie.

Fred tucked the letter addressed to Cora Dunton into the pocket of his jacket, along with his mother's outgoing mail, which he would post tomorrow. He wondered why Tallie hadn't sent the letter directly to her aunt?

If only he had found Tallie's letter, which his mother had hidden beneath stationery in the small desk drawer, Fred would have known that the letter to Cora had to be sent with secrecy and haste. He did not know that his mother planned to send Tallie's letter to her agent in London, who represented her in bids at the antique auctions.

He could not possibly have known as he arose from the desk and made his way back into the company of family and friends that his simple act of directly posting the letter would bring the most heinous kind of monster into Tallie's life.

The following morning

"Where on earth did you get that bump on your head?" Sister Pete nearly threw Tallie back against the cot in her efforts to inspect the injury to her forehead. "Did someone strike you?"

Tallie dodged out from under Sister Pete's hand and made her way to her feet. "It is nothing, Sister Pete. I forgot to duck beneath Fanny Collins's clothesline post." She felt a pang as she lied to her friend. "You know how clumsy I can be at times."

"Clumsy, in a pig's eye! I've never seen you clumsy!"

A frustrated Tallie clicked her tongue. "Oh, for heaven's

sake, do not make such a fuss over one little bump. You would think my limbs were hanging off!"

"Harumph!" Sister Pete had now crossed her arms, and her foot was tapping upon the rough, planked floor. "What were you doing under Fanny's clothesline post in the first place? I thought you were ministering to the poor and needy."

"Do not be sarcastic, Sister Pete . . . you know I went to the winter ball in Granger."

"And so you did! Sister T, your soul is in great jeopardy!"

"Blast my soul, Pete! I am not in a mood to fuss with you." Drawing her fingers to her mouth, she looked apologetically at Sister Pete. "I just do not understand why you keep picking at me. I get so frustrated at times."

Sister Pete was silent for a moment. She didn't like outbursts, especially ones that lent harshness to God . . . or souls. "Forgiveness is our Lord's." Sister Pete now resumed the short trip to the door she had begun minutes ago, before discovering Tallie's misshapened forehead. "It's your turn to prepare breakfast. I'll be at chapel with the sisters."

The door slammed resoundingly, giving Tallie no chance to again apologize to the woman who was her friend. Oh, why couldn't she control her temper?

She had a bit of a headache and one, she was sure, not caused by the bump on her head. She had consumed too much of the spiked punch last evening, and she wondered if that was why she'd been so bold in Storm Phillips's arms as they'd danced. She remembered the way he'd looked at her, and it melted the very core of her soul all over again. Almost by instinct, she moved toward the window to look out at the familiar location where he cut logs for their stove and hearths. He was not there; she wondered if he might have a headache himself.

Then she saw it resting on the sill . . . a single, long-stemmed red rose, just beginning to open.

As she drew it through the window, then touched the velvety softness of the petals to her mouth, she thought that Fanny was right . . . he *did* know that she had been Cleopatra last night.

And, she couldn't help wondering whose garden the charming rogue had stolen the rose from.

Storm Phillips had a hell of a heartache. He could scarcely remember placing the rose on Tallie's windowsill, let alone where he might have gotten it from. He had vague recollections of driving past Mrs. Kingsley's house, and of moonlight washing over the few roses clinging to one of her prized bushes.

He now sat on the cot beneath the canvas covering of the tent he shared with Old Potts and held the tiara almost lovingly between his strong hands. He studied its intricate detail, touched his fingers to the smooth enamel giving color to the cobras and imagined it perched atop the golden hair of Tallie Edwards. It was all he could do not to rush to the kitchen window, hide and spy upon her as she performed her duties in the kitchen. He felt that he would die if he did not again set his gaze upon her exquisite female form and draw in a heady, intoxicating whiff of the perfume she had worn.

"You have stolen my heart, Miss Tallie Edwards!"

"Thinkin' about your Egyptian queen again, eh, Storm?"

His muscles jerked; he had not heard Old Potts enter the tent. He had not told the man that Tallie had been his Egyptian queen. "You should have seen her," Storm reflected after a moment. "She was the most beautiful female creature I've ever seen. This morning I woke up, and I didn't know if I'd dreamed her. Then I found this, and I knew she'd been in my arms. She was as real as you are . . ." His sentiments suddenly embarrassed him, and he grinned, "but a hell of a lot better looking, old-timer."

Old Potts got to the subject that had brought him into the tent. "Sister Joseph's marching over here, Storm. Says you should have been at work two hours ago. Ya know that's when the sun came up."

"Why the hell didn't you tell me right away?" bellowed Storm, coming to his feet and hiding the tiara beneath a blanket just as Sister Joseph entered the tent without announcing herself. "Good morning," he said, meeting one narrow, disapproving eye and a mouth pinched so tight she might have poured glue between her lips.

Sister Joseph hesitated until Old Potts had left the tent. Then, rather than return his greeting, she said, "Sister Tallie is waiting for wood for the stove, Storm. Or have you decided to take the day off?"

"Could I?" he asked with just a touch of sarcasm.

The sagging old chin rose a tad. "That's enough, Brother Storm. I'll not have any of your insolent ways."

His defiance waned immediately; she was, after all, the one person in the world who could cause him to go back to prison. She need only tell Judge Isaac Grisham that he wasn't working out, and he would be back in the state penitentiary, being beaten on a daily basis simply because he was part Cherokee. "I apologize," he said momentarily. "I suppose I got up on the wrong side of the bed."

Sister Joseph saw the knot on his head when he stepped into the light of the single opening. She approached, her one eye critically narrowing to study the wound. "That's an ugly bump, Brother Storm," she said. "Tallie has one just like it . . . said she got it on a clothesline post!"

His hand rose to the painful bump, then quickly withdrew. "I forgot to duck when I went under a low limb. Careless of me." Then, "I'd better get that wood cut or there won't be any breakfast for any of us."

He did not want to leave first, lest she take the opportunity in her solitude to nose about. He didn't like anyone going through his personal belongings. So, he held open the tent flap and stood patiently by. She looked around the tent, taking notice of its messy appearance, then pivoted sharply and entered the cool morning. Storm was behind her.

They parted company at the wood pile and Sister Joseph began wondering about the coincidence of identical bumps on Storm and Tallie's foreheads. One might almost have thought they'd inflicted the wounds on each other, though she couldn't for the life of her understand how such a mishap could occur.

She entered the kitchen where Tallie was preparing breakfast, and gave her approval to the cuisine. She noticed the rose, now stuck in a small vase, but said nothing. Then she went to the other cabins and gathered the sisters together. Soon, Tallie watched them moving as a group toward the overhang of oak trees, where they would pray loudly and with full, healthy lungs, cry, speak in tongues, and sing praises to the Lord. She was free for a couple of hours to dawdle about, get her chores done, and not be leered over by one of the women.

But then she saw Sister Michael rushing back to the cabin.

The door opened and Sister Michael said, "Sister Joseph requests that you tidy the tent occupied by the men after you have prepared breakfast."

"I'll do it this afternoon," Tallie responded with a slight note of defiance. "I don't think any of us are in the mood for cold scrambled eggs and bacon." A pretty eyebrow arched upward. "I'll give your prayer session a couple of hours, then I'll start breakfast."

"And in that time you might clean the tent?"

Tallie lifted her chin slightly. "I shall clean our *own* quarters first, I think."

Sister Michael giggled, though her following words did not indicate that it was appropriate. "Very well, Sister T. At least I brought the message as it was given me."

The door closed once again. Tallie absently separated the slices of bacon she had cut from the large slab and set them aside in anticipation of breakfast.

She moved to the bed, fully intending to make it up . . . but it seemed so inviting and she was still so tired. So, she dropped upon its softness. For an hour or so, she lay very still, not sleeping, but resting enough that when she arose, she felt refreshed and ready to face the day.

She could see through the window that Sister Joseph was swaying, as she usually did when the prayer session had been unusually raucous and exhausting. So, she began dropping the bacon into the frying pan. The sizzle was almost soothing, and while it cooked, she broke the eggs into a large tin bowl, added a little milk and salt and beat them until they were a creamy white.

It was Saturday; Tallie was thinking about what she'd be doing if she were back in London. Ellie would want to do something special, even if it was simply walking down Whitechapel and hugging the heads of all the cart horses. She especially liked the dapple pony Mr. Kearns drove on his milk route.

She remembered the time she'd taken Ellie to see the queen's palace at Buckingham. Ellie had been so excited, thinking herself a princess and imagining that she was "going home to Buckingham. Oh, but I do hope grandmother, Queen Vicky, won't be angry that I've soiled my dress!" She had fantasized. They had enjoyed a wonderful day, eating ham and cheese sandwiches that Mr. Glynn, the vendor, had given them, drinking sarsaparilla imported from an American company that had sent them to dreaming of the wild lands of that far and distant land. They had held hands, she and Ellie, and had sung a little song Aunt Cora had taught Tallie, and that she had taught Ellie in turn. *The wind, the wind, the naughty wind, that blows the skirts on high . . . but God was just and blew the dust, right in the bad man's eye!*

She missed Ellie so much. If she could only be with her and hug her and whisper a mother's sweet endearments to her and see a smile light her small, angelic features. If she could sit and do her hair the way she liked, plaited and twisted around her head, then adorned with Tallie's favorite "gem"-studded combs. Ellie liked to pretend that the paste emeralds, diamonds, and rubies were pirates' booty and that the captain of the pirate ship was going to come up from the bottom of the sea to reclaim his treasure. Oh, what an imagination she had! Tallie smiled, knowing that it had come honestly. For Tallie could remember being Ellie's age herself and dreaming her dreams and thinking that a handsome prince would come riding up Whitechapel on his splendid armor-coated stallion and take her away to his castle in the hills.

Tears flooded Tallie's hazel gaze so that she could scarcely see the milky liquid in the bowl. "I love you, Ellie, my dear, sweet, precious child. I love you so much that my hearts breaks with wanting to be with you."

"Who is Ellie?"

The tears staunched immediately in her surprise at being overheard, Tallie spun away from the tall Storm Phillips, putting the wood he'd cut into a small wood bin. She gritted her teeth as she drew in a cold breath, then managed to say in the smallest of voices, "A relative back in London. I was thinking of her and missing her."

"Oh." Then, "I brought wood, but I see you had enough." A short pause drew into the moment. "I told Old Potts I'd check to see how much longer until breakfast."

"Fifteen minutes" came Tallie's short reply as she deliberately kept her features from him. "I'll call you when it is ready."

She did not protest when he approached, his hands closing over her shoulders. Against her hairline, he whispered, "My Cleopatra . . . my Tallie . . . why do you wear this ugly scarf? I want you to stop—" As he drew it down, she attempted to retrieve it at once. But she could not keep her long golden tresses from escaping the coarse fabric. She spun, her eyes dancing as he gathered the tresses in his hand and held them gently.

Tallie put distance between them, then twisted her hair and dropped it into the back of her dress. "So, you know I went to the ball as Cleopatra. But I am not *your* Cleopatra . . . or *your* Tallie, Storm Phillips. And I request that you cease and desist this insufferable stalking. Leave me alone, will you?"

He crossed his arms, then leaned against the door facing as though he proposed to stay a while. "I see you found my rose, Tallie. It reminded me of you."

The defiance sparked, and her eyes challenged him. But she forced herself not to respond to his attempt at flirtation as she began beating the eggs that had already been beaten into oblivion. When he crept behind her once again and whispered, "Come and meet me tonight, Tallie," Tallie spun toward him, immediately hitting him full in the chest with the wire wick. He laughed, then withdrew, and she saw him flip his hat onto his head as he crossed the clearing.

He was the most perfect specimen of man she had ever encountered. A warmth rushed through her body at the lingering aura of him so that she felt her knees go flaccid. Dropping heavily into a chair, she now looked toward the door where he had leaned, and she was sure she could still see the outline of him there, the ghost of his presence remaining as surely as the naughty thoughts flashing through her mind.

Was his invitation to enjoy the cool night? Or did he want more? Would he will her mouth to his, to be captured in a hot, passionate kiss, while his arms surrounded her body to claim her? She wanted to feel herself being eased to a soft, downy mattress and his hard, lean body covering her own. She wanted to feel the sweetness of his breath upon her cheek, taste the honey of his mouth, meet the penetrating gaze of his black eyes and surrender to his passions. Yes, that was what she wanted . . .

"Is breakfast ready, Sister T?" Sister Joseph sauntered into the room, put down her Bible and personal journal in which she recorded her "talks with God," then approached the table where Tallie stood. In a voice totally devoid of criticism, she said, "I do believe you've whipped those eggs into a lather. I see that you've burned the bacon. Are the eggs next?"

With a small cry, Tallie snatched the smoking skillet from the stove, then set it down in the pan of water where she was gathering dirty dishes. The heat sizzled against the water, sending even more smoke into the small room. "I do not know what I was thinking." Then, with a small smile, "I suppose we shall have to finish off the ham, Sister Joseph. Forgive me for burning the bacon."

When the other sisters entered the kitchen, Sister Joseph drew near to Tallie, whispering so that only she could hear, "I wonder what else is burning, Sister T, that is not as visible as the skillet and the bacon."

Tallie lowered her eyes. Sister Joseph was starting to know her too well, and that was something Tallie simply could not allow. She had enough problems without falling more deeply beneath the critical eye of Sister Joseph, and so vowed to stop daydreaming, do her duties, and forget about Storm Phillips.

She might as well will herself not to breathe . . .

Chapter Eight

Bart Johnson hurried into the kitchen of McCallister's ranch house, startling Thea, who almost upset the pot of boiling water she was carrying from the stove to the wash tub. "Come quick, Thea. *He's* . . ." he'd spoken that one word contemptuously, "taken the lash to your boy."

The pan of boiling water scarcely found its way to the countertop beside the tub before Thea was rushing out behind Bart Johnson. She had not known she could run so fast as she lifted her skirts, dashed past the large foreman and rounded the corner of the smoke house. There, she saw her son, Matt, stripped to the waist and tied to that ugly, familiar oak post where McCallister punished his men. The brutal, black-clothed bastard had already whipped him a half-dozen times and her son was tearful and whimpering when Thea threw herself against him, covering the bleeding lashes her boss had viciously inflicted.

"What did he do?" she screamed. "What did he do?"

"I didn't do nothin', Ma," Matt whimpered, his forehead desperately touching his mother's. He knew she would help him; she had always been his protector. "Somebody took my horse, an' Mr. Mack, he tol' me to check those fences on Pearl

Ridge. The only horse in the stable was his Black an' I took him out—"

"Get out of the way, Thea, or I'll whip you till you fall and deal your bastard kid a dozen more!"

Thea ignored McCallister Phillips, whose feet had now widened into an arrogant stand as he angrily hit the whip handle into the palm of his left hand. She couldn't believe he'd whip her boy over a damned horse! "My boy. My boy . . ." she whispered, kissing Matt's forehead, then ruffling the hair that had fallen to his forehead, "Mama won't let this happen to you."

Instantly, Mack's whip whirled out, catching Thea across her shoulders and causing her to cry out in her surprise and pain. A line of blood oozed through the white fabric of her blouse. But she did not flinch when she thought he might hit her again; with trembling hands she moved to untie the twine dragging her son's arms upward. The lash whirled again, and this time she was prepared. She stubbornly refused to respond.

"That's two warnings, Thea. You better get away from him."

"You're not whipping my son anymore!" she hissed, tears stinging her eyes. Thea saw the Englishman approach, his right hand darting out in an attempt to take the whip from McCallister.

As the recuperating Englishman was shoved to the ground, McCallister growled, "What makes your boy any different from the rest of the men, Thea? The others would have been whipped for riding my stallion on that ridge. A valuable, irreplaceable horse could have been killed!"

Thea's movements immediately ceased. Dropping her forehead against the bare, bleeding shoulder of her eighteen-year-old son, she turned her furious gaze and said in a quiet voice, "He *is* different, Mack. He's not only my son . . ." Her teeth gritted so firmly that she felt pain. There had been many times she'd wanted to tell McCallister Phillips that Matt was *his* son, but she had been afraid he'd treat Matt as badly as he treated Storm. But now, he was treating Matt even worse, and there was nothing to lose by telling him. "You're taking the whip to your own son!" Tears of outrage flooded her eyes. "Your own son!" she hissed a second time.

McCallister Phillips and Matt looked as though they'd both been struck again by the vicious coils of the whip. Matt mumbled, "Jeezus Christ, Ma!" and McCallister stood there, his dark eyes glaring between Thea and the boy. Eighteen years ago, Thea had told Matt that his father was a man who had wandered in looking for a job. They had spent one passionate night together and the man had moved on, never again to be heard from. "What do you mean, Thea?" Mack asked in shock.

Her son's wrists came free. As he dropped to the ground at the base of the whipping post, Thea moved cautiously toward McCallister Phillips. She stood for a moment, wishing she could turn the whip on him the way he'd turned it on her boy. Then, her hand lashed out and struck him a brutal blow to the left side of his face. Surprisingly, he did not react, not even to rub the stinging cheek.

"You took the whip to your own son, Mack. I'll never forgive you for that! Never!" Then, sobbing, she returned to her son to help him up. But Matt, his gaze angrily narrowed despite his pain, jerked away from her. The Englishman, finding his footing, had retrieved his cane and eased his shoulder beneath Matt's arm. Thea walked a little behind as he helped the bleeding, scarcely conscious Matt to his cot in the bunkhouse.

McCallister had been shocked into silence. Though he'd treated Matt like the rest of the men, he'd always felt a certain affinity to him deep within his soul. There had been something about the boy that confused him, and he had thought it was because he'd been born to a woman who had once shared his bed. Damn! Why hadn't she told him before that Matt was his boy? Didn't she know he would have treated him like a son, that he would have been special to him?

Of course she wouldn't have! She'd seen the way he'd treated Storm from the moment of his birth, and she hadn't wanted her own son to go through the same horrors. But Matt and

Storm were different. Why couldn't Thea have trusted him and told him the truth?

McCallister Phillips had been standing there like an inanimate lump of coal. Now he became aware of the other men discreetly slipping off to jobs and horses that would take them away from the ranch house. He looked toward the whipping post, noticing at once the droplets of Matt's blood still wet upon the smooth oak. Tears stung his eyes, but as he realized another man was present, he growled, "What the hell do you want?" without looking to see who it was.

Thus, he did not see the undisguised hatred in Bart Johnson's eyes as he walked away from him in disgust.

By midafternoon that day, everyone in Granger had heard that Mack Phillips had put another of his men under the lash, and that his longtime housekeeper had tearfully confessed that "the man" was his son. Marshal Crispin Black had been trying to stop the brutality for years, but in the past, when he brought men in for questioning, not one of those at the Phillips Ranch ever admitted to having witnessed such an atrocity. So, once again, he knew he would have nothing to take to the judge to bring charges against McCallister. If only the victim would come forward!

He was looking out the small, dirty window of the marshal's office onto the main street of Granger. From his perch at the desk, he could see the mercantile, the hardware store, Mrs. Pettigrew's dress shop, and the livery where a few scraggly rental horses moved lazily around a small pen. There were more people on the street today, perhaps because Saturday was the one day wives were able to get their husbands to town to do their weekly shopping. Most of the husbands usually made it to the one saloon in town, Friday McCann's place at the end of Main Street, while their wives went among the few shops, loading up their wagons and buggies. Occasionally there would be a scuffle among the children who came in with their parents, but this afternoon was rather quiet. Too quiet, in fact, and Crispin was restless. He was in the mood to rough up a drunkard, run off a few rambunctious boys, or stop one of the frequent cat fights between the two "ladies" who worked at Friday's.

Now there was something to keep him busy for a while. Pulling slightly back from the window, he watched the familiar wagon that Doc Frick had donated to the church ladies amble down the street. Storm Phillips was at the reins, and as he pulled the wagon up to the hardware store and locked down the brakes, Crispin Black, tucking his Stetson onto the scant remains of his hair, was exiting the marshal's office.

When he moved onto the boardwalk in front of the hardware store, he saw Storm digging into the hoof of one of the team with a pocket knife. Presently, he came up with a rock, which he tossed to the side without noticing that Crispin Black stood there. As the rock rolled off his expensive snakeskin boot, Storm looked up, his dark eyes catching the disdain on the man's face.

Before Crispin Black could speak, Storm said, "I'm telling you again, Marshal, I don't know where the hell it is." Every time he encountered the marshal, the subject of conversation was the same: that damned money the robbers had taken from the train.

"Did your friends spirit it away, Storm?"

"I told you, those men were not my friends. I didn't even know them."

"But you were on the train. Two dozen witnesses saw you get up and leave the car just minutes before the robbery took place."

"I told you, I walked out the back to get some fresh air. I *did not* rob the train." Anger sharpened the line of his jaw. "If I had, I'd tell you where that money is just to get you off my back. Now, leave me the hell alone, or I'll tell the judge about your harassment every time I'm in Granger."

Crispin Black made a rather dramatic effort to shudder. In

a voice heavy with sarcasm, he responded, "Not the judge. *Not the judge!* Please, Mr. Phillips, don't sic the *judge* on me!"

Storm glared at him with all the contempt he could muster. The bastard wasn't worth his efforts. He lightly patted the horse whose hoof he had just freed of the rock and pivoted away from the marshal. Soon, he entered the hardware store and was greeting the proprietor, Mr. Everton.

"What'll you be needin' today, Storm?"

Storm moved into the narrow aisle where buckets of nails sat at an angle to accommodate the customers. "Some two penny nails, another good hammer—Old Potts seems to have claimed mine. Here . . ." He pulled a list from the pocket of his shirt and handed it to Everton. "I have it all written down, and there's a few things Sister Joseph wants sent over."

Everton dragged his glasses down so that they rested on the tip of his nose. He glanced over the list, with an "um-hum," at every item, then shook his head, "Don't have any large iron skillets right now. Sold the last one to Mrs. Kingsley just this morning. You might try Mr. Chadwick over at the mercantile."

"I'll do that," Storm offered, then, "Mind if I have some of that coffee on the stove back there? Smells awful good."

"Help yourself," Everton said. "I'll get these items together for you."

Tallie knew she would never have been a good wife. She stood just inside the tent and looked at the mess the two men had made over the past few days and resented having to clean up after them. The old man she could understand—after all, a man who drank himself senseless was a man who didn't care about others, much less himself—but she could see no physical reason for Storm Phillips to choose to live in such a slovenly environment.

Sister Joseph had directed that she clean up after them, and she would do just that. *Pardon me, though,* she thought, *if I do it quickly and without ambition.* Tallie set about picking up the clothing deposited in piles here and there, straightening the toiletries on a small, rickety table beside a bowl and ewer, and, lastly, snatching the blankets and bed linens off the two cots, which she supposed she would have to wash for them, as well.

Clink! She covered her ears, thinking that a gun, disturbed from its hiding place within the blankets, was about to go off. But it did not; rather, from beneath the edge of the brown blanket she had removed from one of the cots she saw the glint of metal. Moving forward, she bent and picked up the tiara entwined with cobras that she'd lost at the dance last evening. Storm Phillips himself had made off with the vital part of her costume!

The rogue! He had stolen it, and she would just have to steal it back. It belonged to Fanny Collins, and she would return it to her tomorrow when she came to pray with the sisters, as she had made a habit of doing these past few days. Tucking it among the blankets and bed linens she would take away for washing, she left the tent, then nodded politely toward Old Potts, who was hauling lumber to a place closer to the building site. He was bringing one board at a time; at that rate, he would be working well into the night, his favorite time for drinking. Frankly, Tallie was surprised that Sister Joseph hadn't run him off, but she was showing unusual restraint and patience in the face of the one vice she most despised. Sister Pete had casually remarked that Sister Joseph's father and brother had been violent drinking men, both of whom had died early. Tallie herself had seen men who would buy drink before they'd buy food for their children, and she personally thought that all drinkers, especially the ones who beat and brutalized their families, should be put against a wall and shot.

As she entered the cabin, she saw that Sister Joseph was dismissing the sisters from their afternoon prayer session. Pete would soon be back in the cabin, since it was her turn to prepare supper, so Tallie hurriedly hid the tiara among her things. By the time Pete entered, Tallie was stirring up the stove to boil water with which to wash the men's blankets and bed linens.

"Those stink!" Sister Pete said, crinkling her nose in distaste. "How can they sleep on that?"

Tallie shrugged, her tone indifferent. "They are men. I suppose they are accustomed to this kind of odor."

"Cleanliness is next to godliness, the Bible says."

Tallie knew for a fact that the Bible said no such thing, but she did not argue with Sister Pete. There was nothing to be gained by it, and she would simply send Sister Pete on a search through the Good Book to prove her wrong. Tallie wasn't in a mood to spend the rest of the afternoon cooking because Pete was on a wild-goose chase.

Sister Michael burst into the kitchen area, startling both women. She was holding something protectively in the folds of her skirt, and her eyes were so bright that stars seemed to fill the room. "Look what I found?" she announced pertly, peeling back the material to show off the gray tabby kitten in her arms. "Sister Joseph says it would be good to have a cat around to chase off the mice."

Tallie liked cats as well as any of them, but she remembered the time Ellie had gotten a ringworm from one that had shown up in Aunt Cora's flower shop. "We really shouldn't handle it too much," she said, "until Dr. Frick can assure us it doesn't have any disease."

"It doesn't!" said Sister Michael with reproof. Then with less conviction, "I don't think it does." The quiet kitten was now deposited to the rug, and Sister Pete eyed it sternly.

"I'll not have it in here where the food is to be prepared," she quipped. "Take it outside, Sister Michael."

"Could I take a scrap or two, in case it's hungry?"

Sister Pete pulled a loose piece from the ham they would have for supper, quickly dropping it into Sister Michael's proffered hand. "And make sure the *kitten* gets it!"

When Sister Michael had picked up the kitten and left, Tallie said, "It is really unkind to keep on at her about her weight and her eating habits. It must make her feel terrible about herself."

With nary a change in her expression, Sister Pete said, "She once ate a wax plum out of a Christmas arrangement. Thought it was candy!"

Tallie laughed, but ceased when she met Sister Pete's disdainful look. After a moment, she asked, "Did she eat *all* of it, or discover her folly with the first bite?"

"She ate *all* of it, and was sick for a week afterward!" said Sister Pete so seriously that her tone of voice alone made Tallie smile. "Now!" Swiping an apron from a countertop, she began to tie it around her own ample waist. "I'll get to the supper while you're washing those stinking things belonging to the men!"

Tired of being called "The Englishman" he was getting almost desperate to know his identity. Farrand Beattie also knew that he wasn't a preacher, because he didn't know the first thing about the Good Book. He considered that he might have forgotten about all his learning in theology, but he could remember the plots and subjects of any number of books he had read.

The woman, Thea, had been a tremendous help to him. When he'd recovered sufficiently and had regained some of his strength, together they had gone through the few belongings that had been found with him. They had found no evidence as to his identity and place of origin. There were, however, a few oddities mixed in with his belongings. One, a surgeon's scalpel, had elicited a fair share of questioning by Thea, and another, an obviously expensive gold watch had been inscribed, *To F. B., From Eddy.*

No other identification, no papers or documents that might have borne a full name. Nothing! He was beginning to believe that he simply did not exist.

He had, of course, considered the possibility he was a felon running from the law, which would explain why he was traveling without identification. He wouldn't want to come under the auspices of a law enforcement official, who might discover his identity and throw him in the jail somewhere to await execution for a crime he couldn't remember committing. He did not feel like a criminal. But he did feel like a man who had come to this country on a mission, though he didn't for the life of him know what it was.

Thea had jokingly asked him a few days ago—in view of his possession of the scalpel—if he might be "Jack the Ripper" fleeing from his heinous crimes in London. Though he knew in his heart he was not, something about the subject had seemed vaguely familiar to him. Thea had brought him the few newspaper accounts that hadn't been thrown out, and he had read the articles with a grim fascination. Mutilated prostitutes! He bloody well knew that he was incapable of such atrocities. He didn't even like the sight of the blood oozing from his face in the wake of a recalcitrant razor.

He really wasn't sure why the rancher, McCallister Phillips, had offered him the accommodations of his bunkhouse during his recuperation. He wondered if he might have been responsible for injuring him, and, therefore, felt responsible for his well-being. It was a distinct possibility, though it did not anger him. Rather, he was glad to have a place to park his expensive leather shoes . . . an evidence, in addition to the watch, Thea had said, that he was a "fine gentleman, wandered away from his environs."

Though she wasn't the best educated woman he'd ever met—he was almost sure of that—she was one of the finest to cross his path. He couldn't imagine that a good woman like Thea had not married, and had stayed in the employ of a man like McCallister Phillips. Her revelation that he was the father of her son gave him some understanding, but she was too good to be so viciously abused by such a man, *or any* man for that matter. He would have to see that she got a better life, if and when he discovered his own. He had roots somewhere . . . everyone did. He had convinced himself that he was no exception.

He wanted to think that whoever he was, he was a good man. Certainly, he had a kind heart, because Thea had told him he did. He had tenderly ministered to the welts on her back, and she was now sitting with her son. He didn't know where Mack was, but he imagined he was doing a good job emptying the decanters in his liquor cabinet. What he had done was abominable. Someone should take the whip to him so that he could see how it felt. Perhaps one day he would do it himself!

But, he wasn't a violent man . . . simply one who didn't know who he was. Perhaps his memory would return one day soon and he could go on about his business, whatever that was.

In the meantime, McCallister Phillips had told him he could stay at the ranch as long as he wished. And while he was here, he had to have a name. He thought a moment, then smiled. Well, Thea would certainly be amused if he chose the name, Jack. And what about a second name. Ripper? No, he didn't think so. People here called him the Englishman. So, he thought Jack English might be appropriate. He smiled, rising from the chair where he'd perched himself half an hour ago. Slowly, he made his way down the length of the bunkhouse, momentarily swiping back the curtain where Thea was watching her sleeping boy. Catching her attention, he crooked his finger several times, summoning her to him.

"Until my memory returns, I wish to be called Jack."

She smiled her response despite her worry for her son. "Jack will do just fine. I thought you'd get tired of being called the Englishman soon."

Cutting his gaze to the cot, he asked, "How is the boy?"

"He'll be all right. I think his feelings were hurt more than anything. He's a sensitive boy, and . . ." Her voice trailed off, "I'm so afraid he's going to hate me. He's been asking me for years about his father and I've been telling him about the loner who wandered in here before his birth, an ex-Confederate soldier, as I recall." With a serious frown, she added, "And he never so much as kissed me, let alone fathered my boy."

Then, "Shame on me! I gave Matt a photograph of him and told him that it was his father. He values that photograph."

"You've been a good mother, Thea. He'll remember that."

"I pray he does."

A comforting embrace fell upon her shoulders. "What do you suppose McCallister will do now?"

Thea shrugged, but not to dislodge the embrace. "I suppose he'll run us both off, me and my boy."

"I shall wager that he does not."

Thea liked the Englishman. He was kind and considerate, and when he showed affection, it was without demand. Perhaps she, Matt, and the Englishman could leave the ranch together. It was a nice thought.

She liked the idea of that, although the prospects of a new home, away from the ranch where she had spent so much of her life, frightened her. With the Englishman, though, she felt she could face the future.

Noticing the clean blankets and sheets on their two cots, Storm began at once to look for the tiara. When he did not find it, he thought Old Potts had taken it, thinking that he might be able to trade it for a jug of hooch. Scraping back his dark hair, he went immediately to the building site where the old man was working to confront him about it.

"Where is it, Potts?"

A cigarette hung down the old man's chin. He looked around at Storm, muttering, "Huh? Where's what?"

Grabbing the pint of whiskey from his back pocket, Storm held it up. "You know damn well what! The tiara that you traded away for this!"

Potts ceased his labors now, then looked around at Storm Phillips, his features furiously darkened. "I din't find nothing that weren't mine, Storm. I might be a lazy old drunk, but I ain't no thief." *Takin' from a dead man ain't stealin'*, he reasoned in the same moment. Moving just close enough to snatch the bottle away from Storm, he now tucked it into his back pocket, where it belonged.

The fury quickly faded; Storm knew that Old Potts was telling the truth. Dropping his gaze as a moment of shame passed over him, he mumbled, "I'm sorry. I know you didn't take it." Which, of course, left one of the women as prime suspect. He had only to learn which of them had been responsible for cleaning the men's living area, and he would know who the culprit was. But how did one accuse a good Christian lady of being a thief? He was mad enough that the tiara was missing to find a way. He was damned sure of that!

The supper bell began to peel across the clearing; simultaneously, both men looked around to see Sister T standing at the back door of the middle cabin.

"I'm hungrier'n fire ants on a squashed possum," Old Potts remarked, dropping the board and hammer against a pile of lumber. "You hungry, Storm?"

Old Potts had a million bad habits, but he never held a grudge. He slapped his hand to Storm's shoulder just as if angry words had not been recently spoken between them.

Storm and Old Potts always sat at a small table on the back porch, while the women ate together at a table in the cabin. Sister Pete had explained that it was because their sleeping quarters were located in the same long, narrow room. The way the women isolated themselves from men was not natural, though Storm had accepted the practice weeks ago. He would like to be able to see their faces, and perhaps discern which of them was the thief. He thought perhaps it was Tallie, but he could not imagine the young woman readily agreeing to clean up after the two men. If it was any of them, it would be Sister Pete.

Before their filled plates were brought to the table, Storm arose. "I brought a treat from town. Tell the sisters I'm fetching it from the wagon." He returned momentarily with a large platter, carefully covered with a linen napkin. "Mr. Chadwick's wife sent over a cake."

"What kind?" snickered Old Potts. "Devil's food choklat?"

"Angel food," countered Storm, a grin raking his striking bronze visage. "Mrs. Chadwick thought it would be appropriate for the church ladies."

The door creaked. Sister Pete approached and set two plates, brimming with food, before the two men. Spying the covered platter, she said, "What is this, Brother Storm? You have brought your own meal to the table?"

Picking up the platter, he handed it to her. When she hesitated to take it from him, Storm lightly nudged her linked fingers. "The merchant's wife sent over a cake for our dessert this evening."

Sister Pete smiled warmly as she took the platter. Storm was immediately ashamed that he thought she might be the tiara thief. Though she was a bit rough and unrefined, he had seen that she was a good, caring woman. Certainly, she'd stuck up for him to Sister Joseph when he'd prickled the elder woman in some small way. He hadn't actually witnessed her defense of him, but the effervescent Sister Michael frequently kept him up to date on the discussions as they pertained to him. Some of them hadn't been all that flattering and would have been better left unsaid.

"Then I shall cut each of us a piece and serve it when we've finished our meal," announced Sister Pete after the moment of silence.

As she withdrew, Potts poked Storm across the table. "Know what I he'erd from over at the Phillips Ranch, Storm?"

Storm had taken up his fork and knife and was cutting up the big slab of ham Sister Pete had put on his plate. "I don't give a damn what you heard from that place," he said, stabbing a piece of ham and waving it toward Potts. "The only thing I would *ever* want to hear from that hellhole is that—" No! He couldn't wish death on his father, no matter what he had done.

Old Potts continued as if he hadn't been warned. "Ol' Mack, he was takin' the whop to one of the boys over yon on his place, the one what was birthed illegitimate-like to that maid workin' in his house. An' when she run out and slung herself agai'n her whopped-up boy, she tol' ol' Mack that he was diff'rent cuz he was Mack's boy. Yeah, Storm, looks like you done found yourself with a brother, that li'l bastard, Matt, what wuz born to Thea—"

Slinging down his fork, Storm sprang to his feet as if he'd been shot. His tone was uncustomarily loud. "You are crazy as hell, old man!"

Instantly, Sister Joseph was on the porch. "I'd watch my tone, Brother Storm, if I were you."

His glare venomous, he growled, "You're *not* me!" He was now backing toward the edge of the porch, his hands curled into fists against his narrow hips. Then he was gone, before Sister Joseph could demand an explanation for his obvious pain.

Chapter Nine

Tallie had heard the somewhat one-sided conversation. Then she had seen Storm flee just before a silent Sister Joseph reentered the kitchen. She was a little surprised to see through the window that his plate was virtually untouched. Delicately placing her napkin against her mouth for a moment, she looked to Sister Joseph. She had not needed to speak her wishes; Sister Joseph knew that she wanted to find out what had happened between the men to make Storm retreat in such anger. He could be so moody! Sister Joseph's immediate inclination was to report to Judge Grisham that Storm wasn't working out, but, deep in her heart, she didn't want to have to do that. Thus, she silently nodded to Tallie. If she could find out what had upset Storm—

With a bow to the other women, Tallie placed her napkin beside her plate and arose, moving toward the cabin porch. "Where has Storm gone, Mr. Potts?" She had refused to refer to the mountain man as "Old Potts," though he had said it was an affectionate reference and that he "didn't mind a'tall."

Potts politely arose, inclining a tad toward her. Pointing, he said, "He run off in the night, Sister. I s'pose I made him real mad."

"What did you say to make him mad?" Tallie quietly asked.

"I jes' tol' him what happened over at Mack's ranch."

"And what was that, Mr. Potts?"

"I s'pose, missy, you bes' be askin' Storm that. I ain't'a gonna repeat it ag'in. Naw, ma'um . . . folks too sens'tive 'roun' here."

Frowning a bit, Tallie moved off the porch and into the darkness of the night. Against the black sky rested the skeletal structure of the building that would be the Lodge of Sisterhood where the woman would permanently reside. Sister Joseph had explained that the sisters needed decent accommodations before they could concentrate on the church, and Tallie certainly understood that. She stepped through the frame of the convent and looked all around her. A brisk mountain wind ruffled through her scarf, so that she had to place one hand atop her head to keep from losing the dark covering.

Then she saw Storm, standing silently against a pine, his silhouette dark against the moonlight glimmering on the small mountain pond. His hands were tucked into his pockets, and his eyes were either closed or simply cast downward. He looked quite dismal, she thought as she recalled the tremendous light and cheer of his being when she'd danced in his arms last night. Slowly, she moved toward him, pausing half a dozen feet away. When his head turned ever so slightly toward her in acknowledgment, she said in the tiniest voice, "I thought you might need a soft shoulder to lean on—maybe even a warm embrace."

He looked around just as she lowered her scarf. He was, quite frankly, surprised, and the fact that she was going outside convention once again took away a little of the pain he felt inside.

In a voice husky with emotion, he said, "You know, that just might do the trick, Tallie."

He pushed forward, and Tallie hesitated only slightly before moving into his arms. When she breathed deeply of the male scent of him, and felt the powerful muscles of his arms as he held her, she felt that it was so natural to be there. She was being held by the most virile man who had ever stepped into her life. She was being held by the man who had danced with her last night, who had smiled teasingly, dropped his compliments easily, and in the few moments they had spent together, had been as hot and passionate as any hero in any romance novel she had ever read.

Because her body was warming through, and she knew he was the reason for it, she discreetly stepped from his embrace, her glance cast downward. "There, is that better?" she asked with a smile. She lifted her features and immediately saw that he was lazily falling back against the rough bark of the tree, his gaze holding her own.

Quietly, he said, "You're a strange woman, Tallie. A fascinating woman."

Turning quickly away, Tallie brought her perspiring hands up and clasped them before her. "Aowwww," she teased, employing the somewhat vulgar brogue of the East End, "git outa 'ere, eh, bloke! I think I 'ave been insulted."

He couldn't prevent his small smile. "I knew you would take offense. I'm sorry." Her eyes smiled at him. He liked the way her hair was long and loose and free of the scarf. "You're not like the other women, Tallie. In fact, I don't believe you *are* one of them."

"Of course, I am," she lied. "I am just different, perhaps because I am much younger than my dear sisters."

"There's no doubt about that." His mood relaxed a little. "You were beautiful last night, Tallie. I could have danced with you all night."

She knew that Sister Joseph expected her to be out here with a purpose other than just being with Storm and talking about last night. But as she looked at him, at his vulnerability, she knew she could not pry into the source of his distress. So, she said, "And I could have danced all night with you, as well, Storm." She turned from him, thinking that she shouldn't so reveal her pleasure at the memory. ''If you should ever need to talk, I am a very good listener.''

His gaze turned to her briefly. As he redirected his attentions to the moonlit pond, he said, ''How would you react, Tallie, if at the age of twenty-nine you were suddenly told that you had a half-brother?''

''Is that what Old Potts told you that upset you so?''

''I was surprised, more so than upset.''

''I think I would be . . .'' She fought for just the right words, ''—elated but a little angry. I think it would be wonderful to have a brother—or a sister, for that matter—and I think I would immediately begin thinking of ways to make up for the years we had missed together.''

His mouth pinched stubbornly. ''That will be a problem. My father and I don't get along and the boy lives on his ranch.''

''You often go into Granger as, I am sure, the boy's mother does. Talk to her the next time you see her.'' She knew some of Storm's history, from speaking to John and Fanny, and she knew his father was not married.

''Thea is seldom away from my father's house.''

Tallie's hand moved to rest against Storm's forearm. ''You will find a way, Storm.''

He looked to her, attempting to see beneath the cowl she had now returned to her head, but seeing only the shadows of her lovely face. ''You know, English, what I would like to do right now?''

She thought they were still discussing his half-brother. ''What is that?''

''Take you in my arms and kiss you.''

She would not have protested, and though she wanted him to kiss her again, she would not move closer to him to invite it. ''I do not think Sister Joseph would approve of that, Storm.'' She was a little disappointed that he continued to stand against the tree. ''Come back to the cabin and finish your meal.''

''I'm not hungry.''

"Then retire for the night. Perhaps a good rest will help you feel better."

"You know what would make me feel better? If I could enjoy . . ."

When he hesitated, she prompted, "If you could enjoy what?"

He had wanted to say, *being in your arms, loving you, tasting the sweetness of your lips.* "Nothing," he mumbled. "I think I'll retire for the night."

"I cleaned up your bedding this afternoon."

Which, of course, reminded him of another subject. "So! You must be the one who snatched the headpiece! I suppose, by right, it is yours."

"No, it belongs to Fanny. And, yes, I did *snatch* it." Tallie turned, taking a few steps away from him. But she had second thoughts and slowly returned. When she stood within reach of him, she asked, "Will you mind if I tell Sister Joseph the reason for your upset? She is very worried about you right now."

"Yes, it is all right." Then his hand darted out and captured her slim one. He held it warmly for a moment, his eyes dark and glazed, his mouth unsmiling, the shades of the night clinging to his slim, masculine form. He drew her to him, his hands covering her shoulders, his mouth touching her cool forehead.

She lifted her chin, her mouth parting as though she would scold him. But she did not. Tallie was speechless, her heart begging for the intimacy of his kiss, the blood teeming through her veins so hot she thought she would burst into flames. When his mouth dipped to hers, she savored the soft heat of it, and when it deepened, she accepted it almost hungrily. But when his hand scooted to the small of her back and she felt the hardness of his groin against her heavy skirts, she pulled free, stood there for a moment regaining her balance, then turned and fled toward the compound.

Tallie reached the cabin, glad to find that the sisters were together in another cabin. She closed the door, then leaned against it for a moment, tasting Storm's kiss upon her mouth.

She looked around the small, neat cabin. The dinner dishes were washed and sitting in a small pan, the plain curtains at the windows pulled back with a short length of ribbon. And she could imagine the woods and the mountains and the tall, commanding Storm Phillips, standing in the darkness, alone.

That is where she wanted to be, even as she moved toward her bed in the back of the cabin.

Storm had returned to the tent, listened for a moment to the snoring of Old Potts, then had grabbed several blankets and headed back out into the woods to sleep.

Though he was in cool peace, beside a still mountain pond, staring at a moon that had the power of hypnosis, Storm found that he could not sleep. He was troubled in his heart, and every time he closed his eyes, he saw either the boy, Matt, whom the old man had said was his half-brother, or the beautiful woman, Tallie, he wanted in his arms. So, he lay there for an hour, or two, or three—it really didn't matter how much time passed—and he thought of them both. Eventually, his thoughts focused on the past. He knew his mother, Rachel, only through the eyes and heart of Doc Frick, in whose care she had died that night while giving birth to him. Her death had been one of those tragic things that he'd apologized to Storm a thousand times over for when he'd reached adulthood. *She might have lived,* he'd said, *if she'd been in the care of a big-city doctor.*

Storm knew that he'd never have survived his childhood and adolescence had it not been for Doc Frick and his two sisters, who had raised him, educated him, and had cared deeply for him. After his graduation from college, he had attempted to acquaint himself with his mother's people, the Cherokee who lived near Caymen's Ridge, but the elders of the tribe, though polite, had let him know in no uncertain terms that he was an "outsider." So, he had returned to the people in Granger, hoping to be accepted, even attempting to go into business for himself using the money Doc's sister had left him in her will. Doc had encouraged him to go to medical school at the age of twenty-two, but Storm knew that the people of Granger would never have allowed a half-breed Cherokee to examine their white wives and daughters. He had told Doc so, and Doc had apologized for the attitudes of his neighbors in Granger, without offering excuses. All these years, Storm felt that he'd let Doc Frick down by not making something of his life.

A twig cracked underfoot. Storm's body grew rigid; even his thoughts flew off with the wind. He waited, wondering if it was, perhaps, a doe, or just a rabbit scurrying across the clearing, possibly a raccoon foraging for food at this midnight hour. Then he realized they were human footsteps, light and delicate, like a woman's!

He watched her suddenly cross his line of vision, her gown so filmy that the moonlight beyond did not recognize the barriers of fabric and revealed to him a slim, alluring female form. She was standing in silhouette, easily three feet of wheat-colored hair trailing down her slim back and fluttering oh so delicately in the mountain breeze that brought to him the aroma of her perfume . . .

He sat forward now, watching her, waiting for her to move and prove to him that she was not a vision. Her breasts were high and round, peaking so erotically that he wanted only to touch them, to feel them against the palms of his hands. But he was afraid if he moved, if he arose and approached her, that she would vanish, like the genies of the Arabian tales he had read, and he would once again be alone, wallowing in his miseries and in the fury of his personal demons.

The night was cool, but Tallie did not feel it. She wanted only to be away from the cabin that was as hot and suffocating as the sisters' old stove. A thick shawl hung across her right arm, but she did not yet feel the need for it. She stood, looking into the night, tears sheening her hazel eyes, and her thoughts many, many miles away.

She needed this solitude, so that she could nurture thoughts of Ellie and Aunt Cora and England and home. She needed to cry, and she could not do so in the comfort of her bed without Sister Pete hearing her. So, she dropped to her knees, giving in to her tears, the tips of her pale, golden tresses settling upon the ground as she buried her face in the thick threads of her shawl.

When she heard a sound very close by and her head snapped up, the tears immediately staunched. She shot to her feet and stood like a doe, too startled to run, but too frightened to stand still. Then she saw him, sitting forward on a blanket, the shroud of darkness suddenly whisked away by a shaft of moonlight. She draped the shawl over her filmy gown and tried to decide what to do.

She knew that she should flee, but her feet would not move.

She was tragic and beautiful, and he was speechless. Tears sheened her eyes; he wanted to kiss them away. Slowly, he arose, approached her and closed her shoulders within his hands. He did not notice that she modestly tried to cover her gown with the thick shawl. "Why are you out, Tallie? And why are you crying?"

She could not find her voice. She dragged the shawl slowly over her shoulders, trying to form some sensible explanation. But none would come, and she was sure she must look the perfect dolt. The gentle rogue was closing the distance between their mouths.

Because she could find no words, she touched her kiss to his own and breathed deeply of him—

Her hair was like a cloud surrounding him, her eyes like twin diamonds caught by the stir of moonlight. Storm sank to the ground with her, his kisses upon her eyelids, tasting the saltiness of her tears and trailing over her smooth, flushed cheeks, to seek the treasure of her mouth once again.

Tallie lost herself in his gentle, and yet commanding,

strength. Drawing back from the kiss, her soft, warm palms rested on the broad expanse of his chest. She looked into his dark eyes, the mirrors of his soul, and she felt her grief fly off with the wind. She smiled, though it was hardly discernible in the darkness. "I must admit, Storm, I would not have come out here had I known you were here."

A dark eyebrow arched. "I supposed that you wouldn't." He shrugged, enjoying the embrace she continued to allow. "I don't like seeing women cry. Do you need to tell someone what troubles you? If so, I am willing to listen."

"Lonely for my family" came her brief explanation.

He'd never asked about her family. "Would you like to talk to me about them? I can offer a shoulder to you, just as you offered to me."

She wanted to tell him the second reason she had walked out into the night. Not only was she lonely for her family, and needed to cry, but she almost hoped that the killer she feared would get it over with so that her suffering could end. But now that she was in Storm's arms, she felt stronger, and able to face the perils threatening her life. She wondered if she should tell him the source of her distress, and solicit his protection.

She had just spoken his name, "Storm," when she heard the voice of one of the sisters across the forest separating them from the building site. Drawing in a quick, surprised breath at the loud call of her own name, she arose so fast that she nearly fell. As she prepared to dash for the cover of darkness, Storm grabbed her wrist so tightly that she could not pull away.

"Let me go, Storm. They cannot find me here like this." She wrenched her wrist so viciously that he was both surprised and wary of her panic. As she fled eastward around the pond, the moonlight catching the allure of her flight, Sister Joseph was entering from the trail.

As she moved cautiously through the darkness toward Storm, she asked, "Is that you, Brother Storm?"

"It's me," he growled, annoyed by her untimeliness. "What are you doing out?"

"I can't find Sister T. When she has trouble sleeping, she often takes a walk, and I'm afraid she might have become lost on one of the trails. Will you help look for her?"

"Yes, Sister Joseph," he said, coming to his feet, then discreetly buttoning his shirt, thankful for the cover of night. "I am willing to wager, though, that even as we speak she is back in her bed." Then he issued the warning, "You really should be careful in these mountains. Bears roam the woods at night, and though they would be as frightened of you as you would be of them, they have been known to attack in their panic."

Failing to respond to the warning, she said, "Good night, Brother Storm."

Now that he was alone again, Storm nurtured his intrigue for the lovely Tallie. One moment, she shielded herself from him like a vestal virgin, and the next, she was no less than a tempting seductress. Most times she dressed in drab, unattractive fabric, but last night, she had been the Queen of the Nile, dressed in gold and jewels, and dancing in his arms. One moment, she was shy . . . the next she was bold and daring, and yet still vulnerable enough to seek his shoulder in comfort. Sitting upon the blanket, he crossed his legs, then dropped his wrists across the fabric tightly covering his bent knees.

His thoughts were deep and complex. Moments later, a startling revelation came to him. The lovely Tallie was definitely *not* one of the sisters, as she kept insisting. She was seeking their protection . . . but from what menace?

He fell back, closed his eyes and wished to the stars that she would return to claim the night and the lusty passion of his arms.

Scotley House, just east of Liverpool, England

Ellie had certainly wondered why she'd been sent to stay with the Pippens family in Liverpool. "Auntie went to heaven, and Mum went to America?"

A pretty, blue-eyed Ellie looked up into the kind, melancholy features of Mr. Leggett, then tucked her hand into his own trembling one. "Don't worry, Papa Leggett . . ." She had given him the nickname Papa when she'd first begun to talk, and it didn't matter that he'd never had children of his own, "Auntie will be happy in heaven, and Mum will see cowboys and Indians in America."

Peter Leggett was glad that Mrs. Pippens had given him time alone with Ellie. She had promised to be close enough, though, to respond in the event that hysteria ensued in the child when she received news of her great-aunt's death. Peter was surprised at how maturely she had accepted the news, though tears filled her pretty eyes. All that mattered to her was that her aunt Cora was happy in heaven and that her mum was enjoying adventures in America. Tallie had done a marvelous job of raising the child. She was like no eight-year-old he had ever met.

Scotley House was a charming old building made of quarrystone sitting among seventeen acres of lush gardens, pretty meadows that would soon be in profuse bloom, and orchards of apples and pear trees that were popular with the children from the surrounding area. Frequently, Mrs. Pippens had said, they walked along the stone wall, plucking apples, then scurrying for the closest stand of trees to eat their stolen fare. Mrs. Pippens had tried mightily, or so she'd told Peter, to stop the thieving little buggars, but Peter suspected that she'd turned her back more than one time.

"Ellie, I've chatted with Mrs. Pippens and she says that you can stay here until your mum returns to get you. Would you like that?"

If it wasn't possible to be with her mum, she couldn't imagine anywhere she'd rather be than with William and Georgina Pippens and their son, Roland. They often rode their Shetland ponies—Roland his Soapy, and Ellie the new pony Mr. Leggett had brought to her his last trip as an early birthday present. Mrs. Pippens had promised that when the weather grew warm, she could accompany them on their annual holiday to the Isle of Wight. She wanted to see her mum very much, but if that was not possible right now, she would stay with the Pippens family, who were very kind to her.

Her tone was appropriately reverent as she responded, "Yes. I will remain here with Roland and Mr. and Mrs. Pippens. But when you see Mum, will you please tell her to write me a letter? And . . ." The maturity became visible once again. "Who is taking care of Auntie's flower shop?"

"I have been taking care of it, Ellie. And Mrs. Muncie helps out."

"I like Mrs. Muncie," said Ellie, quite without a smile. "She has chubby, pink cheeks with dimples and eyes like little stars. And . . ." She leaned close now, in the event that Mrs. Pippens was eavesdropping, "She digs under her bosom quite frequently, don't you think?"

Laughing in response to her apt description of Mrs. Muncie, Peter Leggett hugged Ellie tightly. He suddenly noticed her pretty blue dress, white pinafore and stockings, and the new patent leather shoes whose toes now tapped rhythmically against each other. Touching his hand to the bow holding back her waist-length hair, he remarked, "You are just as pretty as your mum, Ellie, and she would be so proud to see you in such a fine dress."

Ellie was glad to be hugged by her auntie's old friend. "Papa Leggett?"

"Yes, Ellie?"

"Where is Auntie sleeping now?"

"In the church cemetery on Dorset."

"Papa Leggett, when you return to London, will you give her some flowers? She likes the wild ones Mr. Hanley brings from the countryside."

Emotion swelled in his throat. "Yes, I will, Ellie."

"And will you tell her that I love her?"

"Yes, Ellie."

"And please . . ." She looked up now, noticing at once the sheen of tears behind the wire-rimmed spectacles. She wanted to tell the kind man not to be sad, but she was feeling rather sad herself. ''Will you ask Auntie to take care of Roland's rabbit? The coal cart ran over him when he got loose from his cage.''

''I am sure she will'nt be too busy to take care of Roland's rabbit.'' He pulled away now, the hour growing late enough that he needed to catch some sleep in Georgina Pippens's guest room before his trip back to London in the morning. He had a hundred things to do, announcements still to be written to Cora Dunton's friends, and he was desperate for news from Mrs. Hawley in New York that Tallie had arrived safely. ''Now, you go on up to bed. I'll give you a kiss in the morning before I leave.''

He was the only link Ellie had to London, home, and her mum right now, and he was especially important to her. ''Promise?'' she entreated. ''Even if I am still asleep.''

''I promise, Ellie.''

''And you shan't forget to tell Mum to write me a letter?''

''No, child.''

Ellie rose from the settee, gave Papa Leggett a big kiss, then moved across the large, warm parlor. Presently, Mr. Leggett heard the rhythmic tap of her new shoes upon the planked floor. Until this night, he hadn't realized what a sensitive child she was, in heart and in character, and he was determined to do whatever was possible to see that she was always happy.

Even if he had to go to America to find her beloved mother.

Chapter Ten

In the following weeks, Tallie was not sure whether she should return to England or stay in the mountains with the sisters. Sister Joseph bluntly hinted in her every conversation with her that she felt she had reacted excessively to Mr. Beattie's presence. If the man had come to the mountains, it was surely for a reason other than to harm her. *But why would he be here?* Tallie often thought. Sister Meade, on one of her sojourns through the mountains, had heard about a fellow staying at the Phillips Ranch, rumored to be English, who had been grievously wounded. The man was supposedly having some trouble remembering his identity. Tallie harbored her doubts about Sister Joseph's reassurances. If the gentleman were English, and he was also Farrand Beattie, then he might be biding his time, waiting to get close enough to Tallie to do the business that had brought him to America.

Although the spring season was now gently upon them, Tallie felt deep in her heart that she was still in danger. She often sought the company of Storm Phillips, something she had to do in secrecy, because the sisters did not approve. Each night, after the sisters had said their prayers and retired to bed, Tallie walked in the forest with Storm, as she was doing on this clear, mild night. She was not wearing her shoes, and she liked the way the cool earth felt beneath her feet.

Storm drew her into his arms and held her tenderly, his fingers tunneling through her long, loose hair and his mouth oh so gently against her ear. ''Dammit, Tallie—'' He sounded angry all of a sudden, and Tallie felt her body stiffen within his embrace. ''Do you have any idea what you do to me? We take these blasted walks almost every night, and we hold each other, we laugh, we share our thoughts for the day—and yet we keep from each other the most important aspect of our lives.''

She thought he was speaking of intimacy, of being together, that way. ''But—I am not ready, Storm. Why must we rush it?'' She was ready . . . she had been for weeks, but she could not initiate what she thought must come from him. She would make love to him tonight, if it was what he wanted. ''Why must we spoil this time we spend together? Suppose we were to, ummm, be with each other, and tomorrow not be able to face each other.''

He completely misunderstood the direction of her response. Pulling slightly back, he said, ''But I don't care what is in your past, Tallie. I don't care if you murdered a hundred Englishmen and ran all the way across the ocean to get away from the law. Hell! I just want you to share your secrets with me.''

Tallie mentally slumped, terribly embarrassed by the misunderstanding and praying to the night that he did not, after he'd had a moment to think about it, catch the drift of her thoughts. ''Oh . . .'' Then, quickly composing a small narration, she added, ''We cannot do it, Storm. It might spoil everything. I do not wish to burden you with my troubles, though I admit I seek your protection, even now—and whatever is in your past is your business. Let us not spoil our time together by brooding over the past.''

He held her close, remembering the first time he had seen her, standing over two small graves near Fanny Collins's house.

He imagined that she'd been weeping then, and he remembered that he had wanted to approach her, to make himself known to her. Somehow, even then, he had felt an attraction to her . . . yes, even before he knew she was slim, youthful, beautiful . . . and tragic.

He didn't understand her association with the sisters. They were stern and narrow-minded, overly critical and prudish. Sister Meade frequently remarked to Storm that "he should not become too familiar, that he was both a civilian and a male. It is a business arrangement you share here," she had said emphatically, "and you must remember that!"

"What are you thinking, Storm?"

"Silently putting myself in my place," he responded quietly, drawing away, then turning his back to her on the dark trail. When her hand touched his shoulder, he felt his muscles tense. "Perhaps we shouldn't spend so much time together, Tallie. It could—" He'd been about to say, *it could land me back in prison,* but she did not know the follies of his past.

"Pardon, Storm? What harm are we doing by spending time together? We certainly are not hurting the sisters. And, it makes both of us happy. Certainly, I am happy being with you . . ." A thought came to her, one she did not wish to consider, and really did not believe was possible. "Unless you are tired of me? Is that it?"

He spun back, one hand moving up to his dark, unkempt hair. "Tired of you, Tallie?" His fingers closed gently over her shoulders. He hated the drab fabrics she wore. He wished she would wear calico and lace, snug enough to show off her slim, alluring figure. "Yes, I suppose I am tired of you." Before she could issue a small protest, he continued with haste, "I am tired of having to turn my eyes from you when one of the sisters is nearby. I am tired of not being able to sit with you at the same table when we eat a meal. I am tired of us having to sneak out at night to spend time together. And I am damned sick and tired of being lectured by one of the sisters every time I speak to you in their presence—"

"Then, perhaps, Brother Storm, you wish to terminate the agreement that brought you to God's mountain?"

Tallie and Storm both spun toward the familiar voice. There, half a dozen yards down the trail, stood the cowled Sister Joseph, her hands hidden in the wide sleeves of her dark, heavy gown. Tallie put several feet between herself and Storm, her eyes downcast in shame. A rebellious Storm closed the distance to recapture her closeness. Easing his arm across Tallie's shoulder, he overlooked her instinctive cringe.

Then, before he could prevent it, Tallie slipped from beneath his arm, rushed past Sister Joseph, and disappeared onto the trail toward the compound.

Sister Joseph stood there, glaring at Storm with her one exposed eye. "You are compromising Sister T's virtue, Storm. I must insist that you leave her alone."

He approached, his muscles so tense he thought they'd shatter like glass. "And you, Sister Joseph, are compromising her happiness. For your information, Tallie and I have done nothing more than walk, talk, and laugh together." That wasn't quite true: they had also kissed and held each other close—but that was not for her to know. "And don't you ever threaten to send me back to prison, simply for spending time with Tallie. You will only be justified in sending me back if I kill, steal from, assault, or threaten you or any of the others, and I hardly think that's going to happen. Now . . ." He had managed to maintain his calm thus far, but now his voice was slightly affected by his inner rage, "I'd appreciate it, Sister Joseph, if you and I could get along a little better from now on. And if you make Tallie's life miserable . . ." He left the threat hanging as he stepped past her and retreated on the trail.

He was almost glad that Old Potts, who'd had a couple of teeth pulled at the barber shop, had stayed overnight in Granger. His shoulders slightly quaking, he stood for a moment outside the tent he would occupy alone this night. He had lit a lamp before walking into the forest with Tallie, and now entered the canvas dwelling and moved toward its soft glow. But as he turned toward his small bed, he saw Tallie sitting upon it, her eyes glistening with tears. She moved quickly into his arms, even as he was angry enough at Sister Joseph—and her threats—to evade her in the name of self-preservation.

"I am so sorry about what happened, Storm. I know that she must have embarrassed you terribly. Certainly, she embarrassed me."

To have pushed her away would have been unnatural; he could not force himself to do it. "Why the hell are you with these women, Tallie?" Though his words were harsh, his tone was not. He pulled her down to the cot, his fingers gently clasping her own. "You know, if I could, I'd leave this mountain and take you with me—"

Tallie's head cocked sweetly to the side and a world of questions took away the tears. "Why would you do that?"

He seemed frustrated, standing, then moving away from the cot, his hand again sweeping back his long, dark hair. "Hell if I I know. Sometimes I think you and I are in the same boat. We're both stuck somewhere, unable to get out, unable to go on with our lives."

"You could leave the mountain anytime." When he did not immediately agree, she asked, "Could you not?"

He fought with his emotions, with the ugly truth that he had one day asked Sister Joseph not to tell her companions. He couldn't bear the thought of Tallie knowing the head of the clan had the power to send him *back* to prison, and so said, "I suppose I could leave." He did not feel that he had lied, because he *could* leave the mountains, although he would then be considered a fugitive. "But I don't want to leave, Tallie . . . not while you are here."

"What am I to you, Storm Phillips? We have known each other only a few months." He had turned to face her now, his feet apart in a careless stand, his thumbs tucked into the pockets of his Levi's. "Or do you attach yourself to every woman you meet, Storm? Is that it? The male possessing the female? The way things are supposed to be?"

He frowned darkly, his mouth pressing into a grim line. "The male possessing the female," he echoed her words. "Hmmm . . ."

Tallie thought at once that he was mocking her. She shot to her feet, stepped within his reach and said, "I think I shall go back to my cabin, Storm Phillips, before you and I get into a tiff. I really am not in a mood to argue with you, and I am also not in a mood for your . . ." She fought for just the right word, "moods!"

He grinned now, and when she pivoted, his hand darted out, capturing her wrist. His gentleness coaxed her back. "A tiff is not exactly what I had in mind, Tallie Edwards." He pulled her to him, his hands moving to her back to roughly embrace her. "Want to know what I *do* have in mind?"

"And what is that?" The tilt to her voice was more accentuated. She shrugged off the hand he would have dropped to her shoulder. "I was thinking that I would love to completely, and without reserve, be possessed by a certain female."

The way his eyes darkened and narrowed, even as his mouth fought a smile, made Tallie smile herself. She pivoted from him, her fingers traveling through the folds of her skirts. "Pardon, sir," she gently mocked, "if I do not know who this certain female is?"

"It is you, Tallie . . . only you."

Her tone became mocking. "Only me, Storm Phillips? And how many ladies have you made this pledge to?"

Rather than reply, Storm crossed his arms and leaned against a supporting post in the middle of the tent. He should be stubborn and belligerent, and express his fullest disdain, but he was humored that in her words he had detected the smallest hint of jealousy. With a silent smile, he said, "Well, my love . . . none in the past couple of weeks. But this is now—and you are the woman in my tent." It was all Storm could do to continue suppressing his smile as Tallie backed toward the tent flap and stood there in utter silence. Then his dark, steely eyes turned toward her, his mouth pressed into a line appropriately grim, as though he were silently berating her for rebuffing his advances. He approached, his hand scooting along her waistline and to her back, and he pulled her roughly toward him. Against her loose, disheveled tresses he whispered with husky emotion, "There *are* no other women, Tallie . . . there has *never* been a woman who has stirred me the way you do."

"And what have I stirred within you?" she asked, a little flippant, her efforts to dislodge herself from his embrace meeting little success.

"Passion!" he responded. "It is passion you stir within me!"

"Or, perhaps, it is a lusty male's cravings?"

"That, too," he replied with a gentle chuckle.

Though Tallie knew she should draw away . . . that these moments with him were different from all their previous moments together and could lead to something . . . she could not bring herself to do it. Rather, her flushed cheek touched his strong chest, her hands circling his waist and her fingertips tucking into his beltline. "Pardon my boldness, kind sir," she said, "but may I assure you that I would rather be with you, than to have some other woman with you. Call it jealousy, if you will. I choose to think of it as . . ." Lifting her bright, hazel eyes to him, she smiled as she added, "Well, perhaps it is the little green monster, after all."

"And a lovely little green monster it is," he replied, hugging her tightly, possessively. When her gaze flitted boldly over his finely chiseled features, he caught her chin between his fingers and lifted her mouth to his own. "Damn, Tallie . . ." he said, suddenly spinning away from her, "what if Sister Joseph should—"

"And so what if she does? I am an unmarried woman . . . I have a right to be with you, if I wish." At the moment, all she wanted was to be within the strong circle of his arms, in sweet rapture . . . caught in a whirlwind of passion such as she could only find in his arms. She felt that her destiny, at this very moment in her existence, was to be with him., fully and completely.

But Storm was now turning toward her, his gaze dark, brooding, and angry, his hands drawn tightly to his slim hips. There was suddenly a decisiveness in the way he stood there, and she was not sure how to react to him.

A pain had grabbed Storm within; he saw that the top button of Tallie's ugly dress had come unfastened and a feminine undergarment, pristine white and edged with lace, was exposed to his naked view. He didn't know if she deliberately exposed the garment, or whether she was unaware that it had become exposed in her movements. Should he tell her of the undoing, or enjoy the ivory flesh, hidden only by the lace of the garment, that swelled, almost with purpose.

"Pardon, but why are you looking at me like that?" Tallie attempted to muffle her indignation, but it was somewhat futile. He approached, his fingers moving upward to fasten the garment. "Oh," she added, then with a smile, "but I knew the button had come undone."

Was this the beginning of a splendid seduction? Storm wondered.

When he closed her in his arms, she felt the hardening of his body against the soft contours of her own. Suddenly, the oil in the lamp burned down, leaving the tent in darkness, except for the golden shale of moonlight filtering through the canopy of trees. Storm entwined his fingers through Tallie's pale tresses, then lifted her chin and touched a sweet, gentle kiss to her mouth. He felt impatient for her, wanting to have her in his arms, where he felt she also wanted to be.

In the following moments, the button undone once again, Storm touched her in places that had felt the caresses of a man only once. When Tallie realized that his hand had boldly scooted beneath her lacy chemise and was cupping her right breast, she attempted to break away.

"Don't . . . don't, Tallie . . ." he murmured huskily, his fingers moving to unfasten the tie holding the garment together. "You know I will never hurt you."

Her body went rigid in a pleasant mixture of desire and anticipation as her breast was suddenly free of the tight-fitting lace and his mouth was seeking the pink rosebud he had exposed. Tallie felt an icy heat, a fear . . . a desire . . . and she wanted to break free from him and run, and yet she wanted to rip the heavy garment she wore down and pave the way for his bold, commanding naughtiness.

Suddenly, Tallie wanted to be free of her clothing, for Storm to be rid of his own. But she was afraid, though she knew not what of. Would she displease him . . . would he displease her? Momentarily, she broke away, attempting to right her clothing as she settled heavily onto his cot. He stood between her and the tent flap and he was slowly removing his shirt, then his boots, as casually as he might remove them in preparation for a good night's sleep. She wondered what he would do if she scooted past him and made her escape into the night. Would he go after her, recapture the spirit of the moment, or would he simply shrug his shoulders and dismiss her as a loss?

Almost as if he read her thoughts, he stepped aside, his hand outstretching. "If you wish to leave, Tallie, now is the time to do it."

She looked into his dark, somber eyes, then at the triangle of moonlight below the tent's opening. As she looked down at her disheveled clothing, she absently pushed her hair back from her shoulders. Then she became aware of his movements, as he dropped to the floor between her knees, and his mouth found her own in a deep, searing kiss such as she had never experienced. His fingers moved deftly to free her breasts of the coarse black fabric and the white lace chemise she wore, and then he pulled her gently to him. The musky, manly scent of him filled her senses and she was oblivious to her partial nakedness.

Then their gazes met and Tallie was sure she had never before seen such lusty passion, frightening and yet alluring, and she wanted only to be with him. But even as his eyes glazed with desire, she sensed a certain hesitation. He arose; she thought he would part from her, and she wasn't sure how she felt about that. She was experiencing a deep, painful heat in the pit of her stomach.

She watched him as he turned from her, then unfastened his trousers and dropped them down the length of his lean, muscular legs. When he turned, fully exposed to her, she could scarcely cut her gaze from his masculinity.

She was holding her garments over her nakedness. But as he fell across her body, easing her to the cot, his hands took the fabric at the shoulders and pulled it down the length of her arms. Then his lips were brushing her cheek, touching gently upon her eyelids, his hands were easing beneath her waistline to free her of the heavy gown. She gasped as his cool palm fell to her abdomen and when he moved lower, his fingers easing into her most intimate place, she opened her mouth, as though in protest, only to have it covered with his kisses.

In the moments to follow, as all reason was abandoned, Tallie allowed his sweet caresses, the boldness with which he eased her skirts down, so that no barriers existed between them and the way he lay the length of her slender form and held her close. Storm whispered sweet endearments to her, then captured her face between his palms as he added, "Tallie . . . Tallie, I have dreamed of this for weeks." Then, in a low, husky growl, he echoed, "for weeks . . ."

Moving upon her, Storm's knee gently eased her own apart. He lay lightly upon her, looking deeply into her eyes, hoping there would be no fear. There was not; her eyes were glazed and loving, and when his hand slipped beneath her buttocks to lift her against him, she did not protest . . . rather, she volunteered the intimacy, her trembling fingers now moving to the coarse dark hairs covering his chest.

A muffled groan emitted from her as his hand moved from her flat stomach to the heat of her inner thighs once again. She felt a tightening in her abdomen and a fire raging through her veins that made her body go rigid beneath his tender ministrations. She wanted him . . . wanted this moment, and her fragile movements against him were erotic, then almost desperate as she closed the distance between them.

Storm thought his body would explode; he wanted her so badly that he was ready, even now, to take her.

Tallie was trying to be sensible, to remember how this compromising moment might have occurred, but she knew that part of it was rebellious hostility against the overly protective sisters. She knew she shouldn't be here, but for the life of her, she could find neither the strength nor the will to leave this dark, brooding rogue who was awakening her passions as they had never been awakened. She loved the way his expert caresses explored every part of her body, fanning and exciting the flames of her desire. She wanted only to have him close the distance, claim her fully, completely, wildly.

She was almost sure their thoughts had melded together, as he positioned himself against her . . . there . . . then began a very gentle penetration. She closed her eyes, catching her bottom lip between her teeth and opened her thighs to him. As his penetration deepened, her hands curled desperately into the blanket beneath her body, and when he thrusted almost violently, a small gasp escaped her mouth. But there was not a moment of pain and her hips moved instinctively, matching his rhythm and pace and enjoying the completeness of him within her.

Storm was wondering if he had hurt her, as logically a first time should, but she had no tears, and no pain glazed her hazel eyes. Assured, his mouth claimed hers and his hands rose, to tunnel deeply into her golden tresses. His hips suddenly stilled, then moved oh so gently as he enjoyed the heat of her body surrounding him . . . and the way her fingers gently clutched the hard muscles of his back.

Tallie was thrilled by the strong, masculine hardness of Storm upon her, his thrusts growing in intensity and she wanted their union to go on forever, into the stars and the universe. She wanted to be forever in his arms, to be joined to him in sweet naughtiness. Her body rose in wondrous agony, her heart quickening its beat, and as the gyrations of his hips against her grew in intensity, she felt a wondrous swelling within her own body. The remarkable explosion deep within her, simultaneous to his own, drew her against him in these final, tormenting seconds.

Storm collapsed above her, allowing a moment to pass before he lifted his head and gently laughed. "You . . . blast, English . . . you're a fine girl . . . a fine girl, indeed!"

She, too, laughed, her kiss touching the tip of his nose. "An' you, eh, bloke! Ye'r a fine tumble in the 'aiy," she teased.

"Don't you use that Whitechapel brogue on me, English," he continued to laugh, even as he immediately groaned in his withdrawal from her. Easing along the length of her, he pulled her lightly to him. "So . . ." She had closed her eyes against him, but he nudged her with his shoulder. "Are you going to sleep here with me . . . or will you return to your cabin to face Sister Pete?"

Almost absently, and in a very tired voice, she replied, "Well . . . I cannot sleep here, Storm. The sisters shall have an apoplectic should I be seen leaving your tent at dawn. No . . . I suppose I must return tonight."

"And what will you say?"

Her gaze lifted, her eyes smiling. "Sister Pete will be sound asleep . . . I do not suppose a blizzard would awaken her. And if she did awaken, I would simply tell her that I was walking in the woods and got attacked by a big, old grizzly bear." Sighing deeply, she added, "And what a wonderful old grizzly it was!"

She hopped up from the cot quickly, so that he could not catch her and prevent her escape. Dragging on her dress, she buttoned it, then stuffed her delicate lace underthings into the overly large bosom of the dress. As she moved toward the tent flap and looked out, she forced fear into her eyes as she gasped, "Oh, good Lord . . . here comes Sister Joseph!"

Storm jumped up so quickly that he caught his foot in the mattress and half fell. "Dammit!" he growled, turning over on the ground at the same moment that he grabbed for his Levi's. Then he looked up, saw the mischievous smile molding her mouth and he sat, contemplating dragging her down and shaking her but good. Rather, he grinned, then accused, "You lied through your teeth, English. Sister Joseph is not on her way over here at all!"

A laughing Tallie skipped from the tent, and he heard the delicate patter of her bare footfalls on the path. Momentarily, the cabin door gently opened, and she was gone from him for the night.

He climbed into his cot, wishing she were with him, relishing the memories of the wonderful night they had spent together.

And as sure as he knew his own name that they would have many more.

Chapter Eleven

Storm enjoyed the warm, lazy Sunday afternoon. If he could not be with Tallie—who had claimed a need to catch up on important needlework for the sisters—then he was content to be here, on the pond and away from the bustle of the compound.

The small, flat-bottomed boat floated lazily along, taking Storm into the reeds at the edge of the pond. The sun was hot, piercing his flesh in thin, hot shards, and he instinctively moved to cover his bare chest with the shirt he had carelessly thrown in the bottom of the boat. The ethereal peace of sleep was quietly overtaking him, and he did not fight it; rather, he succumbed to the needs of his body and mind, to escape, even temporarily, from the aggravation of work and enjoy thoughts of his beloved Tallie.

The boat ground against something just under the currents of the shallow water, causing him to force open a heavy eyelid. He saw nothing but sand on a high spot of the pond. Nothing to worry about.

Blue skies, just beginning to darken with the approach of night and the threat of an approaching storm, calmed his queasy insides; he shouldn't have consumed the "medicinal" spirits

Sister Joseph had given him to quell his queasy stomach. He was sure that the treeline surrounding the pond was draping its long fingers over his small wooden vessel. Another day in the woods, as drudgerous and mundane as it might be—would soon come to a close—

Singing! His eyes snapped open, his head quickly turning to the direction giving rise to the beautiful notes. Parting the reeds instantly betrayed to Storm the slim, ivory back of the woman who made life in the compound wonderful for him.

Her waist-length hair floated on the glassy surface. Her song pierced his heart and his soul as he watched her hands fan the currents in rhythm with the tune. He was surprised that she had come into the lake so boldly, since *she* was the one who wanted to hide their relationship from the sisters.

She had lain her garments out neatly on the bank, placing the shoes just beneath the hem of the skirt, so that it looked suspiciously like a very flat woman lying against the boulder. Her undergarments were discreetly hidden—or so she apparently thought—beneath the voluminous skirts she had discarded moments before. White lace . . . sensuous, filmy, transparent, tight-fitting, and tiny—

He could imagine that if she knew he was close by, she'd have one of her pretty English fits, which he found oh so charming.

Something moved very close by. Tallie spun, instinctively crossing her slim arms over her breasts just below the surface of the water. Her hazel gaze swept the bank, halting for a moment at the neat stack of clothing and the towel Sister Joseph had given her for her bath. It was the first day warm enough to bathe in the clear pond and she did not want to be disturbed, neither by man nor beast nor slithering creature beneath the water's surface. Beyond the treeline she could see the tall oak that would have to be toppled to make way for the church, and she thought that the sky above it seemed ominous and threatening all of a sudden. She had the feeling of eyes upon her, though she saw no one. Storm had gone into Granger, so she knew he wouldn't be spying on her. She had heard him tell Sister Joseph that he'd be gone half a day; what she hadn't heard just moments later was Sister Meade asking him to postpone the trip for a day until a proper inventory could be made of their building supplies.

Reassuring herself that she was very much alone—though she'd much rather be with Storm—Tallie returned to the pleasant task of bathing. The water was clear and cool, and she liked the way the very lust of the sun's rays teased her cheeks to a crimson hue, and made her eyelids feel like soft, cozy blankets. She liked this place, this wild, untamed mountain range in Tennessee, and if it were not for Ellie and Aunt Cora she would never want to return to London's East End. Perhaps she could one day compel Aunt Cora to come to America, bring Ellie with her, and they—with her beloved Storm, of course—could set up house in this clean, beautiful land. She could imagine Aunt Cora lifting a long, haughty nose to the air and breathing deeply, then smiling because the stink of refuse did not invade her powerful lungs as it did on the streets of the East End.

Oh, how she missed dear Cora Dunton! She had been a mother to her for these twenty-six years and she couldn't imagine never seeing her again. The very thought made her heart almost cease to beat. Cora Dunton was one of the most important people in her life, and a very good part of her being, enough so that she thought she might whither and die without the dear woman.

She should return home, since she had not sensed danger these past few weeks. But the sisters dissuaded her from making such a decision. She wasn't sure if it was because they were genuinely worried about her, or whether it was because the extra pair of hands made the necessary work easier on them.

Then she thought of Storm Phillips. She knew she was falling in love with the handsome rogue. She enjoyed the long, evening walks, the kisses, the way his body pressed to her own . . .

their lovemaking. He had said that he wanted her, but she wasn't sure in what context he had meant it. He hadn't mentioned marriage, but he *had* mentioned staying with her forever. He filled her dreams at night and her thoughts in the day.

A stir in the currents quickly reached her; she whirled in the water, making something of a splash, then gently scrutinized the line of reeds. It would be just her luck if an alligator came out of the flora and fauna to chew off one of her legs. But she saw nothing menacing, and so breathed a little easier . . . that is, until she saw a pair of smiling black eyes staring at her from a part in the reeds.

"Storm Phillips, you stop spying on me this instant! I thought you were gone to Granger!"

His smile now matched the humor in his eyes. "Spying on you?" he drawled in a pleasant masculine tone. "Why, little filly, I was looking out for you. I saw the way those eyes widened when you thought it might be a big old snake or something slipping and sliding toward you."

"I thought no such thing," she easily lied. He had propped his chin on the back of one hand and was using the other to stir the boat through the reeds. "And just what do you think you're doing?" she asked with a note of firm indignation. "Pardon, but I am in my altogethers—" Then, with a smile, "—and I am not quite sure how close the sisters are. If they see me here like this . . . and you as well."

When he was just out of touching distance of her, he stopped the movement of the small boat. Grinning, he said, "Don't think for a moment they are blind to the feelings we have for each other, Tallie." With a twisted grin, he added, "I *know* your altogethers are more pleasant than that white lace undergarment you attempted to hide on the bank—I suppose from the other sisters, since I have seen it many times."

She turned away, pulling herself down into the water in an attempt to hide herself from him. Instinctively, her gaze cut toward her pile of clothing and she saw immediately that she had dismally failed in her attempt to hide the coveted lace garments. What if one of the other sisters, beside Pete, who already knew of her penchant for feminine wear, were to discover the secret she hid beneath her clothes? Sister Joseph, especially, would never understand and would admonish her for days. She could feel the heat rising in her cheeks, and she knew it was not the effects of the sun this time.

Tallie's moment of deep thought had given Storm an opportunity to discreetly maneuver his cane pole into the water. The smaller end now wriggled through the water just below the surface toward an unsuspecting Tallie. When it suddenly touched her just above her knee, she screamed, spinning toward Storm and caring not a whit that she was exposing herself as she thrashed the water—and the unknown sea monster attacking her—with two balled hands.

Storm started laughing, at the same moment pulling the pole—Tallie's sea monster—up from water, peaceful except for the beautiful Englishwoman's thrashing. She cut a lethal, glaring gaze toward him, then accomplished the most pitiful pout Storm had ever seen. The laughter suddenly ceased.

Storm had caught only a glimpse of her before she'd sought the cover of the dark water once again. He was aroused anew by her alluring and womanly figure, her full, firm breasts, their tips the color of his bronze chest, her waist so tiny that he wondered how her backbone could be wide enough to support her. Her skin was like the flawless ivory statue he had seen in the foyer of his father's house the one time he had visited there . . . and her pert, oval features were now as colorful as an impish child's. His body reacted, and in view of her hostile glare, he turned onto his back and supported his head against his linked hands. He would have to wait until the night to have her in his arms again, and he cursed the slow passing of the day.

"I told you to 'go away,'" Tallie repeated, the annoyance in her voice beginning to heat now.

"I'm not looking at you," he pouted with boyish indifference. "You have nothing I haven't seen before."

"The sisters, Storm," she entreated. "They will catch you here, and there will be hell to pay—for both of us." Treading water toward the boat, she quietly promised, "Tonight, Storm. Go away now and we shall be together tonight."

That was certainly a promise he would take her up on. In silence, his dark eyes pierced the approaching darkness, settling on one particularly frothy thundercloud as he watched it tumble toward the lagoon. In a tone quite matter-of-fact, he said, "It is your night to cook and clean up, as I remember."

"I promise to do it quickly."

In a deep, low voice, he said, "I think I want you right now, Tallie, and if the sisters see us . . . well, so be it."

There she was, naked as a newborn in the cool waters of the pond, while a dark rogue of a man lay on his back in a small boat just an arm's length away, making a most indecent proposition. "Storm, you are an exasperating man. Be thankful that I was schooled away from the East End, because I might call you some names that would turn your ears green!"

He pivoted so quickly that he nearly upset the small boat. When their gazes met, he thought her charmingly hostile; she thought him reptilian. Quietly he said, "Green ears! Now, that would be interesting." When he had propped his chin on one balled hand, he asked, "Would you still love me?"

She knew he was teasing, because they had never spoken openly of love. She imagined, though, that it was understood. "It would be difficult, Storm Phillips," she replied demurely, batting pale eyelashes at him.

Storm fought the small smile playing at the corners of his mouth. He liked playing with her like this. He should fear the sisters; if he rebelled against their authority, they could easily send him back to prison. "I suppose, Tallie, that I should go, so the old sisters don't scalp me."

"It is your people, Storm, who scalp people," she reminded him without malice.

Were she anyone else, the remark would have spoiled his mood. "My people don't scalp, English," he responded, a little surprised that he remained so calm. Such slurs against the character of his brethren normally infuriated him. Nothing, however, had been normal since he'd first met this beauty, who hid vast, wonderful treasures beneath the coarse threads of ugly clothing. When he picked up the oars to put distance between them on the pond, she called to him. His dark, glaring eyes turned full to her.

"What time tonight, Storm?"

"After the sisters go to bed."

"About eight then."

"Eight it is." Then he halted, turning back to watch her.

"I want to get out of the water. Will you please go away?"

"I'm not stopping you."

He had seen her unclothed many times in the past, but she really did not want to leave the water in front of him, simply because one of the sisters might see her and she would never live it down. The sisters, who had frequently scolded her for not being more private in her dressing, would accuse her of "unseemly exposure." She simply was not ashamed of her body, though Aunt Cora had hinted many times that modesty in matters of the flesh was the "moral way of things." Tallie remembered the stern lecture she'd received from her dear aunt when their only boarder, Mr. Pringle, had come into the pantry for a potato while she'd been in the tub. The very fact that Tallie hadn't ordered him out had left Cora Dunton with the impression that her niece had "no morals." Poor Mr. Pringle, under such tremendous pressure to "recant his sin and his wicked lust," had been compelled to seek lodgings elsewhere in the Whitechapel district. After that, he'd never been able to look Tallie in the eyes when they'd chanced to meet on the street.

Her thoughts might have spanned the miles and deposited her longer in her familiar streets of Whitechapel had she not looked around to see if Storm had withdrawn. He had not; rather, he had dropped his strong, square chin onto his hands and was looking at her with a strange, dreamy look in his dark eyes.

When her gaze narrowed threateningly, he sent one black eyebrow arching upward. "I am *not* a canary," he pouted with boyish charm, "and I, Storm Phillips, won't be gobbled up. So, don't look at me like a self-satisfied cat!"

"Then will you please leave?"

His hands moved suddenly, his palms bracing against the sides of the small boat to heft himself to his knees. "Since you asked so sweetly, my Cleopatra, my Tallie, your wish is my command."

"Don't call me that."

"My Cleopatra? Why not?"

Rather than answer, she decided to play on his sympathy. "The water is growing colder, Storm, and I will catch my death if I do not get out. Will you please leave, or must I scream for help?"

Tallie had grown very fond of the black-hearted rogue in the several weeks they had been together. Looking into his dark, humored eyes, she felt free and alive, wanting him enough that she didn't really care who saw them. Storm Phillips made her want a lot more from life than delivering flowers for her aunt's small shop.

Because he knew nothing about her personal life, Tallie was a puzzle Storm wanted very much to solve. He would never let her leave the mountain until she was fully, completely his, body . . . and spirit. But for now, he had other things on his mind, and one of them was seeing if she would be so bold as to leave the water beneath his watchful eye.

"*Are* you going to leave, Storm Phillips?" she asked after a moment.

"No" came his short reply, to which he could add nothing to relay the finality of his decision.

"Very well," said a shrugging Tallie, moving calmly through the water and fanning the coolness out of her way.

Storm watched in awe as her glistening body emerged from

the water. Hastily, she dried off, wrapped the towel around her dripping hair, then pulled on her lace undergarments; when she finally covered herself with the bulky dress, she turned to face him as she worked to bring some order to her appearance.

She smiled. "I do hope the little show shall hold you until the evening, Storm Phillips."

"I would love to have dried you off, Tallie."

"I'd as soon be slithered upon by a snake," she teased.

He grinned mischievously. "I slither passionately, as you have found out."

She caught her own grin, holding it back with some effort. "And I can kill passionately, Storm Phillips." Turning away, she took her first step to rejoin the women busy at work in the Lodge of Sisterhood. Then she turned back, piling the small towel atop her head when it began to fall. "The next time you spy on me at my bath, you'll be spying on Sister Joseph as well. I'll put her on lookout duty, and I wonder how passionately you'll slither when she is glaring down your neck! And now you'll see no more of me till we meet at eight this evening."

She turned, moving quickly *now,* so that to have called her back would have drawn the attention of the other women.

Sister Joseph had assumed a stance of disapproval, tapping of toe and big, bare knuckles resting against bony hips. Tallie attempted to lower her gaze and scoot past her, but the taller woman cleared her throat, loudly and with only one intention.

"Yes, Sister Joseph," said Tallie, turning to politely meet the stern gaze of Sister Joseph's good eye.

"It's none of my business, young lady, we have vowed to protect you, but Mr. Phillips should be avoided." In a quieter voice, she added, "Especially when you are bathing."

So! At least one of the women had seen her playful bantering in the pond. Sister Joseph was aware that she and Storm spent a lot of time together, but Tallie felt reasonably sure she didn't know they were intimate. "The meeting was accidental," explained Tallie. "I can take care of myself. I always have and always will."

"Which is why you have sought the protection of four aging women who haven't a single weapon between them! Which is why you are so frightened that even a chance encounter with your own shadow causes the blood to drain from your cheeks. Yes indeed, you can take care of yourself!"

Tallie hated it when Sister Joseph gave one of her mean, insensitive lectures. Her bottom lip trembled and she caught it severely between her teeth, hoping to staunch any show of emotion. Dropping her eyes, she managed to release the trembling lip long enough to say, "May I go now? I wish to dry my hair and get back to my work. And . . ." Her tone grew rebellious, "perhaps I might even give myself a good dose of courage! Will that make me less of a burden to you, Sister Joseph?"

Sister Joseph crossed her arms. Momentarily, she said, "Go," and made a point to watch Tallie disappear into the small cabin in search of solitude.

Tallie had just finished drying her hair and putting it in some semblance of order when Sister Pete knocked on the door. Tallie called for her to come in, at which time, Sister Pete entered the small room. Tossing herself upon the bed, Tallie pressed her palms against the coarse blanket. Now she looked toward the small table Sister Pete settled onto the planked floor, along with several sheets of sandpaper.

"It surely is a scorcher out there . . ." Then with a twinkle, "As you know, Sister T, it is your job to sand the furniture our Mr. Phillips is constructing. I thought you'd like to do it indoors until the day cools."

"Thank you, I will." Tallie rolled her head several times, then dropped her chin to her neckline before looking again to Sister Pete, now straightening toiletries on a small table she shared with Tallie. "Sister Pete?"

"Ummmm?"

"What do you think of Storm Phillips?"

Sister Pete looked toward the young, pretty woman, her eyes narrowing slightly. "More importantly, what do *you* think of him?"

"I think I am in love with him, but . . ."

When she paused, Sister Pete prompted, "But?"

Tallie had expected more reaction from Sister Pete. Were the sisters more aware of her relationship with Storm than Tallie thought? "There is a certain rough charm about him, and I do not think he would fit in well with a London crowd. Do you?

Sister Pete turned, smiling, her hands settling on well-endowed hips. "You will never drag that young man away from these mountains, Tallie. If you love him, then you must begin adjusting to *his* way of life here. Cleave unto your husband, the Bible says, and follow him where *he* wants to go." Then, with a gentle grump, she added, "Doesn't make sense to me, since women should be ruling this world, and the men should be obeying the rules!" They shared a laugh then, and when Sister Pete soon closed the door to the small cabin, Tallie attacked the table with the sandpaper as though she were on a mission of vengeance. Thoughts of Storm Phillips filled her thoughts and made her sigh wistfully.

Storm left early for Granger, before the sun set, because he wanted to get back in time to meet Tallie at eight. Sister Meade had made an inventory in the early afternoon, and had presented him with a list for Mr. Everton's Hardware. Storm had busied himself around the settlement for an hour or so, hoping to see Tallie one last time, but she had stayed in her cabin. He wished now that he'd equipped the blasted thing with a peephole, so that he might have looked upon her angelic features one time before he left for Granger.

He kept to the road as far as Leakey's Gap, then cut through a ravine of maples painted in blinding spring greens. Thinking that he'd have the peace and solitude of the sparsely populated area, he was surprised to run across Doc Frick fishing the healthy waters of Blue Creek.

Storm dismounted, then moved down the shallow incline toward the old gentleman. "Storm!" called Doc Frick as the young man moved beside him. "What brings you out—" Then with a wink, "Escaping the wagging tongues of the women, eh? Probably wanted to throw you into the lion's den. Does the judge know you've left the building site?"

Storm laughed, then replied, "I'm picking up supplies at Everton's."

The man cast a dubious look in the direction of Storm's grazing horse. "Without that wagon I donated, young man?"

"Broken wheel. Old Potts is working on it now. I'll borrow one of Everton's." Storm squatted, then dropped to the cool, dry ground. Taking up a twig, he began dragging it back and forth among the fallen leaves. In a casual, complacent tone, he said, "I've met a remarkable young woman, Doc . . ."

Doc Frick cast him a sideways glance, then threw his line back into the swift current of the stream. He tried to concentrate on the soft filligre of thinning oaks across the stream as he thought of the torrid life Storm Phillips had led. He remembered the day, almost twenty-eight years ago now, that he'd dragged the protesting child into the world. He remembered the horror of his father, McCallister Phillips, as he'd stared into the squealing bronze features of the dark-haired, dark-eyed child who bore no resemblance to him.

He had held the child away from the disappointment of the wealthy rancher as he had then recalled the day McCallister had married the pretty, slender Rachel Spencer, who had died before the child could be placed in her arms. McCallister had fallen head over heels in love with Rachel, a woman he had not known was the adopted Cherokee Indian child of a kind, gentle and loving white family who had taken her in when her parents had been slaughtered by bounty hunters. She had not looked Indian . . . her skin had been as fair as that of her adoptive parents.

Hiram Frick had left the rambling ranch house of McCallister Phillips that night with an unwanted child tucked securely beneath his jacket, a child he had named Storm, because of the emotions that had surfaced in the man who had turned his back on him.

He had attempted to raise Storm himself, but being both a bachelor and constantly out in the mountains following one patient after another, child-rearing had been mentally and physically draining. He had turned Storm over to his aging sister, who soon became ill, and was unable to care for him. Hiram wished that he and Martha could have taken him, but after Martha's own child, born just weeks after Storm, had been stillborn, she had refused to take Storm, because she felt that she'd been cursed by the heavens, and any child would die in her care. Hiram had then taken Storm back to the ranch of McCallister Phillips, hoping that sight of the child might spark some small degree of compassion in him. McCallister had been as cold and unrelenting toward the child as he'd been toward the crying infant. Leaving the ranch, Hiram, hoping that Martha would have a change of heart, as well, had again attempted to provide a home for Storm. But the boy had refused to go to school and was involved in one ruckus after another. Finally, he'd stolen a horse from his father's stable, and Judge Isaac Grisham, pressured by McCallister Phillips to ''get him out of the way,'' had compelled Hiram to take the boy to the home of his younger unmarried sister in Charleston, South Carolina. There, Storm had prospered, attended private school, entered a small, local college, and when Patricia Frick passed away suddenly, the grieving twenty-two-year-old had come back to the Blue Ridge mountain range and approached his father one last time, hoping to be accepted as his son.

Even then, facing a strong, grown man, McCallister Phillips made no bones about the fact that he wished Storm had never been born. Doc Frick had been at McCallister's the day Storm had visited and he would never forget his moisture-sheened gaze as he'd subjected himself to his father's vicious verbal attack. Doc had known that the future would not be bright for Storm, and he hadn't really been surprised when he'd ended up in prison for robbing a train.

"I said I've met a remarkable young woman, Doc."

The nerves raced through Hiram Frick's shoulders as his thoughts flew off with brutal force. He dragged in his fishing line, set the pole beside a strapling oak destined to die for lack of sun, then settled onto the ground beside Storm. "You've been free for only three months and in the company of women dedicated to their Good Book, Storm. How did you meet this person?" He had heard the sisters complaining about the time Storm spent with Tallie, but he had hoped it wasn't true.

Storm said nothing for a moment. Then with a small shrug, he said, "It's Tallie, Doc." Grinning now, he continued apologetically, "But I think it's all right, because she's not really one of them."

Hiram Frick did, of course, know that. The young one with the soft, youthful features was very different from the sisters whose company she kept. Momentarily, Doc Frick warned, "I'd be careful around the women, Storm. You don't want Judge Grisham getting wind of any hanky-panky. She's a pretty girl, sure enough, but you keep your distance and stay out of trouble."

Storm stacked his hands beneath his dark, shoulder-length hair. "You said I'd never live to be thirty, Doc," Storm reminded him. "I've got half a dozen weeks to live, by your calculations." Attempting to throw some humor into the conversation, he continued, "Can you think of a better way to die than to surround myself with soft, womanly skin?"

Doc laughed, then dropped a friendly hand to Storm's shoulder before withdrawing it. "I'd get on to Everton's and pick up those supplies, if I were you. And don't forget to go by Isaac Grisham's. If he finds out you were in Granger and didn't report to him—"

Storm moved quickly to his feet. "I know," he cut Doc off. "He'll throw me back in the pen. I'm going to play my cards straight, Doc. He said I'll have to work for the women for five years, and that's fine. But, by damn, I'm going to make it enjoyable." Slowly, he moved toward his horse, then turned back when he heard Doc's footsteps. "Why don't you visit on Friday." He offered Doc the invitation before Doc could launch a protest to his last statement. "The sisters will cook up a big batch of fish and fries and they'd love to see you again."

Doc staunched the sermon he'd been prepared to give. "Just might do that, Storm."

Returning to his waiting pole and the fish he had not yet caught, Doc Frick did not see Storm's horse mount the hill and disappear into the deep woods.

Chapter Twelve

It was really beginning to grate on Storm's nerves that Tallie wouldn't tell him what trouble had driven her from England, or why she had sought the protection of the sisters. They had made sweet, wonderful love earlier that night, lying together in its aftermath upon a blanket in the forest, and she evaded even his small questions about her family.

"One day, Storm . . . yes, one day soon, I shall be able to tell you . . . but not now." Then she had arisen, hastily dressed and returned, alone, to the compound. He had slept in the forest, thinking about her, loving her, and nurturing his hurt that she refused to confide in him. Blast it! What was she so afraid of?

The following morning, he and Old Potts went to work on the new buildings with a vengeance.

The Lodge of Sisterhood was almost ready for the ladies to move into. The mahogany boards that made up the interior walls had been pleasing to the sisters, and they had joined hands and prayed for three hours over its solid strength capable of "keeping the Lord within and the evil without." Frankly, Storm was beginning to have doubts about the validity of the women's divine mission. Sister Meade was an imbiber of liquor—Storm had seen her sneak behind the wood shed frequently—and yet she was the arbiter of social behavior. She was also loudest in her prayers. Just last week, Mrs. Lee, their closest neighbor, though still a good half-mile away, reported that she'd heard a banshee howling at the moon and was considering calling in an exorcist. Storm hesitated to report that the banshee was Sister Meade, swarthy and unadorned, who claimed to have a bad leg when it came to doing her share of the work, yet could ride their old work horse. She also liked to ride among their neighbors in the mountains, worrying them with tales of woe and need so that they went into their cupboards and storage areas, searching for "love offerings" to send back to the compound with her. Storm had heard from Judge Grisham that the neighbors had been complaining of her mooching, and were requesting that the judge issue a restraining order against her wanderings. Likewise, curses were being put on Dr. Frick by the more superstitious, since he was the one who had donated the land to them. Sister Joseph had been unable to control Sister Meade's journeys into the mountains to annoy their neighbors. Old Potts had taken to calling her Sister Crazy.

"What are you thinking, Storm?"

The hammer Storm was wielding came abruptly to a halt. He looked down from his perch on the small ladder to see Tallie standing there, holding a glass of lemonade up to him. "Sister Meade," he mumbled, turning to sit on one of the steps of the ladder, then taking the lemonade she offered.

"Why her, in particular?"

He smiled, taking a sip of the lemonade. "Good," he said, then, "because she's causing trouble in the mountains and I wish I could talk to her and make her see that her place is better kept here on the mountain."

"She would not listen," Tallie responded with a note of worry. "She feels that she is failing in her divine mission if she does not reach all the people."

He grinned. "She's making people angry, Tallie, and if they dislike her, they won't come to the church anyway."

Tucking her hands into the small of her back, she eased against the wall. "I would not worry too much about it, Storm. I shall ask Sister Joseph to talk to her."

Storm looked at Tallie as if she hadn't been standing there for the several minutes. "You're wearing a proper lady's dress."

Tallie's hand rose, then felt along the lace at the bodice of her dress. "Sister Joseph insisted that I continue to wear the drab frocks, but I cannot bear it any longer. I should be able to wear my own clothes, especially in the heat that is upon us now. And I feel the danger to me might be passing."

He frowned, the rim of the glass resting against his upper lip as if to cool it. "When are you going to tell me about that danger you constantly feel?"

"Do you like the color?" She looked up. "Yellow is a bright, cheery, springtime color, do you think?"

"Don't want to talk about your danger, do you?"

"No," she said a little tersely, immediately softening her voice. "There are things I do not think I *should* talk about." She had only mentioned that she was in danger, she'd never told him about Collar and Cuffs and his agent, Farrand Beattie, the letters she'd written to Mrs. Hawley that she wasn't sure she'd received, and, most of all, missing Aunt Cora and her dear Ellie.

"Then . . . yes, the color of your dress is most becoming," he responded, tearing her from her array of thoughts, "and the view from here is simply wonderful."

She pulled up from her slumped position, her hand smashing flat against her bodice so that the material hugged her bosom. "Well, it is not as if you have not seen them before, Storm Phillips!"

"And a lucky man I am that I have," he said, his voice teasing, and yet sincere. He sipped the lemonade, his dark eyes watching her, admiring the color that rose in her pale cheeks, admiring the light wisps of hair that had pulled loose of the ribbon tying her magnificent tresses of gold back from her face. "Tallie, what is happening between us?"

"What do you mean?"

His hands covered her shoulders for a moment. "You and me, Tallie . . . where will all of this lead us?"

He was apparently referring to the intimacy they had shared. "We have had nights, Storm Phillips. Have we not shared long, enjoyable walks, have you not held my hand, and have we not kissed and—" She turned slightly away, her fingers linking against the folds of her skirt. "I do not know what you want me to say, Storm."

"I want you to marry me, Tallie."

Tears popped immediately into her eyes and she spun from him so quickly she hit the ladder. Luckily, it was held in place by Storm's weight, though the glass of lemonade sloshed, spotting the bare floorboards. "Marry you, Storm? I do not even know you."

"You know me well enough to make love to me, Tallie. Do you think that's all I want from you? I want to be committed to you for the rest of my life." The emotions causing tears to spring to her eyes angered him. "Unless you wouldn't consider me as a husband because I am part Indian?"

"I do not care about that, Storm!"

Just at that moment, the cat Sister Michael had found came rushing through the open door, threatening to topple a gallon of paint resting atop a narrow stool. No one could have been happier about its arrival than Tallie. She didn't want to argue with Storm, and she certainly didn't want to think about marriage, when she had too many other worries on her mind right now.

Storm liked the cat, probably because it had made itself king of the compound. Sister Meade's dog often hid from its prowling fury that had even sent their work horse scattering into the mountains a couple of times.

Storm, too, was relieved that the cat had interrupted what could have become an argument between them. Quickly drinking down what remained of the lemonade after the spill, Storm handed the glass back to Tallie, who was now chasing the cat away from the paint, and doing it so gracefully. "You know, pretty English lady, you sure do know how to make a man smile."

She turned, her eyes cutting him a coy glance. With the cat now in hand, she replied, "I had better get back to the kitchen before Sister Joseph thinks we are doing something we should not. You know how suspicious she is."

He laughed. "If a man and woman are merely looking at each other, she thinks it's something they should not." He had mimicked her English accent, which bothered her not at all.

Dropping her gaze, she tried not to react to his assessment. Moving toward the door at the end of the corridor, she turned, saying to him in parting, "I shall see you tonight, Storm? You said we would walk in the moonlight."

He had returned to the higher step of the ladder, then carefully removed the nails he had tucked between his lips. "Tonight it is, Tallie Edwards. And don't get caught by Sister Meade sneaking out."

"It is Sister Pete I must worry about, since she is the one who shares my cabin."

At that, she was gone, and Storm turned, so that he could watch her through the empty room, running along the well-worn path back to the cabin where all the cooking was done.

Mr. Leggett held the letter, dropping the others onto the counter in the flower shop. He knew the handwriting as well as he knew his own heart, and that heart was now thumping so hard he thought he might collapse from the sheer pain of it. Sitting on the stool that happened to be right behind him, he turned the letter over, at once alarmed to see that it had been opened and then resealed, with little care to conceal the fact. Why would Tallie have been so reckless as to send the letter directly to her aunt? Didn't she understand that someone might be watching the post?

Mrs. Muncie waddled into the flower shop, then settled onto

the customer's stool. "Mr. Wardlow says you got a letter from Tallie?"

Mr. Wardlow was the postman, and a notorious gossip. "Yes," he said simply, "and I haven't yet read it. It is addressed to Cora." Shaking his head, he said with regret, "I had no way to let her know that her aunt was dead."

Mrs. Muncie waved a thick hand at the slight man. "Go on . . . go on and read it. Cora would want ye to. Anyway, chap . . ." She leaned close, hiding her mouth behind one palm. "You know who—he ain't been in the district . . . at least not since poor Mary was cut up and strung about."

Mrs. Muncie was neither tactful nor refined. She lifted her heavy left breast with one hand and scratched beneath it with the other. Mr. Leggett turned slightly away, opened the envelope and began to read Tallie's letter. Seconds later, he said, "Thank mercy she is safe. Our Tallie is safe and in the company of kind, caring women." He looked up at Mrs. Muncie, "Watch the shop for a time, will you? I'll fetch paper and pen so that I can dash a letter off to her right away. She needs to know about Cora, and that Ellie is safe and happy."

"Ern't ye goin' ta read it, chap?"

"I did read it," Mr. Leggett reminded her.

"But to me, chap. Ye know I cain't read."

"Later on," he said, and soon moved onto the narrow steps toward the small upstairs apartment that had been shared by Cora Dunton and Tallie and Ellie Edwards . . . in happier times.

Sister Meade ambled into the corridor of the Lodge of Sisterhood and stood silently by, waiting for Storm to acknowledge her. When he did, she said, "There's a young man out here wishing words with you, Brother Storm." Then, "You know you're not to have visitors between the hours of seven and five. Those are your prime hours of work."

As he climbed down from the ladder, then tucked his hammer into his belt, he said quietly, "And I don't remember inviting company, Sister Meade. You could have easily told him to leave as come here to lecture me on my duties."

Small, dark eyes narrowed hatefully. "Well," she said in departing, "keep the visit short."

Soon, Storm exited into the morning, then saw a young man standing idly, holding the reins of a dapple mare. He thought perhaps that it was someone bringing a message from either the judge or the doc, but when he turned, he saw a similarity to an older man that took him quite by surprise. The young man did not have to introduce himself.

"You're Matt, Thea's son," said Storm, and didn't really intend for it to sound like an accusation.

He nodded. "Yeah, I am."

He was almost as tall as Storm, and his manner was nervous, almost as if he expected some kind of showdown. "What brings you here?"

"Curiosity, I reckon," he responded truthfully. "Ma tells me you're Mack's son, and I wanted to see you for myself."

"More important than the fact that I'm Mack's son is the fact that I'm your half-brother." Storm tucked his thumbs into his waistband, his feet moving slightly apart. "How do you feel about that?"

Rather than respond, Matt moved to the back of his saddle and untied a long, narrow wooden chest. "My ma, she says this here box belonged to your ma. She found it in a storeroom, under some old clothes, and she wanted you to have it. Mack, he don't know I'm bringin' it."

Storm had never had anything belonging to his mother. He took the elaborately carved chest, similar to a letter box he had once seen in a store window, and gazed first upon the name engraved there—*Rachel Spencer*—then upon the small, tarnished lock. Noticing the direction of his gaze, Matt's hand went into his shirt pocket. "Here's the key," he said. Without hesitation, he remounted his horse, asking as he did so, "You reckon it would be all right if I come see you again?"

Storm's imperceptible nod gave him an answer that brought

a quick smile. He reined around, then nudged the mare into a gallop toward the trail.

Sister Meade approached, standing behind and slightly to the right of Storm. "It is time now to get back to your work."

To which Storm replied, "I'm taking my noon break early." When the terrier growled, then approached to sniff around his boots, Storm warned, "Bite me, you little demon—" then held back the threat, since Sister Meade was glaring at him.

Storm went straight to the tent with the chest. He sat on his cot and held it in his lap, his trembling fingers moving over the worn etching on its time-darkened lid. His index finger traced the indentation of his mother's name, his eyes misting as he wondered what she might have looked like. Doc had said she was very pretty, but as far as he knew no pictures existed of her.

Unless there was one in the chest.

He knew that it could contain treasures—money, jewelry, gold and silver, though he doubted it—but if there was even one photograph of his dead mother inside, that would be all the treasure he wanted from it.

He didn't know how he felt right now. He was holding the first tangible evidence in his hands that his mother had ever existed. Though he'd always had the memories provided him by Doc Frick, he'd had a difficult time making her solid and real, a woman who had actually *lived* once, who had owned a few possessions, who had laughed and cried—a woman who might have looked forward to the birth of her child, a woman who would have been a wonderful mother—

"Storm?"

He looked up, then immediately turned away as his hand came up to his glazed eyes. "Damn, there must be smoke in the mountains somewhere. My eyes are itching madly enough that I could dig them out." He wasn't sure how he'd managed to say so much without choking up.

Tallie went to sit on the cot beside Storm. "What is this?" she asked, knowing that she hadn't seen it before when she'd made up their bunks. "It is beautiful."

"The boy from my father's ranch thought I'd like to have it since it had belonged to my mother."

"Oh . . ." Then, "Where is your mother?"

"She died years ago," he responded, but did not go into detail. Rising, he scooted the chest beneath his cot, then dropped the key into his pocket. "I'd better get back to that building before Sister Meade sends the cavalry for me." Folding his arm over her shoulders, he escorted her back into the sunlight. "What are you ladies fixing for lunch today?"

"Kidney pie," she responded, and when she saw the utter disgust in his face, she laughed. "But we are cooking you and Potts a steak each, since we did not think you would like kidney pie."

"Revolting! No wonder you are so slight!"

Without any warning at all, Tallie turned, drew her hands gently over his shoulders and touched a warm kiss to his mouth. "One day, Storm Phillips, will you trust me enough to talk to me? I feel that you have a very troubled heart, and I would like to help if I can. Perhaps . . ." She smiled now, "we can share our secrets soon."

"What brought this on?" he asked.

To which she replied, "The story of your mother, I suppose. I hope that one day you will tell me about her."

Her warmth and sincerity brought a sad smile to his mouth. "I had always heard that the English were cold and unemotional. Tallie, you're nothing like that. I am a different man when I am with you. I am happy, and contented . . . you make me think that the future isn't nearly as dismal as I thought it was. You make me want to love, and to be loved." Then, drawing back with a small shrug as he tucked the tips of his fingers into his pockets, he ended softly, "I trust you, Tallie. And . . ." He looked to her now, noticing how lovely she was, how sincerely she listened to his every word, how her hand came to rest on his forearm, to comfort him, "we *will* talk soon. I promise. There's a lot I would like to tell you, and ask your advice on."

Her hazel eyes misted; dropping her gaze, she immediately recaptured her waning composure. "Then I shall see you this evening, and I shall tell you about my life in London, my family . . . and what I am fearful of."

His hand closed over hers, giving it a tender squeeze. "I'll get back to my work now. Sister Meade thinks I am wasting too much time."

Then he was gone, and Tallie stood just outside of the tent flap, watching his long strides put distance between them before she moved toward the kitchen. Storm and Old Potts would have the accommodations of the cabins when the Lodge of Sisterhood was completed and ready to move into, and she was taking special care to get them in order, mending the better blankets Sister Joseph had said they could have, and erasing all evidence of their occupation, including the lingering fragrance of her perfume. Men, after all, would not want to live in a cabin reeking of women's toiletries.

Tallie lazed away the afternoon, catching up on some reading, mending and just plain thinking. She went through the stack of newspapers Judge Grisham had brought over on his latest visit, and was suprised to read that the Ripper had not struck since the murder of Mary Kelly. It was being presumed that he had drowned in the Thames, returned to a native country, or was locked up in an asylum, with no one knowing his true nature and identity . . . and not a word about Eddy. Could she have been wrong about him? Perhaps she should consider Sister Joseph's hypothesis, that Eddy had come upon the murder scene, after the fact, just the way she had. Surely Farrand Beattie was guilty, and if he were still on her trail, he would have found her by now. He hadn't, and that should be some small indication she should consider all the possibilities . . .

A sound erupted behind her; she turned quickly, seeing Old Potts at the stove, fork in hand and sampling the kidney pie.

He had not seen her in the doorway, but now turned at the sound of her delicately clearing her throat.

"Sorry, miss," he said, grinning. "I just had to see what this here stuff tastes like." He swallowed the morsel in his mouth that had shifted around as he'd spoken. "Ain't bad, neither, miss. Wouldn't want it every day, but it ain't bad."

"You need only have let your wishes be known at lunch and it would have been served to you."

"But ya might'a took my steak," he reasoned. "An' the steak, it seemed a mite more appetizin' than this here kidney pie." Grinning again, he wiped his mustache. "Storm says you and him'll be walkin' tonight again. Storm's real fond of ya, miss. Real fond of ya, fer sure." He should have stopped there, and simply accepted Tallie's shy smile. But he did not. "Yep, I reckon Storm'll be pokin' ya real good tonight, miss. Fer sure he don't poke jes' any ol' gal."

She gasped. "What do you mean . . . poking?"

"Ya know, miss . . . hump-hump." He made a crude thrust with his groin area. "Hell, what do ya call it over there in British land?"

Tears misted her eyes; she couldn't believe Storm had told this man what they did at night. A lump as large as Buckingham rose in her throat, and her fingers moved upward in a desperate attempt to squeeze it away. She found it difficult to be polite as she said in dismissal, "Good day, Mr. Potts."

"Good day, miss." He moved toward the exit, then turned back. "Ya'll enjoy yer walk tonight, ya here." A guttural laugh echoed in his retreat across the lawn.

And Tallie felt sick at her stomach. Whatever Storm had said to Potts had been insulting, and she would never forgive him for making her a vulgar joke between them.

She could just hear them now, sitting in their tent, possibly swigging out of the same whiskey bottle, Old Potts telling Storm of his female conquests in days long past, and Storm bragging about his own.

How dare he be so despicable, so reptilian . . . so . . . so . . . she fought for the proper words. So traditionally *American!*

She began to clean up the lunch dishes, washing them in the pan of soapy water with such force that it was a wonder the delicate floral pattern did not wear off the rims. She noticed the plates for the first time. Where had they come from . . . Ah, yes, one of Sister Meade's missions into the mountain community. She'd probably nagged the dishes out of some poor soul who'd been saving them for a daughter's trousseau.

Well, there was no sense in trying to concentrate on plates, when her thoughts were clearly on the irascible Storm Phillips. He was not as she had thought he was, a caring, sensitive man.

She was so angry that she contemplated never speaking to Storm again. But could she keep away from him? When he looked at her with his deep, hypnotic eyes, would she be able to look away?

Tallie didn't think so.

Storm worked throughout the afternoon as though everything still to be done had to be done in just these few hours. He wanted only for the night to come, and to walk through the forest with Tallie. He wanted to tell her about his father, and a recently revealed half-brother who might want a relationship with him. He wanted to tell her about the tragedy surrounding his mother, and the unhappy life she had lived. He wanted to tell her about his life with Doc Frick, and his two sisters, without whom he might not have lived to be a man. He wanted to tell her everything, clear his heart, his mind, and his soul, and he wanted to give her comfort, hear about her own life, and tell her that he would protect her and keep her safe, that he would never be farther away than the sound of his voice. He wanted to convince Tallie that he loved her enough to make her his wife, and he wanted her to know that she made him feel life was worth living.

He thought her like a butterfly, fragile and yet hardy, able to flit nervously among a stand of wildflowers and yet still able to perch for hours in motionless peace. But there were menaces out there for her. He had never met such a strong, indomitable woman who was so fearful of something unseen. No more peaceful place existed on earth than the top of this mountain, and yet she constantly watched over her shoulder, expecting danger.

What could she have witnessed, or experienced, that had frightened her so? She frustrated him with her secrets, and confused him with her erratic moods. One moment, she acted as self-righteous as Sister Meade, at others, she was as tearful as Sister Michael when the dog got after her kitten, and no matter that the kitten was a lion against the cowardly terrier. Sometimes she was quiet and thoughtful, reading her books and dreaming her dreams, and her world was as inaccessible to him as the moon. Then she was the Tallie he favored—fun-loving, her laughter filling his heart, her arms surrounding his shoulders, her mouth touching his own. He had watched her skip childlike down the mountain trails, then turn and stoop forward, her palms pressed to her knees as she dared him to try to catch up to her. She often grew quiet and almost tearful when he mentioned a particular child in the region, and he thought that perhaps she had left a niece or a young relation back in London whom she dearly missed.

Tallie, Tallie, Storm's heart cried out, *you are everything I think of, in my dreams at night, in my heart always. I think of you and I am glad. I dream of you and I wake refreshed. I am yours, to do with as you please.*

Chapter Thirteen

At first, Tallie's feelings had been hurt. Now, she was simply angry that he had boasted to Old Potts of the time they spent together. The more Tallie thought about it, the madder she became. She had cleaned the cabin until it was spotless from ceiling to floor, and was now in the one occupied by Sister Joseph, scrubbing floors, washing down walls and brushing the spider webs out of the high corners with the use of a small ladder she'd found out back. The more she worked, the madder she got, too, and the madder she got, the more she worked. It was a vicious cycle that had left her exhausted by the time supper was ready that evening.

Rather than face Storm Phillips, Tallie asked Sister Joseph for permission to borrow the workhorse to ride over to the Collins house. She and Fanny had become good friends and they often did delicate needlework together. Both were working on samplers, and Tallie thought it might be nice to have her own finished by the time she returned to England.

These past few weeks, Fanny often gave her small things, a music box, an Oriental fan covered with brightly colored peacocks and pagodas, and once, she had given her a small journal to record her thoughts and experiences in America. Tallie had given Fanny a cameo brooch Mr. Leggett had given her on the day of her marriage to David Edwards. She didn't think Mr. Leggett would mind that she'd given it to her friend. The dear gentleman had, after all, gifted her with several other cameos over the years, which she exhibited in a glass display case in the apartment she shared with Cora and Ellie.

She lingered along her way to Fanny's house, admiring the deep woods, the gentle greening of the trees and underbrush, a pileated woodpecker hammering out its oval nest in a dead tree, a hawk circling, its raucous calls filling the cloudy sky. She often let the mare she rode upon nibble at new growth in a dell or along a trail, and was almost unseated when it startled at the sight of a rabbit scurrying into underbrush.

Weeks ago, she would never have ventured away from Storm and the protection of the sisters, because she would have expected danger. But today, she was much too angry to even think about the menace she still so deeply feared.

She couldn't get Storm Phillips off her mind; it was almost as if the Blue Ridge Mountains and the moody rogue were one and the same, sharing the same heartbeat and life force. She could see him everywhere, in the sturdy strength of a fir tree, in the deeper gray characters of the clouds moving briskly across the sky, in the trail that seemed to bear the impressions of his footprints.

She hated him today, but she knew that she could love him as deeply forever. Before talking to Old Potts, she had thought that she might stay with him, be his woman . . . perhaps even marry him and allow him to be a father to her beautiful Ellie.

Startled by a gray fox, Tallie eased the clumsy mare into a trot along the trail. She didn't relish the idea of being eaten by the indigenous creatures of the Blue Ridge mountain range.

Soon, the high, brick chimney of Fanny's house came into view, and she turned off the road onto a narrower one winding around to a wide, spotless porch.

* * *

"You said *what?*"

Old Potts looked into eyes so darkly narrowed that he thought daggers would explode from them. "I tells Miss Tallie that you wuz lookin' forward to pokin' her. Ya are, ain't ya?"

"Hellfire!" Storm balled his hands, though he would never in a thousand years have struck the old man. "You have probably destroyed the closest thing I've ever had to a true relationship with a woman, and I would suggest that you get the hell out of my way."

Storm and Old Potts had been lounging around the back of the tool shed—the only place the old man was allowed to smoke one of his big cigars—and Storm had been rolling a piece of hard candy around in his jaw. He hadn't realized that he'd swallowed the candy, until he felt a painful lump in his throat as it was going down. So angry was he with Old Potts that he could have choked him to death.

"Din't mean ta make ya mad, Storm. I figgered if the lady knew how ya wanted her, she'd be mighty willin' to oblige."

"You don't know women," Storm retorted. "It's no bloody wonder you never got married. You have the tact of a startled skunk!"

Old Potts grinned. "An' smell as bad, too, huh?"

Storm wasn't in a mood for the old man's humor. His dark eyebrows sank even lower, so that it seemed they would completely erase his eyes. "If I can't undo the harm you've done," Storm warned, "it'll be a while before I'll want you in my line of vision."

"You'll still be givin' me my two dollars a week, huh, Storm?"

He turned away, his inner fury causing his body to quake from head to toe. "I'll give you your damned two dollars, so you can buy your hooch and rot your guts. You bet I will, old man!"

He walked off, swiping at the odor of Potts's cigar smoke lingering on his clothing.

Tallie had just told Fanny Collins what Old Potts had said, and now solicited her feelings about the matter. She had not, however, admitted that she and Storm spent intimate time together. "Do you think Storm would have used such foul language?" she asked Fanny.

Fanny paused a moment, then, quietly gathering her thoughts, responded, "I suppose that a man who was in prison just days before you met him might have said something vulgar."

Tallie almost upset her tea, righting it just as it would have spilled onto her lap. "He *what?*" she whispered harshly, looking to Fanny as though she hadn't heard her correctly.

"You heard me, Tallie. Storm Phillips was in the state prison just days before he came to work for the sisters up on the mountain. He robbed a train, or so a jury agreed that he did."

Tears popped into Tallie's eyes, instantly sheening across them so that Fanny's features became a blur. Still, she could see her eyes well enough to know that this was not a mere jest. She was being very serious. "I know you are telling me this because you are worried about me, Fanny, but . . . I do wish you hadn't."

Seeing that Tallie's hands were now trembling, so that the tea in the cup trembled also, Fanny took it from her hands and set it on the small side table. "You have every right to know Storm's past, Tallie. But if it is any consolation to you, John and I believe he is innocent and that he did not deserve to be imprisoned."

Tallie's eyes gently closed; dropping her forehead against her now moist palm, she quietly shook her head. "I just don't know what to think, Fanny." She knew he had a problem with his father, but she would never have believed that Storm Phillips was a criminal. She certainly could not imagine him locked away from his beloved mountains. "I do not want him to know that I know this until he is ready to tell me!" Rising, Tallie forgot about the needlework she and Fanny had prepared to work on. She needed to be away from the stuffy interior of Fanny's parlor. She needed to see Storm. Her fierce anger with him before hearing Fanny's news completely eluded her now. "If you do not mind, Fanny, I would prefer not to work on the samplers today."

Fanny, too, arose, her hand gently closing over Tallie's wrist. "Please, don't be annoyed with me."

"I am not annoyed at all . It was something I did need to know." Then, "I must leave. I do not know when I shall be back. We shall move into the new quarters very soon."

As she mounted the horse and turned about, Fanny said, "Tell the sisters I will be out to see them soon." Tallie simply nodded.

The sky was beginning to darken as she urged the mare quickly onto the road, cutting onto a narrow trail five hundred yards to the east. She wanted to reach the compound, and the comforting arms of Storm Phillips, before the night became heavy darkness. She cared not that twigs bit at her tender flesh. She knew only that her anger had flown off with the wind and she wanted to assure Storm that, no matter what he might have done in the past, she loved him.

Then she heard something strangely, horribly familiar . . . a voice, detached and yet part of something very real and menacing. She felt her heart suddenly cease to beat.

"T-a-a-a-l-l-i-e-e . . . T-a-a-l-l-i-e-e . . ." the horrid voice called, the whisper of it haunting the woods and tightening in her throat. The darkness hung low, and all at once, a snap in the underbrush a few feet away caused her horse to startle. She scarcely had a chance to clasp a small hand over the pommel to gain her balance before strong, muscular hands were closing around her waist. With a strangled cry, she jerked the horse around, aware that as it loped down the trail, the dark figure was folding to the darker earth, like a creature that had sprung from it, only to return again.

A now crying Tallie ducked low to the mare's neck and dug her heels into her haunches. Within moments, she had reached the compound, and as she jerked back on the reins, she stumbled from the saddle with such force that the startled mare pulled free of her grasp. She was sobbing hysterically as she entered the kitchen and stood, trembling and faint, against the table.

Then the sisters were surrounding and smothering her with their concerns, and Storm charged through the kitchen door. At once, she was pulled into his arms, to be held tightly enough that she almost had no room left to nurture her sobs.

"Tallie . . . Tallie, it was me in the woods. I was playing with you." The sobs died at once; Tallie looked at him as if he had suddenly metamorphosed into some hideous creature before her very eyes.

"You? That was you on the trail calling my name?"

His brows furrowed, his mouth pressing into a thin line for a moment. He failed to notice the sisters shaking their head in disapproval at his boldness. His eyes were only for Tallie, and when she drew back her hand and slapped him very hard, he did not blame her. He simply held her until her renewed sobs died away.

Tallie was so upset with Storm that she left early the next morning for Fanny's house. They enjoyed the day, engaged in their needlework, and cooked a meal, which she, Fanny, and John shared, and in the afternoon, John took her on a tour of his furniture shop. He promised to make a new dresser for her room at the Lodge of Sisterhood, as soon as the building was completed.

Tallie had told John and Fanny what Storm had done, and they both agreed that it was horrible of him.

She left their house just after five and loitered on the way home, enjoying the fresh breeze rushing through the forest, the scampering of woodland creatures, and the new growth and fragrance of wildflowers through the hills.

Her beloved Ellie would like these wonderful woods. She could just see her flitting among the wildflowers in profuse bloom, gathering them up for her mum and all her friends. *Oh, Ellie . . . Ellie, I am so lonely for you.*

Finally, she reached the line of spruce, beyond which the Lodge of Sisterhood and the cabins sat and she thought that she really did not want to return there yet. So, she dismounted, untied the blanket, and slapped her hand to the horse's rump to send her home, then moved into the woods to find a log to sit upon. As she dropped her face into her hands, it never occurred to her that she would worry the residents of Sister Joseph's mountain.

Storm caught the skittery horse by the reins and calmed it. Sister Michael came running, soon followed by Sister Meade and her terrier.

"Was she thrown?" asked a panicked Sister Michael.

To which Sister Meade responded, "Couldn't have been. She's a good rider, and the horse is old."

"Why would she dismount on the trail?"

Storm handed the reins over to Sister Meade, ignoring her inquiry. "I'll find her and make sure she's all right."

Under normal circumstances, the familiar horizons of the mountains would have sheltered and soothed Storm's thoughts, but now he could see them only as a dangerous maze of valleys and dells into which Tallie might have stumbled. Perhaps the horse had skittered at the Collins place and Tallie was safe in their parlor.

He had to know for sure. With that thought in mind, he returned to take the horse from Sister Meade before she could turn it over to Old Potts. In a matter of moments, he was easing the horse onto the trail for the three mile trip to Fanny Collins's house.

Both Fanny and John came out to the porch when he rode up. "Is Tallie here?" asked Storm. "The horse returned to the settlement without her."

Though she was angry with him for what he'd done to Tallie, Fanny managed to be civil. "She left almost an hour ago." She wondered at once if Tallie had kept her word, not to let him know she was aware of his imprisonment.

Storm returned immediately to the vicinity of the settlement. For an hour or two, he searched the surrounding woods, calling her name, following every thrash in the underbrush, every stir on the mountainside. She was nowhere to be found and he began to panic, feeling in his heart that he would never see her again.

He couldn't bear the thought of it. Returning to the settlement, he inquired of Sister Joseph if she'd returned. She had not, so he set out on foot into the vicinity, determined that before he emerged, she would be tucked beneath the protection of his arm.

Tallie sat quietly beneath the canopy of a towering tulip tree, the fragrance of its orange-and-yellow blossoms heady in the deepening mist. Her tears of loneliness for Ellie had stilled, so that all she felt inside was a numbness, an emptiness that made her feel that she could float off, as light as the fog creeping through the trees. Her mind was a flood of memories, her heart beating so lightly now that she scarcely thought it was beating at all. Perhaps that was why she didn't feel alive; perhaps she had settled here against this tree and allowed herself to die. Perhaps she had yet to realize it, and a spiritual presence would come along to take her hand and lead her away somewhere, to a place peaceful and calm, a place where no harm could come to her.

Her pain, heartache, and erratic thoughts made her so tired that she sunk down to the blanket and rested her head on her bent arm. Her eyes closed; she was scarcely aware of the tangled wisps of hair clinging to the tears resting upon her cheeks. She knew that sleep was overcoming her, she felt warm and safe, as she had these past few weeks Storm had been with her. She was horrified that one negative word from Sister Joseph could send him back to prison. And she remained horrified at the events of yesterday, both over what Potts had told her and what Storm had done on the trail last evening. Of course, he had not known how she would react.

But here she was, thinking about herself, when she should be worried about Storm! She wondered if she should go away, so that Sister Joseph would not be inclined to turn on him. Tallie was well aware that all the sisters disapproved of their relationship.

Suddenly, the past two days had never happened . . . not the thoughtless remarks of Old Potts, not her talk with Fanny Collins, not Storm's folly on the trail. It was a new day, her heart and her mind had no worries, except those constantly inside for Cora and Ellie. She was looking forward to walking in the dark woods with Storm, accepting his gentle kisses, the protection of his strong embrace, the light, masculine laughter that had become so much a part of her that she could not imagine him laughing like that for another woman, or whispering the teasing affections against her ear that made her wish for the lingering command of his caresses. *Oh, Storm . . . Storm . . . you are everything I want . . . everything I need—*

"Tallie?"

Yes, there you are, my gentle rogue, my sweet one with the teasing laugh, there you are in my dreams and my heart, sharing our lives and our hopes and our happiness. I knew I had only to empty my mind and you would walk into my dreams. I knew if I was patient, you would be here.

She awoke at once, amazed that he did not disappear into a misty cloud, to be swallowed up by the dark forest. So she surrendered to his arms, to the musky, masculine scent of him, to his caress and his quick breath tickling against her cheek.

"Tallie, I was worried sick for you."

"I am here, Storm. I knew you would come to me." Her arms moved to his back, her fingers closing over her wrist to give strength and prevent him from drawing away. She was thankful she had not awakened and found herself alone in the deep woods of the Blue Ridge Mountains. "Oh, Storm, Storm . . . I am sorry they sent you to prison. I am sorry you were locked away from your mountains."

She felt him go rigid against her. "Fanny told you?"

"Yes."

"This is what has upset you so?" When she nodded, he growled, "I thought you were still angry about what I did last night!" Then, "Fanny had no right!"

Sweetly, her kisses covered his mouth, erasing the tight line of his anger. "Make love to me, Storm. Make love to me as though dawn will never come. Make love to me the way you would make love to the woman you cherish and love—"

"Tallie, wake up."

"I am awake."

Storm was a little surprised at that declaration. After what Old Potts had told him he'd said to her and the little trick he'd played last night on her, he imagined she would be waiting to slap his face again. Rather, she was in his arms and wanting him to make love to her.

She drew back, her eyes, even in the partial light of the moon, permeating the thick canopy of the forest, narrowing in near laughter. "Do you really think I am still asleep, Storm? You do not think I am capable of initiating passions while I am awake?"

He shrugged boyishly. "I thought you . . ." He'd been about to remind her of all the reasons she should be angry, but he rather liked this mood. He hated, though, that she knew he'd been in prison. Roughly, he pulled her into his arms and held her tightly. "I didn't know where you were, Tallie. I thought something had happened to you. All kinds of horrors were flying through my head, wondering where you were, if a bear had killed you, or you'd stepped into a trap! I thought I'd never see you again. And it made me sick at heart!"

She wanted him, wanted his arms around her, his mouth covering her heated flesh, his maleness inside her.

But . . . what was this? He was drawing away from her; she could see his shoulders lightly trembling and his hands moving to tuck in the hem of his shirt that had pulled loose from the waist of his trousers.

"What are you doing, Storm?"

"I'm tidying myself, Tallie Edwards, so that Sister Joseph won't think there's been any hanky-panky when we return to the compound."

"But—" One of her long, slim legs stretched out, the other bending upward and taking the fabric of her skirts with it. "Don't you want to make love to me?"

"That's a preposterous question, Tallie. You know I do. But not when you are upset . . . and especially not if I am the reason you are upset." Dark anger hung on his brow for a moment. "I know Old Potts said something vicious to you yesterday that might not have settled well with you. I sure as hell don't want you to think he's right. I wish you'd remember that never once have I taken a kiss from you that you fought off. Never once have I embraced you that you did not return it. And I certainly don't tell an old drunk what you and I do when we're alone." His hand went out to her. "Let's get back to the women."

Tallie pulled herself forward, drew in a deep breath, then climbed to her feet. Turning her back to him, she retrieved the blanket and took an inordinate amount of time folding it just right. She knew her hesitation was annoying him; he put a few feet of space between them down the face of the hill. Then she turned, her chin held high, her eyes as flaming as his own, and within moments, her rapid footfalls had outpaced his on the hill as she broke into a run.

He never caught up to her, so he could not say good night to her before she'd charged into the cabin she shared with Sister Meade. He stood for a moment on the trail against the dark timberline, his hands tucked into his pockets as he watched the light at the window suddenly disappear.

* * *

The Englishman who had dubbed himself Jack was having a terrible dream. He awoke, perspiring heavily, when he lurched from the small cot in the bunkhouse at the Phillips Ranch. Regaining his orientation, he threw his feet to the rough, planked floor and bent forward, to drop his forehead onto his damp hands and close his eyes tightly. He had been dreaming of a tall, slender man with a pencil-thin mustache, dressed to the hilt, with a cape thrown across his left shoulder. He'd worn boots to his knees and a strange cap, much like the Hessians might have worn, and he had drawn his knuckles lightly to one hip to strike an imposing figure.

Who is he? thought the Englishman, now pressing his fingers to his mouth as he fought for memories lost in the fog of his mind. *Could I dream such a face? Such a man?* He knew it could not be a son, or any relation at all, because the man's station had, obviously, been far above his own humble place in society. But it was a man he knew, a man very close to him, and a man . . . yes, he knew that it was a man he must protect. But how? And why?

He had to capture the face while it was still fresh in his mind. Lighting the gas lamp on a table that was little more than boards nailed together, he took the paper and pencils he had neatly arranged on the far right corner. For half an hour he drew the figure, the thin face, the mustache, the bland, lifeless eyes he had seen in his dream. As near as possible he reproduced the clothing the vision had worn, shading in the dark areas, rubbing his finger across it and blending the planes and shadows of the face that had appeared to him from the deepest recesses of his conscience.

Soon, he had the impression on paper, and yet the familiarity was as distant as the stars. He sat for the longest time, staring at it in the flickering light of the lamp, trying desperately to assign a time to the face, a place, an environment. Could it be a person he'd seen in a photograph or an oil painting?

But why did the face drawn in pencil seem to leap out and grab his attentions as surely as a wild animal leaping from the cover of the deep forest? Why did he feel an unbidding loyalty to this nameless face?

He continued to stare, taking in every feature that his art, which he did not consider accomplished, reflected to him from the paper. As he stared, a woman's face began to take form. A pretty face, pale hair, smooth skin, young, a body slim and well proportioned, a woman who carried herself like a queen . . . and yet wasn't.

He had seen neither of the faces rotating through his mind in these mountains; he was sure of that. Perhaps in the country of his origin? In England? Perhaps he should return there. It was a small country; perhaps while traveling, someone would recognize him and return his identity to him.

But, he sighed deeply. He felt safe here at the ranch owned by McCallister Phillips. He enjoyed the company of the woman, Thea, who kept his feet firmly rooted to the ground when vague memories might carry him away to places of danger and uncertainty.

"Mr. Jack?" The Englishman looked up, a smile instantly lighting his face as Matt moved in and sat on the bunk beside him. "I done what you suggested. I went and talked to Storm, and I took him that box Ma found." Matt grinned. "An' I think he ain't goin'ta mind if I come see him again."

"Just remember that he's your half-brother, and that half is just as good as a whole," said the Englishman. "It'll take time, and you began on the right foot, by taking him something belonging to his mother. I imagine that means a lot to him."

"Sure hope so, Mr. Jack. Sure do." He paused, his hands wrapping around the thin mattress on the cot. "You know I was real mad at Ma 'cuz Mr. Mack was my father, 'cuz he's a real mean bastard, but, if I had my druthers, I wouldn't want *not* to be born, even if he had to be the one that helped make me. So, I can't stay mad at Ma, 'cuz she loves me. But, Mr. Jack, I really hate my pa. I hated him even before I knew he was my pa. He's tryin' to shine up to me, but I jus' don't want none of it. I 'spect I understand better'n most anyone how Storm hates him. He's treated Storm real bad, just 'cause he's got Indian blood in his veins."

In the pause, the Englishman wrapped his arm around Matt's shoulders. "You know, Matt, you just referred to yourself as a boy, but if I could remember my past, I know I would not be able to remember anyone your age who deserved to be called 'man' more than you do. I am as proud of you as if I had known you all my life. As proud as a pa would be of his lad. I sure am."

Matt grinned shyly, his gaze cutting to the planked floor, then toward the blanket separating Mr. Jack's bunk from the sleeping quarters of the other men. He knew his ma had left the blanket up, so that Mr. Jack would have his privacy, and at the moment, he was glad the other men were still out in the mountains. "Mr. Jack, do you reckon you an' my ma might get married up. I know Ma's real fierce fond of you. Sure would make her happy."

The Englishman had thought of it constantly the past few weeks. He was fond of Thea, as well, perhaps already loved her. But how could he take a woman to his heart when he didn't even know who that heart belonged to? He could be some nefarious rogue—though he didn't think so—or he could be a criminal. Would it be fair to the gentle Thea to pull her into a life being lived on the run? He had to find out who he was before he could have a life with Thea. He knew that.

And, of course, the silence told Matt the same thing. He was quite a perceptive young man, as the Englishman was soon to find out. Rising, Matt said, "I s'pose ya need to get your life in order, Mr. Jack, before you think about my ma. But . . ." He turned to face the Englishman, his hands tucking into his pockets, "you *are* right fond of her, ain't ya, Mr. Jack?"

"As fond as I am of the tea your dear mother brings me every morning. Fonder, Matt, because I only *like* the tea." When Matt entered the room, the Englishman had folded his drawing discreetly upon the table. Now he brought it forward, handing it to Matt. ''Look at this.'' Matt took the drawing and held it to the light. ''Have you ever seen a man who looks like that?''

Matt immediately handed the drawing back. ''I promise, Mr. Jack, there ain't nobody in the mountains that looks like that.'' Then, ''Did'ya remember somethin' that made you draw that? An' it's a real fine drawin', at that.''

''It did come to me,'' he replied after a moment. ''I do not know who it might be.''

In departing, Matt said, ''You still goin' ta ride out in the mountains with me in the mornin', Mr. Jack?''

The Englishman stretched out on the bunk and pulled the one blanket over him. ''Get me up at the crack of dawn, young man. I shall be prepared.''

''Dawn!'' said Matt, chuckling. ''I'll fetch you at four o'clock, way before the dawn.''

''God forbid!'' mumbled the Englishman, and closed his eyes to snatch a few hours of sleep, at least.

Chapter Fourteen

Tallie had made a very important decision. It was time to return to England. No matter how she felt about Storm Phillips, she had to pick up her life and do what she'd always done best . . . be Ellie's mother. While Sister Pete slept, and when her usual snoring indicated to Tallie that only an exploding cannon would awaken her, she packed her one small canvas bag, preparing to leave the compound. Once arrived in London, she would dodge any impending danger, collect her daughter, say farewell to her aunt, and go to a place where she and Ellie could be safe, and together.

She had missed five months of Ellie's life that could never be recaptured. Five months gone forever, five months that Ellie must have missed her terribly and wanted to be with her . . . five months of grief and tears that she'd attempted to staunch against the shoulder of a handsome American rogue.

Thinking of Ellie made her smile, even as she wanted to weep in loneliness for her. The child could be like a firecracker one moment, and the next, she was the sweet, charming little lady who said and did no wrong. She could be as ladylike as she could be tart, and her actions were always appropriate to the circumstances.

"Oh, I miss you, Ellie—"

Though she'd softly whispered the sentiment, she immediately clamped her hand over her mouth and looked to Sister Pete. The woman merely grumbled in her sleep, and Tallie, with her meager belongings firmly packed, moved toward the door. She had written a short note, which she would leave in the kitchen, so the sisters would know she had gone voluntarily. They were such sweet worriers!

Soon, she moved into the brisk night air and breathed deeply of its mountain freshness. She would borrow the horse, ride into Granger, and entreat the judge to provide accommodations for the night. She was counting on a small loan from him, as well, to pay for her travel to England, which she imagined was terribly brazen. Though she wasn't quite sure why, she was certain the judge would understand why she was leaving.

The small shed where the horse usually stayed at night was empty. Dropping her canvas bag near the fence beside it, she lifted the wire latch and moved into the darkness against the timberline. The horse was not there!

She looked around frantically, thinking it might have gotten out and was wandering about, nibbling at new grass. But she saw no movement, not the horse, not the slightest breeze through the forest, not even the cat that usually appeared out of nowhere to pester whoever might be around. The world was strangely still and she stood for a moment, trying to rethink her plans, and dreading the seven-mile walk she might have to make to Granger.

She knew she would not find the horse when she saw that the old wagon was gone, as well, from its usual place beside the new lodge. At least, she didn't have to worry about Storm catching her, since he was the one who usually went into Granger for the supplies. Old Potts, with so much booze in his veins, slept like a hibernating bear. She dragged up the canvas sack, drew her shawl more firmly around her shoulders and moved across the grass toward the road that would take her into the valley where Granger sat nestled amidst spruce and firs. It would be a long, long night, and she imagined that when—or if—she reached the judge's house, she would be a bundle of exhausted nerves.

As she entered the road, she stood for a moment, then looked back at the cabins, at the soft glow of the lamp in Sister Joseph's quarters, at the small tent where Old Potts was sleeping. She looked toward the new building where the sisters would move in the next few days, and beyond, at the purple sky above the dark timberline.

Warmth rushed into her eyes; she knew she would miss the sisters . . . and the wonderful rogue whose dark eyes had pierced her heart and her soul.

Storm Phillips had stood rigid against the rough boards of the shed, watching her turn in place, seemingly disoriented and trying to gather her thoughts. He'd seen the canvas bag she carried and had a pretty good idea what she was up to.

Normally, he would have been the one to go into Granger for supplies, but he had sent Old Potts so that he could have the tent alone for the night. He had wanted to go through the box Matt had brought to him, but though he'd held it on his lap, fingering the key in his right hand, he still had not opened it. He wasn't sure what had held him back, but all these years the mystery, myth, and allure of having a mother had been very important to him. He had visions of her and had even imagined the sound of her voice. Somehow he feared that the contents of the box revealed would take away all that.

Suppose he found evidence that she was not the sainted woman he had envisioned. Suppose there was a picture, and she had a mean scowl, rather than the sweet smile that had always been there in his dreams.

Suppose the box was a cruel joke perpetrated by his father?

Suppose he unlocked it, opened the lid, and a rattlesnake leaped out to sink its fangs into his cheek, bringing an agonizing death?

He simply didn't want the dream to end, to lose the sweet image of his dear mother, the woman he had heard about from Doc Frick and the judge. For a little while, he had to hang on to the dream, so he had dropped the key back into his pocket and slipped the box under the bed again. He would know when the time was right to open it.

For now, he watched Tallie move cautiously toward the road. She would not get away that easily. Skirting the dark woodline, he kept pace with her as she moved along the mountain road, so lightly lit by the veiled moon that he wasn't sure how she kept her footing over the deep wagon ruts and potholes.

He had walked every trail of these mountains over the years, knew every hill, valley, and dell. He knew where every pond was, the lagoons of clear spring water, the falls endlessly splattering glassy surfaces. He knew every rut and every pothole, and he watched her move steadily along, knew when she might trip, and kept just enough distance between them that he would be there to catch her before she hit the ground. He made no sound, as evidenced by her lackadaisacal manner as she moved along the road, and so confidently closed the distance a little more.

She was, undoubtedly, attempting to walk to Granger, possibly to Doc Frick's house. Though her destination might be the judge's house, Doc Frick's was a good half-mile closer. He didn't imagine she would make it to either house. The seven-mile journey was arduous, especially now, since it had rained several times in the past few weeks and the roads had yet to dry out. It was simply a matter of time before she found a log to collapse upon and rethink her folly.

So, he followed, watched her struggle with her canvas bag and fought the urge to rush to her aid.

He was good at stealth; Doc Frick had teased him more than a few times that his Indian blood was good for something. He kept against the shades of the woodline, scarcely two dozen feet from where she walked, and yet she did not detect his presence. A slight wind rustled through the treetops; occasionally her gaze would drift in that direction. Once, a scurrying in the woods very close to him had caused her to turn her head, but he had merely stopped dead in his tracks. To her, he was probably nothing more than a series of knobby shadows on one of the trees.

The air was heavy with the threat of rain. Storm thought that she'd picked a bad night to run away. Perhaps in London it only rained when it was convenient, but here in the Blue Ridge Mountains, the sky could open up on a sunny summer day and flog the earth with rain. He didn't relish the thought of being caught in such a downpour, and worse yet, he didn't relish the idea of her being caught in it alone.

So, he fought his better instincts to capture her attentions, then drag her back to the compound. They would both be caught in the storm, but at least she would not be alone. He knew that she was getting close to the trail leading to the cabin where the Mackenzies had lived; it was a dilapidated place, but if the rain began soon, he would be able to take her there, talk to her, and find out why she was running away. Of course, he knew that he was part of the reason, but surely not the whole of it.

Just as he had predicted, the rains came. As he sought shelter beneath the canopy of trees on his side of the road, he heard her utter an expletive, a particularly naughty one certainly from the alleys of the East End. Watching her run for cover on the other side of the road, he stood against the tree, watched her drop to a seated position on the canvas bag and attempt to shield herself from the rain with the knitted shawl. It accomplished naught; rain dripped from the loose strands of her hair, gleaming like diamonds in the flashes of lightning.

In a quick, even tone, he called, "Caught in the rain, little girl?," then smiled as a small cry broke from her throat and she darted to her feet. He moved across the road now, ignoring the rain that pelted against his skin with such force it stung.

When he stood before her, attempting to see her features below the limp edges of the shawl, he said, "You picked a hell of a night to run away from home."

Tallie was instantly furious. "How long have you been spying upon me?"

"Since you walked out the kitchen entrance and began looking for the horse."

She merely plopped herself down on the canvas sack, ignoring the water soaking through to her underthings. In the flashes of lightning, she thought Storm Phillips resembled images she'd seen of the devil. He was not, however, menacing enough to silence her. "Well, you could have said something then."

"And spoil all this fun? I was waiting for you to get attacked by a bear so I could rescue you."

She pouted prettily, her arms crossing in her attempt to ward off the cold she now felt. "You are teasing me. I do not think I appreciate it."

Instantly, he groped for and captured one of her hands before she could evade him. Pulling her up, then grabbing the canvas bag, he said, "Come. I know a small cabin close by where we can seek shelter from the rain."

For lack of the strength to break his hold, she stumbled along, her brittle protests filling his ear. "Let me go. It cannot be that much farther to the compound."

"The cabin is closer," he argued. "You need to get out of those wet clothes—"

"In a bloody pig's eye, Storm Phillips!"

He pulled her toward the dark, rectangular shadow sitting in a tangled grove scarcely three hundred yards ahead on the trail. The door protested on rusty hinges as he pushed it open, then pulled her inside. Immediately, the stink of whiskey filled her nostrils, and she stood, hugging herself and shivering against the cold as Storm moved confidently through the remains of furniture and lit an oil lamp. His familiarity with the cabin was evident, and when his face was suddenly illuminated by the pale gold glow, she thought he seemed inordinately pleased with himself.

"Your little hideaway?" she queried. "Or did some sort of Indian intuition tell you there were matches on that mantel?"

"It wasn't Indian intuition," he said, setting the lamp on a small table. "Old Potts and I sometimes come here when we want a drink that won't require our souls being prayed over for half a day."

"The sisters have good intentions," Tallie mumbled as she dragged off her dripping wet shawl and attempted to smooth back hair that felt as if it must weigh a hundred pounds. She looked around for a moment, at broken, water-damaged furniture, a rotting, braided rug, various implements that might once have had a useful purpose, tatters hanging at the two small windows, a cot she was sure should logically be infested by every creepy, crawly thing that lived. And Storm Phillips was now tossing himself upon it as though it were the most casual thing in the world to do. He had tucked his hands beneath his soaking-wet hair and his dark eyes were merely smiling at her.

"Aren't you going to climb out of those wet clothes? I'd imagine the contents of your getaway bag are still dry."

Her eyes became livid, like pale flames leaping into a raging forest fire. "I see no other room, Storm Phillips!"

He laughed; it felt wonderful. She was as wet as a bean left on a straggly vine, and she was beautiful. Turning on a mattress that scarcely had an inch of unripped fabric left on it, he stretched his arms out and dropped his head back. He did not look to her right away; if he had, he'd have seen her drawing her knuckles to her slim hips and her mouth parting in her instant rage.

He imagined that her rage might be as dark and lethal as the storm dropping upon them, flashing into the small cabin as though it fully intended to take over their lives. Then . . . he knew he shouldn't have . . . he opened his eyes, to see her own mere inches from him. She had bent toward him, fully intent on exhibiting the extent of her rage as she opened her mouth to release a barrage of insults and degradations. But she did not have the chance, for swiftly did his hands dart out, firmly grip her upper arms and pull her onto the shaky cot. She did not react beyond her initial surprise, but narrowed her eyes and held his gaze, transfixed. It became a standoff to see who would look away, or even blink, first.

Her anger ignited him. He thought he should at least get the satisfaction of a hot, moist kiss before she left nothing of him but a mangled mess. But when his mouth lowered to scarcely an inch of her own, she growled, "You do and I shall be spitting out your bottom lip while you scream in agony!"

"You don't mean it, English," he murmured. "Your body is like a boiling cauldron—"

"A boiling cauldron!" She fought her instant smile. "I have never heard it put quite like that before," she said with mock severity. "I should know you *have* to be different from other men to come up with a silly comparison like that!"

He grinned, his hands now circling her wrists to hold them above her head. "Aw . . . was it silly?"

"Quite silly," she began, rolling her eyes as if she was quite bored. When her gaze made the rounds of the cabin, she continued, "I really should be angry with you for bringing me here, when the compound was just as close." Her mouth puckered like a child contemplating mischief. "Or did you wish to be alone with me this night?"

Tallie thought the rogue quite handsome, the way his features darkened, his wet hair glistened and gently invaded his forehead, the way his mouth twisted as he fought his show of humor. He could be so charming at times.

"What are you thinking, Tallie Edwards? Or are you still contemplating relinquishing me of part of my anatomy?"

"Oh, for heaven's sake! I would not have ripped off your lip. Not—" Again, her eyes rolled, but this time downward, "At least, not before I have had my way with you—you despicable rogue!" Her body moving atop his own on the narrow cot, she said, "You are my prisoner, and I do not wish to have to subdue you."

Instantly, his cheek eased against her own, his mouth moving to her hairline. "I am your prisoner then, and willingly so. Do with me as you please."

"Remove your shirt."

He drew slightly up, releasing her as he did so. In a moment, the wet shirt was being dragged from his arms and discarded to the floor. He stood now, his hands drawing to his hips. "Your turn. Remove something."

Tallie sat forward, the shawl being dragged from her shoulders with a little effort. She dropped it onto his soggy shirt. "All right. Next."

His belt whipped through the loops, clinking as it fell to the floor. Tallie's black shoes . . . his boots . . . her blouse, exposing at once the lacy chemise hugging her bosom.

His socks . . . her bloomers, whipping from beneath the hem of her skirt . . . and now . . . his pants.

They stood facing each other now. Her in her lacy chemise and skirt . . . him in his long johns. They stared each other down like taunting children.

"What now?" teased Tallie. "Or was this your way of getting me out of my wet clothing?" Then, taking a step back, she said, "I shall wager two of your American dollars, Storm Phillips, that you will have trouble taking off those silly drawers held on by those silly little strings."

With a crooked smile, his hands moved to his waist, and just as he ripped down his long johns, she grabbed up the pile of their wet clothing and fled into the storm. In his haste to pull his long johns back up, he tripped, landing firmly on his backside and getting himself hopelessly tangled in the stupid garment.

He laughed, ripping the long johns off, then charging into the storm after her. He could hear her giggling, slipping on the trail, muttering incoherent expletives as he closed the distance between them. Then he was stepping on the clothing that had fallen from her bundle. He stepped on a rock, muttered an expletive of his own, and by the time he caught up to her, he was sure he was shaking so hard in his laughter that he could not possibly have maintained any degree of composure.

He had just caught her skirts when she let out a small scream, and they tumbled down a steep hill, tumbling over each other until they landed together in a heap. He could not see her face, and her laughter was all he could hear right now. He was naked as a jay, tangled in her skirts, and she had clamped a very firm hand over the muscles of his left shoulder.

"Ouch, dammit, your fingernails are sharp as tacks!"

She tried to right herself, but could not get loose of her tangled skirt. Lightning flashed all around them, the rain that was able to penetrate the canopy of trees stung her tender flesh, and she was so exhausted in her short flight over the treacherous trail that she almost could not catch her breath.

Tallie had never in her life had so much fun. She felt as free as a creature of the forest and wanted only to be with him, in his arms, feeling the warmth of his breath against her cheek. But she fought her passions, pushed him away, and when she started to arise, he quickly covered her, throwing her to her back upon the thick cushion of rotting leaves littering the earth. His eyes were like diamonds, gleaming like the devil's own, and her mouth parted as she prepared to protest his imprisonment of her.

But the words would not come, and she became aware of his total nakedness.

She felt the hardness of his manhood against her hip, and when he slipped between her legs, untangling himself from her skirts with a long, low groan,she felt her breathing all but cease. She did not fully comprehend his intentions until she saw the deep, dark, familiar passion glazing his eyes.

"Not here in the rain, Storm. We can return to the cabin." But he seemed to pay little mind as he pressed her to him, her breasts heaving against the wide expanse of his chest. His mouth claimed her own in a gentle kiss that quickly deepened, and his right hand lowered to fumble beneath the soaking hem of her skirt. Then he thought better about it and arose, his hand circling her wrist to draw her up. They were quickly back in the cabin and he was easing her to the narrow cot.

Throwing back her head, she allowed the stays of her lacy chemise to stretch apart, so that his mouth found one of her breasts and claimed it for his own.

She was lost in the erotic passion of him. She felt his fingers finding the moist depths of her, easing into her so that she paled visibly in her passion and surprise. Her hips thrust against the intrusion, wanting more, her mouth now seeking his as her fingers entwined through his dark, wet hair. The lashing of the rain against the tin roof aroused her passions even more, the lightning casting macabre shadows upon his bronze skin. The forest shook in the rage of the storm, and she wanted only the exquisite delight of another Storm inside her.

His groin ached with want of her, and yet he felt that he had to delay, to awaken her passions and make her want him as badly as he wanted her. After all, she had entered the night fully intent on running away, not making love, and now he felt her clamping her legs together as he eased between them. His fingers gently massaged her wrists, his mouth again claiming the hot wetness of her own.

The sporadic flashes of lightning lit the rapid fluttering of her eyelashes. Storm thought again that she was planning to dart away from him, but to accomplish it, she would have to lose her skirt. His full weight was upon it, his hand again easing into the cavern of warmth beneath the heavy folds of the fabric. She gasped; he covered it with a kiss, his tongue tasting the honeyed sweetness of her mouth.

"Storm . . . Storm, I was running away from you tonight . . . why do you want me?"

The husky passion almost took away his ability to speak. "Be still, my English. Of course I want you."

His hands moved to cup her breasts; she felt him moving, his kisses trailing along the opening of her chemise, lowering

. . . popping the stays holding her skirt together. The heavy wetness caused it to fall from her . . . and she was naked beneath his commanding caresses, his kisses trailing over the flat plane of her stomach . . . lower . . . lower. His mouth was against her . . . there . . . his tongue tasting the sweet nectar of her, his hands now moving to the small of her back and down the curve of her buttocks, to lift her fully to him.

Tallie was sure she had been robbed of her mind, that it had been sent scattering into the stars in a million tiny fragments. Storm had never made love to her like this, and if she'd had the capacity for reasonable thought—

Instantly, the wonderful, erotic torment ended, the kisses returned over the plane of her stomach, his tongue teasing a circle around her navel, then capturing each round breast in turn to bring them to peakness. When, at last, his mouth returned to her own, she felt him position himself against her below.

Her body was in a wildly passionate frenzy beneath his touch. Instinctively, her knees fell apart, her hips lifting to accept him. He seemed to hesitate, and she was hardly willing to wait. She was shuddering with joy, and wanting the satisfaction of their joining. Was he waiting for an invitation? she wondered, again arching her body to him.

Storm was in absolute pain, wanting her so badly that he thought his body would explode.

He saw her mouth press rebelliously. She wanted him, but she was too proud to let him know. But those pretty knees did not lie . . . her aroused body told him everything he needed to know! He had felt her legs ease apart, and now they were pressing against his hips as a subtle invitation.

"Do you want me, Tallie?"

When he hesitated, awaiting her answer, her hips moved suddenly upon him, driving his full length deep within her.

The wild mixture of the raging storm and the driving force of this Cherokee drove her to unparalleled heights of passion. She moved to match his rhythm and pace, her fingers clinging to his wet shoulders, moving through the sinewy muscles flexing in his broad back.

He had half drawn up now, so that he was on his knees and her hips were a good six inches off the cot. His hands were firm in the small of her back and they were pulling her so far upon the staff of his manhood that she was sure she could feel it all the way to her stomach. It was wonderful, the fullness, the erotic naughtiness of their joining, and she wanted it never to end. The lightning lit his lusty features, and all the while a wild excitement was bubbling inside her body, covering every square inch of her like a raging river.

She could hear his little groans . . . she could see more in his features than mere lust . . . she was sure she could see ecstasy . . . the same she was sure she was feeling. She wasn't just a conquest to him . . . she *had* to believe that she was the only woman he wanted to be with like this—

The thrusting ceased. With masterful movements he was fully on his knees, pulling her against him, and down more completely over the fullness of him. He seemed content to be joined to her without moving, and it prompted her to ask, "Are you through?"

He drew slightly away, smiling his half-cocked smile. "Hardly! I cannot bear to have this end. I cannot bear to be separated from you."

"And you can just . . . um . . . wait like this?"

"All night, if I wanted to," he laughed, capturing her mouth in a rough kiss. "But I do not want to."

He began to move again, pressing her close, their hips grinding together, his body very close to release.

Tallie felt something wonderful happening inside her. A ricocheting through her abdomen was so delightful that she wanted it never to end. She groaned, throwing her head back, feeling the spasms course through her body . . . and in that moment, she felt his own satisfaction as he filled her with his seed.

He held her even closer, his forehead resting against her neck, his hands firmly holding her hips over him. His breathing was labored against her skin and her hands arose, her fingers tunneling through the limp, wet strands of his hair. "That was wonderful," she gasped. "Could we do it again?"

He put the smallest space between them, his dark eyes smiling while his mouth did not. "I think, my English, that we should wait a little while."

"Oh?" she teased. "Why is that?"

"I must regain my power," he laughed, easing her back and slipping from the hot, moist depths of her. He outstretched his arms as he fell to his back, crooking his arm over her neck when she moved to lie against him. "I hope the rain doesn't let up, because I want to stay here with you."

"But it is letting up," she murmured. "Could we not stay here anyway? The gentle sounds of the forest should be good for your 'power.'"

He laughed, coming to his feet so quickly that it startled her. Taking up a small towel, he dried every inch of her body, touching a kiss to her mouth as the drying was completed. Then she dried him, and quite before she'd reached his back, they were in each other's arms again, his full power restored and the small cot lending support to their entwined bodies.

Tallie couldn't imagine the rest of her life without him.

As she and Storm made sweet, wonderful, wicked love once again, Tallie made up her mind that she would have *everything*. She would have life, dear Aunt Cora, her beloved daughter, Ellie . . . her Cherokee rogue, Storm Phillips . . . and she would have them all in his beloved Blue Ridge Mountains.

Chapter Fifteen

The past two months had been wonderful. Tallie had decided to wait until she'd heard from Aunt Cora before blindly heading back to London, and in that time she had fallen madly, passionately in love with Storm Phillips. There were times she came very close to giving him the answer he wanted to the proposals of marriage he had begun to make quite frequently.

Judge Grisham, who remained a close friend to the sisters—and to Tallie—had discouraged her from such a commitment, though. He reminded her of Storm's own commitment to the new church. The judge sat with them now, at a large table set up beneath the trees, where they enjoyed an early-morning breakfast. Matt had also joined them, and was attentive to the bubbly Sister Michael. He thought she told the funniest stories. When he wasn't hanging on her every word, he was especially attentive to the antics of the compound's dog and cat.

They had just finished breakfast and were chatting when a woman moved across the clearing toward them. She was big-boned, probably in her sixties, and her close-cropped hair was the most brilliant color, like polished copper. She approached the table. "Pardon, dear people, but might ye spare a meal for a poor soul?"

She was English and a recent arrival to America. Tallie knew only because a tag remained on her one canvas bag that read, *Boarded in Plymouth, HMSR.* At once, Storm arose and offered her his chair. "Please . . . sit—" Looking to Sister Joseph for approval, he then offered, "We'll fix you up a plate."

In the next few minutes, the woman introduced herself as Brookie Newgate. She had left England a couple of months ago, hoping to make a new life for herself in America. But she had arrived to find that her only contact had recently passed away, and she did not have enough money to return to England. She wasn't even sure how she had ended up on the mountain and, with a careless shrug, said it might be all the leads for jobs she had been blindly following.

"Ye wouldn't have a job for a poor woman, would ye, eh?" Brookie Newgate had quickly determined that Sister Joseph was in charge, and she looked to her.

Sister Joseph hated to cook and clean, as did the other sisters, because it took time away from their prayers. Still, the woman's disheveled appearance and incredibly bad teeth made her think twice about letting her stay. Then she frowned, thinking that her thoughts were not good ones and the Lord wouldn't approve. "Will you work for little recompense?" she asked Brookie.

"I'll work for meals and lodging," she enthusiastically offered, now setting aside the plate she had emptied three times. "And mayhap a penny or two when a necessity is required."

So, in the matter of a few minutes, the Lodge of Sisterhood had a new cook and Tallie was, effectively, out of a job. She couldn't help wondering whether the sisters would think she had become a liability. Then she looked to Storm, silently standing by, and she thought he would find good reasons to convince the sisters she should stay.

* * *

Tallie helped the new cook settle into one of the rooms in the lodge. Brookie Newgate was pleasant, friendly, quite funny, and Tallie thought she might be nice to have around.

Since Brookie had gotten right to work in the kitchen, Tallie was able to sneak out early. She wanted to tell Storm so many things, and sent a message to him by Old Potts. In the late afternoon, with dusk falling, she met Storm at the cabin in the woods.

When, at last, she lay in his arms, her heart aching to tell him everything, he had other concerns on his mind. ''Somebody's trying to kill Old Potts,'' he said matter-of-factly.

To which Tallie replied, ''What could anyone have against him? He is always here and cannot be getting into any trouble.''

''I think it has something to do with those few weeks he worked out on my fa—McCallister Phillips' ranch.''

Tallie let a moment pass before saying, ''He is your father, Storm. It does not hurt to refer to him as such.''

''Yes . . . I know.'' There was a time he had hated McCallister Phillips, but since he had met Tallie, she had softened him. She made it difficult for him to hate anyone, even the man he had once prayed would die a horrible death. He did not want to think about Mack right now, because he had something important to show Tallie. It had been troubling him all day, ever since Old Potts had given it to him. He sat forward, then pushed himself up, putting a few feet of distance between them.

Storm seemed moody tonight. Tallie watched him pull on his Levi's, then approach the mantel a dozen feet away. When he turned, he was holding something dark and rectangular, and as he moved toward her, he held it close to his chest. When he sat on the cot, he was quiet a moment, his dark gaze holding her own, the fingers of his right hand flipping open the rich leather portfolio. ''Do you remember a few months ago that Old Potts claimed somebody shot a man on the trail, but the body disappeared?'' She nodded quietly. ''Well . . . Old Potts took this before he ran away.'' Quietly, he poured the contents of the portfolio onto the cot, at which time Tallie sat forward.

Storm watched the fear glaze her eyes. Her mouth parted and begin to tremble. "Before I tell you the name inside the portfolio, I want you to tell me what you are running from."

She looked up quickly. "Why?"

"Because I believe this and your fear are connected."

Her mouth pressed into a thin, rebellious line for a moment. She could continue to harbor her secrets, or she could share her fear with him and continue to enjoy his protection. There had been many times in the past when they had planned to tell each other their secrets, but something always came along to interrupt their good intentions. Now they were alone in the cabin, they had just made deliciously explosive love, and . . . what better time to spill her heart? "If the name inside is Farrand Beattie, then, yes, we are connected."

"It is the name," Storm said. "Furthermore, there is an Englishman at my father's ranch who has suffered a memory loss after a wounding. I believe that man and the portfolio belong together."

Tears filled her eyes. She had nurtured many doubts these past few months and had somehow managed to convince herself that Eddy had not killed Mary Kelly. Sister Joseph had been instrumental in posing all possibilities, and she believed that Farrand Beattie had wanted nothing more than to convince her of her folly. Because of that conviction, she had wanted to return to England. She had kept putting it off, because she wanted Storm Phillips to return with her.

Tallie now met Storm's warm, waiting gaze. Quietly moving into his arms, she said, "I want to tell you about Ellie, Storm. I want to tell you about the one person in all the world whose absence crushes my heart and my soul."

"Ellie?" he questioned quietly. This was a name he had not heard before.

She shrugged delicately, moving her cheek to a place of comfort against his fur-matted chest. "Ellie is . . ." The declaration trailed off; she wasn't sure why she hadn't told Storm about her daughter in these few months they had been together, sharing everything as if they were man and wife. Perhaps she was afraid he would be appalled . . . a mother, after all, leaving her own child for this long length of time.

"Who is Ellie?" Storm asked after the short pause.

Tallie had never even told Storm she'd been married once, though briefly. How would he feel to know that she also had not told him of a daughter? He had walked into her life and made himself a very vital part of it. She had lain in his arms and been loved by him in a way that she had never imagined, and now she could not picture a future without him in it. For that reason, she would not deny Storm an answer, even if that answer drove a wedge between them. "Ellie is my dear, sweet, gentle daughter, Storm. She was eight years old in May and I will not be in England to help her celebrate her birthday." Tallie felt his body go rigid against her.

For all Storm knew, she might also have a husband tucked away in the row houses of London's East End.

When Tallie thought Storm might withdraw from her, she continued with haste, "No, Storm, I do not have a husband." Then, "That is not to say I never had one, but he died in India when I was carrying Ellie." She sat forward now, and her soft, hazel gaze turned to hold Storm's dark one. "I am sorry I was not a virgin when we first made love, but if you had asked, I would have been truthful. I am sorry if the lack of my innocence leaves you feeling betrayed."

His strong hands moved to claim her shoulders. Drawing her roughly against him, his mouth was mere inches from her own as he said, "No matter what you have heard, men don't place that much stock in virginity, Tallie. I was afraid you belonged to another man. I couldn't bear it. I . . ." He hesitated momentarily, then drew her even closer. "I want you for myself, Tallie. I want you to be mine."

"I will not be owned, Storm Phillips," she answered, the rebellion, though muted, undeniable. "I do not find the prospect of sharing your life with you altogether unpleasant. But . . ."

When she hesitated, he prompted, "But what?"

"But Ellie and I come together, Storm. I want my daughter with me. And she must be first and foremost in my mind when I chose a man in whose hands I will place our lives."

"Then choose me, Tallie Edwards. I'll be the protector of your lives and the bearer of happiness for you always."

"Are you asking me to marry you, Storm?"

"Again, Tallie . . . yes, for the hundredth time, I am asking you to marry me." Still, the thought of being an instant father brought a moment of apprehension to him. Suppose the child took a dislike to him. Suppose she insisted that her mother choose sides. Could a child cause trouble between her mother and a new husband who was not her father? He thought he was willing to take that chance. "Your little girl couldn't have a father who would protect her more than I will. But—will she like me?"

Tallie was so happy she could scarcely contain that elation. "She will love you. And you will like my daughter."

Storm thought about the kind of daughter Tallie would have . . . delicate of bone, frail and fair-haired, with hazel eyes, like her mother . . . or was she more like her father? Storm wished that Tallie had told him more about her husband, so that he might be able to picture the child, but now he didn't know how to broach the subject once again. If he brought up her husband, would she think him jealous? Or merely curious? Would he open old wounds or would she—

"She must, of course, approve of you, Storm Phillips."

So surprised was he by her declaration, that Storm felt his breath catch in his throat. "And will your answer hinge on that approval?" he asked after a moment. If he could not win the heart of an eight-year-old, then he didn't have the way with the ladies he had thought. When Tallie failed to offer an answer, he said, "Tell me about her."

"She is quite bright—"

"Like you are, Tallie."

"And quite pretty."

"I wonder where she got those attributes."

''Do stop, Storm. You are embarrassing me.'' Quietly, she continued, ''She is slight and pale, with hazel eyes and dark hair.'' Tallie gently laughed, her thoughts of Ellie bringing her sweet pleasure. ''She can be quite charming when it is to her advantage. And I have been fortunate that she has not picked up the vulgarities of the East End. I often let her accompany me on my flower deliveries after her schooling, and she so enjoyed meeting the people of the East End. Everyone has always liked her.''

''And I will like her, too.''

''I like America,'' said Tallie, stifling her crisp English accent in her gentle laugh. ''And I like the Blue Ridge Mountains. It will be very difficult returning to England after being here in your mountains.''

Storm thought for a moment, then said, ''I did not realize returning to England was a choice I would have to make, Tallie. Certainly, I would not want to go there, except to visit. I couldn't—''

''Could not what?''

He'd been about to say that he couldn't leave the jurisdiction of Judge Isaac Grisham's court. ''I couldn't exist anywhere but the Blue Ridge Mountains.''

''I don't think that's what you were going to say.''

He shrugged. ''I suppose not. But . . .'' His arms moved around her shoulders and drew her close. ''We don't need to talk about unpleasantries!''

She gave him a shy glance; he'd been fishing for the source of her fear for the past few weeks, and for the life of her, she couldn't understand why she hadn't confided in him. She should have known that Eddy had neither the strength nor the spirit to be a killer. He was languid and listless and the girls had always tired quickly of him. She knew in her heart that thinking Eddy capable of murder had been her greatest folly, and one that had profoundly changed her life.

She would never forget the grisey scene she'd witnessed in Mary's room at Miller's Court, or the look on Eddy's face as he'd met her ashen stare. She now suspected that Sister Joseph had been right . . . that his horror was the same as her own, that of a witness who'd come upon the scene after the murder. How could she have been so foolish?

Tallie wanted to tell Storm about Eddy, and his bodyguard, Farrand Beattie, who had boarded the same ship as she in Southampton. She wanted to tell him that she had thought she was in danger, because she had witnessed a most heinous crime, but now it all seemed so silly.

Just a few days ago, Storm had jokingly asked her if she'd "witnessed Jack's killings"; had he noticed the blood drain from her features as she'd stumbled about for a response?

"You have a faraway look, Tallie. Are you back in England?"

So deep were her thoughts that, for the moment, she was disoriented as to time and place. She looked into Storm's eyes as though he had suddenly materialized before her, then drew slightly back as she contemplated an answer. But when he gave her a cool, assessing look, she relaxed a little, favoring him with a tiny smile. "I am afraid I was," she eventually responded. "You would think you were not good enough company, would you, Storm?"

A dark eyebrow raised slightly, his mouth moving to gently caress her forehead. "You're a long way from your home, Tallie. I understand that you're lonely."

She snuggled against him. "I cannot be lonely with you, Storm, but I can miss my family. You are the one bright spark in my existence right now." With a tad of guilt, she amended, "You and my thoughts of Aunt Cora and Ellie."

Though she tried mightily to staunch them, tears moistened her eyes as she closed them against Storm's chest. She loved the musky, manly scent of him, the delicate pulse of his heart beating against her cheek. She loved the coarse, tight curls covering his chest tickling against her hairline, the way his hand lifted and possessively covered her shoulder. She loved the way it moved slowly along her arm, then tucked into the small of her back to pull her against him. She loved . . . oh how she loved the way he held her and touched her, expecting no more nor less than she wanted to give.

Thus, Tallie lifted her mouth to his own and accepted the sweet, warm kiss he gave her. Turning in his arms, she eased her hands across his shoulders, then wrapped her fingers through his dark, shoulder-length hair. She knew she would not have to speak her desires; he would know what she wanted.

The moment was sensual and shared; then, without warning, Storm chuckled.

"What is so amusing?" asked Tallie, a little indignant.

He had now pulled the edge of her white lace chemise from beneath the coarse fabric of her gown. "This! White lace! Such a contrast to the disgusting fabrics you were wearing when you first came here. I want—" Releasing the fabric, his fingers grazed her crimson cheek. "I want to see you in satin, Tallie. Yes, satin and white lace, and I don't want you to have to hide your beauty beneath ridiculous disguises. Don't you remember the one day you had on a pretty dress? Why don't you wear garments like that more often. Why these ugly rags?"

"It makes the sisters happy," she pouted prettily.

"Make *me* happy. Don't wear them any longer!"

He looked distastefully at the coarse, black fabric of her tunic lying across a nearby chair. "It is fine for the other women . . . but not for you." Then, dragging his feet to the side of the cot, he quickly pulled on his Levi's and boots.

"I grew up on the grimy, vermin-infested London streets, Storm. I did not wear satin then, and I cannot see why I deserve to wear it now."

"My woman deserves them," he countered somewhat impolitely.

She grinned, unable to suppress the humor she felt in his boyish brooding. "The women are asleep . . . and we are alone. I believe a handsome rogue and a lady might be able to find something to do if the handsome rogue removes those rough trousers. Do you not?"

He gave his best boyish smile. "Again, Tallie?"

"Again," she whispered, touching a kiss to his ample mouth and shifting the contents of the portfolio, so that it fell on the floor."

"I'm a damned handsome rogue," he growled. "Will I do?" He was about to capture her impetuous mouth in a sweet kiss when a stirring of horses' hooves echoed from the trail outside. Instinctively, Storm found his footing, jerked on his shirt, then scrambled for his gun hanging over a chair.

As Tallie arose and quickly pulled on her dress, Storm was already leaving the cabin. Moments later, she scooted beneath the protection of his left arm and watched three men approach from the trail. The older one, a tall, distinguished, gray-haired man rode to the front, pausing a few feet from where Storm and Tallie stood.

"Sorry . . . I thought the cabin was unoccupied. Me and the men were going to rest and grab a smoke."

Storm and the older man faced each other down for a moment. Then Storm said, "You're welcome to stay. The lady and I were just leaving. Tallie . . ." His hand went across her shoulder for a moment. "Get our things, will you?"

The two men accompanying the tall, angry man nudged their horses up to either side of their boss. "You ain't goin' ta do nothin' to him, Mack?" asked the shorter of the two the men.

The older one growled, "Shut up," and to Storm, "Me an' the men'll smoke on the way back to the ranch." He'd always felt bad about framing Storm for the train robbery. He was glad to see that he appeared well . . . and that he had a lady who seemed to make him happy. Tipping his hat, he said, "Good day," and the three of them turned back on the trail.

Only now, did Tallie notice the moisture sheening Storm's dark eyes. She put her hand gently to the back of his shoulder but he jerked away from her. "What is it, Storm? Who were they?"

It was an innocent enough encounter . . . but an encounter nonetheless. Storm felt a painful wrenching in his heart that he hadn't felt in a year now. He wanted to be alone; he didn't even want to be with Tallie right now. So, without answering her, he walked away. "I'll see you back at the lodge, Tallie. Go straight there, will you?"

She stood on the narrow, ramshackle porch and stared after him, a bit dumbfounded by the change in his mood. It was a special night for her . . . she had told him about Ellie. And he could just walk away from her like this because three men had ridden up on their horses?

She simply wouldn't allow it! Putting some order to her appearance, she moved off the porch and entered the trail in his wake. She wasn't sure where he had gone, but she had a good idea. He had taken her a few times to a favorite spot, beside a lagoon, where they had swam. She was not surprised when she entered the clearing, and the shaft of moonlight gleamed across his dark hair.

Storm had dropped against the smooth trunks of a cluster of crepe myrtle trees. Easing to her knees beside him, she looked at his dark, brooding profile for a moment.

In the few moments they had been apart, he had tied the familiar bandanna around his forehead and his dark hair.

Now, she placed her fingers to his cheek, but he moved away from her touch. She would not allow him to put this distance between them, so she tucked herself against him and placed her head upon his shoulder.

He did not rebuff her, but the muscles of his shoulder grew tight beneath her features. "What is wrong, Storm?"

"That man . . . the older one. He's my father."

Her head snapped up, her eyes narrowing as they studied his profile. "I thought, perhaps, he might be." He looked to her now, so much fury in his gaze that she was momentarily taken aback. "Please, Storm, do not put yourself on his level. Do not harbor hatred in your heart, even though he has never been a father to you."

"That's the problem, my Tallie. I don't hate him. I wish I did."

"You love your father, Storm, even though he has no right

to expect you to," she murmured, her fingers easing along the hard muscles of his arm. 'And I love you for it."

Storm looked away again, his gaze penetrating the dark horizon, and beyond, to the thunderclouds rolling toward the timberline where they sat. Presently, he replied, "Do you remember when I told you my parents were dead?"

"I do, but I knew your father was not dead, except, perhaps, in your heart." Tears moistened Tallie's hazel gaze, then she gently kissed Storm's taut shoulder. "You cannot hate, Storm, because you know it is like an acid, destroying the vessel in which it is stored just as surely as the one on whom the contents are poured."

"I stopped hating because of you, Tallie," he argued without pause. "I don't hurt so much since I met you."

She smiled sweetly. "Then I have been good for something, have I not, Storm?"

"Not something . . . many things."

A thought came to Tallie. "When you hated your father, Storm, why did you take his name?"

"He offered to pay me once to take my mother's maiden name, Spencer, but I told him he didn't have enough money. I was McCallister Phillips's half-breed boy, and I was going to make sure that everyone knew it!"

Tallie had to end this discussion, and the direction his thoughts were taking him. Rising swiftly to her feet, she wasted no time in removing her clothing, along with the white lace undergarments he loved to tease her about. Naked within moments, she gave Storm a cool look, then turned and fled toward the lagoon. "You had better come in and get me, Storm," she ordered, making a wild splash in the current. "Or that old gator we saw earlier in the week is going to make a meal of a tasty English female!"

Storm hardly thought so; the gator was hardly bigger than a lizard and fearful of humans. Though he knew Tallie was reasonably safe, he felt an ache crawling through his body that compelled him to rise and shed his own clothing. Soon, he moved into the water, found her splashing like a precocious child and captured her in his arms.

Without prelude, his hand went beneath her thigh and he pulled her close, easing himself into the sweet receptable of her body so swiftly that she had no chance to prevent it . . . if, indeed, that was her first inclination.

Rather, she wrapped her legs around his slim hips and laid back upon the cool water. With a small groan, she allowed him to bury the full length of his manhood inside her. She thought she would burst with enjoyment as his hands roughly held her hips, then moved along her waist until they cupped the soft swells of her breasts rising above the surface of the water. His teeth claimed a dark rosebud, his hips ceasing their movements for a moment as his hands awakened the hot passion within her.

His manhood swelled within her so visibly that she reacted instantly to the wondrousness of it. One of her feet touched upon his own on the sandy bottom of the lagoon and she held him close, loving his kisses and the cool swirl of the water embracing their bodies. The water between their hips splashed hither and yon as their passions grew. Storm's hands pinned her hips, his eyes holding her gaze in a hot mixture of primal lust and gentle passion. He'd never seen her so beautiful . . . so fervent.

The telltale signs of her own lust and desire were deliciously clear to him . . . the tiny moan emitting from her parted mouth, her fingers pressed firmly over the muscles of his arm, then slowly opening and closing . . . the way her hips ground against his own, powered by her own strength . . . the sensual narrowing of her eyes and their hazel sheen of love for him . . .

Then, his breathing grew labored and he scattered his seed within her, his eyes closing as he savored the delicious torment of it.

He collapsed over her, his hands releasing her hips now to move around her tiny waist and draw her close . . .

Then, with a small, pretty laugh, she broke from him and

dived beneath the water. When she came up, her hair was floating on the surface of the lagoon like a fallen cloud. Her back was to him; when he made his way through the short spanse of water and attempted to draw her against him again, she spun in his arms, splashing water on him like a precocious child. "I say, old chap, I do believe we are having a bit of frolicking fun."

He laughed as droplets of rain began pelting the water, followed at once by a clap of thunder that sent her diving into his arms. He held her close, kissing her wonderfully cool cheeks and seeking the honeyed sweetness of her mouth.

When she said, "I love you, Storm Phillips," his mouth pressed into a tight line for a moment. Then he responded in a cool, even tone, "Does this mean that you'll marry me, English?"

She held him close, her wet hair dragging against him. "I want to marry you, Storm, but I must hear from England first. Will you be patient with me? As soon as I hear I will give you an answer." Her gaze now lifted to him. "And I promise it will be the answer you want."

He attempted to intimidate her with a dark, brooding gaze. But he smiled, giving his feigned disappointment away. "Very well." He now moved toward the bank of the lagoon, then covered his nakedness with the familiar Levi's and black shirt. When he'd pulled on his boots, then buckled his holster around his narrow hips, he turned to look at her, any words he might have spoken lost in the silence of her gaze. He wanted to tell her to come out of the water, lest lightning strike, but he knew by now that she didn't like anyone telling her what to do, even when it was for her own good.

"I suppose you're going to swim for a while?"

"I am," she said, gently tredding water. "Are you going back to work?"

"I don't believe anyone knows this lagoon exists, except you and me. But just in case . . ." Quietly, he removed his gun and laid it on the ground. "I'll leave this for you." Moving toward the edge of the lagoon and squatting, a finger went out, motioning her to him. When Tallie was balancing herself against his boot, he touched a gentle kiss to her forehead. "Tonight, Tallie . . . tonight I want you to come to my cabin."

Alarm flashed in her eyes; Storm was getting bold in front of the sisters. "You know that I cannot, Storm."

"Not for that, Tallie. Tonight I will open my mother's chest. I want you with me."

"Why tonight, after all these weeks that it has rested beneath your bunk?"

He shrugged. "I don't know. Perhaps it is because I saw my father today." Then, "Will you come?" She gently nodded, and in a moment of fun, his slim fingers closed over her shoulders, ducking her beneath the water's surface.

When Tallie came up, she saw only the dark form of him disappearing into the forest.

Chapter Sixteen

Because night came quick and deep, feeding the fears that had clung mercilessly to her, Tallie didn't linger long at the lagoon after Storm had left. She returned to the Lodge of Sisterhood, where Brookie had already made herself useful in the kitchen. She had prepared a fine evening meal, and, later, when Tallie popped in on each of the sisters, she found each talked of Brookie in a very complimentary manner. They thought they had made a wise decision in allowing Brookie to stay.

Now Tallie made herself busy in the kitchen. Within the hour, she could see why the sisters liked Brookie so much. Her character was wonderful and she had a grand sense of humor. Tallie had been wrong in her first assessment of Brookie. She was actually seventy-one years old, rather than in her sixties, as Tallie had thought. She had a big, big voice, eyes that smiled so enthusiastically they were swallowed up by the gentle folds of her eyelids, and hair the color of a polished copper pot. "It is that way natural, lass," she said the first time she'd noticed Tallie staring at her hair, "and if ye'll look real close, ye'll not find a single gray one among it!"

So far, Brookie exhibited not a single flaw, except that she didn't like Sister Meade's little terrier. Tallie had seen one of her large feet come out from beneath the hem of her skirt and boot it out the kitchen door. The dog had yapped, more in surprise than in pain, and Brookie, grinning her biggest grin, had smacked her hands together in satisfaction that she'd gotten rid of the "beggin' lit'l bugger!" She didn't mind the cat, though, because "they're English creatures, you know, and have a lot of spunk and usefulness."

Tallie thought her a refreshing addition to the staid and proper sisters; she reminded her a lot of Aunt Cora, in her exuberance for life, friendliness, and willingness to lend a hand where needed. No job seemed too demeaning for Brookie; she said that she wouldn't mind, even, cleaning up after the men.

The sisters were now moved into the Lodge of Sisterhood, each having her own room in which to enjoy personal prayers, sleep, and spend the hours of solitude "the Lord required for a pure heart." Those were the hours, or so they testified, that God spoke loudest to them individually, calling them by their heavenly names. Those names, Tallie was told in not too polite terms, were secrets between them and their savior, and to breathe that secret name to a living soul was a sacrilege He would not forgive, not on this earth and not in heaven.

The antics of the sisters were becoming more bizarre. Sister Meade had taken to screaming her prayers for so long a time that she frequently collapsed in exhaustion, Sister Joseph had begun swaying in rhythm to her distinctly quieter prayers, Sister Michael bounced when she was "filled with exhilaration for the Lord," and Sister Pete, acting closer to normal than most of them, still had her way of praying that grated on the nerves of most human beings.

Having another English woman at the Lodge of Sisterhood made Tallie very lonely for her family. She wanted to return to England, but she did not want to leave Storm. She wanted to be with him, but she also wanted to be with Aunt Cora and Ellie. She wanted a future with her beloved daughter, but she did not want to face the future without Storm. And he was so completely a part of the Blue Ridge Mountains that she knew he would never allow himself to be uprooted. Certainly, Storm moving with her to England was out of the question. Oh, what to do. What to do—

"Daydreaming, English?"

Tallie spun rapidly from the counter at which she'd been peeling potatoes, sure that Storm could read her thoughts as surely as if she'd spoken them. Brookie politely slipped from the kitchen and Tallie heard her footfalls down the corridor and, soon, the creaking of the door to the outside world. "Always," she responded, turning back to her labors. "Do you still want to open the chest tonight after supper?"

"I do." He waited until her gaze lifted to his, before continuing, "You don't mind, do you?"

"I look forward to it, Storm. I suppose I am nosy, because I am curious about your mother, as well . . ." A moment of silence was strangely intimidating. "Are you sure it is not something you should do alone?"

"No." His hands closed over her shoulder, his cheek resting against her pinned hair. "It's something I want to share with my beloved."

Shrugging delicately, she said, "Suppose it is empty. I could not bear to witness your disappointment."

He smiled. "Well . . . in that case, don't you think I would need your arms around me?"

She instantly recalled that evening Potts had told Storm about his half-brother being whipped at the Phillips ranch. She had offered him a hug, and she was sure that was what he was remembering. "I suppose that you might," she agreed. "Yes, I shall sit with you when you open your mother's possessions."

That evening, Tallie and Storm sat on his cot in the middle cabin, the chest perched on Storm's lap. He had carried the little brass key in his pocket for a couple of months; now, he took it out and held it gently between his fingers. "Well, at least if it's a rattlesnake, it would be dead after all this time," he said, attempting humor but feeling, instead, his heart pounding into a fervor. "I'm glad you're here, Tallie."

When he hesitated, she prompted, "Open it, Storm."

His fingers were shaking as they slipped the key into the small lock. With one light twist, it was unlocked, and Storm's right hand moved to the side, preparing to lift the lid. But he again hesitated.

Then it was open, and he looked into contents possibly unseen for almost thirty years. A bundle of letters was tied with blue ribbon, hardly faded at all, and a small velvet box sat in the corner, as soft and smooth as the day it had been put there. Various papers were held together by a bit of twine, and a portfolio, handsewn of floral fabric and edged with gold cord, betrayed the corners of several sheets of paper.

His fingers moved into the box as though fragile crystal were held inside. First, they opened the velvet case, finding a wealth of gem-studded jewelry—rings, necklaces, bracelets, brooches . . . all very expensive, and yet subtle in taste. The portfolio held elegant stationery and matching envelopes with the cursive initials, RS, embossed in the upper left corner. The papers turned out to be a marriage license, a written account of Rachel's birth and adoption papers, and various documents that had belonged to her adoptive father and pertained to his military service. There was a journal, its pages covered with lovely feminine entries, and the letters bundled in blue ribbon had been written to Rachel by his own father; the latest date seemed to have been just days before their marriage.

Storm had lifted the items, one by one, hoping, praying . . . and, all at once, his prayer was answered. There, beneath the portfolio and the bundle of letters, the velvet jewel case and the documents, was a single picture . . . a beautiful, dark-haired, dark-eyed woman with high cheekbones, dressed in wedding finery, her delicate hands filled with a trailing bouquet of roses, bridal wreath, and ribbon.

"She is beautiful," whispered Tallie. "Oh, Storm, this beautiful woman was your mother.'

Tears misted his eyes. He had always suspected his mother had been beautiful, and Doc Frick had certainly told him she had been, but he'd never imagined such perfection. He could see how McCallister Phillips had not known of her Cherokee roots, what with her pale skin and fine features.

How could he not have loved and cherished such beauty, regardless of her nationality?

How could he have turned her back on her, when Storm knew that she'd had a gentle heart. Doc had said so, and Doc had never lied to him.

Storm folded his arm over Tallie's shoulder and drew her close. "Thank you for being with me, Tallie." A gentle kiss touched her hairline. "Could I be alone now? I'd like to read my mother's journal."

"Of course." She arose. "I shall prepare a pot of fresh tea and add a little cinnamon. I know it helps you sleep."

He looked up, a sad smile touching his mouth. "*You* help me sleep, Tallie."

She took no offense, even as she thought she knew what he meant. With a gentle smile, she exited into the moonlight, moved a few feet along a path worn smooth by their footsteps over the months, then broke into a run, soon entering the kitchen where Brookie was cleaning the dishes.

Tallie threw on an apron and took over the job at the wash pan. She remembered Brookie's remark earlier in the day that harsh soaps broke her hands and arms out in a rash. Tallie could see that her hands were already unnaturally red.

"Put some lotion on your hands," she lightly ordered the older woman. "There is a bottle there on the table that I had been using earlier. I shall finish these up in no time."

Brookie sat at the table and dabbed a little of the lotion on her thick hands. She watched Tallie, thinking how pretty she was, thinking how melancholy she seemed since being at the cabin with the handyman. "Tell me a little about yourself, Tallie."

Tallie glanced over her shoulder, smiling. "Where to begin, Brookie? The last few months or my entire life?"

"Tell me about your mother."

Tallie's labors over the dishes suddenly ceased. She drew her hands from the hot, soapy water and wiped them on her apron. Moving to the table, she dropped to a chair across from Brookie. "My mother? I never knew her. She died on Christmas night, 1862, the same night I was born."

"Oh? She was a frail bit of a woman, was she?"

Tallie herself knew very little about the facts surrounding her birth, and Cora had told her very little. "I do not believe she was a frail woman. My aunt said she was slender, but strong."

"Then why do you suppose she died in childbirth?"

Tallie thought it a rather odd subject to be brought up by a woman she'd known for only a day. "Aunt Cora said that a problem arose with the midwife. She had been drinking, was angry that she had been taken from her family on Christmas Day to deliver a baby, and that some negligence resulted in my mother's death." Then, "Why do you want to know?"

Brookie nodded thoughtfully. "I had a similar experience, dear lass. I kept me life, but lost me child. In me case the death was due to the negligence of a physician. My child was a boy, and he would be twenty-nine now, if the dear thing had lived."

"Oh, I am sorry, Brookie. Did you ever have more children?"

"I 'ad me two daughters at the time me lit'l lad died, but I haven't seen them now in more than twenty-five years."

"Did you lose track of them?"

Brookie's wide shoulders shrugged imperceptibly. "I got in a bit of trouble back a few years and the husband took them away. I n'er saw any of them again."

Across the table, Tallie's hand covered the woman's own. "What a tragic life, Brookie. And you are such a dear woman. I am so sorry."

Brookie brightened immediately. "Tragedy is a way of life, dear lass. I've had me fair share of it. But, now I am here, with ye and the dear ladies, and I am happy. I do hope they shall allow me to stay."

Tallie smiled. "They fully intend to. They think you are wonderful, and a much better cook than any of us!" Rising, she moved back to the wash pan. "I must finish these dishes before Sister Joseph comes in."

As she washed dishes, Brookie asked her about her own family. "I have a daughter back in London. I hope to have her with me very soon."

"Ye had to leave the wee lass, Tallie?"

"For a little while," said Tallie, sadly and with a little shrug. "But she is in good hands. My aunt is taking good care of her."

"Why did ye leave London?"

Tallie was silent for a moment. Then she put the last dish on the towel she had laid out, dried her hands and moved back to the table. "I am afraid, Brookie, that I got in a little trouble myself. It will settle down soon and I shall be able to return to London to fetch my dear Ellie."

"And the young man?"

A frown covered Tallie's features. "Young man?"

"Aye, young Storm. I 'ave only been here since the morn, lass, but I can see ye two have a wee thing in the makin'."

Tallie nodded. "I do love him, Brookie. I love him with all my heart."

"Love is good," said Brookie, rising now and swiping off her large apron. "Me thinks I should try out that fine bed the sister has assigned me to. See ye in the morn, lass."

"Yes, Brookie." Taking her hand for a moment, Tallie added, "And we really are so glad you are here. Do prepare your bed, then come back to the kitchen for a cup of cinnamon tea. It will be nice to sit down and drink tea with another English woman."

"I'll do that, lass. Aye . . ." She moved to the door, opening it into the narrow corridor. "I'll see to me bed an' me necessaries, an' I'll be back in a wee bit."

Storm had stared at the picture so long it had eventually become a blur beneath his scrutiny. He was enchanted by the face, figure, the total beauty of the woman who had been his mother. Then he'd gone through the documents tied together by twine. Over the course of half an hour, he had learned much about his mother's family. His mother's real parents, given Christian names of Patrick and Jenny Turnbull at the Indian mission where they'd been raised, had been survived by a brother named Parker Turnbull, whom he knew to be an Indian lawyer on a reservation in Arizona. Ironically, he'd met Parker Turnbull during a trip with college classmates to the South Carolina legislature ten years ago. He had spoken of the plight of the Indians, and Storm remembered being fascinated by the man he now knew to be his great-uncle.

All this he had learned from his mother's adoption papers. He knew there would be much more to learn from his mother's journal and from the letters his father had written to her before their marriage. He wanted to read and absorb everything now, and yet he wanted something for tomorrow and the next day and the day after that. He wanted to know everything, but he wanted to learn something new every day. So, he placed the items back into the chest, vowing that he would read one letter each night and save the journal for last. Now, he wanted to be with someone, and that someone was his beloved Tallie.

He went first to the kitchen, catching the strong, pleasant aroma of the cinnamon tea as he entered and saw Tallie sitting at the small table with the new woman. When Brookie arose and started to leave, Storm attempted to wave her down. "No, stay and have tea with us."

"Three is a crowd," she reminded him. "I've got a bit of tidying up to do in me room." Taking up her teacup, she nodded politely to both of them as she departed.

Storm was glad the sisters had insisted that the lodge be built with several extra rooms. He found Brookie very pleasant . . . and her first meal tonight had been a feast.

He said nothing as he watched Tallie prepare his tea and scoot it across the table to him. It had cooled a bit, and he sipped it slowly, his gaze transfixed to Tallie's own, his thoughts still on his mother's belongings. He had seen a particularly beautiful brooch with diamonds and a single square-cut emerald and was wondering if it would be disrespectful to his mother's memory to give it to Tallie. He remembered the many things Doc had told him about his mother, and he decided that she wouldn't mind at all if he eventually gave Tallie the brooch . . . perhaps as a wedding gift.

Right now, she looked thoughtful. "Are you thinking about your daughter?"

"Actually, I was thinking about you," she responded demurely. "Are you all right?"

"Never better," he said, putting down the now empty cup, his hand going out to her. "Come, let's walk in the moonlight while the sisters are in their rooms."

She arose, pulled her shawl from the back of the chair, then took his hand, moving with him into the warm night. A light breeze, fragrant with honeysuckle, wafted through the forest.

She knew there was something on his mind, and her intuition told her it had nothing to do with the memories of a mother he had never known, nor did he simply want to be with her. He was almost childlike in the way he took her hand and coaxed her down the dark forest trail. This was the trail they were most familiar with, the one that took them to the cabin where they had spent so much time together.

Storm suddenly turned on the dark trail, pulling her into a gentle embrace. His cheek touched against her pale tresses, his hands rising to cover her shoulders. Then, he drew slightly back, his dark eyes catching the gleam of the full moon. "Tallie Edwards, I wanted to be alone with you for a reason."

"Well, it must not be to make love, since we are still a good ways from the cabin."

Again, he pulled her to him, his mouth caressing her wind-blown hair. "Tallie, I. I just want to be alone with you. I hate having to share you with anyone, even the sisters." He held her as if he thought she'd suddenly leave him. "I want to live here in my mountains, with you and your daughter. Tell me that you will stay with me. Tell me that we will never have secrets again."

But they *did* have secrets. She had secrets. He had secrets. She didn't see how they could vow to marry if they could not share with each other. Though she could never imagine spending her life with any other man but Storm, she also had never imagined that she would live anywhere but England.

Perhaps all the rules of life were made to be broken.

"Storm—"

"All right." The way she spoke his name, almost with regret, caused him to cut her short. "Perhaps this is not a good time to speak of such a serious matter."

She stood slightly away from him, her hand slipping into his own. "There are things I have not told you, Storm. And I would imagine things you have not told me, either. Until we learn to trust each other completely, how can we enter into such a serious contract as marriage?"

"I will tell you everything, Tallie. Everything you want to know. Though I have already told you the important things."

"Then tell me who you think robbed that train you were sent to prison for?"

Silence as heavy as the night fell upon them. He grimaced, his mouth pressing into a thin line as he pondered a reply. No matter the feelings he had for his father, casting aspersions on his character did not rest well with him. "I suppose I will never know for sure, but I think Mack had something to do with it."

"Your father robbed a train?"

"Not my father . . . but a couple of his men, I'm sure."

A thought came to Tallie and she moved away, soon lighting

upon a fallen log. "If Old Potts is to be believed, someone tried to kill him. Since he worked at your father's place, is it possible he might have seen the money stolen in that robbery?"

He hesitated only a moment before replying. "I don't think Mack would be that stupid. He'd never bring evidence back to his ranch. No . . ." He nodded thoughtfully, "Mack is smarter than that." Still, he was not so sure. Mack had done dumb things in the past, if the judge was to be believed.

Tallie turned away, her gaze lifting to the violet haze above the treeline. "Storm, you must have had an alibi for the time. Surely, someone saw you . . . someone who could have told a jury where you were when that train was robbed?"

He approached, his hands closing over her shoulders, his cheek again touching the coolness of her long, loose hair. "If I didn't know better, I would think you were doubting my innocence." When her eyes avoided contact, he continued quietly, "As I love you, I swear I did not commit that crime, or any crime for that matter, except . . ." A sardonic laugh was short-lived, "Except for the rock I chunked through Mr. Everton's store window when I was visiting Doc Frick after leaving college. I swear, Tallie, that I am not lying."

She turned into his arms, her cheek resting against the smooth fabric of his shirt. "I believe you, Storm. And it need never be mentioned again between us." Still, she wondered . . .

"Does this mean you'll marry me?"

"As I said, I have to hear from England before I give you an answer."

"So you did," he agreed on a light note. "You're saying, then, that it isn't the right moment?"

"It is too soon, Storm. I must get my life in order before I can make you a part of it. I have to think about Aunt Cora and Ellie. I have to . . ." She shuddered to even think about it, "somehow dispose of the troubles I'm having."

He was glad she'd brought it up, these troubles that had darkened her moods. But just as he was about to attempt to pry some information from her, the soft clop of a horse's hooves echoed on the trail behind them. He turned just in time to see the large, dark form of a horse and rider appear in the stream of moonlight.

"I do beg your pardon," called the Englishman from the Phillips Ranch. "But I thought I was taking a short cut and I have gotten myself hopelessly lost."

Before Storm could even prepare to give him directions back to the road, Tallie had ripped the shawl off her shoulders and charged at horse and rider with an almost maniacal cry. Immediately, the horse reared back on his haunches, and before the Englishman could gain control, he was unseated and dragged back through the forest, one foot caught up in the stirrup. He cried out as he bumped along the trail and Storm, momentarily confused by what Tallie had done, gathered up his wits and ran through the woods, cutting off the horse as it rounded the trail to the right. Grabbing up the reins, he attempted to still the spooked horse and the Englishman managed to free his foot from its iron-and-leather prison.

He sat there for a moment, shaking so badly that Storm feared for him. "I don't know why she did that!" He could not even begin to make excuses for Tallie, and so felt compelled to say, "I'm so sorry, mister. I hope you're not hurt."

The Englishman took a long, deep breath, trying to calm the quake rocking his insides. "Sir, this action is a good indication the young lady might know me. You cannot imagine how happy I am about that."

Storm was further confused. "What do you mean?"

"I had a bit of bad luck a few months back." He now took the hand Storm offered, "I have been living at the Phillips Ranch since I was shot, and I bloody well do not know who I am. If the young lady knows me, I simply *must* talk to her." A thick eyebrow arched dramatically. "I would entreat you, sir, to take me to her, and to make sure she does not have some weapon on her person before I confront her. It seems that the young lady does not care much for me, as attested to by the attack upon me moments ago."

Storm couldn't help but notice the man's refined English accent, and he wondered if this was the man Old Potts had been with the night a volley of shots had been fired at him and a stranger. Was this man the owner of the portfolio?

"The young lady also is English," informed Storm. "Apparently, she does know you well enough to have tried to kill you, and perhaps it would be just as well that we talk to her." Storm had imagined Tallie had returned to the lodge; just as well, because he was so damned mad he couldn't see straight. She might have killed this man! And no matter what he'd done, there was no sense in such viciousness. Perhaps he didn't know Tallie as well as he thought he did.

"Are you sure you're all right?" asked Storm, handing the reins of his horse back to him.

"I imagine I shall live," he replied.

"Come on then." Storm began to move back down the trail. "I'll take you to the lodge to talk to Tallie. You deserve an explanation."

Tallie was throwing her possessions into her one canvas bag. Her heart was beating so quickly that she thought she would faint. Having run so fast on the trail, she had been almost breathless when she'd stopped at the cabin and told Old Potts to get the wagon ready for a trip into town.

Now packed—and she didn't care what she'd forgotten—she moved into the corridor and toward the back entrance. Immediately, Sister Joseph emerged from her room, her loud voice as she spoke her name catching the attention of the other women. Tallie heard Sister Meade's raucous prayer quickly cease as she, too, joined Tallie in her flight to the wagon.

Potts was just pulling up to the entrance when Tallie threw her canvas bag in the back. Now, she turned, Sister Joseph's fingers so firmly over her arm that they caused pain. "I asked you where you are going, Tallie."

"He found me, Sister Joseph," she rushed the confusing

explanation, accepting the hand Old Potts offered her. As she settled onto the seat, she continued, "I was walking with Storm, and Farrand Beattie rode right up to us. I must leave. I swore that I would not put you and the other sisters in danger."

"We will protect you," Sister Joseph said. "Haven't we done so up to this point?"

"I will *not* put you in danger. I must go!" Then, "I shall go to the judge's house and leave on the first stage tomorrow."

Sister Joseph would not argue; she had no hold on Tallie, and she was free to go where she wished. Stepping back from the wagon, she ordered of the other sisters, "Let us get back to our prayers."

And immediately, protests began, tears fell and farewells were said as the wagon pulled away.

Tallie turned, watching the sisters until the lodge was swallowed up by the trees.

She hadn't seen Brookie, and she wished she could have said farewell.

As they moved onto the road, a tearful Tallie said to Old Potts, "I think I just caused a man's death. Do you think I will go to hell?"

Old Potts calmly asked, "Were it Storm what you kil't?"

"No."

"Then I reckon you won't be goin' to hell. 'Cept fer Storm, ain't no man worth goin' to hell over." Curiosity compelled him to ask, "How'd ya kill a feller, Miss Tallie?"

"I spooked his horse, he fell off and his foot got caught in the stirrup."

Potts clicked the reins at the pair of horses he'd hitched up. "Now, that won't be a purty way fer a man to die. Why din't ya just shoot 'em, Miss Tallie?"

Old Potts had obviously been drinking; Tallie turned her delicate senses away from the stink of whiskey. "I would have shot him if I'd had a gun, Mr. Potts."

"Is he why you be runnin' away? What you runnin' for if ya think ya kilt him?"

"Storm cut through the woods to catch the-horse. It will be just my luck if the chap only has a few scrapes and bruises. Besides . . ." Tallie shrugged her slender shoulders, "what makes you think I am running away?"

"Ain't ya, Miss Tallie?"

To deny it would be to lie. "I suppose I am. But . . ." She turned to the old man now, giving him a shy smile; "would you mind not asking any questions? I really am doing the only thing there is left to do."

"This fella what you spooked, is he after ya or somethin'?"

"Or something," Tallie mimicked his query without meaning insult. "It is a long, long story and I really cannot go into it."

"Storm knows ye'r leavin', eh?"

Her eyes dropped in shame. "No, he doesn't. Please, please, do not tell him you are taking me to the judge's house. Will you promise?"

"I promise, missy. But you'll have to talk to him sooner or later. Ol' Storm, he's a mite fond of ya, miss."

She chose not to tell Potts that she was fond of Storm as well, and that, right now, her heart was breaking. Now that the shock of seeing Farrand Beattie was over, tears welled in her eyes so that she had to look away, the countryside passing them by little more than a blur.

She would miss Storm.

But she silently vowed that when her troubles were over, she would return to him.

She wanted to be with him always, and she could only admit that now that she was leaving him.

And, though he knew nothing of the menace on her heels, she hoped he would understand.

[illegible]

Chapter Seventeen

Tallie made Old Potts pull the wagon up two miles from the compound. She sat for a moment, the old man's eyes full upon her, her own gaze skittering across the horizon as though answers to unspoken questions might be written there in the stars. She was running away from her problems, as she had run away from them when she'd allowed Mr. Leggett to put her aboard ship in Southampton. Perhaps it had been the right thing to do then, since a mere commoner would have been foolish to go up against such powerful forces, but she was in America, surrounded by friends, with the man she loved, and there was no longer a need to run. She sat now upon the rough, hard seat, dropped her face into her hands and wept gently.

Old Potts, at a loss, hopped down and tucked his hands into his pockets. He wanted to whistle a small tune, but didn't think it appropriate. So, he turned, sobering instantly, and asked Tallie, "Anythin' I can do for ya, Miss Tallie?"

She would have asked for a handkerchief, but she was sure she would not want to put whatever cloth he had in his pocket so close to her face. Potts didn't keep himself very clean, and his clothing was seldom washed. "Take me back to the lodge, Mr. Potts. I refuse to run away."

"Good fer you," he mumbled, hopping up to the seat, then reining the horse to the side of the road, so that they could be more easily turned around.

When the wagon entered the narrower road twenty minutes later, Storm and the Englishman, whose horse had been spooked, were exiting the Lodge of Sisterhood where they had apparently been talking to one of the sisters. Tallie was at once relieved that she wasn't now a murderer. When the wagon eventually came to a stop, the Englishman remained on the wide porch, and Storm approached the wagon.

"Took a little ride, did you, Tallie?"

Tallie found his voice strangely free of anger; a display would have been appropriate under the circumstances, she thought. She moved easily into his arms when he offered them to help her down. "I will not run away any longer, Storm. I shall face him."

He stood for a moment, holding her, ignoring the wagon as it pulled away. "He doesn't know who he is, Tallie, but he wants to know who *you* think he is. He was shot a few months back, and he's the gent who's been living at the Phillips Ranch without an identity. He's hoping you can help him."

Tallie glanced around Storm, her gaze finding the form of the Englishman against the pale light emitting from the lodge. "He does not know who he is?" she whispered, incredulous, refusing to believe such a blessing. "You are sure he does not know? You are sure he is not fibbing?"

"He's not fibbing, Tallie. The fellow genuinely has no idea who he is. They've been calling him 'the Englishman' at the ranch, and he dubbed himself Jack, just so he'd have a name."

Tallie swallowed hard. Jack! How ironic! How horrible—

Gathering up her courage, she said, "I shall talk to him." Tallie stepped away from Storm now, her hesitant steps taking her closer to the Englishman. She stood there, looking at Farrand Beattie, her heart beating so fiercely she could feel it against the fabric of her dress. When only a few feet separated her from him, she halted, one of her hands gathering the other within it, hoping her tremble wouldn't be too noticeable to him. She hated to give him the satisfaction of frightening her—again.

Old Potts had tried to be quiet while he unhitched the team, so that he could eavesdrop on the conversation between Storm and Tallie. He knew who the Englishman was, because he thought he had all his papers in a neat leather portfolio. He still did not know Storm had found the portfolio, and he had never discovered it missing. He thought he'd been killed that night on the trail, and that wild animals had dragged him into the woods to devour him. But there he stood on the porch of the lodge, waiting for Tallie Edwards to give him some clue as to his identity.

It made Old Potts feel kind of good inside that he would be able to provide that information . . . if he had a mind to.

Which he didn't.

Because Tallie Edwards was scared to death of him, so he had to have done something horrible to her.

Now that the team was put back in the pen, he slipped around the corner of the small shed where they sought shelter in bad weather and tried to catch further bits of conversation. He heard nothing, so he glanced around the corner of the shed and saw Tallie standing a few feet away from the Englishman . . . standing there like she was scared to death that he was going to pull a gun and shoot her.

Tallie had never known she could do so much thinking in so short a time. She thought about the past, the horrible crimes that had been committed in the Whitechapel district of London, and the fact that she'd had to leave her aunt and daughter because of him. And now, there he stood, looking the innocent and having no idea who he was or why he'd come to America. If she told him, it might trigger his memory, and then he would know that there was an unfinished job to be done. But Storm himself knew Farrand Beattie's true identity, and she knew she was taking a chance if she decided to lie to him. Did Storm love her enough to back up her story?

Tallie was sick of running, when she'd simply been in the wrong place at the wrong time and seen the wrong face perched over a crime scene.

She had always like theatrics; she had never liked being scared. And if she could put her dual talents to work now, she could end the cat-and-mouse chase and live her life in peace. So, taking these few moments to gather her thoughts—and her wits—she now moved hastily toward the Englishman, hesitating only slightly as she embraced him. "Uncle Paddy . . . oh, where have you been? I have been looking everywhere for you!"

She'd been staring at him long enough, with enough fear in her eyes to last a lifetime, and he knew immediately that she was lying. "Uncle Paddy?" he echoed her greeting. "You are trying to tell me I am your uncle, young lady?"

She drew back, her eyebrows furrowing in her efforts to feign hurt and confusion. "You must remember me! I am your niece, Tallie. You are my uncle, Patrick Edwards, and I have always called you Uncle Paddy. Oh, you mustn't tell me you do not remember me! I could not bear it!" She thought her pout effective, and the pain in his eyes indicated to her that it was, indeed.

He was thinking what an accomplished liar this comely young lady was. "I do not remember." But he must go along with her, until he could determine her motives. "Were we together when I had my accident?"

"I had just walked off in the woods to gather wildflowers and I heard shots. When I returned you were gone, and I could not find you."

She was lying through her teeth, and Storm wondered why.

Even if he didn't know the Englishman's identity, he knew that wild flowers generally closed up at night and were much harder to see beneath the deepening shades of the trees. He stood back, utilizing all the effort in the world to keep him from charging into the middle of their conversation and stop the nonsense.

So, why was she lying? And what was she accomplishing by telling the man that he was her uncle and that they were traveling together? What had the man done that was so abominable that she should so cruelly and viciously strip him of his true identity?

Old Potts knew she was lying, too. He knew the man's name was not Patrick Edwards, as Tallie would have him believe. He might not be too smart, but he damned well could read—even if it weren't too good—and every paper in the man's portfolio said his name was Farrand Beattie.

And neither he nor Storm could believe she was lying like that, and doing it with the talents of the most accomplished actress.

Tallie moved with her "uncle" to the porch of the lodge where they took seats. "I have been here since I lost you, Uncle Paddy, and I have made inquiries here and abouts. But no one seemed to know anything about you."

"Odd," Farrand Beattie said, "because word of mouth has been carried through these American mountains since my accident. Odd that you did not hear about me, and being so close to the ranch." Then, "Where were we going when we were separated?"

"Where were we going?" she echoed. "Well . . ." She tried to gather her thoughts and come up with another lie. "You were escorting me here to the lodge so that I could help establish the church, and then you were going to travel on to—" Oh, dear, what was the name of a city in this big country? "You were going to St. Louis, Mississippi, Uncle Paddy."

"St. Louis? I believe it is in Missouri."

"Oh, yes . . . yes, that is what I meant."

"Did you like me, young lady?"

"Well, of course I did. And I do! You are my uncle."

His bone-thin hands moved onto his knees. "Then why did you spook my horse? I could have been killed. And why are you now lying to me through those pretty white teeth?"

Tallie dropped her eyes, ashamed. "Seeing you startled me so. I thought you were a ghost, come back from the grave to haunt me. And if you think I am lying, then—then—"

"A ghost? You believe in those things?"

"Yes, and so did you."

Storm approached now; he'd had just about enough of this ridiculous exhibit. "Could I have a moment in private with you, Tallie?"

Though she knew what was coming, and dreaded it, she arose without hesitation and moved across the clearing with him. When they paused beside the fence he'd built along the cliff, he asked, "What the hell are you telling that man? You haven't said one true word!"

"I will explain later, Storm. I promise."

"You'd better have a damned good explanation, Tallie."

She suddenly bowed over, clutching her stomach. "Storm . . . I feel sick."

"It is probably guilt," he growled, aware that this was simply the second act of her dramatics. He, therefore, showed very little compassion.

"Will you tell Mr.—*my uncle* that I am not well and that he might come to see me again tomorrow?"

Dark eyes narrowed. "You tell him yourself, Tallie Edwards."

She righted herself immediately, a smug look capturing her features. "Very well." She pivoted from Storm and closed the distance to the lodge. Farrand Beattie came to his feet as she approached. "I am not feeling very well, Uncle Paddy. Might you visit again tomorrow and we shall talk?"

"Better yet," responded Farrand Beattie, wanting to get to the bottom of this farce, "you and the young man should come to the ranch tomorrow and have dinner with me. I have been given unrestricted accommodations, and Thea will enjoy having you to dinner." When Storm approached, he asked, "Will you bring her to the ranch?"

"No!" Storm snapped. "I don't make it a practice to go there."

Tallie turned, moving quickly to him. "Please," she whispered. "Please, it will save him from having to come here. I cannot bear to have him here."

"Tallie," he whispered in return, his brows darkening with pain. "I am not welcome at my father's place."

Farrand Beattie had overheard Storm's more powerful voice. "Mack Phillips is not expected back until later in the week. Do come, Mr. Phillips."

"Please," begged Tallie, looking up to him with the most compelling entreaty.

Storm looked across her slender shoulder, saying to the Englishman, "I'll come, only if Matt and his mother will be there."

"They will," Farrand replied. He moved down the steps now, gave Tallie a small kiss at her temple, failed to react to her physical withdrawal from it, then mounted his horse. "It is wonderful knowing who I am, and that I have family." He would play her little game until she saw fit to tell him who he *really* was. "I shall see you at the ranch tomorrow. Will one o'clock suit you?"

Storm nodded his affirmation, at which time the Englishman turned his horse toward the road Storm told him would take him back to the Phillips Ranch.

Storm was furious. He'd rather go to hell than to his father's ranch, and he wasn't quite sure why he'd agreed. He certainly couldn't allow Tallie to go alone, and there was the chance that he would be able to see Matt, who hadn't been back to the church site since that day he'd brought the box. He had grown accustomed to the idea of having a half-brother, someone who might eventually be true family.

But Tallie! Damn the woman and her lying ways! As she

approached him now, as casually as if she planned to tuck herself beneath the wing of his arm, he wondered about her motives. Who was the Englishman that she should lie to him so callously? He wasn't any more her uncle than he was Satan. She had crossed her arms and was standing beside him, watching the man enter the main road and disappear from their sight. Dammit! He had forgotten to give him the portfolio!

"I suppose you want explanations now?" Tallie queried Storm on a quiet note. "If you do, I am ready to give them. Might we go to the abandoned cabin, so that we can talk without being interrupted?" She had been aware of Potts's eavesdropping.

Storm was thinking that he and Tallie only went to the cabin when they wanted to be alone and make love. He couldn't imagine going there now just to talk. "Yes," he said after a moment. "And, I'll warn you now, if you lie again I will know it."

He outpaced her, then turned back, waiting for her to catch up to him. When she did, he dropped his arm casually across her shoulder. No words were exchanged between them as they entered the trail, then less than five minutes later the small cabin where they'd made wonderful memories. When she dropped to the small cot that had often given comfort and delight to their entwined bodies, she felt that she had decently composed her recitation. She would tell him no lies, no matter what. She looked to him now, lighting the oil lamp on the mantel, then stretching out along the dry-rotted divan as though he'd rather rest than talk. But his countenance was a mere facade, for now his eyes turned to her.

"You have a story to tell me?"

Tallie leaned forward, her elbows coming to rest on her knees, her fingers linking tightly together against the folds of her skirt "I have a horrid tale, so horrid, in fact, that I am not sure you will believe me."

His gaze narrowed. "I told you, Tallie, I will know if you lie. No matter how horrid, if it's the truth, I *will* believe you."

Even thinking about what she'd witnessed had filled her with fear. Now, she was prepared to talk about it for the first time since relating the story to the sisters aboard ship in the mid-Atlantic. "I had a friend in London named Mary Jane Kelly, whom I hadn't seen in about seven months when she sent an urgent message to my aunt's apartment that she had to see me that evening. Since the killings that had been attributed to Jack the Ripper had ceased several weeks before, I did not feel I would be in danger by going to Mary's room at Miller's Court. Late that evening, I went to see her."

"Wasn't it dangerous to be on the streets?"

"Yes, I suppose it was. The East End of London is pitted with thieves' hideouts and coiners' dens—a horrid place, where fighting dogs roam the skittle grounds behind taverns. But you must understand that everyone knew me there and, no matter that I was schooled away from the East End, I was more or less accepted as one of them. So, I went to see Mary that night." She shuddered now, recalling the scene. "When she had sent the urgent note, I had thought she had fallen behind in her rent again, since she was usually three or four weeks behind all the time, so I had taken a little money from my savings in the jar above the cook stove, just in case she needed a small loan. I had also thought that Joe had left her again . . . she had been living with him off and on, and he had a habit of running off to his sister's place in Gray's Inn Road when they had a tiff."

Impatiently, Storm said, "What difference does it make as to the reason for the summons. Tell me what this has to do with the Englishman whose horse you deliberately spooked."

"When I got to Number Thirteen, which was Mary's room, the door was slightly ajar. I pushed it open and called her name, but she did not answer. Then, in the gloom of the unlit interior, I saw a shape on the bed and I thought she had passed out drunk. But as my eyes focused, I saw a most grisly scene. A mass of raw flesh, her face had been skinned and her ears and nose had been cut off." Again, she visibly shook, her hands coming up to cover her own ears, as though to shut out the deadly silence that had greeted her that night. "Mary's throat had been cut so deeply and so grotesquely that her head hung sideways, and I saw that her abdomen had been ripped open. Mary's entire insides had been strewn from every picture rail in the room, and body parts had been neatly piled on a small table beside her corpse."

Storm arose, approached and dropped down beside her. "Was this friend of yours a victim of the Ripper?" When she quietly nodded, the impatience slacked in his voice. "But what does it have to do with the Englishman?"

Her temple came to rest against Storm's shoulder. "The Englishman is an agent and bodyguard to one of the royal family, who was often seen in the Whitechapel district. That night, Storm, as I stood, horrified, over Mary's mutilated corpse, Eddy stepped from a dark corner. I ran away, and when I looked back, I saw Farrand Beattie chasing after me. I lost him in the doorway to the chandler's shop, and when I finally snuck off home, Aunt Cora was awaiting me, and Mr. Leggett immediately drove me to Southampton to board ship and leave England. My aunt said I was in mortal danger even before I was able to tell her what I had witnessed. The first person I saw on the ship was Farrand Beattie, and I knew immediately he was after me."

"Are you saying, Tallie, that this member of the royal family is Jack the Ripper?"

"I thought that he was then, but I have had these few months to think about what I saw. Now, I do not think so. I believe that he came upon the scene after the killing, the same way that I did." Tallie thought she owed some pleasant memory to poor Mary, and so said, "Mary may have been just a plump little prostitute to most people, but she had been a beautiful woman, with raven-black hair hanging to her waist and remarkably blue eyes. She was youthful and attractive and terribly sweet to everyone. She did not deserve to be so horribly murdered." She drew a shallow sigh. "I should have known that Eddy could not commit such a crime. And I now suspect that

Farrand Beattie came after me so that he could convince me how very wrong I was to assume that he had."

"Why didn't you go to Scotland Yard, Tallie?"

"Of course!" she said, her short laugh sarcastic. "And tell them I thought I had just witnessed royalty hacking up a woman in Miller's Court? I would have been sent to an aslyum and given a brain operation. That is what could happen to political enemies. I did not want to be rendered insane!"

He would not argue with her impassioned declaration, simply because he did not know enough on the subject to carry his end of a discussion effectively. He cared only that she'd gone through a horrible ordeal, had been in constant fear, and she'd spooked Farrand Beattie's horse because that fear had been brought back to her in one swell swoop. But how harmful could the man now be? He did not know his own identity, nor did he remember that he'd trailed Tallie all the way into the mountains. He was just another English citizen. Without his memory, what danger could he be to Tallie? By her own admission, she might have been wrong about him . . . and yet she remained fearful.

Standing, he drew Tallie against him. "I wish I could take you away from here, Tallie. I wish I was . . ."

When he hesitated, she asked, "Was what, Storm?"

"Free," he said regrettably. "I may not be behind prison walls, but I am still a prisoner." His mouth touched her own in the gentlest of caresses. "I want to protect you, Tallie. I want you to never know another moment of fear, because I would lay down my life for you. I want you to know how much I love you." He kissed her more deeply this time, his hand at her back pressing her to him. "Damn, but you're a wonderful woman. I can't get enough of you. I want to be with you every hour of every day for the rest of my life. You're everything I've always wanted." He chuckled boyishly, hugging her tightly to him. "Perhaps, even, my love, a little more than I've dreamed about."

The heat of his body against her own swelled through her.

"Let us not talk of the Englishman any longer this evening, Storm," she implored, and her mouth rose to his, instigating a wild, wonderful kiss that completely enraptured both of them.

Within moments, they were free of their clothing, their bodies entwined upon the cot, his hips gyrating against her own as they moved toward fulfillment. His hands covered and caressed her passion-sensitive breasts, his mouth roughly claiming her sweetest kisses. Perspiration molded their joined bodies and when, scarce moments later, he collapsed above her, they fell asleep in each other's arms.

Storm liked the way her full bosom burned into his bare chest, the way her legs entwined through his own as they lay in wondrous rest.

He didn't even care if they were caught like this by one of the sisters who owned the next five years of his life.

The Englishman arrived back at the Phillips Ranch, knowing that he had been lied to by the lovely Tallie Edwards, and still having no clue as to his identity. He didn't feel like a Paddy Edwards, and he couldn't imagine why he'd be going to the city of St. Louis. He couldn't imagine that she would have been so close, and still would not have found him had she been genuinely looking. Furthermore, the expression on the face of the man named Storm reaffirmed his suspicions. He couldn't imagine why this woman was willing to rob him of his identity.

He moved confidently into the bunkhouse where he knew Thea would be cleaning up and related the incident to her with all the enthusiasm he could muster, deleting, of course, the spooking of his horse that might have caused him to be dragged to his death. Thea listened, then bluntly told him she did not believe Tallie's story.

"I mentioned you to one of those church ladies in the mercantile one day, and they said nothing about Tallie looking for a lost uncle. How many English people are there in these hills, besides you and the young lady? Tell me, Jack, how many?

No, I don't believe her! She's lying. You're not her uncle, and your name is not Patrick Edwards." Hugging him now, she whispered, "You're Jack English, as far as I am concerned. I don't believe you were on your way to St. Louis. Why, that trail where you were shot heads north, not west." Pressing him to her with something of a desperation, she whispered, "Oh, I am sorry, Jack. I truly am sorry that she lied to you."

"It is all right, Thea. I cannot believe her, either." Instantly forcing the melancholy from his tone, he said, "I have invited her and the young man, Storm, to dinner tomorrow. Do you mind?"

She drew back, disbelief filling her brown eyes. "Storm agreed to come?"

"They'll be here at one o'clock."

"I don't believe it." She was finished now with her labors and moved to the door. Soon, Jack joined her and they moved toward the kitchen a hundred yards away.

The Englishman smiled. "You must prepare those superb barbequed ribs and the garlic potatoes. And have Matt on hand for the meal. He and Storm might like to talk and get to know each other."

"Mack will be furious if he finds out."

"Poppycock!" snipped the Englishman. "The men will all be at their jobs in the mountains. Who will be here to gather tales? Mack never rewards loyalty, so there will be no motive to tell him anything!"

Thea smiled now, drawing away so that she could pour a cup of tea from the pot she had prepared just before her walk to the bunkhouse. "It will be fun, doing something that he would so highly disapprove of. Indeed, it will be fun!"

The Englishman approached, his arm scooting across Thea's thin shoulders. "That's my dear lass."

Two hours into the night, Storm had returned Tallie to the lodge and was now alone in his cabin, brooding miserably. He remembered a time he had gone to see his father, twelve years ago now, and had been impolitely escorted to the front gate and ordered not to return. Storm had hoped that his father would accept him—something he had wanted his entire life—but that day, all hope of having a relationship with Mack had ended. He'd stopped being Mack's son that night, and he'd stopped believing in dreams.

The thought of going to his father's ranch for something as mundane as dinner made him feel hard and brittle inside. He must be deeply in love to have made such a commitment, though he wished now he could politely bow out, and not lose the benefits of Tallie Edwards's warmth and passion.

And, blast it, the woman had better appreciate the sacrifice he was making! When he'd said he'd rather go to hell than to his father's ranch, it had not been an understatement.

He was furious with her for causing this instance of turmoil in his life, and yet he still wanted to be with her. He wanted to hold her close, whisper endearments against her ear, and tell her how precious she was to him. He wanted to run away with her, and yet at the same time he wanted to stay here with her to face his personal demons. He wanted to hate Tallie, but he wanted to love her more deeply than he already did.

He needed a drink; with that thought in mind, he moved toward the cabin Old Potts was occupying. But he was not there, and Storm thought he might be at the other cabin, although Storm had told him it was off limits to him, so that he could swill his drink without being preyed—and prayed—upon by the sisters. So, he began looking around, hoping he might find a bottle hidden away somewhere.

The cabin was in a shambles and it stank to high heaven. So offensive was it to Storm that he was sure his nose had folded into his face to avoid the stench.

"Where the hell did you hide your hooch, old-timer?" mumbled Storm, jerking the small mattress up by one rotting corner. But he did not find a bottle, and so he knew that Old Potts was somewhere out in the woods, drinking it all by himself.

So much for drowning his sorrows in a bottle.

Chapter Eighteen

That evening, the Englishman who had dubbed himself Jack walked out to the wide porch of MacCallister Phillips's ranch house and looked toward the evening sky. He knew he had been raised in England, but he remembered nothing about it, and he wondered if the same sky looked down upon that far and distant land. He couldn't imagine that such a primitive purple haze would streak the sky of the prudish society he'd been reading about in the books Thea's boy had brought him from town, and he could not imagine actually having lived there.

The door opened behind him. Presently, Thea tucked herself beneath his arm and followed his gaze across the sky. "It's beautiful, isn't it, Jack? Only in the mountains will you see such a wonderful sky."

He looked down now, catching the coy expression in her soft brown eyes. A devilish smile turned up his mouth. "You are a hopeless romantic, Thea. And, I'd imagine, you have a pretty red healthy heart."

"What a strange thing to say," she said, laughing as she pulled away from him. Moving into the pale moonlight, she turned back, her gaze lifting to his own. "And just how many red, healthy hearts have you seen in your lifetime?"

Actually, he couldn't remember. With a parting hug, he said, "I need to be alone for a while, Thea. I shall ride a while in the mountains."

As she watched him move toward the corral, she warned affectionately, "Keep out of trouble . . . and away from other women."

Sister Michael was restless. She'd been thinking about the leftovers from supper, and was sure that the reason she could not sleep was because her stomach protested its emptiness. So, she arose, slipped into her most comfortable dress and crept from her room in the Lodge of Sisterhood. Presently, she was in the kitchen, slicing the leftover roast beef in secrecy and haste and tucking the thick slices between the biscuits with a bit of sauce. If she were caught with the sandwiches, there would be the devil to pay at prayers tomorrow. So, she cradled them into her skirts and made her way to the cut logs at the back of the wood shed. She sat in the pale, warm moonlight and prepared to enjoy her late-night feast.

After she had devoured the four sandwiches much too quickly to have enjoyed them, she sat back to admire the night. She had liked London the least of the many places they had visited worldwide to collect their love offerings. London nights were usually dreary, overcast, and smoggy, but the clear mountain air breathed new life into her. Though she couldn't convince the other sisters of her self-assessment, she really was improving her health in the mountains, and wasn't eating nearly as much food as customary. She'd even lost a few pounds, she was sure of it, and even if she hadn't—as Sister Joseph had suggested—her lungs were clear and healthy, and she didn't cough nearly as much as she once did. Yes, indeed, these mountains were good for her . . . the kind of doctor every soul needed when the Lord was busy with someone else.

It was Sister Michael's turn tomorrow to go into the settlements and witness for the Lord. Though she loved singing his praises, she didn't like having to ride one of the horses and dragging her bulk into the clumsy saddles. She had entreated—actually, begged—Sister Joseph to let Old Potts drive her to the duty, but their leader had said the man had enough to do with the building of the church.

A movement at the edge of the forest caught her attention. "Who goes there?" she called, hesitating to come to her feet and make a dash for safety. The Lord did not like cowards. When no one appeared, she called again, "Is someone there?" At which time a dark form emerged into the moonlight. Narrowing her eyes, she attempted to see the person approaching her. "Oh, it's you again . . . what are you doing prowling in the darkness?" When her query went unanswered, Sister Michael slowly got to her feet, turning to the interloper who had disrupted her solitude. "Have you lost something that you've—"

She did not see the hand lash out at the air until it was too late . . . too late, even, to ward off the small, sharp knife that almost separated her head from her shoulders in the initial attack. Her eyes widened in horror as she sank to her knees, Sister Michael was dead before her body fell slowly, face downward, into the well-worn dirt around the wood pile.

But the vicious killer was not yet finished with Sister Michael. Hefting the body on to strong shoulders, Jack the Ripper staggered toward the smokehouse with the latest victim.

Back in Sister Meade's room at the Lodge of Sisterhood, her little terrior barked in frantic terror.

Tallie was up the following morning before everyone. The sun had not yet lit the sky as she moved toward the clothesline with the basket containing garments she had washed in the last hour. She had been restless all night, hearing noises, worrying that Farrand Beattie had lied about losing his memory and that he was simply waiting for the opportunity to sneak into her room and plunge a dagger into her throat. So, she'd done some reading during the night, straining to see the letters in the light of the single lamp, and as she hung her clothes to dry, she felt a niggly headache behind her eyes.

Over the next fifteen minutes she saw the lights in the sisters' rooms come on one by one, and then the brighter ones in the kitchen where Brookie was gathering up her pots to prepare breakfast. The predawn air was cool and refreshing, and Tallie didn't want the day to come upon them. She was unaccustomed to the heat in these American mountains, and took a moment to remember the heavy smog of London's East End.

The first glimmer of sunlight eased upon the woodline just as Tallie finished hanging out her clothes. Now she moved toward the Lodge of Sisterhood, to help Brookie prepare breakfast. Entering the kitchen, she dropped her empty basket and tied on the familiar white apron she always wore. Through the window she watched Storm Phillips exit the cabin and stand for a moment, his palms pressed to the small of his back as he wrenched back his shoulders. Then, as was his usual practice, he moved the few feet required to take him to the door of the cabin Old Potts occupied. Banging his fist on the door, he yelled, "Time to get up and labor, old-timer!"

Tallie smiled at Storm's casualness, the way he now moved toward the lodge, his eyes holding her own. Then he was in the corridor, moving into the kitchen. "What?" he grumbled insincerely. "Breakfast is not ready yet? What does a man have to do around here to get fed?"

"Get up from your lazy bottom," said Tallie, turning to him with a smile, "And put the bacon in the pan."

Brookie drew in a short breath of surprise. "It isn't the gentlemen who should cook, Tallie Edwards! It is the women!"

Tallie lifted her eyebrow, her smirk now for Storm's benefit. "Oh? Well, I will have you know that I am a woman of the eighties, and I believe that kitchen duties should be shared equally between man and woman."

Storm arose at once, his slim hand snatching an apron off a hook at the wall. Tying it around his narrow waist, he asked, "Where's the bacon?"

"Mr. Phillips, don't ye put on an apron like a woman!" Brookie gasped. "It airn't fittin'."

And Tallie, laughing, pointed out that he looked quite nice in it. "The bacon has been sliced and is lying in that dish, Brookie."

While Brookie grumbled and complained that, "It just airn't fittin'," a grinning Storm set about putting the bacon in the pan. As it began to sizzle, he picked up a fork and stirred it, turned it and watched it until it began to turn brown. And, just as he was about to take it out of the skillet, a blood-curdling scream ricocheted from outside the building.

The residents of the lodge spilled into the early morning. Storm, having jerked the pan off the fire with such haste that he'd burned his wrist, mumbled an expletive as he joined the women and saw Sister Meade rushing toward them. Her little dog was choking on something it had picked up in the woods.

"He's dying," she wailed, not even aware that her head had been uncovered in her hysteria.

Storm couldn't stand the dog, but that didn't prevent him from grabbing it from her and shaking it vigorously several inches above the ground. Momentarily, what appeared to be a hazelnut dislodged and the terrier squirmed to get loose. It had scarcely touched the ground before Sister Meade was swooping it up. With a quick "thank you, Brother Storm," she then walked away, cradling her dog and giving due credit to her Lord.

"That was very good of you, Storm, since I know you dislike the little beast," Tallie said quietly.

"It's just a dog," Storm grumbled. "But Sister Meade likes it. I didn't want her to be unhappy."

When Tallie saw that tears filled Brookie's eyes, she said, "Mustn't be upset. The little dog will be all right."

"It airn't the little dog," she sniffed. "Our bacon is burned to a crisp!"

With a gentle laugh, Tallie attempted to cover the woman's shoulders with one of her long, slim arms, but it would only reach halfway. "Then come along, Brookie. We shall cook up a new batch."

Moments later, freshly cut bacon had been cooked and Tallie now broke eggs into the bacon grease, scrambling them the way everyone seemed to favor.

Soon, breakfast was ready, and Tallie sliced the bread she'd baked yesterday. Now that the butter and condiments were on the table, she went into the corridor and announced breakfast in her usual way.

Sister Joseph entered and took her place at the table. "Sister Meade will not join us for breakfast. She will spend the morning praying in her room." Then, "Where is Sister Michael?"

"It is her duty to witness for the Lord this day," Tallie reminded her. "She must have left already."

"Before breakfast?" said Sister Joseph, finding the moment to sound a little incredulous. Sister Michael *never* let a meal pass without her. "Very odd."

"One of the horses is gone," said Storm, taking his covered plate to return with it to his cabin. "She must have left before anyone got up."

"Odd," said Sister Joseph again, then, "It won't be necessary that you take your meals—you and Mr. Potts—to yourselves. Since we have this fine new kitchen and dining area, we will expect you to join us from now on." Now, this was a startling revelation. Storm and Tallie looked at each other as if they couldn't believe Sister Joseph. She was the one who had always insisted on separation of the genders. As Storm took a chair at the table, Sister Joseph said, "After all, if the son of our dear Lord could extend the hand of friendship to a common harlot like Mary Magdelene, then, Brother Storm, we sisters can extend the hand of friendship to you . . . and to Mr. Potts as well."

The comparison certainly left a lot to be desired. To question her sudden change might embarrass her, so Tallie eased into her own chair across from Storm. It seemed very odd to have him at the table, but a nice odd and one she was sure she could grow accustomed to. Momentarily, they were joined by Old Potts, who explained that he'd had to wash his hands again. When he asked for his breakfast plate, his eyes a little bewildered to see Storm sitting among the sisters, he was invited to join them. He did so hesitatingly, a little suspicious.

Then came Sister Pete, who'd gotten so involved in her morning prayer that she'd almost forgotten about breakfast.

As usual, Sister Pete's blessing was overly long, so that when they finally sampled the meal, the eggs and bacon had grown somewhat cold. With an apology, Brookie offered to cook more, but Sister Joseph said, "Food that is wasted goes to Satan. No, Sister Brookie, we shall eat it." Raising her pale-gray brows, but not looking to Sister Pete in particular, she said, "From now on, the Lord won't mind if we keep the blessing short."

"This a celebration?" asked Old Potts, spooning eggs into his plate. "What we bein' treated like this for, Sister?"

Storm wished that Old Potts could learn to keep his mouth shut. He said nothing, but later on, he would have words in private with the old-timer about his manners.

The inquiry, unfortunately, launched Sister Joseph into a recital of every passage in the Good Book, insomuch as it pertained to friendship and tolerance. By the time breakfast was over, Storm was ready to leave. He excused himself, picked up his plate, putting it beside the wash basin, and cut a gaze to Tallie. When she glanced up, his head made a small movement, a familiar one that indicated he wanted her to meet him outside as soon as she was able. For now, he moved into the morning and toward the skeletal structure of the church he and Old Potts were building for the women.

When Potts joined him a few minutes later, Storm growled, "Why the hell can't you leave well enough alone, old-timer?

The women are trying to accept us, so when they do something nice, don't question their motives."

"Din't mean nothin' by it, Storm," the man responded, his voice free of argument. "But ya gotta admit, it were a strange thing, bein' as we been takin' our meals together an' away from their table. Them's strange women! Sure enough, Storm . . . strange women!"

"Aw, hell!"

"Well, they *are* strange women!" Potts said.

"Not that. We got trouble." Storm had just then noticed their only saddle resting against the pen where the horses were kept, and in which only one horse foraged in the fresh supply of hay. "If Sister Michael lit out of here on her rounds, she didn't ride a saddled horse." Then, "Did you see her this morning?"

"Ya know I weren't up till after you were, Storm. How could I a' seen 'er?"

"You didn't sneak out to that cabin to drink some hooch?"

"Naw. I was dead tired las' night, Storm."

Storm approached, looked over the saddle, then the pen where their team was kept. A post had been loosened near the lean-to, and there was enough room for the one horse to have gotten out without the other finding the same escape route. "I know damned well Sister Michael couldn't have gotten on the horse without a saddle. We'd better go look for her."

"I'll go tell Sister Joseph—"

"No!" Storm immediately softened his voice. "There's no reason to alarm her." Then, "I have a real bad feeling about this, Potts. A real bad feeling."

Brighton Road, London

Peter Leggett pulled the cart up to the wide steps of the townhouse occupied by the Gaynors for the past twenty years. The house was a large brownstone almost overgrown with ivy on its south and east sides, and massive mahogany doors and a welcome mat warmly invited visitors. Peter had sent a request to Mrs. Gaynor that he be given an appointment to see her that day, a requirement of the well-to-do residents in this part of the city.

Now, he knocked at that same door, instantly filled with dreaded anticipation, and presently, a prim and proper young maid answered. "I've an appointment to see Mrs. Gaynor," he announced, effecting a slight bow, a requirement, he was sure, even for the maid of such a family.

Shown into a sitting room off a wide foyer, he stood there with his hat crushed to his chest. The furniture was of rich brocade; he wanted to sit, but he didn't know if it was allowed. The room was much too fancy for the likes of him—a commoner from the East End—to simply make himself comfortable.

So he stood just off the Oriental rug, pacing up and down on highly varnished floors and admiring the rich mantel and the delicate porcelains resting atop it. Then a door opened nearby and presently a diminutive boy entered the room. The child looked surprised to see him, though he did manage a redeeming smile.

"Good morning, sir," he said in a small, polite voice. "I do beg your pardon, but I did not know company had arrived. I do hope you are well—"

Peter Leggett felt obligated to respond to the greeting of the handsome, pale-haired lad. "I've come to see Mrs. Gaynor, young man. And thank you for inquiring about my health." The child was richly dressed, his trousers and jacket of dark-blue velvet and his white shirt neatly pressed. "That is a very nice outfit you have there."

"Yes, it is," said the boy with complete innocence. "Mother is taking us to chapel. Her friend, Mrs. Hepplewhite, is christening a new baby." The child approached, leaning close as he whispered, "I have seven sisters, sir. What do you think of that?"

"Seven sisters? Why, I think that's just fine."

"I am the youngest—well, that is, Annie and me. We are twins."

"Cedric!" The boy snapped about like a good little soldier, his eyes widening as his mother entered the parlor. She smiled sweetly then, dragging the child against her skirts to pat his shoulder and again admonish him. "I do beg your pardon, Mr. Leggett. Children are so precocious nowadays, and he tends to be a chatty little lad." Giving him a shove, she lightly ordered, "Go on, Cedric. See if your sisters are prepared. We'll leave in half an hour."

Of the families he had investigated in the past few days, this one had the most potential. He looked after the child until the door had closed and now turned his gaze to the matronly Mrs. Gaynor, her hands twisting through a lace-edged handkerchief as she moved toward him.

"Do tell me what you wished to see me about, Mr. Leggett? I gathered from your correspondence that we have not met."

"No, Mrs. Gaynor, we have not. The matter I've come to see you about is . . ." He wasn't quite sure how to broach it. "Did you know a woman named Cora Dunton?"

"No, I am afraid I did not."

"Then, a man by the name of Mayfield."

She paled visibly, sitting so quickly upon the settee behind her that it shifted on the carpet. "Mayfield? N-no, I do not believe so."

"Surely, you must," Peter Leggett argued. "He delivered coal in this district for almost fourteen years."

"Yes, oh, yes. Mr. Mayfield. The children called him Piggy, because he always smelled bad."

"That is him. Yes, Piggy Mayfield."

"I understand he died a few years ago. My neighbor, Mrs. Cully, told me they had found him facedown in an alley, consumed of the drink." She was trembling inside, hoping it was not visible to the gentleman standing against the cold hearth, his fingers making a crumpled mess of the hat he was carrying.

"Is there something about Mr. Mayfield that I should know? Or this woman, Cora Dunton, you have asked me about?"

"Actually, Mrs. Gaynor, I believe there is something *you* should tell *me*. Since Mrs. Dunton's death, I am the agent, of sorts, for a young woman named Tallie Edwards, who is presently in America. I believe . . ." There was no way to broach the subject delicately, so Peter Leggett mustered all of his courage and continued with haste, "I believe she is in danger . . . and that you might be able to help her. I believe you have a sister somewhat older than you are, who was at one time married to Mr. Mayfield, and I need to know where that sister is."

For a woman of wide girth, Margaret Gaynor came to her feet with the agility of a cat. "Get out, Mr. Leggett. Get out at once. Or I shall immediately send for a bobby!" When he hesitated, she screamed, "Get out! Get out of my house!"

There was all probability that the woman might charge in her second attack. Peter Leggett moved hastily into the foyer, where the woman's children were rushing down the stairs and a maid and butler were emerging from a long corridor at the back of the house.

Peter Leggett said to Mrs. Gaynor, "Perhaps it would be better if I talked to your husband," then exited into the cool London morning. The woman called his name, but he did not give her the satisfaction of a response. By the time he had climbed into the seat of his cart, a tearful Margaret Gaynor had closed her hand over his arm.

"Please, Mr. Leggett, you must not talk to my husband. He must never be told about my sister. Please . . . he does not know what she has done—or where she spent twenty-five years of her life. He will not understand."

"I want only to protect an innocent young woman who is like a daughter to me."

Margaret Gaynor was almost distraught. "You do not understand. I have not seen my sister in many years. I can tell you nothing to protect the young woman."

"Then I am sorry to have troubled you, Mrs. Gaynor." He handed her a small card. "Should you hear from your sister, will you please contact me at this address?" Then he flicked the reins at the harness horse and slowly pulled it away from the curb. He did not look back at the palatial stone house on Brighton Road, nor at the tearful woman who had long denied the existence of her sister.

Storm found the old harness horse grazing in new clover in a shady dell half a mile from the compound. Wearing only its halter, he knew it had not been ridden by Sister Michael, by her own admission an extremely poor rider. He had been worried before, but now he *knew* something was very wrong. Sister Michael was the one with the robust personality and the one with the tender heart. She was the one, he feared, who was in a lot of trouble right now. And it wasn't trouble that Sister Joseph would bring upon her for her unexplained absence.

He had just entered the compound with the wayward horse when Tallie approached him. He could hear the prayers and incantations of the three women left in the lodge.

"Sister Michael was thrown?" questioned Tallie. "Did you find her?"

"The horse hasn't been ridden," Storm grumbled. "It merely broke out of the pen."

"Then where is Sister Michael?"

"I have no idea," he continued to grumble. "I'll find her, but I don't need you to pester me right now."

Tallie gasped in her surprise. "I'm sorry. I thought you wanted me to come out-of-doors, so I assumed you wanted to talk to me. If you are in one of your moods, Storm—"

He had just released the horse back into the enclosure. Turning, he took Tallie in his arms, sure that the sisters, deeply engaged in their prayers, would not be spying upon them. "I'm sorry, Tallie." She merely shrugged, tucking herself against him. "I'm worried about Sister Michael. She missed breakfast and I can't remember her ever doing that before."

"Well, you don't have to snap at me," she pouted, lifting her gaze to his own dark one, "just because you're worried about one of the sisters."

When Brookie exited the lodge to throw out the dishwater, Tallie pulled from Storm's embrace. She acknowledged Brookie's absent wave with one of her own, then turned as Storm began to speak.

"I know I have a lot of work to do on the church today, but I simply must get away and find Sister Michael before the others know she's missing. Do you mind making excuses for me?"

"I have an idea," Tallie offered. "Why not hitch up the team, take them down the road, and I'll tell Sister Joseph you ran out of supplies. That way, there'll be no need to make excuses. Potts can continue to work. Sister Joseph will be glad to see at least one man on the job today." Then, "Would you like for me to help you look for Sister Michael?" A thought came to Tallie. "Do you suppose John Collins might have driven over to pick her up? She may have made arrangements with him that she didn't tell Sister Joseph about."

"Why don't you ride over there and check with Fanny."

"All right." She hadn't seen Fanny in a few weeks and she had missed her. "If John picked up Sister Michael, I shall track her movements so that we can be assured she is safe."

Storm pulled her into his arms, at once intoxicated by the morning freshness of her hair, of her skin. Worry had robbed him of his senses moments before, or he would have noticed the delicate fragrance of her. "I'll saddle the horse for you."

"Thank you, my love—"

"Sister T! There'll be enough of that!" She jerked from his embrace, turning instantly away from the approaching Sister Joseph so that she could compose herself. "Brother Storm, I'd get on to your work, if I were you."

Storm mumbled, "I'll saddle the horse," then politely drew away.

Before Sister Joseph could get within range, she whispered, "Don't forget the appointment with Mr. Beattie this afternoon."

"I won't forget," he promised, moving into the pen to fetch the horse.

Tallie smiled her widest smile when Sister Joseph reached the spot where she was standing. "Sister Joseph, through with your prayers so soon?"

"Come, Tallie—" A bone-thin hand outstretched. "We'd like for you to join us in our prayers this morning. We believe you have many sins."

Rage instantly flooded Tallie's pretty features, which she suppressed at once. "I am riding to Fanny's to see if John might have—." She'd been about to confess the reason, which Storm had said they shouldn't, and quietly amended, "finished with the dresser he is building for my room." With a smile that immediately stifled any forthcoming argument, she said, "Do you have a message to send to Fanny?"

"No," said Sister Joseph, "and if you find Sister Michael send her back at once."

"I will," replied Tallie, moving toward the horse Storm was saddling.

Chapter Nineteen

At midmorning Sister Joseph was advised of the problem of the horse, and that Sister Michael had not been picked up by John Collins. She seemed to have disappeared from the face of the earth. Sister Joseph and Sister Pete went through her room, finding her canvas sack gone and the journal she had always kept turned to a particular page. Just two weeks before, Sister Michael had written, *It is so difficult. I am ordered to eat only one helping at meals, but I am always hungry. After these twenty years that we have been together, Sister Joseph has accused me of gluttony. If I thought I could go away somewhere and my God not abandon me, I would do so, I cannot bear to go to bed hungry every night.*

Sister Joseph brought the diary to the attention of the other two sisters, and to Tallie's and Storm's when they returned from a ride through the woods in their search of Sister Michael. "She has left us," Sister Joseph solemnly announced. "Our dear Sister Michael has left us."

So, it seemed, the mystery of Sister Michael was sufficiently solved. Storm, reading the page in the diary, grumbled, "So,

Sister Michael was plump. It's a shame she had to be made to suffer daily for it."

For the first time that any of them could remember—even the two sisters who had been with her for twenty years—Sister Joseph began to weep. Thereafter, she closed herself in her room, to pray and beg God's forgiveness for the unhappiness she had brought upon Sister Michael. Storm was, effectively, outcast for the day in the eyes of Sisters Pete and Meade for reminding her of her folly. The young man should learn to hold his tongue and respect his elders.

Alone with Tallie now, he said, "It's after twelve. I'll get washed up, hitch the team, and we'll ride over to the ranch." Then, "You do still want to talk to the Englishman, don't you?"

"Yes. I won't be able to rest until I know that he truly does not remember me. You don't mind, do you?"

Storm was honest. "I don't want to go there, Tallie, but I will go for you."

"Then I, too, will freshen up and meet you here in fifteen minutes."

They parted. When Tallie entered the kitchen, she encountered a very stern-faced Brookie Newgate, scrubbing pots and pans as though she fully intended to remove the surfaces. "I do not believe Sister Michael just *left!*" Brookie snapped at the first person to enter the kitchen. "Someone is trying to make us believe the dear woman departed of her own accord. No, no, no! I do not believe it! I spoke to her yesterday morning, and she seemed pleased to mention how happy she is to be here."

"That is not what she wrote in her journal, Brookie."

"The journal!" The small woman now pivoted about, her hands going into the folds of her apron to dry them. "And explain if ye will, Tallie, why she would have packed her things and left only the journal behind?"

Actually, Tallie hadn't thought about that. She hadn't realized how sensible Brookie was, and immediately dropped her eyes in shame at her own shortcomings. "No, I cannot explain it, Brookie."

"Or how she left the Lodge? Surely, a woman unaccustomed to so much walking would not take her feet to the road! Something has happened to our dear Sister Michael!" Dropping into a chair at the table, Brookie suggested that they call in a bobby to investigate.

"They are called marshals and deputies here," Tallie corrected. "Perhaps you are right. Perhaps we should summon Marshal Black to look into this. When Storm and I leave the Phillips Ranch, I shall have him drive me into Granger."

Brookie rose, her expression now one of satisfaction. "Good! I will feel much better when we get to the bottom of this. Dear, dear Sister Michael. She might be lying somewhere in the woods, injured, or taken off by some grizzly mountain man intent on having his way with her."

A gentle laugh rocked Tallie's voice. "You are like a protective mother hen, and we are all your bitties."

"Harumph! I'll keep ye fed and happy . . . or me name airn't Brookie Newgate!"

Tallie thought she could share the same kind of friendship with Brookie she shared with Sister Pete. She was a godsend.

"Are you ready?" Storm entered the kitchen, his gaze connecting to the somewhat absent one of Tallie Edwards. "The wagon is outside."

Tallie was a little surprised that so much time had passed, when she'd thought it had been only a minute or two. She didn't even realize Brookie had left the kitchen, and she couldn't believe she'd been sitting here alone, absorbed in her thoughts. "It'll take just a minute to freshen up."

Hardly had Storm sat at the table with a cup of coffee before Tallie was returning to the kitchen.

Storm thought she looked as though she'd been primping for an hour. She was wearing a pastel-blue dress with just enough cotton lace to take away its plainness, and it hugged her slim figure most becomingly. Raising a dark eyebrow, he said, "I haven't seen that dress. Is it new?"

"I brought it with me from England. Aunt Cora purchased it for me as a Christmas gift and gave it to me when Mr. Leggett took me to Southampton for the trip here."

"You do look lovely," he remarked, rising, closing her in his arms. "Now, let's get this damned visit over with, shall we?" Politeness eased into his tone despite the words, and he smiled pleasantly.

Spying the portfolio, she said, "You are returning that to him? I wish you would not."

"Why?"

"Because he will know who he is and why he came here. It might trigger his memory."

"I'm returning it to him," Storm said flatly. "We'll deal with the repercussions later."

Tallie couldn't find a single person to tell she was leaving as she moved into the morning and accepted Storm's offer of assistance into the wagon. Soon, they were moving onto the narrow dirt road for the half-hour journey to the ranch of MacCallister Phillips.

Thea had prepared the ribs and potatoes, as Jack had requested, but she was still miffed at his coolness to her this morning. He had gone off in the night and had not returned until the predawn hours. She knew, because she'd sat in the rocker on the porch and waited for him. He had gone straight to his cot in the bunkhouse without ever having seen her sitting in the deep shade of the porch.

At least, when she'd retired to bed at the back of the ranch house, she'd known he was safe. And for that reason she'd been able to snatch a few hours of sleep before arising to face the new day.

She moved around the large kitchen, readying plates for the luncheon she and Matt would have with Storm and the young

English lady. She hoped that Jack would make an appearance, though it was after twelve and he still had not confirmed the plans he'd made with the young people the day before. Thea would not allow him to spoil the day for her, though, and Matt was excited that Storm was coming to lunch. He had spruced up, put on his best plaid shirt, and had polished his old boots so that he'd be presentable to again face his half-brother.

Had it not been for MacCallister taking the whip to her boy that morning, Thea knew she'd never have had the courage to send the box of Rachel Spencer's things to her son. She'd seen the ornate box sitting among rags and old blankets in a storage room for the past twenty years or so, and she'd always wanted Storm to have it. Mack had said, however, that if he ever found it missing, someone would have hell to pay.

She had seen Storm only a few times, because she very seldom left the ranch. He was quite a handsome man, and he always seemed polite to those he encountered on the street. Thea remembered watching him a few weeks ago from her perch in Granger's only restaurant as he'd loaded supplies for the church ladies. She'd been surprised at the number of people who approached him simply to talk, to exchange a greeting, or to share a laugh with him. She'd never heard a bad thing about him from anyone. She didn't think a single person residing in these mountains within a fifty-mile radius of Granger truly believed that Storm Phillips had robbed a train.

Certainly, she didn't, because she knew where the train money was. One day she was going to let everyone know what Mack had done. One day when the time was just right.

"Thea?" So startled was she by her name being spoken, and worrying, for just a moment, that Mack might return to the ranch before he was expected, she almost lost her balance. But when she turned, a very humble Englishman stood in the doorway, dragging his hat off his head. "I did not mean to startle you."

"You scared the wits out of me, Jack! I thought McCallister had returned."

He'd come to the kitchen to apologize for his mood last evening. But the apology was momentarily forgotten. "Do you mind, Thea, not calling me Jack any longer?"

"What then?" Annoyance laced her voice as she turned back to the stove, to stir the beans and bacon in a deep iron pan. "Patrick Edwards?"

"It is not Patrick Edwards."

She turned again, at once surprised by the pain in his features. "What is wrong? I've never seen you like this."

"I remember everything, Thea. I went riding in the woods last evening, and I am afraid I got hopelessly lost on the trails. I dismounted and sat on a fallen log for a long, long time, thinking and worrying and wondering if I would be lost forever in these woods. And it came to me, Thea, as quickly as an inventor's idea. I know who I am and why I am here and—I know the young lady lied to me about my identity." With deep regret, he added, "If I were in her shoes, I would have done the same thing."

"Jack—"

"My name is Farrand Beattie, Thea, not Jack. And I followed the young woman, Tallie Edwards, all the way from London because I was ordered to."

Thea sat at the table, stirring spoon still in her hand and drippings falling to one of the clean plates she had set out for their meal. Dropping it, she stared at her Englishman as though she hadn't believed a thing he'd said. "Who ordered you?"

"By the man for whom I am—was—employed. His name is Prince Albert Victor, Duke of Clarence and Avondale, grandson of Queen Victoria and eldest son of Edward."

This was quite a claim. Was her Englishman having delusions of grandeur brought on, perhaps, by the serious injury he'd received? "Why would a prince care about a girl from a London slum district?" she asked indulgently.

"Who told you she was from a slum district?"

"I heard it from Fanny Collins. She said Tallie was from the East End, and that it was a poor section riddled with crime."

"And so it is. This Collins woman? She does not like Miss Edwards?"

"Quite on the contrary. She brought up the lady's background to show the strength of her character." Then, "Why, I repeat, would a prince order you to come here after Tallie Edwards?"

Seated at the large table, Farrand Beattie's elbows found a place upon the table. Linking his fingers, he pressed them firmly to his mouth to gain a moment. Then he told Thea the story, leaving out none of the details, of his prince going to see Mary Jane Kelly that evening at Miller's Court and coming upon her mutilated corpse while Farrand waited outside for him. Eddy had startled the killer, who in haste had dropped the murder weapon, a surgical scalpel, which Eddy had foolishly picked up. When Tallie had entered the lodging room, she had seen Eddy and assumed him to be the killer.

"Do you see, Thea, the harm she could do if she told such a story to the American press? I wanted only to talk to her, to tell her that she had made a mistake. The American newspapers would make a vicious killer and mutilator of women of my beloved prince. He has problems, Thea, but he is not a killer. He was shocked by what he had seen that night, and even more shocked when Tallie walked in on him before he had a chance to flee before the wrong conclusion could be made." Thea's skeptical gaze instantly caught his eye. "You do not understand. His father, Edward, will assume the throne. After his reign, Eddy is next in line. I have to protect his reputation, for the good of England and the Crown. I have taken a sworn oath to do so."

Thea sat back, feeling a bit listless as she listened to an incredible tale being told by a man who, until last evening, had no memory whatsoever of his own identity, let alone the full history of the ruling family of England. In the moment of silence, she said, "This is all a bit much for me to handle. I'm not—"

Just at that moment a wagon approached and Thea heard her son's voice. She had just forced her gaze from that of the

Englishman when Matt, Tallie Edwards, and Storm entered the kitchen. She could tell that Storm was uncomfortable, and the young lady, clutching Storm's arm when she saw the Englishman at the table, had eyes filled with fear. She was beautiful nonetheless and Thea could scarcely cut her eyes from Tallie's remarkable features.

Storm broke the tense silence. "It is very kind that we are allowed to come to lunch, Thea."

"My pleasure . . . I am glad you agreed to come." Outstretching her hand, she invited them to sit down. "Everything is almost prepared. I was just finishing the beans and bacon, so that I could pour it in a bowl."

She'd set out a pretty table, with an embroidered tablecloth, blue stoneware plates, and cutlery with wooden handles. Matching napkins lay to the right of each plate, one of which she quickly replaced when she saw that she'd dirtied it with her stirring spoon.

"Ma's a great cook!" exclaimed Matt, taking his usual chair at the head of the table. "Come on, Storm, Miss Edwards, let's dig into the grub."

"Grub, young man?" interjected Farrand Beattie. "Your mother's food is hardly *grub*. Do be polite." He smiled, his right hand moving graciously, to motion Tallie and Storm to their chairs. "My niece and her gentleman friend shall sit together—right here."

Thea cut him a narrow look. So, he was going to play the game for a little while. She was curious as to his motives. Or did he simply not want to ruin their meal?

Setting the platter of barbequed ribs on the table, Thea poured milk into their waiting glasses and brought a large bowl of steaming garlic potatoes and the smaller one of beans and bacon, setting them in the middle of the table. Retrieving the warmer of bread rolls, she took her chair, then placed them just above her plate.

"Dig in," she ordered, looking at once to Tallie. "Do you wish to say a blessing?"

"I'll say it, Ma."

Matt had never offered before. Thea gave him a strange, questioning look, nodding her head even as she was suspicious, and a little leery as to what would come out of his mouth.

"Lord . . ." began Matt reverently, his linked fingers pressed beneath his chin. "Although I rounded up this here cow, and Pokey, he was the one that murdered it, an' me an' Bart, we got it all skin't an' chopped up and smoked real nice like, an' Ma, she's been slavin' over the stove a cookin' an' preparin' this here meal the whole blessed mornin', well, we thank ya anyway. Amen."

Stifling a small smile, Storm said, "That was a fine blessing, Matt."

To which a skeptical Tallie added, "Yes, fine, indeed."

The Englishman had remained relatively quiet, his eyes upon the familiar leather portfolio Storm had set against the leg of his chair. Almost at the same time, Storm picked it up and handed it to him, explaining, "It is yours. If we get a chance to talk, I'm sure you'll want to know why I have possession of it."

He nodded, asking no questions as he tossed the portfolio to a side table, and Tallie knew then that he was very aware of his identity. Now, when she looked toward him, it was not the theatrics of a pretend niece looking adoringly into the face of a pretend uncle. It was the mouse looking into the gaze of the cat.

Farrand Beattie had made no move to fill his plate after the blessing, and paid very little notice when Thea began piling hefty portions in front of him. His gaze held the features of Tallie Edwards; there was no anger in the way he looked at her, only pain and regret.

His beloved Eddy was not Jack the Ripper. How could he convince the young woman, who had seen him at Mary Kelly's room that night, of that? He wasn't sure. He imagined that when she learned he had recovered his memory, she might flee once again and he would not get the chance to talk to her.

So, he watched the young people at their meals, eating very little himself. The man, Storm, merely picked at his plate, while the young lady ate nervously, he imagined, so that she would not have to look up at him. He did not know that Tallie ate her heartiest when she was frightened out of her wits. Matt was his usual self, trying to chat in between bites of his meal, his mother fussing at him to "watch your manners proper, young man, or you'll feel a spoon across your knuckles."

"Awe, Ma—" Matt said half a dozen times, always feeling it necessary to explain to Storm and Tallie that "Ma, she don't mean it. She jes' gits a little crabby now an' then."

Somewhere in the conversation, Storm said to Thea, "I want to thank you for sending over my mother's chest. It meant a lot to me."

"Did it contain things that might be of value to you?" When she noticed his strange expression, she hastily amended, "I don't mean valuables necessarily. I mean things that might reveal something about your mother."

"Yes," he replied. "There were letters and a journal, but I haven't read them yet. I do thank you, Thea."

"It should have been given to you years ago."

Matt now chimed in, "If you're finished, Storm an' Miss Tallie, I'll show you the bunkhouse where the men stay, an' show you around the ranch."

To which a solemn Storm replied, "I don't believe your employer will appreciate that."

"He ain't goin' ta be back fer days. Hell . . ." Cutting a look to his mother, he said, "Is it aw'right, Ma, if I show Storm an' Miss Tallie around?"

"If Storm would like to go," Thea said. "I believe our Englishman wishes to talk to the young lady."

Storm looked to Tallie, unsure if she wished to be alone with the man. She nodded imperceptibly, at which time he hesitated, then accompanied his young half-brother into the warmth of the afternoon.

Matt bubbled over with cheer; Storm wished he felt as good.

Still, he managed some semblance of contentment as Matt showed him the stables and the expensive horses, careful to point out the one that got him whipped by his father. Storm cringed at the thought of the brutality, and wondered why Thea and Matt stayed at the ranch. They should have left years ago. He didn't understand why any of them stayed; from what he'd heard, MacCallister Phillips had put every man in his employ under the lash at one time or another.

As Storm climbed into the saddle of one of McCallister's best horses for a tour of the ranch, he wondered what Tallie and Farrand Beattie were talking about.

Thea had politely withdrawn from the kitchen, leaving Tallie and Farrand Beattie alone. Tallie was frightened, but only because it came so easily to her after these few months of constantly watching over her shoulder. She felt reasonably sure her life was not in any imminent danger from the Englishman who had followed her across the Atlantic. Suddenly, she was more than frightened . . . she was angry! And because she was, she looked across the table at Farrand Beattie and accused, "You have ruined my life! You have driven me away from London, from my family, and especially, from my daughter. You have terrorized and intimidated me and made me too afraid to go home. And I hate you for it."

He was silent for a moment, his bone-thin fingers linking together atop the checkered tablecloth. "You saw me aboard ship, young lady. I know that I frightened you. That has been months ago and you did not see me again until yesterday. Where is the terror and the intimidation, and why did you not simply go home when so much time passed without seeing me again?"

His logic left her speechless. She opened her mouth, but no excuse was forthcoming, her eyes holding him firmly, even as she wanted to drop her gaze in shame. When she recovered her thoughts, she said, "Are you saying that you no longer intend me any harm?"

"I am not saying that, young woman. I am saying that I *never* intended you any harm. I wanted only to talk to you, and you foolishly fled England before I was able to do that. Yes, I followed you and, yes, I boarded the same ship as you, but no, I have never meant you any harm."

"You have a very strange way of showing it, Mr. Beattie. Why would you follow me? And why would my aunt insist that I go away, if you were not a genuine danger to me?"

"Have you thought that it was not my threat she was sending you away from?"

Tallie's hazel gaze widened; her mouth falling open for a moment as she contemplated his outrageous statement. "Not your threat, Mr. Beattie? Then who's?"

"Has it occurred to you that you may be the woman the Ripper is after, even as he killed all the others?"

Fear filled Tallie's heart; she thought she would suffocate. "That is preposterous. Your prince killed Mary, and he probably killed the others as well." But even as she spoke, she remembered the doubts she'd had these past few months. She scarcely believed that the thin, languid Eddy could have been strong enough to commit such atrocious murders. Tallie had been watching Farrand Beattie intently, and as he suddenly got up from his chair and fell to one knee before her, she gave a small gasp. He had captured one of her hands and was holding it firmly. "Let me go," she ordered. "You cannot do me harm with Thea in another room."

"I do not intend to do you harm, Tallie Edwards, but I must convince you of the prince's innocence. He did not kill. I would rather you believe *I* had committed these vicious killings. I will confess to it, if only you will believe my prince to be innocent!"

"Why should I? You said yourself I might be the intended victim. How can you know that, if your prince did not tell you that it is me he wants to kill?"

Farrand Beattie released her hand in exasperation. "Because, Tallie Edwards, my prince claims that when he entered the room, he heard the killer growling your name—Tallie . . . Tallie

. . . over and over, and demanding to know where you might be found. Yes, this he demanded of a woman who had already been wickedly mutilated. When the fiend heard my prince's gasp of horror and surprise, he fled, and my prince saw only the dark form of him disappearing into the courtyard. Eddy said that he was very large and wearing a long black cloak."

Tallie thought she would faint. She scarcely moved as Farrand Beattie returned to the chair, bending slightly forward as he continued, "I must know that you have not cast aspersions on the prince's character in any of these American newspapers . . . that you have told no one else of your suspicions, or of what you saw that night in Mary Kelly's room. I swear to you, Tallie Edwards, that the prince is innocent."

Tears flooded Tallie's eyes. "You still worry about the character of your prince, even as I sit here in mortal danger and fear for my very life? What kind of monster are you, Farrand Beattie?"

"A monster who will stay here, Tallie, and protect you," he assured her quietly. "The fiend has disappeared from London, or he would have killed again. I fear he is coming for you, Tallie, and I do not say this to frighten you."

"You could not know he is after me." Then, flicking away her tears in a moment of rebellion, she added in a quieter voice, "Unless you are he."

"I am not!" he responded curtly. "Damn, woman, can you not be reasonable?" His forehead found a place against his palms for a moment. "I beg of you, Tallie, to stay close to the man, Storm, and do not go into the woods alone. If at all possible, stay with someone at all times." He looked up now, his eyes glazed and fearful. "*Never* be alone, Tallie, if you value your life . . . if you will see your daughter again."

Tallie at once misunderstood. "You are threatening my daughter, Mr. Beattie?"

"God forbid!" Farrand Beattie got to his feet, eyes narrowing angrily as he stared at Tallie. "I could never threaten a child! I am merely stating that you must take special care to protect yourself, so that you will be able to return to your daughter." He pivoted, his arms crossing against his waistline. "I see there is no sense in trying to make you see reason, Tallie Edwards, because you are determined to believe what you will. I do not know what else I can say. Blast, woman, but you are stubborn!"

With that, he closed the distance to the kitchen door and left her alone in the room. But only for a moment, for Thea had been listening in the other room. She entered now, sitting across the table from Tallie. The silence compelled Tallie to look up. "You are wrong about the Englishman," Thea said. "I hope very soon you will see that."

Matt and Storm spent a good three hours touring the ranch, and when they returned, they unsaddled and rubbed the horses down, put them in their stalls with fresh hay and sweet feed, then entered the bunkhouse, a long narrow building with bunks on one side and racks for clothing, boots, and accoutrements on the other. The bunkhouse was typically male, as not a single shirt was hung up, and clothing had been dropped into smelly heaps.

Presently, they stretched out on two bunks, hands beneath their heads, and chatted like two brothers who had a lot of catching up to do.

As the sun began to withdraw outside, the two men sat on Matt's bunk, flipping through a small photograph album Matt had taken from a locker at the foot of his bed. There were pictures of a young, somewhat stern-faced Thea, of Matt when he was a boy, and several of groups of cowboys who had worked at the ranch off and on over the past twenty-five years. Then Matt paused at one photograph, of a young Confederate soldier in full military regalia, a Confederate flag prop and cannon in back of him.

"This here's the man Ma said was my pa, an' I thought all these here years that he *was* my pa. But now I know diff'rent. Mack's my pa—" With that, Matthew ripped the photograph from its decorative black corners and threw it across the unvarnished planked floor. "No sense to keep a picture of a man what I don't even know who he is."

Quietly, Storm retrieved the photograph, handing it back to Matt. "I'd hold on to this, boy. One day you're going to be looking at this photograph, and wishing he *was* your pa—"

Neither brother had seen the man standing in the doorway at the far end of the bunkhouse. Storm would not have looked up now if his skin had not suddenly crawled with apprehension. There, in the shadows dragging in from the late afternoon, stood MacCallister Phillips.

Matt, following the direction of Storm's gaze, shot to his feet with a hastily yelped, "Goddamn—"

And Storm wouldn't give his father the satisfaction of seeing fear in him.

Casually, he picked up the photograph album from the floor where Matt's sudden movement had deposited it and began thumbing through it, starting at the first page, where a four-year-old Matt, one strap of his baggy overalls hanging in front of a short, wiry leg, struggled to hold up a spotted pup.

Thea dragged her hand to her throat as though she was attempting to claw away some horrid demon growing there. "Mack has returned. Oh, my God."

When Thea turned with so much fear reflecting in her gaze, Tallie closed a hand over her arm. "He has returned? Will he . . ." She hesitated to speak the words, "will he hurt Storm?"

Thea had turned her worried, watchful eyes back to the window. Momentarily, she saw the Englishman and McCallister part company, with McCallister taking care of his horse, and now the man, who had confessed to a true identity just this afternoon, was moving toward the kitchen. He entered, his eyes softening as they met the worried gaze of Thea.

"Strangely, he is not angry," he said to Thea, then turning

to Tallie, "but I suspect it will be better if you and your man departed at once."

Both men had been surprised when Mack had sauntered casually toward the bunk and stood over them for a moment. Storm, expecting him to pull his pistol and shoot him dead, was a little surprised that he had not. Then he gently laid a package on the cot beside Matt, flipped back his hat and pivoted on the rough floorboards. Presently, he was out of sight.

Storm shot to his feet, allowing a moment of silence to pass before he could collect his thoughts. He wasn't necessarily worried about himself, but he was sure as hell worried about Matt and his mother. "I'd better get out of here." Then, "He won't punish you or Thea, will he?"

"If he does, I'll shoot him plum dead!" boasted Matt, his hand lashing out to knock the package from his bunk. "I don't want nothin' from that son-of-a-bitch!" Storm had moved off a half-dozen steps, but now turned back to await Matt. He felt an emotional stirring deep within when Matt said, "Ya know, Storm, if I had to have a brother, I sure am glad it was you."

Locking his fingers over the younger man's shoulder, Storm moved into the shrinking light of late day.

Tallie was already sitting on the buggy seat. Taking Matt's proffered hand, Storm promised to see him again soon. "Now, you let me know if Mack does anything to hurt you and your mother."

"He won't. An' I will," assured Matt.

"Mr. Beattie said that he was not angry," Tallie told Storm, almost breathless with fear. "When I saw him, he had a strange look on his face, but it wasn't rage. I'm not sure what it was. I even saw him greet the Englishman warmly outside the bunkhouse."

"It really surprised me that he didn't shoot me where I sat."

"Perhaps in his advancing age he is beginning to mellow."

Storm laughed lightly. "Stale tobacco mellows, Tallie. Vicious old men? That's another story."

Her arm went through the crook of his arm, her head coming to rest against his shoulder. "And I hope you remained a gentleman when you encountered your father."

"I did."

"Farrand Beattie remembers who he is. I shall tell you all about our conversation later tonight."

And with that, the return trip to the Lodge of Sisterhood passed in the lovely silence of the mountains.

Dusk was gathering when they pulled up to the small corral.

And the horror was just beginning.

Chapter Twenty

Tallie arrived back at the kitchen to find Brookie in a dither. She'd burned the dinner biscuits, had not yet fetched a ham from the smokehouse, and the milk Old Potts had brought her from "the goodness of a neighbor's heart" had been sour in the pail before its journey into the kitchen. The usually staid and efficient new housekeeper sank to a chair in frustration and tears.

"I din't know what has affected me," Brookie sniffed, her hands wringing through the grease-stained apron that had been white and starched just that morning.

Drawing a chair up beside Brookie, a concerned Tallie asked, "Are you still upset over Sister Michael?"

Her gaze saddened, along with a gentle shrug of her shoulders. "I suppose I am, dear lass. Aye, I suppose I am." Then, with more inflection, "Did you go into town to fetch the copper?"

"That is *Marshal* Black, Brookie," Tallie corrected, her annoyance unintended. "I'm sorry. We were late leaving the ranch. I promise we shall go first thing in the morning." Tallie's forehead dropped against Brookie's for a moment, a comforting gesture that brought Brookie's hand up to roughly pat the younger woman's cheek. "How is Sister Joseph? Did she get past her upset?"

"Aye, that she did. Gave me a lecture about Christian values and trust and taking care of our bodies because the Lord wants us to have the best of life. She said she was only looking out for Sister Michael's good by reminding her daily of the sins of gluttony."

Standing, Tallie asked, "May I do something to get dinner on the table?"

"I've got a fresh batch of biscuits in the oven. If ye'll be a dear, Tallie, and fetch a ham from the smokehouse, I'll be appreciative. Afraid we'll have to drink water, lass, since the milk is sour."

Tallie approached the bucket still resting against the counter, bent to sniff the foul liquid, then laughed. "That isn't sour milk, Brookie. It is buttermilk, and I understand the Americans drink it quite often."

"Have mercy! I'd as soon drink cow piss." When Tallie gave her a surprised glance, she continued, "I'd imagine, dearie, with ye growing up in the East End, that's a *mild* vulgarity." Brookie threw back her shoulders as she moved toward the stove and the fresh batch of biscuits. "Fetch that ham, lass, if ye will."

Tallie took the key from the nail and dropped it into the wide pocket of her skirt. The hazy dusk greeted her as she stepped off the porch, and she looked about, thinking she might see Storm. Many times he slumped against a porch support while Potts smoked one of his nasty cigarettes. But she saw neither man, and the gentle glow of a lamp from within Storm's cabin indicated he was possibly engaged in examining the contents of the chest Thea had sent over to him.

Soon, she reached the lean-to where the horses sought shelter from storms and the night and found the lantern hung over a bent two-penny nail. On a low rafter, she found the matches Potts often used to light his cigarettes and soon had the lantern burning brightly. When she resumed her journey to the smokehouse against the line of spruce trees, she hummed a happy tune, one she'd learned at Aunt Cora's knee, and one she had taught, in turn, to her beloved daughter. She would return to Ellie oh so soon. After her talk with Farrand Beattie, she knew there was no need to postpone her trip.

A movement at the cliff caught her attentions. Feeling rather brave despite the descending darkness, she moved toward the fence Storm had built. For a moment or two she stood beneath a pitch pine overlooking the eastward-sloping foothills, though she could see nothing but the lingering shadows of the night. She could stand there for hours, imagining the gentle beauty of the rolling foothills she often gazed upon in the early morning, watching the mist swell up from the ground to encompass the trees, the clouds above seeming to descend to meet it halfway. But now she had to think about dinner and hungry residents, and so turned away from the mountain range she was growing to love with a passion that matched Storm's. Soon, she stood outside the smokehouse, digging in her pocket for the key she had dropped there.

Pulling the door open, she stepped inside, then set the lamp on a small counter just to the left. She didn't like the smokehouse with its donated meats hanging from large iron hooks, nor did she like the wild, pungent smell of hickory and pine. Moving to the rough shelves, she chose a medium-size ham and turned to retrieve the lamp.

In the pale light emitting into the small room, she saw feet and familiar black-laced boots. She saw dark skirts dragged upward . . . and her heart ceased to beat then. Raking her knuckles against her teeth, she took one step forward, the screams she wanted to scream gathering so painfully in her throat she thought she would suffocate.

It was an all too familiar sight, bringing back the horror of Mary Kelly's murder. There, lying on her back was Sister Michael, her palms upward and slightly bent, a sickly, almost blue, tinge washing over her face. Her throat was cut, the upper part of the dress had been pulled open a little way and her abdomen was exposed.

Tallie wasn't sure how she maintained her composure, nor how she stopped herself from fleeing into the safety of the Lodge of Sisterhood. Calmly, she set the ham on the table, took the few steps that would remove her from the smokehouse and stood for a moment, gathering her senses. All at once, she was disoriented as to time and place; in her mind, she could picture Miller's Court and Mary's lodging room—

And yet she was not afraid. Remaining calm, she moved toward Storm's cabin, knocked gently at the door and heard the stir of his footfalls within. Soon, he stood at the door, an almost macabre darkness in his features as he looked down at her. "The smokehouse, Storm . . ."

Fear claimed his dark gaze, his hands immediately on her upper arms. "The smokehouse? You need to get in and you don't have the key?"

Her senses gathered swiftly. "The smokehouse . . . Sister Michael. Oh, my God—"

Though he hadn't intended the roughness, he released her so quickly that she merely slumped against the wall of the cabin. Grabbing up the lantern, he half ran toward the smokehouse, and when he emerged he sank to his knees, his horror and revulsion so immediate that he was not sure he wouldn't lose his stomach then and there.

Brookie had been watching for Tallie's return at the kitchen window, surprised that she had stopped along the way to visit Storm. She had watched him take the lantern and move toward the smokehouse; had Tallie failed to find a proper ham for their supper?

Annoyed now, she moved to the porch and called, "Tallie, do ye have the ham, lass?" She did not answer. Again Brookie called to her, and again she did not respond.

She was at once impatient. As she descended the three steps, she began to move toward the smokehouse to retrieve the ham herself.

As she approached, Storm Phillips came immediately to his feet, his arm whipping out to catch Brookie's arm as she moved past him.

"Don't go in there," he ordered.

"I need a ham for ye supper, lad. I sent Tallie, but—"

"Damn it! I said *don't go in there!*" When he saw hurt fill her eyes, he quietly explained, "Sister Michael has been killed. Her body is in there."

"Sister Michael . . . killed?" she echoed, and quite before Storm could offer any words of comfort at all, her fingers raked through her frizzy copper-colored hair and, screaming now at the top of her lungs, she began to run in small, haphazard circles.

Which, of course, drew the attentions of the three sisters, who emerged from the lodge in a group.

Confusion ran amuck. Storm tried to explain to Sister Joseph what had happened, Sisters Meade and Pete set up a barrier in Brookie's path to capture her flaying arms and halt her hysterical display, and Tallie, now somewhat composed, approached to tuck a trembling hand into the crook of Storm's arm. An inebriated Old Potts staggered out of his cabin, and Storm barked the order, "Ride into Granger and fetch Marshal Crispin, Potts. Sister Michael's been murdered in the smokehouse."

That news sobered him immediately. With quick efficiency, he saddled one of the horses and within minutes was edging the beast into a clumsy lope toward Granger.

Now that the initial shock was over, the residents of Sister Joseph's religious compound gathered in the kitchen. The weeping sisters huddled at the table, their hands clasped in prayer, Tallie was sitting beside a still sobbing Brookie on the deacon's bench and Storm stood against the counter, both palms pressed firmly to the solid wood, his gaze watching the darkness outside. The lantern was still on the ground beside the smokehouse, catching the shadows of the square mortar-and-stone building in its macabre glow.

It sickened him that he'd casually lunched at the Phillips Ranch, gazing at photographs in the bunkhouse with Matt, riding over his father's lands . . . and all the while, poor Sister Michael had lain dead in the smokehouse. He recalled every square foot he and Tallie had covered in their search of her this morning. He had not even thought to check in the smokehouse.

He would never get out of his mind the vision of her mutilated corpse, the eerie white cast to her skin, as though no blood had remained in her body, and her throat slashed from ear to ear, like a grotesquely smiling mouth. Tears came to his eyes; so that the women would not be aware of his emotions he quietly slipped to the outside, to stand in the darkness of the mountains he so dearly loved.

News traveled fast; by midnight dozens of men loitered around the lodge, drawn by morbid curiosity and the gruesome details of the murder that had swelled far beyond physical capabilities. *A three-hundred-pound woman was hung in the rafters from a single wire . . . her limbs were spread about, severed from the torso . . .* and so on and so on, until Storm thought he'd like to fetch a rifle and shoot the lot of spectators dead in their tracks.

He didn't like Marshal Crispin Black, who, months ago, had enjoyed the spectacle of hauling him to his trial manacled hand and foot. But he had to give the man credit for the investigation he now made at the scene of Sister Michael's murder. He had even had the forethought to inform the town's photographer, Mr. Searle, who had brought all his equipment despite the darkness that would require him to wait until morning. The coroner was among the men lingering, waiting until light when the pictures could be taken, so that he could gather together all parts of the corpse for its journey to the mortuary, where some effort would be made to put it in some semblance of order for display in the coffin.

Marshal Crispin Black talked to all residents at the compound. By the time the haze of dawn began to erase the dark, he had put together a somewhat logical outline of the murder of Sister Michael. Dr. Isaac Frick said she had been dead for twenty-four to thirty hours, which would have put the death at between six and midnight of the preceding day. She had not struggled, so death had been instantaneous. After taking statements from the residents, he felt that the killer must have had some knowledge of the layout of the compound, as well as access to the Lodge of Sisterhood.

The marshal had to have a suspect. But when he looked at the women, their faces dragging in agony and eyes red from weeping, he quickly eliminated them, as well as Old Potts, whom Crispin Black had known all of his life. Who was left?

Storm Phillips . . .

But why would he do something so evil? Even Crispin Black, who disliked him immensely, thought that to rule Storm out was the sensible thing to do.

So, for the time being, and because elections were coming up soon and he needed to maintain some degree of popularity, he would eliminate Storm from the list of suspects. The judge had given him a good word, which the people of the county valued, and Crispin Black would not contradict that character assessment.

As he finalized his investigation, he took possession of Sister Michael's journal, thinking it might reveal a clue. Perhaps she had a personal enemy, someone who would kill and mutilate her body so heinously. He would have to find this monster, or he could forget his job at election time.

After the harrowing night of investigation, which lasted well into the morning, the crime scene was finally cleaned up. Sister Michael's corpse was loaded into the mortician's wagon for the journey into Granger, where it would receive a complete autopsy. When, as the last duty of business before departing with his men, the marshal ordered the huge mob of morbid spectators back to their homes, some normalcy returned to the Lodge of Sisterhood.

Sick at heart, Storm moved across the clearing, past the skeletal structure of the church being built, and sought the solitude of the woods. Naturally, no work had been done that day, and Sister Joseph, following the direction of Tallie's gaze, quietly said, "It is some time to himself the young man needs. We'll be tolerant of Brother Storm, in memory of our dear Sister Michael."

Though she'd discovered the body, had sat through the ordeal of weeping women and the wretched sobbing of poor Brookie, Tallie had somehow managed to maintain her composure through the day. But now, hearing Sister Michael's name spoken once again, she quietly succumbed to her own grief.

Because she knew, now that she was able to think sensibly for the first time since last night, that a very familiar killer was at loose in the mountains. There was no other explanation.

For lack of another suspect, she felt that it had to be Farrand Beattie.

Bart Johnson returned to the ranch, having spent almost the entire day among the spectators at the site of the new church. He'd stayed well back from the buildings, so that Storm would not know he was there. Now, he moved into the kitchen to make fresh reports to Thea and the Englishman, who had been receiving news every couple of hours, along with the rumors abounding.

Bart had felt like a damn spy, and he let the Englishman, who'd requested that he go out there, know it.

"Why did you not say something this morning?" asked Farrand. "I would have gone myself."

"Weren't just you. Mack wanted me to go out there, too. Thought maybe it was Storm what killed that woman."

"He thought no such thing!" Thea's retort was quick and

heated. Though she knew Mack didn't like Storm, and had been upset about finding him at the ranch yesterday, he would never believe Storm to be a killer.

Bart shrugged, taking up the cup of coffee Thea had been bringing to him, and that was now half tossed on the table in her anger. Without comment, he wiped up the bit that had spilled, quietly tucking the soiled handkerchief he'd used into the back pocket of his Levi's.

"Any speculations as to who committed the crime?"

"Sure," said Bart, his laugh without humor. "Ol' Jack the Ripper, fer one. An' somebody overheard Crispin Black askin' if Storm could do somethin' like that, an' one ol' codger said maybe it was a bear come in, sliced the lady's throat real clean-like, then took to cleanin' out her innerds." Looking over the rim of the coffee cup held to his mouth, Bart continued, "Some even think it was *you*, Englishman." Then, "Where were you night before las'? Thea's boy said you didn't come back to your bunk until well after four yesterd'y mornin'."

"Of course not," replied Farrand Beattie, straight-faced, but straining to keep back his anger. "I was out slashing up a good Christian woman."

Thea had stood quietly back, listening in on their conversation. The Englishman *had* acted rather strangely last evening, and he *had* been away from the ranch all night. Could he have gone to the site of the church, found an unwary woman lingering about and taken a knife to her?

Without fully thinking it all through, Thea asked, "*Did* you kill her, Farrand?"

He stood suddenly, so outraged by the query that he could have screamed a torrent of vulgarities at her. He was, after all, in love with this common American kitchen servant and that she could cast such an aspersion on his character left him cold inside.

He moved into the dying day, saddled his horse and rode off into the mountains, hoping that he might once again get lost, and this time for good.

He had such a vague recollection of the torturous night he'd spent lost on the trails that he bloody well could be Jack the Ripper!

Three days later

Marshal Crispin Black had put together an investigative file so lengthy and filled with details he'd had to buy a special portfolio from Chadwick's mercantile to accommodate it. He was especially intrigued by the newspaper accounts of the London murders, which were very similar to the slaying of the woman, newspaper accounts he had clipped at the time they'd appeared and set aside to read in his leisure.

With elections coming up the following November, he did not want to hurry the investigation and risk an error that might ensure his defeat. Therefore, he sat down, wrote a letter to Sir Charles Warren, the Commissioner of the Metropolitan Police in London, who had been in charge of the Whitechapel killings, and enclosed the autopsy photographs of Sister Michael's corpse, as well as the news account in their own *Granger Weekly* and some of his notes of the investigation into this latest murder.

While he waited for a reply, he'd posted a man at the Lodge of Sisterhood, to protect the women and to keep an eye on Storm Phillips. Though he had not advertised his suspicions, the half-breed Cherokee remained at the top of his list of suspects.

Crispin Black would like nothing better than to see Storm Phillips back behind prison walls.

He'd been found guilty of train robbery and had received a just sentence at the hands of the judge following the verdict of a duly appointed jury.

Judge Isaac Grisham had no business setting him loose in the mountains when the law said he should be locked up good and tight.

* * *

Isaac Grisham and Hiram Frick sat in the judge's parlor, going over the details of the killing. Being a close friend of the county coroner, Hiram had obtained copies of the photographs, as well as the coroner's autopsy report. The one conclusion that he'd reached from viewing the nicks in Sister Michael's ribs was that the killer favored his left hand.

"We've got to find this maniac," Isaac Grisham blew steam across the surface of his coffee, watching it swirl hypnotically. "I fear it might possibly be someone we know."

"You don't think Storm—"

"No!" He had not meant to snap. Setting the cup down, he amended, "Storm cares deeply for those women. And I believe he is in love with Tallie. He hasn't said so, but I see the way he looks at her."

"Potts, then?"

"Potts can barely see to his business over the bulge of a whiskey gut. Even round Sister Michael could have outdistanced him if he'd posed a threat to her. It isn't Potts."

"Then who?"

Isaac thought for a moment. "My money is on the Englishman out at the Phillips Ranch."

Now, this was a surprising revelation. Hiram Frick had looked in on the Englishman the same day he'd learned he was being cared for by the woman, Thea, and he'd been quite a pleasant fellow. Thea had done a competent job of treating the bullet wounds, though Hiram wasn't sure why he hadn't been sent for when it had happened. He imagined that one of the men at the ranch might have been responsible, and Thea hadn't wanted anyone to know. She was, after all, the mother of MacCallister Phillips's second son and fiercely protective of the men who worked for him.

Hiram shook his head. "No, the man isn't a killer. You're wrong, Isaac."

Judge Grisham popped his knuckles slowly, one at a time.

"Two aging old men sitting around talking about a killing. We're a fine pair, aren't we, Hiram?"

"I've got a feeling that Tallie is in danger."

Isaac nodded thoughtfully. "She hasn't told me much, no more than she's told you, I'd imagine, but Storm mentioned to me that she claimed to have witnessed the final Whitechapel killing and knows who the killer is. I wonder if she told that to Crispin Black?"

"I don't believe she did."

"Don't you wonder why?"

"Of course. Perhaps we should have a talk with our Miss Edwards? You up to driving out there, Isaac?"

"Not today, Hiram. Martha is stirring up a fine stew." With a funny little laugh he added, "And if I don't go home, she'll feed it to the dog!" He arose now, with the effort required of a man feeling defeated by advancing age, and added, "I'll fetch my coat . . . and go home to that stew."

Tallie sat on the bed and read the letter again: *miss edwards, i cut the sisters throt let her bled took her kidne fried it and ate it tasty old sister cud be next one to die shoe my letter to anyone old sister die tonite prasarve old sister be me next victim catch me if you can jack the ripper*

She read and reread the unpunctuated note with no capital letters, becoming more horrified at each reading. She recalled that after Kate Eddowes's murder, the chairman of the newly formed Whitechapel Vigilance Committee, a man named George Lusk, had received a similar letter accompanying a box containing what had turned out to be a human kidney.

She didn't know what to do, but she knew she couldn't let anyone know she'd gotten the letter. The killer might be watching her, and she could not put Sister Joseph in such danger.

All through the day, she tried to engage herself in her usual routine, helping a solemn Brookie in the kitchen, watching Storm and Old Potts finishing the framing for the church and stacking roofing materials nearer to the building site. Thereafter, she took her afternoon walk in the forest, taking the small derringer Storm had insisted she keep with her. Unsure of where he'd gotten it, she dropped it into the pocket of her skirt as she sneaked past the guard Marshal Crispin Black had posted for their protection. Soon, she reached the solitude of what she'd jokingly referred to as "the love cabin." She almost hoped the killer would show up, so that she could shoot him and get it over with.

Dear God . . . what was she to do?

Stretching out on the cot, she felt in her pocket for the horrid letter she'd received. She read it again, though she didn't know why she'd felt the need. She'd read it so many times that she knew every word by heart, every lack of punctuation, every half-illiterate curve of the letters. *Jack the Ripper wrote this letter!* she told herself over and over in her mind. *He has followed you here, he knows your habits, and he will kill everyone precious and dear to you. Why does he hate me so much? What am I to do? Where am I to go?*

But she knew she would go nowhere. As she lay upon the cot, she buried her head in the poufed sleeve of her dress and wept quietly.

So distraught was she that she did not hear the approaching footsteps just outside the door.

Brookie needed a cut of beef from the smoke house, but she refused to go into the building herself. Rather, she called Storm down from the rafters of the new church.

"I need a bit of meat to prepare for supper. Will ye fetch it to me?"

He was a little annoyed; since the murder Brookie had refused to enter the smokehouse, claiming that an encounter with Sister Michael's ghost would cause her heart to stop. "Where is Tallie? She would have gotten it for you."

"I saw the lass sneak past the guard half an hour ago,"

Brookie replied. "And I did need her to help me with the cooking. I airn't sure what's got into her today."

"I suppose, Brookie, the same thing that's gotten into all of us this week," Storm grumbled. Sweeping back his black hair, he began to fasten the buttons of his shirt that had become undone in his labors. "I'll get the meat for you, and then I'll see where Tallie has gone."

"Thank ye much, Mr. Phillips."

"Name's Storm."

She made no comment as she handed him the key to the smokehouse. Unlocking the door, he entered without hesitation; the grisly pools of Sister Michael's blood had been completely washed away after the removal of her body. Several times he came to the door with a different cut of meat, until he presented one that Brookie thought would be satisfactory.

Brookie returned to the kitchen, and Storm moved toward the mountain trail that forked off toward their special cabin. He paid no attention to Crispin Black's posted guard, a heavyset man named Sam Kerr, who worked part-time as a deputy, but when the butt of the man's rifle jabbed into his back, he halted, pivoting so quickly toward him that he had to step back.

"Where you goin', Phillips?"

He looked first at the butt of the gun, still nudging against his shirt, then into the watery blue eyes of Sam Kerr. "Tallie Edwards has gone off in the woods alone and I don't believe it's safe."

"You just get back to work. I'll find her."

In one swift move, Storm's fingers gripped the rifle and snapped it from the startled man's hands. By the man's yelp he thought perhaps he had broken his index finger when it had ripped away from its resting place against the trigger. Slinging the gun back at him, Storm hissed, "I will find Miss Edwards. You, Sam, need to keep a watchful eye around here like you were told to do!"

With that, he entered the woods, soon leaving the trail to take the short cut toward the cabin.

Dusk was only an hour away, and yet the woods were deep and dark, almost eerily alive as a summer breeze wafted through the treetops. Storm paused for a moment upon the blanket of rotting leaves in a shallow dale, looking for the menace he could feel crawling through his skin like fire. For the first time that he could remember in his lifetime, the woods he loved so much were sinister and foreboding, almost as if evil hung on every limb and bramble. He didn't like the fear he felt inside; he thought that if he took a step, some treacherous thing would snake out of the ground to capture his foot and drag him into the bowels of the earth. The sky became purple above the treetops, the wind wailed like a banshee—

And just as he thought he might sink to his knees, he heard a high-pierced scream rake the forest and leave the gleam of frozen fear, like a winter blizzard dragging limbs to the ground beneath the packed weight of snow.

Chapter Twenty-one

The nightmare had seemed so terribly real.

Tallie, who had fallen asleep on the cot, now sat quaking in her fear. She had grown somewhat fearful, in view of everything that had happened these past few days, that she'd have one of the nightmares that had plagued her months ago. Orienting herself quickly as to time and place, she now heard the crackling of twigs outside the door. Pressing a palm to the mattress, she found the small weapon, then bolted upright, her pale hair dragging against her damp cheek.

"Who is there?" she called tentatively, and when the crackling suddenly ceased, she tightened her grip on the derringer and pointed toward the door. "Is anyone there?" she called again, and still there was no answer.

She *knew* someone was outside; she could hear the deadly, suspicious silence in the small clearing around the cabin. Then the door stirred and she shot to her feet, the little derringer now taking steady aim as she awaited the intruder.

The door opened wide. Relief swept immediately over her as the dark, familiar outline of Storm Phillips hovered against the withdrawing light of day.

"What are you doing here, Tallie?" he asked. "It was foolish to come here alone, what with a killer in the mountains."

She shrugged as she responded, "I needed solitude, and I was quite willing to take the risks."

"Foolish," he mumbled, taking her in his arms to hold her close. "I don't know what I would do if anything happened to you. I would take off into these mountains, become a grizzled old bear reeking of whiskey—just like Old Potts—and never would these eyes set sight on mankind again."

"You are being rather dramatic, are you not? Why, I shall wager you have any number of lasses waiting to warm your bed."

"I want you, Tallie. Only you." Drawing back, he dropped his gaze to the derringer. "Would you really have shot me with that thing?"

"Not you, but anyone else who might have come through that door."

An amused gaze skittered onto his face. "Of course, Tallie. And I can see horses flying, too." She wrapped her arms around him and her cheek moved to his chest, so firmly that the pressure was like a brick.

"I'm so glad you are here, Storm. I was feeling terribly blue . . . and I needed to be with you."

"Are you upset over Sister Michael's funeral tomorrow?"

She was, of course, but she was also upset over the horrid note she had found under her door. A note she could not tell Storm about, because it could cause Sister Joseph's death if the killer found out she'd shown it to anyone. So, she simply responded, "Yes, I am," and left it at that. Now looking up into his dark, brooding features, she said, "May we spend some time alone, Storm? I really do need to be with you."

His fingers caressed her shoulder, his mouth capturing her trembling one in a gentle kiss. "I think time together will do us both some good," he replied, sinking to the small cot to hold her close.

Storm held Tallie against him, his cheek against her pale,

damp hairline, his fingers gently massaging her arm through the cool material of her dress. He knew he had work to do before nightfall, and Old Potts was probably wondering where he'd gone off to—or was he?—and that the guard, Sam Kerr, might possibly come looking for them. No! That wouldn't happen; he was under orders from Crispin Black not to leave the church women alone at the compound.

So, Storm held her close, enjoying the warmth of her, wanting to lie there beside her and never have to move a muscle as long as he lived.

He could see that she was worried; a fear clung to her features that was so tangible he could almost reach out and grasp it. Had she learned something about the killing and was afraid to tell him? If she still did not trust him enough to confide in him, that was something he did not feel he could tolerate.

Tallie was wondering what he was thinking. His eyes had darkened to the color of a storm-tossed sky, and his mouth was pinched tightly, the way she'd seen it when he was annoyed, or angry. She didn't want him to worry. Rather, she wanted him to find warmth and comfort in her arms and think of nothing but their being together, being in love, and facing the future together.

Almost as if he had read her thoughts, Storm now turned, propping his head on his palm. "I was thinking, Tallie, if you're willing to listen to another of my aggravating proposals, I would like to tell you what I plan for our future."

"Oh? What *you* plan? Why not what we plan?" When his gaze darkened even more, she gently shrugged. "All right, I will listen to another *aggravating* proposal as you tell me what you plan for our future—"

Suddenly, he turned and pinned her beneath him, his mouth mere inches away from her own as he murmured, "I wanted to talk about our tomorrows and all our tomorrows thereafter, but Tallie, in view of your sarcasm, now I just want to think about the next few minutes. I . . ." A rough caress grazed her cheek as his mouth came to rest at the corner of her own. "I want to be surrounded by you, Tallie, to be inside you, to love you and have you love me. That is the only future I want to discuss right now."

Normally, such talk would have met with her annoyance, since she considered it vulgar. But she found her body responding to the naughtiness of his narration, and wanting much, much more than mere words. She wanted to feel his powerful, commanding hands moving to her back with rough passion to draw her close to him. She wanted to feel his hot breath against her cheek as he whispered endearments, and to tunnel her fingers through his thick, dark hair and drag his mouth to her own hungry, willing, waiting one.

"Conquer me, Storm. Take me into battle and conquer me."

He drew back, slightly amused, his eyes smiling, even though his mouth did not. "Conquer you? I see you more as a parlor with a warm hearth beckoning me, Tallie, not a cold, ruthless battle. Besides . . . I thought it was *you* conquering *me* this time."

The searing, never-ending kiss she now enjoyed caused fire to race through her veins and she responded almost impatiently, hating with a vengeance the barriers of the clothing separating their bodies. She loved the way his strong, protective arms surrounded her, pulling her to him, and when the buttons of his shirt were suddenly within reach, she used her teeth to unfasten them. His chuckle put an immediate halt to her erotic diversions.

"And what is so amusing?" she asked, a fine eyebrow arching slightly upward.

"I was just wishing *you* had buttons—"

She pulled slightly back, a smile skittering onto her mouth. "Buttons? I have something much better than buttons." Boldly taking his hands, she moved them to her breasts, so that he sat before her, gently cupping them. "Do you agree?"

His lusty growl was low; she almost did not catch it. Then he stood away from her, ripped his shirt down his arms and tossed it across his left shoulder. Where it fell he did not know and did not care. Now, he bent over her once again, his mouth assailing her willing one, teasing it beneath his hungry caresses, trailing over her crimson cheeks and along the fringes of her disheveled hairline. When he lowered his mouth to the edges of her bodice, he found something much more enticing to undo than buttons: long, thin satin ribbons crisscrossing her bodice, and he began to unfasten them with his tongue. Soon, oh so wonderfully soon, he was holding her slim wrists between his fingers and easing away the fabric of her gown. When his tongue began to trace a circle around her supple breasts, which had been freed from the tight bindings, she lifted herself against him.

She was so excited by the passionate caresses that she wanted only to be free of her gown, which had now twisted among her legs, when she would rather have his own twisted among them. As he fondled her bare breasts, she eased her body beneath him, her hands moving to the back of his neck to coax him down to her.

As she molded herself to the commanding rogue who had stolen her heart, she remembered the frightening letter tucked into the pocket of her skirt. The image of a vicious murderer caused a shudder of revulsion, and at once Storm drew away from her, his dark eyes grazing her own now tear-sheened ones.

"You do not want to do this?" he questioned grimly. "Why didn't you say so?" His hands lifted to cup her face as he looked deeply into her eyes. How lovely she was, her high-rose-colored cheeks, her sensual mouth slightly trembling, the tiny curls held to her forehead by dampness. With something akin to desperation, he pulled her to him and held her close, her passion-peaked breasts crushing into his bare chest. "Tallie, I am content to lie with you, to breathe the gentle fragrance of your skin, and to dream of our future. If you do not want to make love, I will understand."

Her hand moved, almost absently, to rest against his denim-covered hip. As her hand pulled away, it grazed his hard groin, and a sad smile touched her mouth. "You would be content to simply lie beside me? I think not, Storm Phillips. Certainly, I would not be content if you and I—"

Without words, he turned to pull off his boots, then his Levi's, which he dropped to the floor. Then his knees pressed into the cot's mattress and he pulled Tallie against him. For a moment he held her close, unmoving, feeling that if he let her go he would lose her forever. His body burst with want of her. When he let her fall back to the cot, he looked into her pale, oval face, his gaze instantly lowering to her small, milk-white breasts and the rosebuds that beckoned his caresses. How could he deny himself the taste of such sweetness, when one look into her eyes was all the invitation he needed? His fingers easing into the thick, tangled masses of her hair, he moved his body against the length of her own.

He was spellbound by her elegance, by the graceful way her hand bent and rested against her cheek as she looked at him. Slowly, erotically, stirring his passions to a height he thought would end in fireworks, he removed her clothing, his patience subsiding at once when she was fully naked beneath him.

Though he hungered lustily to be joined to her, he took the time to caress every inch of her exquisite loveliness, to love her the way he knew she wanted to be loved, to taste the honeyed sweetness of her mouth . . . and there . . .

Tallie knew he was aching; he had to be. His taut, well-endowed groin pulsated against her hip, his eyes as dark as the storm that was his name. The cabin was now in near darkness, and yet he was as visible to her as the love in her heart. She could imagine being with him nowhere else but this humble, run-down cabin, and when his hands caressed an arousing trail toward her back, her legs eased apart, an invitation to him. She saw his features darken, his mouth press the way it always did when they were ready to join, and as he slipped between her knees, lifting her buttocks slightly, she relished the velvet hardness of his complete masculinity easing into the depths of her as though he feared hurting her.

Now that he was inside her, he gently covered her body, his

fingers tunneling through her long tresses. "I love you, Tallie Edwards," he murmured against her neck. "I want to spend an eternity with you."

A kittenish moan escaped her mouth; he trailed kisses over her pert chin, along the slim column of her neck and the pale buds of her breasts. He loved the way her hazel eyes glazed with desire, the way her long, beautifully manicured fingernails gently crept over the hard muscles of his arms as she sought to draw him close.

Deftly, wanting only to satisfy her as completely as himself, he began to move within her . . . ah, the sweet agony of her, the seductive, arousing movements that made his body feel like a boiling cauldron. For a moment he paused, his hands cupping her flushed little face, his body remaining part of her own, and his gaze skittering lustily over her eyes, her mouth, her nose . . . then he was moving again, slowly, working to a hard drumming against her tender thighs, and when her legs lifted and her ankles crossed against the small of his back, she was offered fully to him.

It seemed that a thousand hours passed in the few minutes they remained joined to each other in joy and passion, before their breathing moved in ragged rhythm together and their hips melded as they moved swiftly in the rapture of their passion. Soon, oh so soon, their desire culminated, his seed scattered within her, and his damp forehead collapsed against her waiting shoulder.

Even now, her features darkened by the fall of night outside, Storm saw an illusion, an alluring woman whose pale tresses were like spun gold. He saw the woman of his dreams, of his future . . . of his heart . . . the woman he would sacrifice all to be with for the rest of his life. With a small groan, he withdrew from her, lay against her length and pulled her against him.

"Marry me, Tallie. I'll do anything, take any vow, if you will be my wife."

Her eyes were suddenly like pools, tear-sheened, deep, the pain almost as evident as the falling night. "Oh, Storm . . .

Storm—" She could think only of the threat she had received, not only to herself but to Sister Joseph as well. She loved Storm, and ultimately, she would be with him—she and Ellie—but she could not commit to marriage until this vicious killer was torn from her life.

"You didn't answer me, Tallie."

Her chin propped on his hard chest, her fingers easing beneath it. "I know."

"Will you give an answer? Or should I take your lack of one as a very firm no?"

"No, you should not do that." She attempted to brighten, so that he would not see the pain in her features. "You know that I want to be your wife, Storm, but I have asked that you wait until I have heard from my aunt. There are so many loose ends in my life—"

He drew away so quickly that it startled her. When he'd carelessly tossed her gown atop her naked form, he began to dress. "I suppose you have many loose secrets as well, Tallie, that you've taken special care to keep from me?"

"Do not be like this, Storm."

His words were hot and angry; his tone was cold and detached. "Don't be like what, Tallie?" Dropping to the cot, he pulled on his boots, then retrieved his shirt from the corner where he'd tossed it. "I'll wait outside until you dress. Don't be long. I've got more important things to do than molly-coddle evasive females."

When the door had closed, Tallie mumbled, "What will I do with you, Storm?," then began dressing. She loved him, but she hated his moods, hated that he was impatient and needed immediate commitments, and always had to have his own way. She hated that he thought of himself before anyone else and . . .

But that wasn't true. She was angry with him, but she knew that he was kindhearted and that she always came first in his thoughts, and his worries. She was being unfair and, she had to admit, he did deserve an answer to his proposal, since he'd asked several times now. Always, she'd put him off, and once had even managed to change the subject without his being the wiser.

He probably thought she was playing with him, mercilessly teasing him, and that she had no intentions of ever marrying him. Perhaps there were even times that he thought she did, indeed, have a husband back in London.

Since Marshal Crispin Black was riding out to the lodge anyway, Mr. Chadwick at the mercantile, who was also Granger's postmaster, sent the mail out that had come for the residents there. He now tossed the few parcels onto the table where the old cook was sitting and sat across from her to await Sister Joseph. Mrs. Newgate arose to summon her.

As Sister Joseph sat down to confer with the marshal, she took a moment to flip through the mail, thinking that a money order might have been sent from one of their supporters. None had, but she did notice the letter for Tallie from a man named Peter Leggett. Dismayed that Tallie had disobeyed her and let someone in London know where she was, Sister Joseph could scarcely concentrate on Crispin Black's inquiries.

She managed somehow to dutifully answer his questions—which she remembered answering several times before during the course of the marshal's investigation—but she was thinking about the letter still held in her hand. If Tallie had, indeed, defied her and written to London, could the killer she had been eluding have found out? The heinous killer from Whitechapel might have intercepted any correspondence Tallie had sent to London and followed her here. Sister Joseph believed that the man who had thus far killed half a dozen women in London was the same man who had killed poor Sister Michael. And now, from the questions Crispin Black was asking, there left no room for doubt that his thoughts were running the same course.

"So, you don't believe Sister Michael had any enemies who would have done this to her?"

The interrogation was winding down; this was the fourth time in the span of the last half hour that Crispin Black had asked her this question. "No, I do not. Sister Michael was loved by all. She had no enemies. She was happy with her life, content to be the Lord's servant and to engage in her daily prayers. No, Sister Michael did not have any enemies."

"Do *any* of you have enemies who would do this kind of harm to you?"

"No." Her response was flat, unfeeling; she was growing tired of the interrogation.

"What about the young woman with you? Tallie Edwards?"

Sister Joseph pressed her mouth firmly for a moment. "Miss Edwards has no enemies that I know of."

Startling both people sitting at the table, Brookie Newgate suddenly impaled the cutting board with her knife. Now she ripped the apron from her waist, wiped the vegetables she'd been paring aside with her forearm and exited the kitchen.

"And that woman?"

"Brookie? I don't know. She hasn't been with us very long."

"Where did she come from?"

Sister Joseph felt a solid moment of embarrassment as she realized she did not know, nor had she asked. She had claimed to have no home, and so Sister Joseph had welcomed her with open arms. After all, that is what the lambs of God were brought here for, to open their arms to the needy and ask no questions. "I don't know where she came from," she responded momentarily, "and it doesn't matter. She needed us and we opened our hearts to her." Then, "I will find a way to question her later in the evening. If you wish to visit tomorrow—"

"I'll do that." Crispin Black looked toward the window just then, and did not see Sister Joseph slip the letter addressed to Tallie Edwards into the deep folds of her skirt. "I won't trouble you any longer today."

When the gentleman looked toward the cooking pot Brookie had left on the stove, Sister Joseph, wishing to be polite, offered, "You are welcome to share our supper, Marshal Black. We normally eat at seven."

He patted his stomach. "It's past that now, and I see a pile of uncooked vegetables on that counter over there. I think you'll be late sittin' down to your supper this evenin', so I reckon I'll be on my way." When he reached the door, he turned and asked, rather exuberantly, "Did you hear some fellow's made an electric motor? Read it in the paper today." He wasn't sure why he felt the need to engage in small talk, and he really didn't need the old sister's opinion on the matter.

Sister Joseph held her skirt so that she would not lose Tallie's letter as she arose. "An electric motor, Marshal Crispin? Why would mankind need an electric motor when the Lord provides our every need?"

Crispin Black groaned inwardly, even as a smile forced its way onto his face. Nodding politely, he now moved into the outdoors.

When Brookie returned to the kitchen after the marshal and Sister Joseph had left, she looked for the letter addressed to Tallie she had seen Crispin Black drop to the table upon his arrival. It was not there now and she tried to reason why Sister Joseph wouldn't want Tallie to have it.

She and Tallie had talked at length; she knew about the murder Tallie had very nearly witnessed, about the dear child she had been forced to leave behind, and the aging aunt living in a small apartment in London's East End. She knew that Tallie had a lot of pain in her heart, and she had tried to be a friend to the young woman, to offer hope and encouragement and to always be nearby when she needed someone to talk to. Tallie had been waiting for a letter from London with so much hope that Brookie had silently joined in that hope. Now the letter had been spirited away, and for what reason?

But Brookie could not cause trouble at the lodge by telling Tallie about the letter. She would simply have to wait until Sister Joseph came forward with it. Perhaps she simply wanted to wait until after the funeral of Sister Michael tomorrow before turning the letter over to Tallie. Yes, that had to be it.

Brookie would say nothing for now. She had made the lodge her home, and she would not risk the wrath of the sisters and be forced to leave.

Returning to the cutting board, she resumed her labors over their dinner. Presently, Tallie entered, scooted past her toward her room, then emerged minutes later, her hair tidied and a clean dress pulled onto her slender frame. Brookie didn't have to wonder why Tallie felt the need to freshen up; without a doubt, she'd been wallowing somewhere with her young man.

But that was Tallie's business, and not Brookie's place to criticize.

"What can I do?" asked Tallie as she tied on her apron. "How long have the biscuits been in the oven?"

"I'd give them a few more minutes," responded Brookie, the reservation in her voice drawing Tallie's attention at once. "The potatoes need to be whipped, and don't add so much milk this time, dearie."

Tallie raised an eyebrow as she moved toward the steaming potatoes in the large stoneware bowl. "Is something wrong, Brookie?"

She was annoyed that Sister Joseph had taken the letter addressed to Tallie. She was annoyed that a funeral would take place tomorrow, because she hated such events, hated the feigned grief and sobbing they produced, the curiosity mongers who would appear from every crevass of the woods, hated the thought of the sisters wailing and praying for Sister Michael's soul, when she had unquestionably been the most righteous of the four. Yes, indeed, she hated the whole melodramatic business and wanted only for tomorrow to be over with.

But she did not tell Tallie that. Erasing the silence with a smile and a haughtily clipped "No, indeed, lass, nothing is wrong!," she turned to Tallie. "Shall we get this American grub on the table before the sisters send our souls to hell for lack of it?"

Tallie merely smiled, thankful for Brookie's exuberance for life and her gentle love for everyone, no matter their faults.

Chapter Twenty-two

Storm did not come to the table for his supper that night. Under questioning, Old Potts, told by Storm to keep quiet about his plans, admitted that he'd taken the wagon into Granger, to pick up supplies in the morning. He would stay the night at the judge's house.

Tallie missed him; she wished their last moments together had not been so tense, especially after they'd made such wonderful love together. Now that the supper dishes had been washed and she'd retired to her room, she had time to think about their short, solemn walk along the trail when they'd returned to the lodge. Storm's long strides had easily outdistanced her, and he'd seemed annoyed the few times he'd paused at a bend in the trail to await her. When he'd said good night at the front of his cabin, she had thought then that she wouldn't see him at the supper table. There had been a certain finality in the way he had left her, though she was well aware that he had stood in the darkness of the porch, watching her until she had entered the kitchen door of the lodge. Even when he was quiet and moody, he still worried about her.

Now, she threw herself on her bed and tucked her hands

beneath her tousled hair. Supper had been a solemn occasion, and Sister Joseph had gone over the details of Sister Michael's funeral tomorrow, delayed these few days because the coroner had insisted upon an autopsy. Sister Michael would wear one of her customary dark gowns, but Sister Joseph, having sent the garments to the mortuary early yesterday morning, had also included a small white cap, with an indulgence of modest white lace on its rim, which Sister Michael usually wore to bed at night. Tallie remembered how Sister Joseph had left the table in disgust when Sister Meade's concern had centered on whether or not the coffin would be opened during the service. It was the first time she'd ever heard Sister Joseph mutter an expletive, though it had been a relatively tame one. She imagined that Sister Joseph was now begging the Lord for forgiveness, though she could hear no muttered prayers beyond the boundary of the walls.

Storm had left the lodge for the night and Tallie was glad of the time she'd spent with him at the cabin. She wished she could have shown him the letter she had received from a killer she had fled from in London . . . a killer who had followed her to the mountain, just as Farrand Beattie had said that he would—

A knock sounded at the door. Pushing herself forward, Tallie's nerves jumped sky high. She was frightened of every little sound. "Who is there?"

"It is Brookie, dear lass. Might I have a wee word with ye?"

"Yes, come in, Brookie," and at once she entered, giving Tallie a small, apologetic smile.

She sat on the cot beside Tallie and dropped her large hands into her lap. She got right to the point. "Something is bothering ye, lass. Do ye wish to talk to me about it?"

Tallie shrugged. "What makes you think so, Brookie?"

Brookie smiled again, though sadly this time, her hand now covering one of Tallie's. "I can tell, lass, just as sure as ye be me own flesh and blood. Ye're like a child to me. Me own child, to be precise."

Tallie hugged her tightly. "Brookie I have really been much happier since you arrived. I . . ." Her hand now moved into the pocket of her dress and brought forth the note. "You must keep this to yourself. I found it under my door this morning."

Brookie took the letter and read the cryptic, threatening lines that almost boasted of the writer's power to cause the fear she now saw in Tallie's pretty features. "Ye don't believe this, lass? T'isn't from Jack, to be sure. Could it be the Mr. Beattie ye told me about?"

"It *must* be from the Ripper, Brookie, though I have my doubts about Mr. Beattie being him. Who else would write this? Who else could have killed Sister Michael? Brookie . . ." Tallie didn't like thinking that perhaps Mr. Beattie had been right, and so hesitated to speak the words to the likable woman she had known only a short while. "Is it possible the killer is after me, personally, and that the others simply got in his way?"

"After ye personally, lass?" She paused as if considering it. "Why?"

Another light shrug affected Tallie's shoulders, "I do not know." Dropping her head against her drawn-up knees, she exclaimed with more emotion, "Oh, I really do not know!"

"Pardon me impertinence, lass, but I'll pertect ye with me own life if must be. Ye, an' the old sisters, ye be kind to me. Brookie, she will'nt forget."

Surprise jumped into Tallie's eyes. "Brookie, you are in as much danger as the rest of us."

She visibly shuddered. "I din't think of that, lass. Nay, I din't think of that."

"Do you think some mean person sent this to me simply because I am English? Could it have been sent simply to frighten me? Oh, Brookie, please, tell me what you think about it. Is it because it is an English crime and I am an English woman? Or could it truly be a letter from the Ripper?"

"Because we are English," Brookie began on a quiet note,

"we tend to keep up with things that be English. We have kept up, ye and I, with the murderous rages of this Jack the Ripper. We know things about him, because he, too, is English, that most people din't know. And I tell ye, lass, this letter did not come from the Ripper. It is some bloke's idea of a joke, in very poor taste, I might add, and if I were ye, I'd toss it with the trash."

"I cannot take that chance, Brookie. If I ignore it, and if Sister Joseph is killed, I will never forgive myself. I must find this treacherous fiend myself and end the horror, both to me and to the women here at the lodge."

"A wee snip of a lass like ye, Tallie?"

Tallie's voice suddenly became hard, almost mean, as she took the letter from Brookie and stuffed it back into her pocket. "I have been afraid, Brookie, thinking only of my own safety. Now, I have made the decision to find this fiend, and I shall not change my mind. After the funeral tomorrow I shall begin a little sleuthing of my own."

The gentle old cook arose, moved to the door, then said in departure, "Good night then, sweet lass. Do what ye must."

Storm returned in time for the funeral at ten o'clock. People were arriving in wagons and on horseback; a family of eleven arrived on foot, and everyone stood around the grave Potts had dug early that morning, waiting for the hearse to arrive with Sister Michael's body. Soon, the black-and-glass-enclosed bier on wheels pulled into the clearing. The judge and Hiram Frick arrived together, and Tallie made it a point to speak with them before the funeral. She could tell by the judge's mood that he and Storm had spoken at length last night, and she was a little embarrassed by the way he looked at her in silence, as though he couldn't quite understand her. Imagining what Storm might have said twisted her inside, bringing a moment of anger that she found very difficult to hide.

Sister Joseph had ordered a nice wooden coffin with brass

trimmings to take Sister Michael into eternity. Considering herself something of an ordained minister, she had decided she would speak the sermon herself. Tallie imagined that many in the region, getting wind of Sister Joseph's officiation over the rites, had come out of curiosity, since many thought that only a man could speak directly to the Lord on behalf of another's soul.

During the service, Tallie watched Storm's bronze visage, the reverent bowing of his head, the way he deliberately refused to meet her gaze. He was almost inanimate until a male voice far at the back of the crowd yelled, "Let's see the sister's corpse," and then he moved in that direction, his hands balled into fists as he sought out the source of the interference. Seeing the dark anger in Storm's expression, several men departed then, so Tallie never really knew which of them had been so irreverent.

Sister Joseph spoke a fine service over dear Sister Michael, and when the coffin was eventually lowered into the ground by four of the men present, the crowd began to disperse. Tallie looked for Storm, but he had disappeared into the woods.

She needed to talk to someone she cared about—someone besides Brookie, who was a little annoyed that she would try to find the Ripper herself—so she decided to go to Fanny's house.

Old Potts saddled one of their horses, issued an order to Tallie that she was to shoot anyone who got closer than ten feet to her, which she promised halfheartedly to do. Soon, she moved onto the road for the short journey to Fanny's. She caught up to the buggy bearing Hiram Frick and Isaac Grisham, chatted with them for a few minutes, and then left them at the road leading to the house shared by John and Fanny Collins. When she reached the porch, she pulled up, then sat atop her horse until Fanny emerged from the house.

"Tallie, it is so nice, to see you."

"I was afraid you were ill, since you and John didn't come to the funeral."

Fanny's hand moved up to the bodice of her dress, to fumble with a cameo brooch she had pinned to her dress. "I have not been able to attend a funeral since I lost my twins, Tallie."

Tallie now hopped down, tied the reins of the horse and swished out her skirts to dislodge them from her ankles. When she stood before Fanny, she quietly replied, "I am so sorry . . ." then captured Fanny's hand and held it warmly. "And I do understand."

They entered the parlor, where Fanny had just placed a tray of freshly brewed tea. Fanny smiled as she said, "John is out at his work bench, so you can have his cup. I'll make him another when he returns." She could see that Tallie was troubled; quietly, her hand dropped to Tallie's cool one. "You look like you need to talk, Tallie." Then, "I'm glad you came here. I care deeply for you, as you know."

Tallie smiled. "That is why I am here, my friend." Accepting the cup from Fanny now, she held it for a moment, then set it back on the tray. "Fanny, I am in a lot of trouble." When Fanny started to question her, Tally's hand went gently up. "I do not wish to talk about the trouble right now, because I have a much more important issue on my mind. Fanny . . ." Her eyes dropped, her hands settling into her skirts. "Fanny," she began again, "if something should happen to me, will you contact my aunt in London?"

Her hand went into her pocket and brought forth several letters and a small bit of paper. She handed the paper to Fanny. "This is her address on Bergen Street."

A tremble settled into Fanny's mouth, even as she smiled her reassurances. "Nothing is going to happen to you, Tallie, and if it did—God forbid—wouldn't one of the sisters notify your aunt?"

"I suppose that they would, but they have trouble enough of their own right now and . . ." She balked noticeably at continuing, because she could not reveal that her danger was imminent, but she needed a confidante. "Should it come to contacting my aunt, I have written letters, both to my aunt and to my daughter, Ellie. Will you see that they are posted? I shall be so appreciative."

Fanny had never seen Tallie like this; it frightened her very much. Taking the letters, she attempted to make light of Tallie's request. "It is better to be overly cautious," she said, putting the letters on the table, then handing the cup back to Tallie. "Now . . . drink your tea and tell me what is worrying you so much."

Tallie was in tears by the time she returned. She dismounted the horse and turned it over to Old Potts, then moved swiftly into the lodge, disappearing into her private room. Brookie would expect her to help with the day's cooking and baking, but she really wasn't in a mood. There were times when she felt she was simply getting in Brookie's way, because half of what she did, the dear woman undid when she'd sent her off on a errand.

She wanted only to be alone, and so was a little disappointed when someone knocked on her door. She gave permission to enter, and at once Sister Joseph moved into the room. She stood beside Tallie's bed, her gaze critical, and Tallie felt that the polite thing to do would be to stand. So that is what she did.

Sister Joseph's hand went out, her fingers pinched tightly over the letter Tallie had received. "This came yesterday but I decided to wait until after Sister Michael's funeral to give it to you. If it is good news, it would not be appropriate at the same time as a funeral. If it is bad news, I did not want to add this additional worry. I hope you understand."

She had waited months for a letter from home; a day really didn't matter one way or another. "Thank you, Sister Joseph," she replied, taking the letter to give it a quick examination. She was immediately alarmed that it was from Peter Leggett and not from her aunt. Had Cora been too upset to write herself when she'd received Tallie's letter? It wrenched her heart that she might have caused her dear aunt even more pain.

When Sister Joseph hesitated, Tallie looked at her, at which time she explained, "Do you wish that I stay while you read your letter?"

"If you will not mind, I think I should rather be alone," Tallie replied. "But thank you for offering."

Sister Joseph immediately withdrew and Tallie, her hands trembling now, sat on the edge of her bed to open Peter Leggett's letter. It read:

My dearest Tallie,

How happy I am to hear from you, though I am distressed that your letter came directly. Cora and I had both expected you to be discreet and I pray that your dear letter was not intercepted.

I am happy to report that Ellie is well and happy with the Pippenses, loving the pony I gave her, and looking forward to going on holiday in July to the Isle of Wight. She sends her love and asks that you write her.

It is with a broken heart that I inform you our dear Cora passed away in April. She did not suffer, Tallie, and she loved you with all her heart.

Tallie immediately dropped the letter into the folds of her skirt, the sobs now wracking her body making it physically impossible for her to sit up. She sank against her pillow and wept for her dear aunt and for not being with her in her final days and for the worry she had brought upon her and that might possibly have contributed to her death.

"Oh, Aunt Cora, Aunt Cora . . ." she sobbed, and at once a large, familiar hand touched upon her shoulder, then stroked her hair affectionately. Pushing herself up, she accepted Brookie's tender hug. "Brookie . . . my aunt . . . died," she whispered brokenly. "My dear, wonderful aunt, who raised me as her own."

"Lass, I am so sorry for yer pain." Then, "And what of yer wee lass?"

"She is safe with friends near Liverpool," Tallie managed to reply. "Please—" She handed the letter to Brookie. "Will you read the last paragraph of the letter?"

Brookie took the letter, skimmed over the almost feminine handwriting of the man named Peter Leggett, then concentrated on the final paragraph. *'My dear Tallie, there are matters that I urgently need to discuss with you, that cannot be discussed in this letter. It is imperative that I see you soon. If I must, I will come to America in the early part of July and journey to Granger to see you. Please expect me between July fifth and tenth, and please, dear, be careful. Do not trust anyone, no matter how kind to you. Keep your guard constantly up, and when we talk, you will understand.*" Brookie continued to look over the letter. "Your Mr. Leggett signed it, *'Your lifelong friend, Peter Leggett.'*"

Brookie stood, the move almost mechanical. "I'll return to me kitchen duties now. I am sure ye wish to be alone for a while."

Tallie smiled sadly. "I would like to be with Storm, but he is angry with me."

"Shall I fetch him to you?"

"He is not allowed in my room," Tallie said. Then, "Brookie, will you ask him to meet me at the cabin this afternoon at three o'clock?"

"O'course, lass."

Storm came down the ladder, peeved as hell. "What makes Tallie think she can issue orders that I meet her at a certain time? Tell her I'm too busy."

"I am simply delivering a message," said Brookie, turning away from the building site. "Needn't get flip with me, young man."

"I'm sorry," he ground out the apology, "but I am too busy to answer her summons."

Brookie continued to put distance between them. "I'll tell

her. It is just as well. Since she received news that her old auntie passed away in London, she should really spend some time alone."

"What?" Storm immediately caught up to Brookie, placing a hand over her wide shoulder. "Her aunt Cora died? Is that what you said?"

"Tallie received a letter today. She is quite melancholy. But . . ." Physically removing Storm's hand, Brookie continued, "but I wouldn't worry about Tallie, if I were you. Go on back to your important work."

"Tell her I'll meet her at the cabin at three, Brookie. And please don't tell her I was annoyed."

Brookie was quickly approaching the kitchen entrance. Across her shoulder, she called, "Very well, Mr. Phillips. I'll not tell her."

Brookie went straight to Tallie's room and knocked on the door, then patiently waited for her to stir within.

A weeping, heartbroken Tallie had fallen asleep. At first she had not heard the knock, but as she slowly reached for the conscious world, the knock came again, like the pounding of a drum in her ears. She arose, found her footing, then approached and pulled the door open.

"The young man said he is much too busy to meet ye," Brookie said. "He was quite annoyed that ye'd summoned him like a servant. He said to leave him alone for the remainder of the day and he'll see ye when it is convenient to him."

No emotion moved Tallie. "All right." She could understand if he was still angry with her; she had, after all, turned down his latest proposal of marriage and she was sure his pride was wounded. Nonetheless, Brookie's news came as somewhat of a surprise. "Did you tell him that my aunt had passed away?"

"I told him, lass. He said he was sorry for yer loss, but he is still too busy to see ye today."

Dropping her gaze, her bottom lip beginning to tremble, Tallie drew back from the door. "Thank you, Brookie."

Tallie closed the door, then moved back to her cot and fell heavily to it. Immediately, a knock sounded again at the door. When she arose, approached and opened it, Brookie was standing there once again. "I took the young man yer message. He said he will meet ye at the cabin at three o'clock."

Tallie was so confused that she felt she'd been hit with a hammer. "What? But you just told me he was too busy to see me. Not even a minute ago—"

Brookie's head cocked to the side. "Tallie, are ye all right, lass? I've not been to yer room before."

"Yes, you—" Tallie's argument immediately ceased. She *had* been asleep; perhaps she had merely dreamed that Brookie had come a moment ago, bearing ugly news of Storm's rejection. Certainly, she preferred to think that Storm was going to make time for her this afternoon rather than hearing he was much too busy to see her. "All right, Brookie," she said after a moment. "Thank you for bringing me the message."

Brookie retreated down the corridor toward the kitchen and Tallie closed herself in her room, shaking her head to dispel the bewilderment clinging to her like vines.

Brookie returned to the kitchen. Soon, the familiar humming reverberated through the large building as she put together the makings of a sandwich lunch, then began preparations for a supper they would not soon forget.

Storm was already at the cabin when Tallie arrived. When she entered and saw him sitting on the cot, his eyes pressed into his palms, she gently closed the door, then stood against it until he looked up. Their gazes met; his were free of any anger, showing sympathy for her loss.

"Thank you for coming," Tallie said, now pushing herself up from her slumped position.

He arose, momentarily closing her in his embrace. "I am so sorry about your aunt. I know how precious she was to you." Then, "Your Ellie is all right, Tallie?"

''She is fine and with friends.''

''Is there anything I can do?''

''I just want you to hold me.''

''I'm always here for you, Tallie,'' he responded sweetly against her hair, ''even when I'm not too happy with you.''

''Which seems to be often,'' she said with a halfhearted laugh. ''I am so sorry that I annoy you. My life is in such an upheaval right now, and it would be so unfair to drag you into the middle of it.''

''Did it ever occur to you that there is nowhere I would rather be than in the middle of your life?''

''I know, Storm. We both have our problems. Me with the Ripper, and you with your father.''

''And my criminal past. If I don't toe the line to the judge's liking, I could be back behind prison walls.''

Tallie drew slightly away, a small smile easing onto her face as she gazed into his dark eyes. ''I think the judge approves of the way you are toeing the line, Storm. And you said yourself that you are not guilty. That will come out eventually, to be sure.'' Tucking herself back into his arms for a final embrace, she said, ''I know you have work to do. Shall we return to the lodge?''

''I suppose I must,'' responded Storm, unwilling to relinquish the velvety softness of her within his arms. ''Let's leave here, Tallie, and vow not to be angry with each other. I know things are hard on you right now, and I won't push you to make a decision until you are ready. My proposal will remain valid.''

Tallie accepted his gentle kiss, and when they entered the trail a minute or so later, she felt guilty that she had not shared her greatest fear of all . . . the Ripper.

Crispin Black was just leaving the marshal's office in Granger when he made a startling discovery. When a spraddled Crispin turned over on the boardwalk to see what he'd tripped over so that he could give it a good cursing, his other part -time deputy, Kit Everly, was already examining the item in question.

"Well, I'll be daggumed," Kit Everly muttered in disbelief. "Looks like the box from that train robbery." They dragged it into the office and, momentarily, the lamp was lit and Crispin Black was digging in his desk drawer for a hammer and chisel.

The lock was soon broken loose. When Crispin opened it, shocked to see the stacks of money and sacks of loose twenty-dollar gold pieces, he pushed his hat back from his forehead. "Hell, Kit, this is the train money. What do you reckon Storm Phillips returned it for?" Before a response could be given, he ordered, "Go get the judge."

"And leave you alone with all that money?" Kit replied, his laughter ceasing when Crispin Black narrowed his eyes in certain threat. "All right, I'm going."

Alone now, Crispin Black sank into his chair, wondering what surprises would come next in this job.

Brookie had set a fine table, using the white linen tablecloth she'd found in a pantry. Though only three plates actually matched, the setting looked wonderful, and she had put a large bowl of wildflowers in the middle of the table. The occupants of the compound had taken their places, Sisters Joseph and Pete at the ends, Sister Meade and Brookie on one side, and Tallie and Old Potts on the other. Storm was absent from the gathering, and Old Potts mentioned that he'd ridden into Granger.

Sister Joseph said the blessing, keeping it short, then explaining immediately after that "there is no sense to be made of letting this wonderful food get cold."

Tallie accepted their glasses one at a time and poured the cold milk. Brookie cut the roast beef and served a hefty portion to each plate, and then began passing the bowls.

Sister Meade commented on the wonderful mushrooms, placing a large portion on her plate. Sister Joseph took a few, as did Tallie, who tasted one, didn't care for it, and eased it discreetly to the side.

Tallie had a habit of cutting all of her meat in small pieces at once. As she did so, she noticed that Brookie had not taken a helping of mushrooms. "Do you dislike them?" she asked.

To which Brookie, with a coarse laugh, responded, "I ate so many while I was cooking that I almost cannot bear to look at them now. I'ave had me fair portion. Now, eat. Eat! All of you."

"Well, I ain't a gonna eat them thangs," Old Potts grumbled. "They's disgustin'. I seen 'em out in them woods with bugs a walkin' all over 'em. No, sirree, I ain't a gonna eat 'em!"

Sister Joseph's spoon immediately rapped upon the table. "Silence," she ordered, "let us observe our meal with dignity."

By the time Tallie pushed herself from the table, she thought she would pop all the buttons of her dress. While the sisters moved back to their rooms, Sister Meade with a small bowl of leftovers for her dog, Tallie helped Brookie clean up the dishes.

Brookie's silence compelled Tallie to ask, "Something wrong, Brookie?"

To which she replied, "Feelings a bit hurt, Tallie dear. Ye hardly touched the mushrooms . . . an' I spent all the afternoon hunting them special, because I thought ye'd like them."

"I *did* like them," Tallie lied effectively. "But I like roast and potatoes better. I was afraid if I ate too many, then I would fill up too quickly. I am sorry." With a small laugh, she added, "I promise the next time we have mushrooms I shall eat a very big portion, just for you."

Brookie now turned to her with the bowl of scraps. "Give this to the cat, will ye, lass?"

Tallie looked over the bowl. "No mushrooms for the cat?" she asked.

"Cats din't like mushrooms," Brookie replied.

A laughing Tallie moved toward the door. "Selective scraps for the cat, Brookie? Why, you are a dear, aren't you?"

"Don't dawdle out-of-doors long, Tallie. I'll allow ye to hurt me feelings . . . but I'll not allow ye to make me worry!"

Chapter Twenty-three

News of the money box left at the marshal's office spread fast, and motivated Old Potts to make a very startling confession. As the old man had spoken, Storm had felt the darkness of rage enveloping his features.

"You're telling me, Potts, that you saw that money box out at the ranch last summer? Almost a year ago?"

"Sure did! Mack, he had me a doin' small jobs, cleanin' out stables an' storerooms, an' I saw that box under some ol' blankets an' junk in one of them thar rooms in the barn. Shur 'nuf, I seen it." It was all Storm could do not to grab him up by the lapels and reduce him to a bloody pulp. He remained calm, and he was certain that his love for Tallie had a lot to do with that. He had bowed his head now, and his fingers were tightly clasped against the smooth top of the kitchen table. "Storm, you reckon that bullet the Englisher took out thar on the trail that night, you reckon Mr. Mack was aimin' fer me 'cuz he knew I seen that money box an' he figgered I'd tell somebody, maybe even the marshal? He was real mad, said I wuz snoopin', an' I'm shur if Bart Johnson hadn'a rode up to the stable right then, he'd a lifted up his rifle and shot me dead, right thar an' buried me before anybody ever know'd I was missin'."

If Potts was not lying—and he had told some whoppers in the past—then it was a good possibility that the bullets *had* been intended for him. Storm recalled the rumors circulating that one of Mack's men had been whipped the morning after the shooting. Could it have been his punishment for missing the intended target and shooting an innocent man?

He had to think of something else, so that he wouldn't spring and kill this stupid old man who kept the secrets he shouldn't and blabbed the ones he should. Looking around the kitchen, he muttered, "Where's Brookie? She usually has breakfast ready by now."

Just at that moment, Brookie entered the kitchen, doubled over, her features etched in pain. "I'll be sorry about breakfast . . ." She had apparently overheard, "but I'll be feeling a wee bit sick this morning." At that moment, she collapsed to her knees, her hand moving to the edge of the counter for support.

Storm was immediately at her side, helping her up. He had never seen a person in such agony. He realized then that he hadn't heard the morning prayers of the sisters, and Tallie was usually up early, hanging out her washing in the predawn hours or simply enjoying the rise of a new sun.

Old Potts had not moved from his chair at the table, and an aggravated Storm ordered, "Help Brookie to the table. I'll check on the others."

He found each of the sisters ill and in bed, Sister Meade more ill than the others. Tallie, too, was ill, but still making an attempt to rise. All of their symptoms were virtually the same: severe abdominal pains, unquenchable thirst, and Sisters Meade and Joseph had a bluish tint to their skin and told Tallie other symptoms they had not told Storm because "they were too embarrassed." When Tallie was withdrawing from Sister Meade's room, she made another discovery. The sister's little dog lay dead on the blanket she had put for it in the corner of the room.

Old Potts was sent into Granger to fetch Dr. Frick, while Storm found himself playing nursemaid to five sick women, wondering what on earth had caused such a situation.

They had in common the supper they had eaten last night, and Tallie said that Brookie had prepared mushrooms she'd picked in the woods. Storm now questioned her about the mushrooms.

"Picked them in the woods. They were good, were they?"

"Where in the woods, Brookie?"

"Near the pond where the old doctor frequently fishes. I ran upon a good bunch of them while I was walking and I thought they would make a pleasant addition to the meal." Then, "Do ye think they were poison? I would slice me throat in shame if I am responsible for poisoning all of us." At that point, her face grimaced in pain and she laid her head on the table.

"Will you be all right while I go check out the mushrooms? Doc Frick will be here soon."

"Yes, lad, I'll be all right. I believe I'll make a bit of tea to purge our insides, just in case I've done the poisoning."

Storm didn't want to leave the women, even for the short while it would take him to reach the area of the stream and look at the mushrooms. On his way out, he stopped by Sister Meade's room, saw Tallie sitting beside her since she was the one who seemed to have the worst symptoms, and quietly removed the dead dog. Sister Meade always fed them the leftovers from their meals, which reassured Storm that the mushrooms were poison. Potts, who was not sick, claimed he had not eaten any of them. The old man said he had seen Tallie take a small bite, wrinkle her nose in distaste, and then leave them virtually untouched on her plate. That was probably the reason she wasn't as sick as the others, Storm surmised.

Soon, he left the lodge, put the blanket-shrouded dog on top of the woodpile until he could find the time to bury it, then moved off into the woods. The kitten Sister Michael had proudly brought to the compound one morning, now a half-grown cat, bounced playfully at Storm's feet.

Brookie watched him from the kitchen window, smiling a slight smile as he disappeared into the woods.

Now she moved through the lodge checking on each of the women. When she reached Sister Meade's room, she saw Tallie, looking a bit peaked herself, sitting beside her and holding her hand. "How is the poor dear?" asked Brookie. "The doctor will be here soon."

When Brookie dropped her hand to Tallie's shoulder, and the grip was very strong, Tallie doubted that Brookie was as sick as she would have her believe. "Are you all right, Brookie? Perhaps you should lie down."

"I'll be all right, lass. And ye?"

"My stomach hurts, but other than that, I am well enough."

"I'm brewing a spot of tea. I believe it'll help if ye drink some of it."

Tallie couldn't shake the feeling that Brookie had deliberately poisoned them. "All right." Rising, she said, "I must look in on the others."

Brookie nodded, then exited the room and moved toward the kitchen. But she was not quick enough to be halted in her journey by her name being spoken. She turned back. "What is it, Tallie lass?"

The pain in her abdomen almost doubled her over. She wasn't sure how she maintained so much strength as she stood upright and said to Brookie, "You're acting strangely. I heard you humming right after the funeral . . . right after I'd received news of my aunt's death. There is a sarcasm in your voice I haven't noticed before."

"Sarcasm, lass?"

There it was, again, the way her voice lifted at the same time as her left eyebrow, a gleam that was almost cruel in her gaze. "Brookie, did you deliberately poison us?"

"Why, no, lass," she replied, strangely unaffected by Tallie's accusation. "I see beyond the drapes that young Storm is returning, Tallie. He's dismounting now with a small sack. I do hope and pray that I have not poisoned all me dear ones with the mushrooms I picked in the forest."

When Tallie reached the outside, Storm was just moving onto the porch. "Are they poisonous?" she asked.

To which Storm replied, "I don't know for sure, but I think so. I brought some back for Doc Frick to look at." His arm going across her shoulder, he asked, "How are you?"

"I shall live," she responded. "Sister Pete is not too sick. But Sisters Joseph and Meade are terribly ill. I do hope the doctor gets here soon." Then, and she hesitated to make such an accusation, "It is possible that Brookie deliberately poisoned us, Storm?"

Scarcely had she made the statement before buggy wheels clicked on the rocks Storm had put in the deep mud holes on the road earlier in the week. He met Doc Frick at his buggy just as Old Potts was turning his horse into the road some way behind him. Tallie wondered if he had even heard what she'd said.

"Thanks for coming out," Storm said, handing him the sack as soon as he got down from the buggy. "Look at these. I believe they might be what made everyone sick." Then, "If they're poison, there's a possibility it was deliberate."

So! He had heard her.

Doc Frick could smell them through the canvas sack. "Mushrooms? You think they were poisoned by mushrooms?" When Storm nodded thoughtfully, Doc Frick opened the sack and removed one of them. Smelling it, turning it over, then turning it toward the sun so that he could see it better, he said, "You're right. These are Jack-o'-lanterns, extremely poisonous, and similar to the chanterelle, which is a good mushroom." Then, "If they ate many of them, Storm, the sicker ones could—" He'd been about to say "die" but thought better when he saw Tallie.

Before the doctor entered the lodge to check on the women, he said, "Storm, that train money was turned in anonymously at the marshal's office."

"What?" He turned, his dark features visibly paling. When

he saw the way Doc Frick pressed his mouth, he said, "You don't think I took it there, do you?"

"Hell, no!" Doc Frick now moved past him and toward the lodge. "I think Mack—or one of his men—took it in."

Over the next half-hour Doc Frick examined everyone, found Sister Pete sick, but not to the point of concern, Brookie had only a complaint and no true symptoms, Tallie was cramped, but Sisters Joseph and Meade were critically ill. He prescribed an emeric of saltwater to make them vomit up anything that might remain in their stomachs, a purgative of senna to empty the bowels, and cascara as a tonic for the intestines. He stayed throughout the day, hoping to see the two older sisters through the crisis.

All that day, Brookie hummed her familiar little tune as she boiled water and added the salts, kept fresh tea made, and mixed up a pot of porridge for those who might want something in their stomachs. Strangely, though, everyone claimed they were not hungry.

Old Potts buried the dog, Storm decided to cook some steaks out-of-doors, since none of them trusted Brookie to prepare a meal that wouldn't kill them—and they certainly were not going to eat her porridge. Tallie, feeling much better now and helping Doc Frick take care of the sick ones, peeled potatoes and saw to their cooking, whipping in a little butter and milk, the way the men liked them.

She simply could not understand what had gotten into Brookie. Could she have ingested enough of the mushrooms to affect her brain? Tallie thought it an important enough issue to solicit Doc Frick's opinion.

"You say she's been acting strangely, Tallie? How is that?"

"She seems to delight in the misery today, Doc Frick. She has been very sarcastic, and she has been humming, which seems terribly inappropriate in view of the funeral, the bad news I received, and the fact that everyone is ill." Then, because he didn't know what she meant, she hastily added, "I learned that my beloved aunt passed away in London."

"I am sorry, Tallie." Doc Frick was nursing a cup of strong coffee she'd poured for him. He looked across the rim of his cup and saw a puzzled expression on Tallie's face. "I don't know what to tell you about Brookie. I suppose she hasn't been here long enough for anyone to really know her."

Just at that moment, Brookie entered the kitchen, her arms loaded with wood. Tallie took several of the logs from her arms, setting them in the log bin beside the stove. "One day we will have an electric stove," she said, "and I weren't be having to worry about wood for this old thing." Looking into the watery eyes of Doc Frick, she continued, "You two were talking? Should I be leavin'?"

"No, Brookie. We were discussing you—"

Tallie felt her heart fall to a level somewhere around her knees. She didn't want Brookie to know of her suspicions. "Yes, we were discussing your luck, since you are not as sick as the rest of us. And you claimed that you ate a good portion of mushrooms before our meal last evening."

"I cain't understand it," Brookie said, shaking her head. "Perhaps me constitution is much too stubborn to accept poisons." In an effort to solicit sympathy, she tearfully added, "Perhaps it was those oft' forages through the waste bins of London."

Or perhaps you did not eat them! Tallie was instantly ashamed of her unspoken response. Cutting a look to Doc Frick, which surely told the old gentleman what she'd been thinking, she moved into the outdoors for a bit of fresh air. She saw Storm cutting a fresh supply of wood for the stove. Approaching in silence, she soon dropped lazily against the woodshed and tucked her hands into the deep pockets of her skirts. She did not notice the note from "The Ripper" fall to the ground and become wedged between the uncut logs.

She watched Storm work, aware that he knew she was standing there. The sweat of his labors glistened across his bronze, muscular skin. She liked the way he looked, dark, brooding, lean and hard, and she loved the way he treated her, tender, loving, and passionate. And he was good in so many ways, having the capacity to care for so many people when even his own father had not cared for him. Logically, he should have been mean, bitter and carrying the biggest chip on his shoulder imaginable, but he did not. She knew he was sick with worry for the sisters, because she only saw him working this way, as though he could not get enough done in the span of half an hour, when he was worried.

Presently, the axe paused against the stump and he looked around at her. For the first time that day he managed a smile that seemed almost genuine. "Like watching me work up a sweat, do you, English?"

"I just like watching you," she responded demurely, her eyes smiling, even as her mouth did not.

He approached, wiping the sweat from him with his dark shirt. Then he closed her in his arms and held her tenderly. "Are you feeling better?"

"Quite a bit," she said, her hands easing around him, her fingers tucking lightly into the waist of his trousers. "I should go on back to the lodge and help out. The good physician is looking rather exhausted, and Brookie . . ."

When she hesitated, he prompted, "And Brookie what?"

She shrugged gently. "Nothing. I do not even know what I was going to say." When he mumbled something, she asked, "What is that?"

"I'm just grumbling," he responded. "We all should, since Brookie poisoned us." He started to say something else, then shook his head, drawing one of her hands up to touch a kiss to a pretty white knuckle.

"Do you truly think Brookie might have done it? Please, tell me what you really think?"

He drew a shallow breath, his eyes cutting beyond her shoulder, to the forest growing dark with the approach of day's end. "I agree with you. She poisoned everyone deliberately."

Just at that moment, a high-pitched wail echoed from a few feet away. Both turned just in time to see Brookie, sobbing and flailing her arms, pick up her apron-covered skirts and dash for the forest. Neither Storm nor Tallie were quite sure how much she had heard, but her actions were those of a woman crushed by accusation.

Doc Frick called to Storm from the kitchen entrance. Before Storm responded, he growled at Tallie, "Dammit, we were wrong about her! You go on and bring her back. I'll see what Doc wants."

Tallie moved quickly onto the trail where Brookie had disappeared and followed a respectable length behind the woman she could not see but whose sobs echoed in the forest like a drum. She called her name, but she did not answer, and the fact that her stomach was aching fiercely only made her a little more furious at Brookie for being so dramatic.

Tallie followed the sobs, she was sure, for a good mile until she was so deep into the woods that she recognized none of the scenery. She had never walked here with Storm; she was sure of it. The dales had a musky, rotten smell, and the undergrowth was thick and tangled. Even the trail frequently grew so narrow that her skirts were snagged by the brambles.

And there, sitting on a fallen log in the darkness of a stand of pines, she found a sobbing Brookie. She settled onto the log beside her.

"I am so sorry, Brookie."

The woman was dabbing at her eyes with a small towel from the kitchen. "I'll tell ye a story, lass. Would ye like to hear it?"

"Yes, I would," Tallie responded, and failed to notice how quickly Brookie had stopped sobbing.

"'Tis about a poor woman of approximately forty-four years—disowned by her sister who married wealthy, and who herself married a dirt poor coal cart driver named Piggy Mayfield. The poor woman helped make a meager living for her sick and crippled husband and half-grown children by occasionally bringing a baby into the world. One night, lass, but it was a cold, cold night, she was called from her family and the hearth of her poor little room to deliver a child who was having a wee bit of difficulty coming into the world. The poor woman, it bein' a holiday and all, she'd had a bit much to drink, and she really wasn't up to midwifery that night. But the messenger insisted that she come along, and so she did. Well, to get on with the story, lassie, the midwife was blamed for negligence in the death of the poor woman who was birthing a babe that night, and the law, they didn't take kindly to her, even though it was Christmas and the only time of the year she took a wee bit of spirits. The poor woman was taken away from her husband and her children and tossed into a prison cell for twenty-five years."

When Tallie started to rise, Brookie grabbed her wrist. So firmly did she hold it that Tallie thought she was being held in a vise. "You're talking about the death of my mother, Brookie. But how can you know all these details? I told you only that she had died and that the midwife was blamed—"

"Now, lass, sit. Brookie is not finished telling her tale."

"Brookie, it was not—" Tallie was horrified. "It could not have been you. Aunt Cora learned last year that the woman had died just days before she was to be released—"

"Do not ruin me story with interruptions. Do sit still and be a good girl. Ye'll be wanting to hear how she languished in prison, her poor, crippled husband delivering coal up to the day he died, her only son shot by a man whose pocket he was picking. Her four daughters eventually married, then got so bent up in their own miserable lives that they forgot about their mum. Soon, she was alone, with only her fellow prisoners—a motley crew they was—for company. The guards put her to work in the kitchen and she became a good cook, and she never really had to go hungry like some of the others did. But she was unhappy, friendless and without a family, and only one thing kept her alive. Aye, lass, one thing—the wee babe born that night. The poor old woman grew old in prison, but she kept herself strong and fit, because she knew she would need her strength when at last she saw freedom outside the gates again. I do believe, lass, that the reports of her death were greatly exaggerated, an' mayhap the poor old woman herself had a bit to do with the exaggeration."

"Brookie, please . . ." Tears rolled over the gentle curves of Tallie's cheeks. At the moment, she was almost too emotional to be afraid. "I don't want to hear more—"

"But there is so much more, lass," said Brookie, holding tight to her wrist. "Ye'll be wanting to hear how no one in the East End wanted to tell the poor old woman where ye could be found, even those stinking dodseys who said they knew where ye were but weren't going to tell. She didn't know yer name, lass, since ye'd married, and yer old aunt, why the poor old woman remembered when she came to the court and she wasn't named Dunton then, and she was havin' the dickens finding her. But those stinking dodseys, when they didn't tell the poor old convict what she wanted to know, well, she carved them up into little pieces. The last one, Mary Jane, was going to tell, so she said early that morning, but when she went to her room at Miller's Court, she'd changed her mind. The poor old woman scarcely made it out of there before the young prince came to see Mary." When Tallie tried again to free her wrist from the viselike grip, Brookie's other hand pinched her cheek so hard that Tallie cried out. "Now, be good, lass. Brookie needs to finish her tale." Brookie drew a long, deep breath. "Ye see, the poor, mistreated woman found out what she wanted to know that night, and she went to the wee flower shop and she saw Cora through the window—and Cora saw her. The door was locked and the woman could not get in. She would have waited there all night, but the coppers they was everywhere, so she hid until the morning. Then she learned that the babe born that night, who was now a fine-looking young woman of twenty-six, had been spirited out of the East End. The poor woman was angry. She thought she might kill the aunt, but how then would she find out where the lass had gone. So she waited and she watched the mails and she befriended the postman, and sometimes he would let her take the mail to the flower shop. And one day a letter came. It was from the young lady. She opened it and she read it, and then sent it on its way. But by then, poor old Cora was dead and the old gentleman got the letter. O' course, the poor, mistreated woman took passage to America, and she came to the mountains and befriended all who were there, and she found the wee babe that had grown into a fine woman, and she took her into her heart." Brookie fumbled in the pocket of her skirt. "Do ye know why she befriended the beautiful young woman, lass?"

"No," half-whimpered Tallie. "No, she doesn't. Dear God, why did you kill Sister Michael?"

"Sister Michael? *You* think *I* am this poor, tragic woman, lass?" The sarcasm eased into her strong voice. "How could ye think old Brookie a murderer? I'm speaking of the woman who delivered the wee babe that night and lost her freedom for it."

"Why did you kill Sister Michael?" Tallie repeated, her voice stronger this time.

"Sister Michael? She was good practice after all this time since the whores in the East End. She wanted to do it right and cleanly when ye were in front of the knife, dearie. Because, ye see, it is ye she wants, poor old thing." With an ugly cackle, she added, "The mushrooms, they was a little special treat I tossed into the pot, lass . . . the poor old woman, she was glad ye ate nary another after that first. How then, could she save ye fer the knife which ye deserve so mightily? An' the lit'l note from *'The Ripper,'* lassie? Did it grab ye guts like the poor ol' woman thought it would?"

A long knife came up from Brookie's pocket at the same moment that her fingers closed even more firmly over Tallie's wrist. She could almost feel her bones cracking. Her eyes wide with horror, she watched the knife move almost playfully through the air, until its tip was just an inch or two from Tallie's waistline.

"Don't, Brookie—"

"Don't what, dear lass, split ye open from here . . ." The

knife moved fluidly upward, its tip coming to rest between Tallie's breasts, "to here." Another maniacal cackle broke the morbid silence of the moment before she continued, "They say in the papers that the Ripper is a doctor, lass. It is because the poor old thing what quartered the whores worked as a nurse in the prison infirmary for a little while and got to know things. I thought that bit of nonsense rather amusing, didn't ye, lass?"

"None of this is amusing," said Tallie, attempting again to twist away from this demented woman. But she was as strong as two men.

And Tallie, in love with a wonderful man, having a daughter who needed her, and wanting very much to live, simply had to stall for time until she could find a way to outwit this murderous fiend.

But it was too late. The knife drew back as Tallie watched in mute horror.

Storm was confused as hell. When he got to the porch, Doc Frick said, "I don't know what's up, but Brookie asked me to call you away from Tallie. She said they needed to talk and she didn't want to interrupt you."

"I don't like it," Storm said, turning his dark eyes to the woods, then to the gathering dusk across the timberline. "I'd better go after them."

He moved toward the woodpile where he'd left his sidearm—a sidearm Judge Grisham had directed he wear in view of Sister Michael's murder. He wished to blazes that Sam Kerr, the marshal's deputy, had stayed on but the marshal had given him the day off to be with his family.

As he moved onto the trail, he had an uneasy feeling. Brookie must have known that someone would go after her, and that the someone would be Tallie.

The *why* of it urged his booted feet into a faster pace and occasionally he would pause at a fork in the trail to look for the stirrings of their footsteps.

* * *

Mack sat in the large study of his rambling ranch house and sorted through the papers on the top of his desk. Since he'd returned from his trip—a trip that had not produced the results he had wanted—he had tried mightily to make up for the things he had done. He had anonymously turned over the missing train money, had tried to befriend Matt, but he couldn't blame the boy for wanting no part of him. And now, here he sat, adding his signature to the last will and testament he had just written.

The doctor in Nashville had said that he would be dead within a year, that the cancer in his lungs was in its final stages. All those years of smoking, the doctor, a young fellow fresh out of medical school, had said. He'd said that one day the world would be aware of the dangers of smoking, and how it killed people in droves, and how it would kill even the people in the same room with the smoker.

Mack had laughed in his face.

And accepted that, for whatever the reason, he would die a slow and painful death.

He didn't want to suffer, the way he'd seen others suffer. He remembered a ranch hand some years ago, an old fellow whose name he couldn't even recall now, laying in the bunkhouse for half a dozen months, dying of a cancer of the brain. It had been horrible, and if the fellow hadn't been at the ranch for ten years, Matt would have sent him someplace else to die.

Now, that same kind of death was threatening him.

And he wouldn't allow it.

He'd put a single bullet in his revolver, which lay to the right of the papers he was arranging.

A knock echoed at the door. Hastily covering the revolver with some papers, he called for the person to come in.

Thea opened the door, one eyebrow slightly raised as she looked at him. There was that familiar hatred she had nurtured for him since he'd whipped her boy that morning, and he knew that it would never go away, not even when he was dead. "The judge is here, Mack."

"Send him in." When she started to withdraw, he again spoke her name. Her gaze returned to him, and the loathing, though he understood it, wrenched what little heart he had. "I'm sorry about Matt. I truly am. I promise to make it up to him."

She said nothing; at once, the judge entered, closing the door behind him. "What do you want, Mack? You know I don't like coming out here."

"You'll like being here now." Mack's hand outstretched. "Sit, and let's get this business over with."

Judge Isaac Grisham despised this man. He didn't want to sit in his plush leather chair, and he certainly didn't want to pass small talk with him. He did take a seat, because he wanted to get this meeting over with. "I don't know why you sent for me, Mack, and I frankly don't care."

"Why are you here, then?"

The judge's tone was grumpy. "Curiosity, I suppose."

Mack leaned across the desk, then pushed a document toward him. "You'll want this, Isaac. I suppose you could call it a confession."

"Of what crime, Mack. Being a murderer . . . or being a bastard?"

"A little of both, Judge." When the judge hesitated to take the document from the desktop, Mack's hand brushed out. "Go on . . . take it. It lets that boy of yours off the hook."

"Storm? You mean *your* boy, don't you?"

"What the hell. I suppose he is."

Judge Isaac Grisham now swiped the document off the desk and read it:

To Whom It May Concern. I, McCallister Phillips, did on the 17th day of May, 1888, hire two men by the names of Soapy Lawrence and Jess Forbes to rob the Tennessee-Blue Ridge train out of Nashville, for which I paid them four thousand dollars. I then paid them an extra two thousand dollars apiece to commit perjury in the court of Judge Isaac Grisham, to bear false witness against Storm Phillips.

Possibly as a means of redeeming himself, he had added, *The reason I did so was to avoid a court proceedings threatened to be filed against me by Storm Phillips, to claim part of the Phillips Ranch.* He had then signed the document, *McCallister Phillips.*

When the judge looked up, Mack asked, "Will that confession get Storm out of his troubles?"

"It will. But, by damn, Mack, I think you owe Storm something!"

"You let me make it up to Storm in my own way." Mack climbed to his feet, his hands pressing hard to the desk as he leaned across it. "Now . . . take that confession and get out."

"I'll send Marshal Black back here to arrest you," Judge Grisham said as he arose.

"You do that. I'll be right here."

Judge Grisham withdrew, slamming the door behind him, at which time Mack fell back to the chair. He steadied his breathing, then took a moment to check the papers he'd organized on the desktop. Impending death made a man think more clearly, and he knew deep in his heart that he'd never had just cause to hate Storm, his first-born son. He should not have hated Rachel, either; she had not been responsible for what had happened to his own parents.

Then he bowed his head for a moment, closed his eyes tightly, and prayed for forgiveness . . . prayed for the first time in his long, contemptible life.

He took the gun now and placed it against his temple.

For a moment, he remembered his past, his cruelty, his mother and father who were killed by the Cherokee in front of his eyes, he remembered the love he'd had for Rachel, until he had learned of her Cherokee roots, and for Thea, even though he'd never admitted it to her, a love that had produced a son he hadn't known existed until a few months ago. He thought about the Englishman, glad that he was here for Thea.

He thought about his wife, Rachel, and the misery he had brought into a life so filled with hope and expectations . . . and of the vicious injustice he'd inflicted upon that gentle soul.

And without hesitation—

Chapter Twenty-four

Just moments after Storm had left the lodge, Doc Frick returned to find Sister Meade dead. He sat beside her bed for the longest time, remembering the first time he'd met the sisters and listened to the excitement and praise in their voices as they had looked to the future in these beloved mountains. They had wanted only to bring God, as they knew and interpreted him, to the people here, and it seemed that the Blue Ridge Mountains hadn't treated them too kindly. For the first time, Doc Frick wished he hadn't donated this land to the sisters. Perhaps they would still be following their quest and collecting their love offerings from around the world.

When he checked on Sister Pete, he found her sitting against her pillows, and though a light pain etched her features, she managed a smile for the doctor. "How are the others?" she asked weakly.

"Doing just fine," Doc Frick lied. "Now, you don't worry about them and just stay in bed. We'll get you through this crisis."

"Was it the mushrooms?" Sister Pete asked.

To which Doc Frick replied, "It was."

"Thought as much," Sister Pete said, nodding weakly, "when I was strong enough to think, that is." Then, "Brookie must feel badly about the mushrooms."

Doc Frick didn't tell Sister Pete the suspicions all of them had about Brookie and the mushrooms. "You just stay in bed," he repeated.

"Jesus will see us through this," said Sister Pete in a voice strengthened by her love of God. "He takes care of the righteous."

Doc Frick nodded politely, declining to tell Sister Pete that righteous Sister Meade had been yanked across the threshold and was standing face to face with her Maker.

Instantly, he was ashamed of his cynicism. He had always considered himself a God-fearing man, but he could not understand why God would allow this grief. He looked in on Sister Joseph, who seemed a little improved, then moved into the fresh air of the approaching night. He liked to see the sun setting on the horizon.

He walked slowly, without purpose, frequently looking toward the woods and expecting three people to emerge. Soon, he sat on a log behind the woodshed and pressed his thumb and forefinger to his eyes. Then he arose, and in a moment of rage, his foot kicked out at a small pile of logs.

He saw it then, a single piece of paper oddly out of place. Picking it up, he attempted to see the words in the cover of light darkness, but he saw only the vague shape of the letters. So, he returned to the kitchen, dug his spectacles out of his pocket and read the note that had been signed *Jack the Ripper*. It was horrible and graphic enough in its details that Doc Frick thought it might be genuine.

Tallie, who had run all the way across an ocean fleeing from her personal demons, must have been trying to face them alone. Doc Frick tucked the note into his pocket.

He heard a horse, only now remembering that he'd sent Potts back to his house in Granger to get another bottle of cascara. He arose just as the good-natured old drunk entered the kitchen.

Before he could say anything, Old Potts said, "Just met Bart Johnson on the road, Doc. Mr. Mack shot hisself in the head and scattered his brains on the wall."

"You've been drinking again, Potts," the doctor responded critically. "McCallister Phillips would never do that! He enjoys tormenting people too much!"

"He kil't hisself graveyard dead, Doc, not more'n hour ago. Heard it from Bart Johnson myself!"

It was really too unbelievable, and Doc Frick didn't have the time to think about it right now. "You need to go back into Granger," he said, accepting the brown bottle of cascara Potts was handing to him now, "and fetch the coroner."

"One of the sisters died?" Potts questioned, his voice grim. "Which 'un, Doc?"

"Sister Meade."

"Didn't like that 'un," Potts responded without hesitation, and certainly, without an iota of guilt. He'd always thought Sister Meade picked on him without just cause, simply because he drank a little too much.

Just as Potts was leaving to fetch the county coroner, the small, familiar surrey owned by John and Fanny Collins drove up. Doc offered a hand to Fanny when she pulled up to the porch. "I heard the sisters were ill, Dr. Frick. I came to offer my help."

"It's kind of you, Fanny," he replied politely, though he was a little annoyed by the way news traveled in these hills. "Sister Meade has died and I've sent Old Potts for the coroner."

"Tallie is all right?"

"Tallie is fine. So is Brookie. Sister Joseph is very ill, and Sister Pete is feeling better."

Reentering the lodge, the doctor sat at the table and let Fanny make rounds between the two ill women. Now she returned to the kitchen and began tying on an apron. "I brought a bowl of soup. Will you fetch it from the surrey, Doc?"

He did so. When he returned, he set down the bowl and

before Fanny could pick it up, he said, "Sit for a moment, Fanny." Then he asked, "Didn't you see Tallie recently?"

"I saw her yesterday. She came by . . . but she seemed troubled and didn't stay very long." Fanny was thinking that Dr. Frick had a strange sadness in his eyes. She sat across from him, then dropped her hands into the folds of her dress. He said nothing as his hand went into his pocket. Momentarily, the folded bit of paper was being slid across the table toward her.

"Did she show you this?"

Fanny unfolded the letter and read it, her eyes widening in sheer horror. "No, she didn't. We talked about her family . . . and she left letters and asked that I post them to the members should anything happen to her. Now I see why she was so fearful." With a small shrug, she added, "For heaven's sake! Why can't our Tallie trust us to help her? If she is in trouble—"

"She has turned to Storm for that protection—"

Fanny shook her head. "I believe that loving Storm has given her strength she did not heretofore possess."

"I can see that she's fond of our Storm." Then, "Do you have a rifle in your surrey?" She nodded lightly. "I would suggest, Fanny, that you go home and stay with your husband until the terror on this mountain has been resolved. Will you do that for me?"

She did not argue. When she was on her feet, she took off the apron and retrieved her bonnet from the counter where she had dropped it. "I'll leave the soup." And without looking back, she stepped into the night. Presently, he heard the surrey clattering onto the roadway.

Tallie wasn't sure how she broke away just as Brookie drew back the long knife she planned to drive into her heart. Tallie came alive, a fierce longing to live propelling her onward. She screamed in her rage that this evil woman would take her life

. . . a scream that gave her the strength of a dozen men. She saw the surprise in Brookie's wide, watery features, and determination in the way she stood her ground, refusing to let Tallie, pinned against a thick, impenetrable woodline, get past her.

Tallie suddenly became a she-cat, wrenching her arm away and lashing out at Brookie with a balled fist. When the murderous fiend began to fall, Tallie gave her a hefty shove, then darted past her. But she halted at once when she saw horror instantly replace the surprise as Brookie fell to the ground, her arm bending beneath her and driving the knife all the way through her body.

Unwinded by her fear, Tallie dropped faintly against a tree trunk, preparing to dart away if Brookie came up again. But she did not; slowly, cautiously, Tallie moved toward her.

There she lay, upon a bed of blood and rotting leaves, her dull gray eyes seeming to hold Tallie even in death.

Weeping strongly now, Tallie sat upon the log, stunned and disoriented, feeling that every sensible thought she'd ever harbored had suddenly flown off with the mountain wind. When Storm came upon her, she looked at him as if he'd materialized out of nowhere, and when his gaze narrowed in the deepening night, she saw nothing but the past flooding her in wild and angry torrents.

"Where's Brookie?" he asked. "Didn't you find her?"

She felt Storm's strong hands closing over her arms and she was gently shaken. "Brookie?" she whispered. "She's . . ." A slim hand attempted to point, but then fell weakly, "over there."

Storm went immediately to the crumpled form; she was dead, no doubt about that. He stayed crouched on his knees for a long moment, trying to imagine Tallie killing the woman, and being completely unable to picture it in his mind. So, he asked her what happened.

"She was Jack the Ripper," Tallie began quietly, and over the span of a quarter-hour, she told him everything, beginning with her birth on a cold Christmas night and the death of the mother she had never known. When she had finished, she quietly began to cry and at once Storm was drawing her into his strong arms.

"I could not bear for anyone to know those women in London were killed because of me, Storm. And Sister Michael . . . poor Sister Michael. Please, please . . . could we bury Brookie here where she died? The others need never know that she is dead. We must tell them that she simply vanished."

He drew back, appalled by her suggestion, his dark eyes raking her features as though he thought she'd gone completely mad. "Bury her, Tallie, and not tell anyone?"

She attempted to shrug but his hands were so firmly around her upper arms that she could not accomplish it. "Why not, Storm? No one would know except you and me. And Brookie . . . what about her memory? Is it so necessary that everyone know what a fiendish murderer she was? That she killed in London . . . and she killed Sister Michael? We must say she ran away because she felt so guilty over the mushrooms." When she thought his anger and revulsion was deepening, she continued with haste, "What would be the harm of it? This could end now, Storm, in this gentle dale, in these mountains where Brookie died . . . where all the horror can die forever."

Actually, he was beginning to see the sense of her entreaty. This poor old demented woman had hacked up five women in London looking for Tallie, had followed her to the mountains where she'd killed a righteous woman. He had read the newspapers, and he knew the world was fascinated by these grisly murders in London. He knew it would continue to be a fascination, and a subject of conjecture and speculation, unless the identity of the killer was revealed. And Tallie! Did she deserve to be dragged through the sordid details of the crime once again, and for her daughter to be dragged through it as well?

He thought not.

So, he drew her to him for a gentle embrace and said, "All right, Tallie. Let's fetch a shovel and a blanket to wrap her in. The world need never know how this has ended."

Relief swept over her as she closed her eyes against his shirt.

* * *

They returned to the lodge to learn that Sister Meade had died. While Storm was outside, Tallie went to her room for a blanket, meeting Hiram Frick in the kitchen as she was exiting. When he looked questioningly at the blanket, she explained, "Sister Meade's little dog. Storm doesn't want to shovel the dirt directly onto it." The dog, of course, had already been wrapped in a blanket and buried, but Dr. Frick need not know that. It was a small lie, and one she was sure she would be forgiven for. "I shall take it out to Storm." Then, "Do you mind if I sit with him for a little while? He is very upset about Sister Meade."

Hiram Frick wondered if Old Potts had told him about his father's death, and how it was affecting him. Nodding with understanding, because he had brought Storm into this world, had seen him through his life, and knew that he was a sensitive, caring man, he replied, "Go on . . . it won't hurt for you two young people to be alone for a while. I'll be here in the event that Brookie comes back." As Tallie was exiting, he said, "Don't worry about Brookie, Tallie. I'm sure she'll come back when she is thinking clearly."

Dropping her eyes in her moment of guilt and shame, Tallie said nothing. Presently, she was wrapped in the haze of the night, moving toward the clearing where Storm waited.

Aware that Doc Frick saw them move toward the forest, though she was reasonably sure he could see little detail and certainly not that she had taken the blanket with her, Tallie said, "I told him I wanted to spend some time with you because you were upset about Sister Meade."

"That isn't a lie," he replied at once, his fingers firmly clutching the shovel he had taken from their toolshed. "I *am* upset over Sister Meade." He was also upset about his father's death, though he did not want to complicate this burden with that news, if Tallie had not already heard it.

They moved as swiftly as the darkness would allow, the only

light provided by the beams of the full moon permeating the canopy of trees. When they reached the area where Brookie's body lay, Tallie sat on a fallen branch while Storm pulled the knife from the body, then placed it against her when he wrapped her in the blanket. He took off his shirt in the sweltering night and she watched him dig the long, narrow hole that would be Brookie's grave. For an hour he labored in the ground thankfully softened by occasional rains and its protection from the harsh sun in this damp, musky glen. When he'd finished digging the hole, he dropped beside Tallie, pulling her into his sweaty embrace. She didn't mind; her cheek fell to his bare shoulder.

"Do you want to say anything over her?" he asked.

She arose. "A word or two might be appropriate. It seems that I am the one who knows her best."

Storm had positioned the blanket-covered body beside the grave. Tallie now stood on the other side of the hole and gently clasped her hands. Quietly, she said, "You were my first contact with the world, Brookie, and I must give you credit for giving me life, even as my mother died. I forgive you, because I really, really do not believe you were an inherently evil soul. Our story ends here, in these gentle woods, and no one shall ever know what you have done. This is my promise to you, Brookie—mine and Storm's—as you step into eternity." Then she looked across at Storm, and nodded.

Within moments, Brookie was lying in her grave and Storm was easing the dirt atop her with extreme gentleness. It didn't take long to fill in the hole he'd dug to a depth of five feet.

Now they stood together, looking reverently at the grave and sealing a secret bond between them.

No one would ever know.

"Did she have any family?" Storm asked quietly.

"If she was telling me the truth, she has grown daughters somewhere in England."

"Shouldn't they know about their mother?"

She moved beneath the wing of his arm, her hand going up

to take his own, which dangled across her shoulder. "I think this is something her daughters would not wish to know."

On Wednesday, two funerals were held in the mountains. Sister Meade's drew a large crowd of mourners; MacCallister Phillips's only a handful of men who worked for him, men who had remained loyal despite his brutality. Of course, Matt, Thea, and her new husband, Farrand Beattie, were present at the gravesite.

On Thursday, the judge sent for an attorney from Nashville, and when he arrived on Saturday, sent him to the ranch to oversee the reading of Mack's will. There, in the parlor of Mack's ranch house, a startling provision was read by the attorney, Mr. Portland.

The ranch and all assets were to be shared equally between Matt and Storm, with the elder son to have controlling interest. The judge quietly smiled. So . . . that is how Mack planned to make it up to Storm.

Storm received the startling news just minutes before he sat on his bunk to read the letter his father had written him, and that had lain, untouched, upon the foot locker in his cabin since this morning when Matt had brought it to him.

He had not read his mother's journal, nor the letters Mack had written her in the months preceding their marriage, and he felt that reading the letter his father had written him would be giving him precedence. So, he retrieved the chest Matt had brought to him, brought out the journal and the letters, and for the next three hours read every word that had been written. When, at last, he set them aside, he was astonished at his mother's goodness, her capacity to forgive, her refusal to be bitter, and he'd been equally moved by the gentle words MacCallister Phillips had written to her.

Now, he took up the envelope and looked at his name written there by his father. He was annoyed that his hand was shaking, annoyed that his father could intimidate him, even in death, and he wanted to be able to put a match to the letter and never read what the man had written.

But he could not do that. He had to know.

He simply had to know if Mack had continued to hate him right up to the moment of his death.

But hadn't he left him controlling interest in the ranch?

Perhaps the letter explained why.

So, hoping to get an answer to that question, and to the long-standing question of "Why?", Storm swiftly opened the envelope and removed the single sheet of paper folded in thirds. He held it for a moment, then slowly unfolded the crisp piece of paper.

If someone had called his name right then, he would still have had time to read the letter and answer the summons without hesitation. For on the page, in writing that was only vaguely familiar to him, were the words, *Forgive me, Son.*

Storm's eyes misted. McCallister Phillips could not have said anything more important to him if he'd written a thousand pages. Storm's gut wrenched, because he wished he could have heard his father speak these words that didn't make him hate him any less but, perhaps, made him love him a little more.

For there was never a moment that Storm hadn't loved his father.

Never a moment that he hadn't hated him.

Never a moment that he hadn't wished him dead.

And the moment, now, that he wished to God he was still alive.

Sister Pete sat in the kitchen, fussing beneath her breath. If Sister Joseph made one more domestic demand, she was going to do something she hadn't done before, and though she wasn't quite sure what it would be, she was reasonably sure it wouldn't be a pleasant thing to witness! It had been, "Bring me a bowl of soup, Sister," "Pray with me, Sister," "Bring my Bible, Sister," "Tell Tallie this, Sister . . . tell Tallie that, Sister,"

"Ask Brother Storm to bring in wood, Sister," "Tell Mr. Potts we'll need etc., etc., etc!" 'Sister, Sister, Sister!"

Several times Sister Pete had punctuated one of the demands with an expletive, and she had prayed for forgiveness each time. But she was still too weak from her illness to do much heavy praying.

Tallie entered the kitchen. "Sister Joseph wants to see you."

"Damn!"

"Sister Pete!"

The shawl-draped woman raised an eyebrow. "Didn't think I was capable of that, did you, Tallie girl?" She arose, moving at a slow pace into the corridor. "I'll see what she wants. Before I strangle her!"

Tallie had been preparing their supper before Sister Joseph called to her. Now, she commenced her labors, all the while looking out the window at the pale glow of lamplight in Storm's cabin. She wasn't sure what he was doing, but she knew that whatever it was, it had something to do with the letter his father had written to him. She wanted to be with him, in case he needed her comfort, or even a soft shoulder to rest his head against, but she would not disturb the solitude he seemed to need right now.

So, she waited and worried . . . worried and waited. She wasn't sure how much time had passed, but when she heard the sisters praying loudly from the direction of Sister Joseph's room and saw that she had already put the potatoes on to boil, she was reasonably sure her thoughts had taken more than a few minutes.

Then Sister Pete returned, quietly dropped into a chair at the kitchen table and watched Tallie at her labors.

Presently, she said, "You're a good person, Tallie. I will miss you."

Tallie was now chopping a head of lettuce and some fresh tomatoes one of their neighbors had brought after the funeral. "What do you mean, you will miss me? I am not going anywhere, at least not right away."

"Sister Joseph and I will abandon this new church. The Lord is calling us to the Midwest."

This was a startling revelation. "But why? The church is near enough to completion that services can soon be held. You said yourself a few days ago that Sister Joseph had received an inquiry from a local preacher, who wishes to have an active part in the church—"

"We were not meant to be here," Sister Pete cut her off, dropping her eyes. "We have lost Sister Michael and Sister Meade. They will stay on, dear girl, dust to dust, ashes to ashes, but the living must follow the call of God."

Moving toward the table now, Tallie sank into one of the chairs. "Are you admitting defeat? Are you going to give up your dream to establish a church here?"

"It isn't my decision, Tallie, but, yes, Sister Joseph and I are going to give up the dream." Sister Pete took Tallie's hand and gave it a gentle pat. "When you and your new husband take a holiday, perhaps you will come see us."

A blush came to Tallie's cheeks. "I'm not married, Pete. You know that."

She smiled now. "You will be, girl."

Matt came to see his older brother that evening. The two men sat in Storm's small cabin, talking about the death of their father, and the future of the Phillips Ranch.

"You'll be moving over there, won't you, Storm? Ma an' me an' my new pa, we'll be livin' in the house, but there's plenty enough money in the bank to build another house for you an' Miss Tallie. You will be comin' to the ranch, huh?" Before Storm could give an answer one way or the other, Matt continued with haste, "I found a letter Mack had got from a fella in Mexico, an' it seems this fella, he's been raisin' some horses that Mack paid for when they was jus' colts an' fillies, an' it's time to be bringin' 'em to Tennessee. You an' me, Storm, after you spend some sweet time with Miss Tallie, we could go to Mexico an' get them horses. Ship 'em back on the train, an' make a good trip out of it, git to know each other, Storm, since we'll be brothers for life. What do you say?"

"What makes you think I'm going to marry Tallie, Matt, or spend 'sweet time' with her out at the ranch?"

Confusion settled immediately in the man's youthful features. "Ain't ya, Storm?"

"No." Storm grinned now. "Tallie and I will be spending that sweet time on a ship, going to England to fetch her daughter back here. Hell . . ." Pride lifted his voice, "when I marry Tallie, I'll be a ready-made pa. What do you think of that? Ready to be an uncle?"

"You bet I am, Storm. When you an' Miss Tallie goin' to tie the knot?"

"As soon as she says yes," Storm replied. "She's turned me down every time I've proposed."

"She won't turn you down now."

Storm startled at the sound of Tallie's voice. He hadn't heard her enter, and now his dark eyes were holding gentle, loving features. "What do you say, mountain man? Propose to a lady again? Give her another chance?"

Matt arose. "I better git out of here an' let you an' Miss Tallie spend *this* sweet time together."

Storm's hand went out, catching Matt's arm. "Don't go. She wouldn't embarrass me by turning me down in front of my own brother." A dark eyebrow raised with humor. "Would you, Tallie?"

Her arms went around him as she gently leaned into him. "Try me."

Releasing Matt, whom he knew felt a little awkward witnessing this intimacy, Storm gathered the woman he loved in his arms for a moment, then drew back just enough to see her magnificent eyes. "Tallie Edwards, would you do a loathsome creature like me the honor of becoming his wife and making a civilized man out of him?"

Damn! he thought. *She's going to turn me down again! This is going to be embarrassing as hell.*

"Storm Phillips, you loathsome creature, whom I love with all my heart and all my soul . . . the answer is *yes,* I will marry you!"

A smile widened his mouth. "You're not fooling, are you?"

"Not fooling!" she responded, laughing. "You are my witness, Matt. Your brother asked me to marry him and I accept. If he backs out now, it will be breach of promise and I shall take him for everything he has got when I sue him in court."

With a delighted yelp, Matt threw his hat into the air. "Can I be the best man, Storm?"

The prospective bridegroom held Tallie's gaze, transfixed. "Hell, yes."

"An' can Ma bake the wedding cake?"

"Well, *I'm* not going to bake it."

Buggy wheels clattered outside, drawing Matt to the window. "It's the judge, Storm. Can I go out and tell him about you an' Miss Tallie?"

"Go," he said, and when the door thumped against the outer wall in Matt's haste to carry the good news, he gathered Tallie to him once again. "I love you, Tallie Edwards. Now and forever. You're everything I've wanted in a woman . . . and more." He grinned boyishly. "And I don't even have to wait to be a pa."

"Why, Storm Phillips, you're just an old softie."

A thought came to him, clouding his face at once. "I do hope you don't think I'm moving to England. You do plan to stay here with me, Tallie, you and your Ellie."

"Where else, Storm Phillips? I would be insane to choose the crime-infested streets of Whitechapel, when I can have the wide, open air of your beloved mountains."

In those few moments before they were interrupted by well-wishers, they sealed their love with a kiss, a caress, a promise that their love would last forever.

Chapter Twenty-five

A letter came for Tallie on a hot July morning. She had been sitting at the woodpile, keeping Storm company while he planed freshly cut wood boards he'd picked up at the mill near Granger, when Old Potts returned with the mail for the lodge.

Tallie breathed a sigh of relief as she read the letter from Peter Leggett, who had said that he would have to postpone his required trip to America until October because Mrs. Muncie was ill. She thought it rather sweet that Mr. Leggett had looked out for her since her husband had passed away last year.

Though she was sorry Mrs. Muncie was ill, she was glad of the extra time it gave for her good friend in London to receive the letter she'd written a few weeks ago, telling him that his trip would not be necessary, "because her personal crisis was over."

Now she looked to Storm, sweating profusely beneath the high sun. "Why are you still working on the church, Storm? You know that the sisters are leaving the end of the month."

"I'm hoping they'll stay," he grumbled, and set the planing tool against the board once again. She arose, and when she tucked herself into his arms, he was required to turn away from his labors. He didn't seem to mind, though, as a boyish smile crept onto his face. "What do you think? Can we persuade them to stay?"

"Storm Phillips, I do believe you're getting a bit of religion. You really want the sisters to stay?"

"I don't know about the religion," he said, "but yes, I do. I believe they're needed here. I believe they could do some good." His grin widened, his hands playfully moving to pull her more completely against him. "Given time they might even be able to convert me!" Rocking her playfully against his body, he continued, "Besides, I want the inside of the church to be as near completion as possible for our wedding on the twenty-seventh."

They'd chosen a Saturday afternoon for their marriage ceremony, the invitations had been sent out, and Judge Isaac Grisham would officiate at their exchange of vows. Fanny Collins was sewing Tallie's wedding dress, and Mr. Chadwick, sending a bit of the fabric Fanny had provided him to his supplier in Nashville, said that her shoes, his gift to her, could be dyed to match her dress.

"Do you realize how wonderfully our lives are working out, Storm?" Tallie reminded him. "We can live at the lodge until you decide whether you wish to move to the ranch. Soon, we will travel to England and bring our daughter to her new home, and the state has restored the money they seized from your bank account, since you really did not rob that train. Oh, Storm, everything is coming together beautifully!"

"You are such a romantic, Tallie Edwards—" He drew back, so that he could see her soft, loving features. "Soon to be Mrs. Phillips, what do you say we go to the kitchen and snack on some leftovers?"

"You hardly ate a thing at lunch," she said, laughing. "It's no wonder you are hungry."

"I was too excited to eat, Tallie, after my journey to the ranch."

A pretty eyebrow raised quizzically. "And what at the ranch brought on so much excitement?"

"A gift at the stables there for our daughter. Matt picked her up in Memphis last week."

She loved the way he referred to Ellie as "our daughter." "A horse?" she questioned, worry immediately settling onto her brow. She hadn't really wanted Ellie to have the Shetland pony Mr. Leggett had purchased for her, because she was so fearful she would fall off, but now, the possibility that Storm would allow her to have a *horse*—

"Yes, a horse," he said strongly, turning toward the lodge and drawing her into his arms as they walked. "It's a small, gentle mare, from extremely good stock, I might add, and it'll be perfect for her. Everyone rides in the mountains, and Ellie will enjoy riding with her new father."

Hugging him tightly, Tallie said, "You're the best, Storm Phillips. What a lucky girl I am, and my Ellie, too." Then, "I know you will not let Ellie fall off."

He laughed. "Is that an edge of doubt I hear in your tone, English? And you're right! I wouldn't let her fall off. I'm looking forward to escorting her down the aisle when she's as lucky as her mother and finds such a wonderful man as me!"

Sharing in his laughter—and his love—they entered the kitchen, continuing their small talk as Tallie shredded lettuce and sliced a new tomato, while Storm cut several thin slices of beef from the leftover roast.

They loved each other, the future was theirs, and that was all that mattered now.

It had been three weeks since Brookie and Sister Meade had died. Storm and Tallie spent a few quiet moments at the graves of Sisters Meade and Michael just after sundown, then walked the night-cooled trails of the forest. Almost with deliberation in their movements, they came upon the deep, musky glen where they had buried Brookie in secrecy. The light of the full moon could scarcely penetrate the overhang of trees, and so they stood on the trail, gazing in silence toward the grave. In the veil of darkness it almost appeared as if a hole existed where the grave should be, almost as if the darkness of leaves decaying in degrees was the blanket in which they had draped her corpse dragging from the hole. They shivered simultaneously, and Storm wrapped his arms around Tallie's narrow shoulders.

"Let's get out of here," he said lightly. "It gives me the jeebies."

"Me, as well," she responded, and they turned away from the grave.

That night a rain storm pelted the mountains in all its vicious wrath.

Washing the rotting leaves and loose earth—

Back into the empty grave.

The afternoon of July twenty-seventh

As Tallie stood in front of the mirror perched above her dresser, she knew all that was missing from this wonderful day was the presence of Ellie and dear Aunt Cora. Oh, if only her aunt could have lived to see her so happy.

Though her dress was peach-colored, it was a bridal dress in every other detail. Fashioned of fine handkerchief linen with a high neck and pleated yoke, it was lavishly trimmed in rosepoint lace, satin, and hand-sewn faux pearls. Fanny had given her a pair of pearl earrings and her beloved Storm had provided the pearl choker. A parasol had been made to complement the ensemble—a new fashion of the day, Fanny had told her—and a veil of tulle cascaded from her matching linen-and-satin hat. Sister Pete fussed with the soft waves of her hair, tucking in a wayward lock and giving her hat a final straightening. When, at last, she handed Tallie her bouquet of roses and gardenias, freshly picked from Martha's flower garden and bound in delicate lace, the bride knew she was ready for this very important moment in her life.

"You should have worn the corset!" Sister Pete fussed without pause. "It would make you look more mature, and give your hips a little . . ." She hesitated, then said curtly, "Thrust!"

Tallie laughed. "Sister Pete, I tried on the ungodly thing. The *thrust* was in my bosom and my hips were thrown back. My Storm would think I had developed some spinal contortion. There is no sense in offering myself to him as something I am not—an ample-bosomed, round-hipped matron! I am sorry I am so unfashionably thin!"

Sister Pete smiled only when Tallie cut her humored gaze to her. "Corsets are quite the *in* thing," she pouted. "And Fanny went to all the trouble to dig it out of her wardrobe."

"She dug it out of an ancient burial chamber!" Again, Tallie laughed, her fingers closing gently over Sister Pete's wrist. Touching a kiss to her sweet old cheek, she added affectionately, "Shall we go get married now?"

"Thank God you'll be the one taking a husband! I'd as soon take a thousand irrascible skunks as that dark, brooding rogue you'll take to your bed!"

Leaning ever so close, Tallie whispered mischievously, "Skunks are not nearly as entertaining!"

Sister Pete, clasping her hands, took a bit of time for a small prayer before their short journey to the altar. On the way to the chapel, she said with a little indifference, "Oh, by the way, Tallie, I have a small gift for you and your husband. Not a material gift, but a few words you might want to hear." Tallie turned, her warm, loving gaze holding Sister Pete's. "Sister Joseph and I have decided to stay on the mountain. We're not going to give up."

With a delighted squeal, Tallie hugged her tightly. "Oh, I am so happy . . . so happy, Sister Pete!"

* * *

Storm was a nervous, uncomfortable wreck. Judge Grisham had made him wear a suit, when he'd just as soon worn a pair of Levi's and a shirt. The pleated vest was just a tad too tight, and the heady fragrance of his gardenia boutonniere was adding to the butterflies in his stomach. His brother, Matt, standing beside him as best man, leaned over and said, "You look all hot under the collar, Brother. Still time to run, ya know."

Storm smiled nervously, saying nothing, but for a fleeting moment, he considered Matt's advice.

The judge stood silently at the altar, looking across the sea of guests sitting in the unvarnished pews. Mrs. Kingsley was cooling herself with a delicate lace fan, and even Crispin Black had dressed up and sat just behind and to the right of Hiram and Martha Frick. Mr. Everton and his wife, Mr. Chadwick and his widowed sister, Sam Kerr, the deputy marshal, John and Fanny Collins, and a multitude of others whose names he knew but hadn't seen in a while waited expectantly for the ceremony to begin. Thea and her husband, Farrand Beattie, sat in a front pew, chatting pleasantly and occasionally looking toward Storm and Matt.

With exception, curiosity had brought most of the guests to the wedding, especially the men, who had heard about the bride's uncommon beauty.

For a moment, with the mutterings of the guests disturbing the silence of the occasion, Isaac Grisham thought of the document MacCallister Phillips had shoved across his desk toward him. That same day, Isaac had taken the letter to the governor's mansion in Nashville, waited from eight in the morning until ten at night for the governor to return, and didn't leave until he had in his hands a fully executed pardon, and an apology from the State of Tennessee.

Now, here he stood, Bible in hand, waiting for the young man to be married to the prettiest girl ever to set foot in these mountains. Storm deserved a wonderful woman like Tallie

Edwards. Isaac knew his life would be good from this point forward. He and Storm had spoken at length yesterday about Storm's father, and a lot of things were settled now. Strange, how the words *forgive me, Son* could erase thirty years of bitterness. It merely attested to Storm's character.

A stirring at the doorway caught his attention, and at the same moment, the head of every guest turned. There, Sister Pete easing past her, so that she could take her place for the walk alone down the aisle, stood the most beautiful female vision Judge Isaac Grisham had ever seen.

And Storm thought so, too. Pride lit his dark features like a beacon, and the fingers of his right hand gently closed over the ring he'd been fumbling between them, the ring he would slip on his beautiful bride's finger in just a few moments. He saw her eyes, the pride in her own features, the way her fingers rose to nervously tuck back her peach-colored veil.

And the world stood still for him.

Mrs. Kingsley arose and took her place at the organ that had been lent by the Lutheran church in Granger for this special occasion. Now, the wedding march began to play, and Tallie, his bride, his love, his woman, slowly paced in rhythm to the music, closing the distance between them. When she stood beside him, her gaze holding him fully and lovingly, he instinctly touched his fingers to her cool cheek. "You are beautiful," he whispered so that only she could hear.

They now turned to face a proud, beaming Judge Grisham.

He had chosen a simple exchange of vows, as Storm had requested.

Tallie was so happy. She heard every word the judge spoke, every word her beloved Storm repeated, and his special vow to her, spoken so lightly that their guests were straining to hear, *Tallie, I promise to be a good husband, to always be there for you, to be a good father to your beloved Ellie, and to grow old with you, and to take care of you, even into eternity.*

Tears misted her eyes. Emotion prevented her from saying anything beyond, "Me, as well." He smiled then, sweetly, mischievously, and when he slipped the ring on her finger, their fingers then locked gently together.

Judge Hiram Grisham, holding back his own emotions and a pride that almost burst inside him, pronounced them man and wife and introduced them to the guests as "Mr. and Mrs. Storm Phillips."

Following the reception, at which their guests gorged themselves on food brought from throughout the mountains, Storm and Tallie retired to the small cabin he had been occupying since the sisters had moved into the lodge. There they found a brand-new iron bed and feather mattress set up where his humble cot had been, with fresh white linens and a wedding quilt sewn by Martha Frick as a gift for the bride and groom.

But an unwelcome guest had sneaked in, and a laughing Storm took a moment to displace the cat Sister Michael had dragged into the kitchen on a cool February morning and Sister Pete had immediately evicted. As Storm drew his bride into his arms, the cat jumped onto the windowsill and howled to be let back in.

"I hope you're ready to howl like that, English, and let me know how pleased you are to have me as a husband."

"Oh?" she teased, accepting the gentle kiss he gave her. "I thought *you* were the one pleased to have *me* as a wife!"

"I am," he whispered affectionately. "How about if you and me climb out of these clothes, Mrs. Phillips."

She had purchased a filmy red gown at Mr. Chadwick's store, much to the consternation of the proprietor, who had thought it been more suited to one of the women at Friday's saloon.

Storm helped her out of her bridal dress and into the provocative garment, and when they climbed into bed, he still had on his long johns, an oversight that Tallie noticed right away.

She knew that something was up—

Just at that moment, the door burst open and a dozen yelping men flew into the cabin. As she watched in surprise, and near shock, they picked up the bed and began spinning around the room with it. The room was still spinning when, with a thud, the bed was again deposited to the floor and the men withdrew as suddenly as they'd charged upon them.

"Why, I do think we have been attacked!" She feigned annoyance, even as her mouth eased into a gentle smile. "I do hope that will be the end of it."

"It will," he said, laughing, immediately pulling off the long johns and tossing them to a chair. "The night is ours from this moment on—"

She could hear the chattering of the pranksters outside, and a slight frown exposed her doubt. "It would be rather embarrassing if we were engaged in wedding-night amusement, and a dozen boisterous men burst in upon us. I think I would die a thousand deaths if that were to happen."

"It won't," he promised, claiming her mouth in a gentle kiss, which deepened almost immediately. As he put the merest breath of space between them, he asked, "Do you want me to slip the bolt on the door?"

She pretended to think a moment, then quietly answered, "I will feel much safer if you do."

He arose from the bed, his dark, muscular body slim and perfect against the light of the single lamp. She sat against the plush pillows, watching him, the broad expanse of his back, his narrow hips and tight buttocks. Presently, the bolt slipped and he turned full to her, standing there for a moment, posing as though he knew she watched every movement he made.

She thought him perfect, tall and incredibly handsome. She reveled in the way a gleam lit his dark eyes as he met her gaze, the way he now sauntered toward the bed and one knee moved upon it. Pressing his palms to the downy coverings, he bent over and playfully touched his nose to her own, his eyes smiling, his mouth trailing kisses over her translucent eyelids, his hands now moving to gently enclose her shoulders.

"Are we going to live at the ranch, Storm, when we return from our trip to England?"

He drew back, humored, a little surprised at the subject she'd brought up when they had a wedding night to enjoy. "We'll talk about it tomorrow, Tallie. For now . . ." His fingers eased beneath the filmy fabric at her shoulder, "all I care about is you being out of this godawful thing."

"Oh, you dislike it?" Resting back against the pillows, she moved her shoulders seductively, then against his mouth when he touched a hot kiss to the skin he had uncovered. "I think it quite appropriate for the evening."

"Your altogethers are much more appropriate," he murmured, his hands now easing the loose fabric down her arms so that he could cover her with his lean, hard body. Presently, he dragged her wrists up and caressed them lightly. Gazing into her hazel eyes, passion-sheened beneath the thick fringes of her lashes, he couldn't believe his good fortune. No man in the world had such a wonderful wife, one so good of heart, so beautiful, so sensual. As he pulled her against him, then held her for a long, long while, without movement, without demand, he tried to imagine his life without her . . .

But it would be no life.

He tried to imagine an eight-year-old girl who would one day very, very soon be calling him "Father," a child he would feel was his own, because of the love he bore for her mother.

The first thirty years of his life had been filled with bitter uncertainty. The next thirty, and beyond, would be wonderful. He felt it deep inside.

His new wife playfully nuzzled against his neck now, her teeth gently capturing an earlobe. "Make love to Mrs. Phillips . . . Mr. Phillips. Make love to me as though this is our last night together."

He chuckled, drawing back just enough to see her face. "Like condemned prisoners waiting to be shot at dawn, hmm? Is that how we should love each other tonight?"

A coy smile; now that was a wickedly delightful comparison. "Yes, like condemned lovers, Storm Phillips, loving away the long, hot night. Or do you have it in you?"

He growled, pretending to dig his teeth into the tender flesh of her shoulder. "You'll be begging me to end the torture, English! I'll wager you that."

His gaze locked to her unwavering one. She loved the way he moved atop her, like a panther suddenly taking possession of its prey. She loved the way his hands cupped her face, as though he could not get enough of looking at her . . . she loved the way his gaze lowered, and his mouth moved to capture the dark circles peaking her breasts. She loved the way the heat of the night glistened on his bronze muscles as her fingers traced a path along his arm, his back, his neck, to tunnel through his thick, dark hair.

He loved her—they loved each other—with a fierce desire, with an urgency that served only to arouse their passions beyond mortal capacity. His hands caressed her so completely that she thought she would melt beneath them, and when he was within her, claiming her, she heaved her hips mightily against him, again and again and again, until she was almost too exhausted to breathe. And yet, his mastery gave her strength . . . and her love for him gave her new life.

The sweet, intoxicating arousal of their first moment together as man and wife seemed to go on forever . . . through the night . . . through the stars . . . through the universe.

She had known for months, since the moment she had first seen him, that she would be his wife.

That he would be her husband.

And these wondrous nights would be theirs over and over, until they were old and gray, sitting on a porch somewhere and still . . . yes, even then . . . looking at each other with a love that could only happen once in a lifetime.

As their passions soared mightily, then crashed back to earth, their ragged breaths slowed in harmony. In a moment—or two or three, neither was really counting—Storm eased against her side and drew her close. "Give me a bit of time," he murmured sweetly against her hairline, "and we'll do this again." Then, with an exhausted chuckle, "I think within a year I'd like to have a bouncing baby boy nestled in my arms."

A boy," she echoed dreamily, closing herself in his arms. "What would we name our little boy, Storm?"

"Clarence, I think. Or perhaps Merlin, like the ancient magician, or maybe Ebeneezer."

"I think not!" she said, laughing at his terrible choices. She thought about a little boy cuddled in her arms—Storm's little boy—her gaze cutting to the dark eyes of a proud father standing by, waiting to take charge of the infant. Then she quietly said, "Paul. I would like to name him Paul."

"An old suitor, little wife?"

"I do not think I've ever known anyone named Paul. It is a nice name, is it?"

"Paul it is," he murmured, touching a tender kiss to her temple. "Paul Phillips. How about a middle name?"

"You do not have one, do you? Why does he need one?"

"I never said I didn't have a second name."

In her moment of surprise, she stared deeply at his darkly handsome profile. "You have another name, Storm?" When he did not answer, she asked, "What is it?"

His mouth puckered, a thin line gathering over his brows as he frowned. "I suggested that I had one, Wife. I did *not* say I would tell you what it is."

A slim, well-groomed hand instantly pounced upon his chest, her fingernails walking over taut muscles and gently touching his chin. "I think you will, Husband, because I know a sensitive spot on this hard, well-nurtured body of yours that could reduce you to a whimpering beggar!"

"You tickle me, woman, and you'll suffer dearly." Without warning, he turned upon her, his hands imprisoning her wrists against her sides. "You'll not be tickling me, because I have other things in mind for our entertainment."

At that moment, a playful breeze stirred against the gauze at the window, touching their skin and wrapping them together in its coolness. His mouth claimed hers in a kiss so tender that it might not have touched her at all.

"I love you, Mrs. Storm . . . Phillips."

He had eased between her knees, his mouth trailing kisses over her flushed cheeks.

As they became one again, Tallie thought of a little boy named Paul, who would look to them one day for love, guidance, and protection, a little boy for Ellie to mother like a protective hen.

"I love you, Tallie," Storm murmured, as he became one with her again, "yesterday, today, and tomorrow."

The mountains spoke to them then . . . an eerie but gentle vow floating on the midsummer breeze and stirring their passions again and again.

The Blue Ridge Mountains of Tennessee—
Promising to protect them,
Promising forever.

Epilogue

London, 1892

Ironically, Tallie and her family had arrived in London on the day that Prince Albert Victor, heir-presumptive to the throne of England, died of what his physician called influenza. There were rumors that syphilis, contracted at a Paris brothel some years before, had finally caught up to him, but the fact remained: Eddy, or ''Collar and Cuffs,'' as he'd been known both in intimate circles and the slum streets he frequently inhabited, lay dead at the age of twenty-eight.

A Tennessee family intent on a happy holiday arrived in a country stunned and grieved by the young prince's death. Tallie thought that perhaps the death had come as a blessing in disguise, since the future of the monarchy might have been unpredictable had Prince Eddy succeeded to the throne of England.

A week had passed now since the state funeral, and the country was returning to some degree of normalcy. Tallie and her family had been staying in Aunt Cora's apartment above the flower shop, which Mr. Leggett had maintained since taking over operation of the small, thriving business. Though the weather was overcast and bleak, it was the most pleasant day they'd had in a week. Tallie and Storm had decided to bundle up the children, Ellie and two-year-old Paul, a dark-haired, dark-eyed boy, and venture onto the streets for some entertainment. Ellie, at twelve, had become quite the little lady, caring more about the tidiness of her attire than playing with her dolls . . . or riding her horse in the mountains. Her bright red dress and white woolen coat and leggings had been a gift from Mr. Leggett, and Mrs. Muncie had sewn red and white rosettes onto the rim of the matching tam.

"Are we ready to go out, Mum?" Ellie bubbled forth. "I want everyone to see me in my new frock."

"We shall be leaving in a minute," answered Tallie, tucking fur-trimmed blankets around her squirming son. "Your father is still dressing, so do be patient."

"Father—" she always called him *Father,* "takes much longer than the ladies," Ellie fussed, throwing herself into a chair and making a dramatic statement by thumping her heel against the floor.

Peter Leggett called from downstairs, "The carriage has arrived, Tallie."

"Thank you, Papa Leggett," she called. He'd taken special care to arrange this outing, even paying extra for the cab company to send one of its own into the crime-ridden streets of Whitechapel, and Tallie did not want to keep the carriage waiting so long that the driver might have a change of heart. Calling out to Storm, "Hurry, Husband, the carriage is here," she hardly had time to finish the statement before he was sweeping her into his arms. He was clean-shaven, his heady cologne filling her senses.

The last four years as his wife had been exhildirating. "I do think, Husband, that you smell like a man visiting a place a wife would not approve of."

To which the precocious Ellie, turning up her nose in dramatic flourish, added, "Father, you do stink terribly."

He laughed. "Thank you, Ellie. Just what I needed to hear."

Soon, Storm gathered up his son and they began the trip down the narrow stairs to the flower shop where Papa Leggett awaited them. After morning amenities, the old gentleman said to Tallie, "Might I have a moment of your time, Tallie?"

The young wife and mother looked to her husband. "All of you settle into the carriage and I'll be right out."

The kind old gentleman took a moment to pin a small bouquet of hollies and berries to the lapel of Tallie's fur cape. With a rough, paternal pat on one of her gloved hands, he said, "I just wanted you to know how pleased I am that you are here. We—Mrs. Muncie and I—have missed your bright face in Whitechapel." Then, "Go out with your family, Tallie. Have a grand time." Instantly, he called her back, to ease a large holiday wreath onto Tallie's arm. "This is for Cora. Will you put it on her grave?"

She had said nothing about visiting the cemetery; Peter Leggett knew her well enough that it would be her first stop of the day. Soon, she was climbing into the carriage with her husband, tucking Ellie beneath the wing of her arm and listening to Paul's baby talk. At two, he still said very little that could be understood, though her mother's intuition usually picked up on the important things.

When they pulled up to the cemetery of St. Patrick's church to visit Aunt Cora's grave, not very far in the cemetery from that of Tallie's friend, Mary Kelly, Tallie could almost feel the saintly shield protecting their graves from the harsh winter. Thankful for the peace and security they had at last, she stayed only a few minutes, just long enough to say a special word to each of them, and to assure Mary Kelly that "the killer got hers, my friend." She thought it lovely the way the shadow of an angel on a nearby mausoleum touched upon Mary's grave, and as she withdrew from the cemetery to rejoin her waiting family, she was sure she'd heard the angel promise to watch over them. She smiled, remembering the wonderful years she'd had with her dear aunt, and the friendship she'd shared with poor Mary.

Soon, she, Storm, and the children were traveling the length of Whitechapel and Commercial streets, visiting the bleak, almost vacant Covent Gardens, driving by the queen's palace, where Ellie indulged in a favorite fantasy.

The day was wonderful. To save Papa Leggett the cost of the hired carriage, Tallie had suggested that they call it an early day. Storm, in turn, had been required to admit that he'd contributed a good part of the fare himself, and the carriage was theirs for the day, to go where they pleased.

So, they drove by the Royal Opera House, ate winkles from a vendor's art, visited the National Gallery. They saw St. Paul's, drove King Street, saw Somerset House, journeyed across the Waterloo Bridge. Tallie showed them the place where the actress "Pretty Witty Nellie Gwynne" had enchanted a king. The last order of the day was dinner at a restaurant on the piazza, where they were able to relax for the first time all day.

Ellie was too excited to eat. With Paul now asleep across his mother's lap, Ellie looked out the window and watched the activity before her. She wanted to go ice-skating, but her mother had said a very firm No!, and Ellie was pouting. She returned to the table where she threw herself down in the chair she'd vacated before her wanderings and tried her best to make them feel guilty. She had such an effective pout that Storm invited her onto his lap, an offer she readily accepted, despite her claim that she was a big girl now. "Don't be upset, Ellie. Perhaps . . ." He'd been about to say that he'd sneak her out one day to ice skate, without her mum being the wiser, but thought that wouldn't settle well with Tallie.

But Ellie knew what he'd hesitated to say, and her mood brightened at once. She and her father shared a conspiratorial look just as Tallie suggested they call it a day.

Tomorrow they would journey to Liverpool to visit the Pippens family and to make arrangements to ship Ellie's pony, which she wanted her brother to have "now that she was much too big for it." They hadn't been able to ship the pony when the newlyweds had first come to England to get Ellie, because the pony had been in "a condition," as Mrs. Pippens had delicately put it. The colt born of that condition would be kept at Scotley Hall in the stable of Shetlands Mr. Pippens had accumulated over the years.

Soon, a very exhausted Phillips family was deposited at the flower shop on Berner Street, where they were met by Mr. Leggett and Mrs. Muncie, who advised that they were taking charge of the children for the evening, "so that you young people might have some time alone."

A light snow was beginning to fall, and Tallie could think of nothing more pleasurable than being bundled up under blankets with Storm, while snow piled high on the ledges outside the windows. She gladly accepted their offer, and ran upstairs to retrieve night clothing and fresh morning clothes for the children.

Since Peter and Mrs. Muncie lived in the same lodging house—and one of the better ones in the East End—they would share the burden of the precocious children. Storm mentioned as he accompanied Tallie upstairs that they might have taken on more than they could chew.

Tallie turned on the stairs and hugged him. "Then let us spend this time alone, before the children are brought back by two frustrated citizens."

Actually, she didn't think the children would pose much of a problem. Paul had slept all the way back in the carriage, had not been awakened by the clatter of hooves on cobbles, or by iron-ringed cart wheels or costermonger cries. He could have slept through a treacherous mountain storm, so exhausted was he after their exciting day. As for Ellie, Tallie imagined that she would talk Peter's and Mrs. Muncie's ears off, telling them about ranch life back in Tennessee, and the black mare her father had purchased for her, and the silver-studded saddle he'd brought back to her from a trip he'd made to Mexico to buy horses, where his brother Matt had met a young señorita he'd brought back to the ranch as his bride.

Tallie imagined Papa Leggett and Mrs. Muncie would hear

about the Cherokees who lived near Caymen's Ridge, where her father often rode horseback with her, and of the lodge the sisters had built and the large, popular church sitting up on the mountain top. She imagined that Ellie would go into detail about the judge, whom she adored, and the kind old doctor who had told her a thousand times about bringing her father into the world.

It would probably be Ellie who was brought back to them, if it was either of the children. Then, perhaps not. Papa Leggett was fascinated by tales of their home in Tennessee, and Mrs. Muncie would probably fall asleep before ten o'clock.

"What are you thinking, Tallie?"

They were now entering the small, crowded apartment over the flower shop, and Tallie saw that Papa Leggett had put fresh logs in the hearth. "I was thinking about the children, Storm . . ." She turned into his arms and held him close for a moment, "and being able to spend this time alone with you."

Soon, she and Storm were holding each other beneath the soft blankets of the wide iron bed that had been Tallie's when she'd lived with her aunt. The snow was falling hard now, and occasional flurries of sleet hitting the windows were like fingers upon the keys of a piano.

The love they shared in those moments was passionate and heart-warming, as Storm claimed her body and her soul, caressed her masterfully and teased her about turning thirty, having two children, and still being a goddess of youth and beauty. He carried her to the pinnacles of wonderment, swept her along in the tide of his masculine strength, and when they lay together in exquisite exhaustion, there was nothing they wouldn't have done for each other.

Soon, Storm eased to her side and drew her against him, his nose nestling into her hairline and his cold feet suddenly planting themselves firmly against her warm thigh. She cried out in her surprise, then laughed and began to tickle him unmercifully.

When their laughter died into loving silence, they held each other, on the brink of sleep but much too excited to seek that blissful state.

Tallie closed her eyes, tucking herself more firmly into her husband's arms. As she began to feel the effects of her exhausting day, she heard the usual children in the dark January night on the street outside. Grimly, she listened to the song they were singing: *Jack the Ripper's dead, And lying in his bed, He cut his throat, With Sunlight soap, Jack the Ripper's dead.*

She didn't want to think about Brookie Newgate and the hideous crimes she had committed. She and Storm had decided not to tell Scotland Yard who the real murderer was. Besides, they would never have believed it.

The world needed the mystery.

Enough of this! Tallie thought, forcing her mind away from that grim, fascinating aspect of her past. It was dead and buried now, and no need to be dredged up.

"Good night, dear husband," she whispered against Storm's dark hair. "I will love you till the end of time and beyond."

"Me, too," he mumbled in his last moments before sleep claimed him, and drew her ever so close beneath the downy comfort of the blanket.